Honoré de Balzac, William Walton

The House of Nucingen : The Secrets of la Princesse de Cadignan

The Involuntary Comedians ; Sarrasine ; Facino Cane ; A Man of Business

Honoré de Balzac, William Walton

The House of Nucingen : The Secrets of la Princesse de Cadignan
The Involuntary Comedians ; Sarrasine ; Facino Cane ; A Man of Business

ISBN/EAN: 9783744782364

Printed in Europe, USA, Canada, Australia, Japan

Cover: Foto ©Andreas Hilbeck / pixelio.de

More available books at **www.hansebooks.com**

Honoré de Balzac

Honoré de Balzac

PARISIAN LIFE

VOLUME IX

BIXIOU, BLONDET, FINOT AND COUTURE

"This is from Fénelon direct.—Thus, those who know the world, the observers, the people comme il faut, the men well-gloved and well-cravated, who do not blush to marry a woman for her fortune, they proclaim as indispensable a complete separation of interests and of sentiments. The others are the fools who love * * * For them, millions are but mud: the glove, the camelia, worn by the idol is worth the millions."

THE NOVELS

OF

HONORÉ DE BALZAC

NOW FOR THE FIRST TIME
COMPLETELY TRANSLATED INTO ENGLISH

THE HOUSE OF NUCINGEN
THE SECRETS OF LA PRINCESSE DE CADIGNAN
SARRASINE   FACINO CANE
A MAN OF BUSINESS
THE INVOLUNTARY COMEDIANS

BY WILLIAM WALTON

WITH FIVE ETCHINGS BY CHARLES-BERNARD DE BILLY,
AFTER PAINTINGS BY ALCIDE-THÉOPHILE ROBAUDI

IN ONE VOLUME

PRINTED ONLY FOR SUBSCRIBERS BY
GEORGE BARRIE & SON, PHILADELPHIA

THE HOUSE OF NUCINGEN

Is it not to you, Madame, whose lofty and upright intelligence is as a treasure for all your friends, to you, who are at once for me an entire public and the most indulgent of sisters, that I should dedicate this work? Deign to accept it in testimony of a friendship of which I am proud. You and some other souls, fine as your own, will comprehend my design in reading *The House of Nucingen* coupled with *César Birotteau*. In this contrast, is there not an entire social lesson?

DE BALZAC.

THE HOUSE OF NUCINGEN

*

You are acquainted with the thinness of the partitions which separate the little apartments, the *cabinets particuliers*, in the most elegant restaurants in Paris. In that of Véry, for instance, the largest room is cut in two by a partition which is removed and restored at will. This scene is not laid there, but in a good locality, which it is not convenient for me to designate. There were two of us. I will say, then, like the Prudhomme of Henry Monnier: "I would not wish to compromise her." We were lingering over the delicacies of a dinner, admirable in many respects, in a little apartment, in which we were conversing in low tones, having due regard for the lack of thickness of the partition. We had progressed as far as the roast without having had any neighbors in the apartment adjoining ours, in which we heard only the crackling of the fire. Eight o'clock sounded. There was a great noise of feet, the sound of words exchanged, the waiters brought candles. It was demonstrated to us that the neighboring apartment was occupied. In recognizing the voices, I knew what sort of personages were these occupants. They were four of the most enterprising cormorants sprung from the foam which tops the incessantly renewed waves of the present generation; good-natured youths, whose support is problematical, who are not known to possess either incomes or estates, and yet who live well. These clever *condottieri* of modern industry, which has become the cruelest of wars, leave all the worries to their creditors, keep all the pleasures for themselves, and have no other care than that of their apparel. Moreover, bold enough to smoke, like Jean Bart, their cigar over a barrel of powder, perhaps in order not to fail in their particular rôle; greater scoffers, even, than the smaller newspapers, scoffers that would not hesitate to ridicule themselves; perspicacious and incredulous, inquirers into the affairs of others, avaricious and prodigal, envious of others, but satisfied with themselves; profound politicians at moments, analyzing all, guessing at everything, they had not yet been able to shine in the world in which they wished to display themselves. One only of the four had succeeded, but only to the foot of the ladder. It is nothing to have money, and a parvenu only knows what is deficient in him after six months of flatteries. Not much of a talker, cold, affectedly grave, without wit, this parvenu, whose name was Andoche Finot, had had heart enough to prostrate himself on his stomach before those who could serve him, and wit enough to be insolent to those of whom he had no need. Like one of the grotesque figures of the ballet of "Gustave," he was marquis behind and a villain in front. This industrial prelate kept a train-bearer, Émile Blondet, editor of a newspaper, a man of a good deal of ingenuity, but ill-regulated, bright, capable, lazy, knowing himself exploited, but permitting himself to be so; perfidious, as he was good, by impulses; one of those men whom you like and for whom you have no respect. Sharp as a soubrette of comedy, incapable of refusing his pen to any one who asked it and his heart to anyone who borrowed it, Émile is the most attractive of these girl-men of whom the most fanciful of our wits has said: "I like them better in satin slippers than in boots." The third man, named Couture, supported himself by speculations. He grafted one enterprise upon another; the success of one covered the failure of the other. Thus he maintained himself on the surface, sustained by the nervous strength of his activity, by sharp and audacious strokes. He swam about here and there, seeking in the immense sea of Parisian affairs an islet sufficiently contestable for him to lodge himself thereon. Evidently, he was not in his place. As to the last, the most malicious of the four, his name alone will suffice: Bixiou! Alas, it was no longer the Bixiou of 1825, but the one of 1836, the misanthropical buffoon, with his mad fancy and biting wit, a poor devil exasperated at having expended so much wit in pure loss, furious at not having picked up his lucky find in the last revolution, giving a kick to each one like a true Pierrot of the Funambules, having the

knowledge of his own epoch and of its scandalous
adventures on the tips of his fingers, ornamenting
them with his own droll inventions, leaping on
everybody's shoulders like a clown and endeavoring to leave a mark there like an executioner.

After having satisfied the first cravings of gour-
mandizing, our neighbors arrived at the station in
which we were in our dinner, at the dessert; and,
thanks to our silence, they thought themselves alone.
With the smoke of the cigars, with the aid of
the champagne, interspersed with the gastronomical
pleasures of the dessert, they fell into familiar conversation. Characterized by that icy spirit which
stiffens the most elastic sentiments, arrests the
most generous inspirations, and gives to laughter
something cutting, this talking, full of the bitter
irony which changes gaiety into sneering, betrayed
the exhaustion of souls delivered over entirely to
themselves, without any other aim than the satisfaction of egotism, a fruit of the peace in which we
dwell. That pamphlet against man which Diderot
did not dare to publish, *le Neveu de Rameau*, that
book, which reveals everything in order to show
the wounds, is alone comparable to this pamphlet
uttered without any after-thought, in which the language does not even respect that which the thinker
is still discussing, in which nothing is constructed
save with ruins, in which everything is denied, in
which nothing is admired save that which skepti-
cism adopts,—the omnipotence, the omniscience, the
all-congruity of money. After having taken stray

shots in the circle of acquaintances, back-biting now began to massacre intimate friends. One indication will suffice to explain the desire which I had to remain and to listen to the moment when Bixiou began to speak, as will be seen. We then heard one of those terrible improvisations which secured for this artist his reputation among a certain number of blasé spirits; and though often interrupted, commenced and recommenced, it was stenographed in my memory. Opinions and form, everything was outside of all literary conditions. But this is what it was,—a pot-pourri of sinister things which paint our time, of which should be recounted none but similar histories, and I leave the responsibility, moreover, to the principal narrator. The pantomime, the gestures, in harmony with the frequent changes of the voice by which Bixiou depicted the various personages brought on to the scene, must have been perfect, for his three auditors uttered from time to time approving exclamations and satisfied interjections.

"And Rastignac refused you?" said Blondet to Finot.

"Flatly."

"But did you threaten him with the papers?" asked Bixiou.

"He just laughed," answered Finot.

"Rastignac is the direct heir of the late De Marsay; he makes his way in politics as in the world," said Blondet.

"But how did he make his fortune?" asked

Couture. "He was in 1819, with the illustrious Bianchon, in a miserable boarding-house of the Latin Quarter; his family dined on scraps and drank raw wine, so as to send him a hundred francs a month; the estate of his father was not worth a thousand écus; he had two sisters and a brother on his hands, and now—"

"Now, he has an income of forty thousand francs," resumed Finot; "each of his sisters is richly dowered, married in the nobility, and he has left the usufruct of his estate to his mother—"

"In 1827," said Blondet, "I saw him still without a sou."

"Oh! in 1827!" said Bixiou.

"Well," resumed Finot, "to-day we see him in a fair way to become a minister, peer of France, and everything that he could wish! Three years ago he got rid of Delphine comfortably; he will only marry under good conditions, and he can marry some young girl of noble rank, he can!—The scamp has had the good sense to attach himself to a rich woman."

"My friends, give him credit for favorable circumstances," said Blondet; "he fell into the hands of a clever man when he escaped from the clutches of poverty."

"You know Nucingen well," said Bixiou; "in the early days, Delphine and Rastignac found him good; a wife seemed to be for him in his house, a plaything, an ornament. And this is what, for me, makes this man so remarkable and decided,—

Nucingen does not hesitate to say that his wife is the representation of his fortune, an indispensable *thing*, but one of secondary value in the life at high pressure of men in politics and the great financiers. He said, before me, that Bonaparte was as stupid as a bourgeois in his first relations with Joséphine, and that, after having had the courage to take her for a stepping-stone, he was ridiculous in being willing to make a companion of her."

"Every man of superior qualities should have concerning women the opinions of the Orient," said Blondet.

"The baron melted the Oriental and Occidental doctrines together into a charming Parisian doctrine. He held De Marsay in horror, as he was not manageable, but Rastignac pleased him a great deal and he exploited him without Rastignac's having the least idea of it: he put on him all the charge of his household. Rastignac took on his back all the whims of Delphine, he drove her to the Bois, he accompanied her to the theatre. This great little man of politics of to-day for a long time passed his life in reading and writing pretty notes. In the commencement of things, Eugène was scolded for trifles; he was lively with Delphine when she was gay, he was melancholy when she was sad; he supported the weight of all her headaches, of her confidences; he gave her all his time, his hours, his precious youth, to fill up the emptiness of the idleness of this Parisian woman. Delphine and he held great consultations over the adornments which were most becoming to her, he sustained all the fire of her anger and the broadsides of her poutings; during which time, in compensation, she made herself charming for the baron. The baron, for his part, laughed in his sleeve; then, when he saw Rastignac bending under the weight of his duties, he assumed *the air of suspecting something* and reunited the two lovers by a common fear."

"I can understand that a rich woman could have made Rastignac live, and live honorably; but where did he get his fortune?" asked Couture. "A fortune as considerable as his is to-day has to be found somewhere, and no one has ever accused him of having invented a good piece of business?"

"He inherited," said Finot.

"Of whom?" said Blondet.

"Of imbeciles whom he met," answered Couture.

"He did not take it all, my little loves," said Bixiou:—

> "—Dispense with your unwonted fear;
> The age with fraud holds compact dear."

"I will relate to you the origin of his fortune. In the first place, let us pay homage to talent! Our friend is not a scamp, as Finot says, but a gentleman who knows the game, who is acquainted with the cards, and whom the gallery respects. Rastignac has all the wit which it is necessary to have at a given moment, like a military man who only stakes his courage at ninety days, three signatures and an

endorsement.   He may seem heedless, scatter-
brained, without connection in his ideas, without
constancy in his projects. without any fixed opinion;
but, if there should present itself a serious affair, a
combination to follow, he will not scatter himself,
like Blondet, whom you see, and who goes off into
discussions for the account of his neighbor.   Rastignac concentrates himself, gathers himself up,
studies the point at which he must charge, and he
charges furiously.   With the valor of Murat, he
drives in the squares, the shareholders, the founders, and the whole shop; when the charge has
made its hole, he returns to his soft and careless
life, he becomes again the man of the *Midi*, the voluptuous, the sayer of nothings, the unoccupied Rastignac, who can lie abed till mid-day because he did
not go to bed at the moment of the crisis."

"All this is very well, but let us get to his fortune," said Finot.

"Bixiou will only give us one charge," added
Blondet.   "The fortune of Rastignac, it is Delphine
de Nucingen, a remarkable woman, and one who
joins audacity to foresight."

"Has she borrowed money of you?" asked Bixiou.

A general laugh broke out.

"You are mistaken about her," said Couture to
Blondet; "her wit consists in saying more or less
piquant words, in loving Rastignac with a wearying
fidelity, in obeying him blindly, a woman altogether Italian."

"Money apart," said Andoche Finot, sharply.

"Come, come," resumed Bixiou, in a wheedling
voice, "after what we have just said, will you still
dare to reproach this poor Rastignac with having
lived at the expense of the house of Nucingen, with
having been set up in his house neither more nor
less than was La Torpille formerly by our friend
des Lupeaulx? You will fall into the vulgarity of
the Rue Saint-Denis. To begin with, speaking
abstractly, as Royer-Collard says, the question may
bring up 'the criticism of pure reason;' while as
to that of impure reason—"

"Now he is off," said Finot to Blondet.

"But," cried Blondet, "he is right. The question is very ancient; it was the great word in the
famous duel to death between La Châtaigneraie
and Jarnac. Jarnac was accused of being on good
terms with his mother-in-law, who furnished the
pomp of the too-much loved son-in-law. When a
fact is so true, it should not be uttered. Through
his devotion for the king, Henri II., who had permitted himself this evil speaking, La Châtaigneraie
took it on his own account; hence this duel, which
has enriched the French language with the expression *coup de jarnac.*"

"Ah! if the expression comes from so far back,
it is then noble?" said Finot.

"You might be ignorant of that in your character
of a former proprietor of newspapers and reviews,"
said Blondet.

"There are women," resumed Bixiou, gravely,
"there are also men, who can saw their existence in

two, and only give away a part of it—observe that I
phrase my opinion after the humanitarian formula—.
For those men, all material interest is outside of the
sentiments; they give their life, their time, their
honor, to a woman, and consider that it is not good
style to spend between them that silk paper on which
is engraved: 'The law punishes the counterfeiter
with death.' Reciprocally, these individuals accept
nothing from a woman. Yes, everything becomes
dishonoring if there is a community of interest as
there is a community of souls. This doctrine is
confessed; it is rarely applied."

"Well," said Blondet, "what punctiliousness!
The Maréchal de Richelieu, who was versed in the
science of gallantry, granted a pension of a thous-
and louis to Madame de la Popelinière, after the
adventure of the chimney plaque. Agnes Sorel
brought quite naively to the king, Charles VII., her
fortune, and the king took it. Jacques Cœur contributed to the support of the French crown, which
allowed him to do so, and was as ungrateful as a
woman."

"Monsieur," said Bixiou, "that love which does
not consist of an indissoluble friendship seems to
me a momentary libertinism. What is an entire
abandonment in which something is reserved?
Between these two doctrines, thus opposed and as
profoundly immoral one as the other, there is no possible conciliation. According to my ideas, those who
fear a complete liaison doubtless fear that it may
come to an end, and then, adieu illusion! Passion

which does not believe itself eternal is hideous.
—This is from Fénelon direct.—Thus, those who
know the world, the observers, the people *comme
il faut*, the men well-gloved and well-cravated, who
do not blush to marry a woman for her fortune, they
proclaim as indispensable a complete separation of
interests and of sentiments.   The others are the
fools who love, who believe themselves alone in the
world with their mistress!   For them, millions are
but mud; the glove, the camelia, worn by the idol
is worth the millions.   If you never find among
them any traces of the base metal dissipated, you
will find the remains of flowers hidden in pretty
cedar-boxes.   They are not to be distinguished one
from the other.   For them, there is no longer any
I.   THOU, that is their incarnate Word.   What
would you have!   Would you hinder this secret
malady of the heart?   There are idiots who love
without any kind of calculation, and there are sages
who calculate in loving.''

"Bixiou seems to me sublime," cried Blondet.
"What does Finot say about it?"

"Everywhere else," replied Finot, settling his
cravat, "I would say like the gentleman; but, here,
I think—"

"Like the infamous badly disposed persons with
whom you have the honor of being," interrupted
Bixiou.

"Faith, yes," said Finot.

"And you?" said Bixiou to Couture.

"Imbecilities," cried Couture.   "A woman who

does not make of her body a stepping-stone to enable the man she distinguishes to arrive at his aim, is a woman who has a heart for no one but herself."

"And you, Blondet?"

"I—I practice."

"Well," resumed Bixiou, in his most biting voice, "Rastignac was not of your opinion. To take and not to give is horrible and even somewhat light; but to take in order to have the right to imitate the Lord, in returning an hundred-fold, is a chivalrous act. Thus thought Rastignac. Rastignac was profoundly humiliated at his community of interests with Delphine de Nucingen. I can speak of his regrets; I have seen him with tears in his eyes, deploring his position. Yes, he wept of it veritably—after supper! Well, according to us—"

"Ah! now you are ridiculing us," said Finot.

"Not the least in the world. It concerns Rastignac, whose mortification would be, according to you, a proof of his corruption; for he then loved Delphine much less. But what would you have! the poor boy had this thorn in his heart. He is a gentleman profoundly depraved, as you see, and we are virtuous artists. Then, Rastignac wished to enrich Delphine, he poor, she rich! Would you believe it?—he succeeded. Rastignac, who would have combated like Jarnac, went over from that time to the opinion of Henri II., in virtue of his fine saying: 'There is no absolute virtue, but there are circumstances.' This is connected with the history of his fortune."

2

"You would do well to go on with your story instead of enticing us to calumniate ourselves," said Blondet, with a gracious good-fellowship.

"Ah! ah! my little one," said Bixiou to him, giving him the baptism of a little tap on the occiput, "you will pick yourself up again in the champagne."

"Oh! by the holy name of the stockholder," said Couture, "tell us your story!"

"I am within a notch of it," answered Bixiou; "but, with your oath, you have brought me to the dénouement."

"There are, then, stockholders in the history?" asked Finot.

"Multo-rich as yours," answered Bixiou.

"It seems to me," said Finot in a stiff voice, "that you owe some consideration to a good lad with whom you find occasionally a note of five hundred—"

"Waiter!" cried Bixiou.

"What are you going to ask of the waiter?" said Blondet to him.

"Five hundred francs, to return them to Finot, in order that I may disengage my tongue and tear up my receipt."

"Tell your story," resumed Finot, feigning to laugh.

"You are all witnesses," said Bixiou, "that I do not belong to this impertinent who thinks that my silence is only worth five hundred francs! You will never be minister if you do not know how to gauge consciences. Well, yes," he said, in a cajoling voice, "my good Finot, I will tell the history without any personalities, and we will be quits."

"He is going to demonstrate to us," said Couture, smiling, "that Nucingen made the fortune of Rastignac."

"You are not so far from it as you think," resumed Bixiou. "You do not know what Nucingen is, financially speaking."

"You do not even know," said Blondet, "one thing about his beginnings?"

"I have only known him in his own house," said Bixiou, "but we might have seen each other in other times on the highway."

"The prosperity of the house of Nucingen is one of the most extraordinary phenomena of our epoch," resumed Blondet. "In 1804, Nucingen was but little known; the bankers of that day would have trembled to have known that there were on the market a hundred thousand écus of his acceptances. This grand financier was conscious of his inferiority. How to make himself known? He suspended payment. Good! His name, restricted to Strasbourg and to the Quartier Poissonnière, resounded in all the exchanges! He indemnified all his creditors with non-interest bearing securities and resumed payment; immediately his papers circulated throughout France. By an unheard-of chance, the stocks came up again, resumed their value, paid dividends. Nucingen was very much sought after. The year 1815 arrived, my hero consolidates his capital, buys

funds before the Battle of Waterloo, suspends payment at the moment of the crisis, liquidates with
shares in the mines of Wortschin which he had procured at twenty per cent less than the value at
which he had put them out himself! yes, Messieurs! He took from Grandet a hundred and fifty
thousand bottles of champagne to cover himself,
foreseeing the failure of this virtuous father of the
present Comte d'Aubrion, and as many from
Duberghe in Bordeaux wines. These three hundred thousand bottles *accepted*, accepted, my dear
fellow, at thirty sous, he caused the allies to drink
at six francs, at the Palais-Royal, from 1817 to 1819.
The paper of the house of Nucingen and his name
became European. This illustrious baron had lifted
himself out of the abyss in which others would have
sunk. Twice his liquidation had produced immense
advantages to his creditors: he wished to get the
best of them, impossible! He passed for the most
honest man in the world. At the third suspension,
the paper of the house of Nucingen was circulating
in Asia, in Mexico, in Australia, among the savages. Ouvrard is the only one who had found out
this Alsatian, the son of some Jew converted through
ambition: 'When Nucingen lets go of his gold,'
said he, 'you may believe that he is seizing diamonds!' "

"His ally, Du Tillet, is well worthy of him,"
said Finot. "You must know that Du Tillet is a
man who, as far as birth went, had only that which
is absolutely indispensable for existence, and that

this beggar, who had not a liard in 1814, has become what you see; but what none of us—I am not speaking of you, Couture,—has been able to do, he has had friends instead of having enemies. In short, he so well hid his antecedents, that it was necessary to search the sewers to find him, no later than 1814, clerk in a perfumer's shop in the Rue Saint-Honoré."

"Ta, ta, ta!" resumed Bixiou, "never compare Nucingen to a little timid gambler like Du Tillet, a jackal who succeeds through his sense of smell, who scents the carcass and arrives the first to get the best bone. Besides, look at the two men,—one of them has the sharp look of cats, he is thin, lank; the other is cubical, he is fat, he is heavy as a sack, immovable as a diplomat. Nucingen has a thick hand and the look of a lynx, which never becomes animated; his profundity is not before, but behind: he is impenetrable, he is never seen to come, while the sharpness of Du Tillet resembles, as Napoléon said of someone, I have forgotten whom, 'cotton spun too fine, it breaks.'"

"I do not see in Nucingen any other advantage over Du Tillet than that of having the good sense to understand that a financier should be no more than a baron, whilst Du Tillet wishes to have himself made a count in Italy," said Blondet.

"Blondet,—a word, my child," said Couture. "In the first place, Nucingen has ventured to say that he has only the semblance of an honest man; then, to know him well, it is necessary to deal

with him.   With him the bank is a very small
department,—there is the furnishing of government
supplies, the wines, the wools, the indigoes, in
short, all that might be made to contribute to any
gain whatsoever.   His genius embraces everything.
This elephant of finance would sell deputies to the
minister, and the Greeks to the Turks.   For him,
commerce is, as Cousin would say, the totality of
varieties, the unity of specialties.   Banking, considered in this light, thus becomes a whole political
system; it requires a powerful head and carries a
man whose metal is well tempered to lift himself
above the laws of probity, in which he finds himself cramped.''

"You are right, my son," said Blondet.   "But
we alone, we comprehend what it is thus to have
war carried into the monetary world.   The banker
is a conqueror who sacrifices masses to arrive at
hidden results, his soldiers are the interests of individuals.   He has his stratagems to combine, his
ambuscades to prepare, his partisans to send out,
his cities to take.   The greater number of these
men are so close to politics that they end by going
into it, and there losing their fortunes.   The house
of Necker was thus destroyed, the famous Samuel
Bernard was there almost ruined.   In every century
there may be found a banker with a colossal fortune
who leaves neither fortune nor successor.   The
brothers Pâris, who contributed to bring down Law,
and Law himself, besides whom all those who float
stock companies are pigmies; Bouret, Beaujon,

all have disappeared without leaving a family to
represent them.   Like Saturn, the bank devours its
own children.   In order to subsist, the banker
should become a noble, found a dynasty like the
money-lenders of Charles V., the Fuggers, created
princes of Babenhausen, and who still exist—in the
Almanach de Gotha.   The bank seeks nobility
through an instinct of self-preservation, and without
knowing it, perhaps.   Jacques Cœur founded a
great noble house, that of Noirmoutier, extinct under
Louis XIII.   What energy in that man, ruined for
having made a legitimate king!   He died prince of
an island in the Archipelago, where he built a magnificent cathedral."

"Ah! if you are going to give a course of history,
we will get away from present time, when the
throne is devoid of the right of conferring nobility,
when barons and counts are made behind closed
doors.   What a pity!" said Finot.

"You regret the *savonnette à vilain*,"* said Bixiou; "you are right.   I return to our subject.   Do
you know Beaudenord?   No, no, no!   Good.   See
how everything passes away!   That poor boy was
the flower of dandyism ten years ago.   But he has
been so completely absorbed that you no longer
know him any more than Finot knew, just now, the
origin of the *coup de jarnac*—it is for the sake of the
phrase and not in order to tease you that I say that,
Finot!—In truth, he belonged to the Faubourg

---

*A proverbial expression in allusion to such posts or offices as were
purchased with a view to nobility.

Saint-Germain. Well, Beaudenord is the first
pigeon that I am going to put on the stage for you.
In the first place, he called himself Godefroid de
Beaudenord. Neither Finot, nor Blondet, nor
Couture, nor I, none of us, will despise such an advantage. The youth did not suffer in his self-
love in hearing his domestics called when coming
out of a ball, while thirty pretty women, hooded
and flanked by their husbands and their adorers,
were waiting for their carriages. Then he was in
the enjoyment of all the members which God has
given to man,—whole and entire, neither film on
the eye, nor false wigs, nor false calves; his legs
were neither knock-kneed nor bowed; knees not
too prominent, spinal column straight, figure slender, hand white and handsome, hair black; complexion neither pink, like that of a grocer's ap-
prentice, nor too brown, like that of a Calabrais.
Finally, the essential thing! Beaudenord was not
a too-pretty man, as are those of our friend who
have the air of making a business of their beauty,
of not having any other affair, but let us not dwell
on that subject; we have said it, it is infamous!
He was a good shot with a pistol, a very good eques-
trian; he had fought for a punctilio, and had not
killed his adversary. Do you know that, to por-
tray that which constitutes an entire happiness,
pure without alloy, in the nineteenth century, in
Paris, and the happiness of a young man of twenty-
six, it is necessary to enter into the infinitely
little things of life? The boot-maker had quite

compassed the foot of Beaudenord and shod him well, his tailor loved to array him. Godefroid did not get fat, did not gasconnade, did not Norman-ade, he spoke purely and correctly, and tied his cravat exceedingly well, like Finot. A cousin by marriage of the Marquis d'Aiglemont, his guardian—he was orphaned of both father and mother, another happiness!—he could go, and did go, among the bankers, without the Faubourg Saint-Germain reproaching him with frequenting them, for, fortunately, a young man has the right to make pleasure his only law, to go wherever there is amusement, and to flee the sombre corners in which chagrin flourishes. Finally, he had been vaccinated—you understand me, Blondet—. Despite all these virtues, he might have been able to find himself very unhappy. Eh! eh! happiness has the misfortune of appearing to signify something absolute; an appearance which leads so many simpletons to ask: 'What is happiness?' A woman of much wit said: 'Happiness is where one puts it.' "

"She proclaimed a sad truth," said Blondet.

"And a moral one," added Finot.

"Arch-moral! HAPPINESS, like VIRTUE, like EVIL, expresses something relative," replied Blondet. "Thus, La Fontaine hoped that, in course of time, the damned would become accustomed to their situation, and would finish by being, in Hell, just like fish in the water."

"The grocers know all La Fontaine's sayings!" said Bixiou.

"The happiness of a man of twenty-six who lives at Paris is not the happiness of a man of twenty-six who lives at Blois," said Blondet, without hearing the interruption. "Those who start from this to rail against the instability of opinions are either knaves or ignoramuses. Modern medicine, of which the finest title to glory is in having, between 1799 and 1837, passed from the state of conjecture to the state of a positive science, and that, through the influence of the great analytical school of Paris, it has demonstrated that, in a certain period of time, man is completely renewed—"

"After the manner of Jeannot's knife, and you think him always the same," resumed Bixiou. "There are, then, several lozenges in this harlequin costume that we denominate happiness; well, the costume of my Godefroid had neither rents nor spots. A young man of twenty-six, who would be happy in love, that is to say, loved, not because of the flower of his youth, not for his wit, not for his appearance, but irresistibly, not even because of love in himself, but even when this love shall be abstract, to return to the phrase of Royer-Collard, this aforesaid young man may well not have even a liard in the purse which the loving object has embroidered for him, he may owe his rent to his landlord, his boots to the boot-maker already named, his clothes to the tailor, who may finish, like France, by becoming alienated. In short, he may be poor! Poverty spoils the happiness of the young man who does not partake of our transcendental opinions on

the community of interests. I know of nothing
more wearying than to be morally very happy and
materially very unhappy. Is it not to have one leg
frozen, as mine is, by the draught that comes
through that door, and the other grilled by the hot
coals of the fire? I trust that I make myself understood. Is there an echo in the pocket of your waistcoat, Blondet? Between ourselves, let us leave the
heart, it spoils the wit. We will proceed. Godefroid de Beaudenord had, then, the esteem of his
haberdashers, for his haberdashers received, with
sufficient regularity, their payments. The woman
of a good deal of wit already cited, and who cannot
be named, because, thanks to her lack of heart, she
lives—"

"Who is it?"

"The Marquise d'Espard! She said that a young
man should live in an entresol, have in his domicile
nothing which smelt of housekeeping, neither cook
nor kitchen, be served by an old domestic, and make
no pretension to stability. According to her, any
other establishment would be in bad taste. Godefroid de Beaudenord, faithful to this programme,
lodged on the Quay Malaquais, in an entresol;
nevertheless, he had been obliged to have a little
resemblance to married people by putting in his
chamber a bed, which, however, was so narrow that
it made but little difference. An Englishwoman
who might have happened to enter his lodging,
would have been able to find nothing *improper*
there. Finot, you will explain to yourself the great

law of the *improper* which rules England! But, since we are united by a note of one thousand, I am going to give you an idea. I have been in England, I have"—in a low tone in Blondet's ear: "I give him wit for more than two thousand francs.— In England, Finot, you become extremely well acquainted with a woman, at night, at a ball or elsewhere; you meet her the next morning in the street, and you appear to recognize her: *improper!* You find at dinner, under the black coat of your neighbor on your left, a charming man, witty, no haughtiness, an easy freedom; he has nothing of the English; following the ancient laws of French society, so flexible, so courteous, you speak to him: *improper!* You accost a pretty woman at a ball to ask her to dance: *improper!* You warm up, you discuss, you laugh, you expand your heart, your soul, your spirit in your conversation; you express in it feeling; you play when you are at play, you talk in talking and you eat in eating: *improper! improper! improper!* One of the most spiritual and most profound men of this epoch, Stendhal, has very well characterized the *improper* in saying that there is a certain lord of Great Britain who, when alone, dares not cross his legs before his own fire, for fear of being *improper.* An English lady, were she of the furious sect of the *saints*—double-dyed Protestants who would let all their family die of hunger rather than be *improper*—would not be *improper* in making the devil of an ado in her bed-chamber, and would consider herself lost if she received a friend in this same chamber. Thanks to the *improper*, some day London and all its inhabitants will be found petrified."

"When one thinks that there are in France simpletons who wish to import here the solemn stupidities which the English commit at home with that fine complacency which you see in them," said Blondet, "it is enough to make anyone shudder who has seen England and who thinks of the graceful and charming French manners. In his later years, Walter Scott, who did not dare to paint women as they are, for fear of being *improper*, repented of having drawn the charming figure of Effie in the Prison of Edinburgh."

"Would you like to know how not to be *improper* in England?" said Bixiou to Finot.

"Well?" said Finot.

"Go to the Tuileries and see a species of fireman in marble entitled Themistocles by the statuary, and endeavor to walk like the statue of the commander; you will never be *improper*. It was by a rigorous application of the great law of the *improper* that the happiness of Godefroid was completed. This is the story: He had a tiger, and not a groom, as those people who know nothing about the world write. His tiger was a little Irishman, named Paddy, Joby, Toby—at will—, three feet high, twenty inches wide, with the face of a weasel, nerves of steel, made by gin, active as a squirrel, managing a landau with a skill which was never found in default, neither in London nor in

Paris; the eye of a lizard, fine as mine, mounting a
horse like the old Franconi, hair as blond as that
of a Virgin by Rubens, pink cheeks, dissembling as
a prince, learned as a retired lawyer, aged ten
years, in short a true flower of perversity, swearing and playing, loving jam and punch, insulting as
a newspaper, bold and pilfering as a gamin of
Paris. He had been the honor and the profit of a
celebrated English lord, for whom he had gained
seven hundred thousand francs on the race-course.
The lord prized very highly this infant: his tiger
was a curiosity, no one in London had a tiger so
little. Mounted on a race horse, Joby looked like
a falcon. Well, the lord dismissed Toby, not for
gluttony, nor for theft, nor for murder, nor for
criminal conversation, nor for failure in style, nor
for insolence to milady, nor for having made holes
in the pocket of milady's first maid, nor for having
been bribed by milord's adversaries at the races,
nor for having amused himself on Sunday, in short,
for no reproachable act. Toby might have done all
these things, he might even have spoken to milord
without being questioned, milord would again have
pardoned this domestic crime. Milord would have
endured a great many things for Toby, so much
milord was attached to him. His tiger could handle
a two-wheeled carriage, tandem, mounted in the
saddle of the rear horse, his legs not reaching below
the shafts, having the appearance in fact of one of
those heads of cherubs which the Italian painters
scatter around the Eternal Father. An English

journalist made a delicious description of this little
angel. He found him too pretty for a tiger; he
offered to bet that Paddy was a tamed tigress. The
description threatened to envenom and to become
in the highest degree *improper*. The superlative of
the *improper* leads to the gallows. Milord was much
praised for his circumspection by milady. Toby
could not find any other situation, after having his
civil status thus contested in the Britannic Zoölogy.
At this period Godefroid was flourishing at the
French embassy in London, where he heard of the
adventure of Toby, Joby, Paddy. Godefroid took
possession of the tiger, whom he found weeping beside a pot of jam, for the infant had already lost the
guineas with which milord had gilded his misfortune.
On his return, Godefroid de Beaudenord then im-
ported amongst us the most charming tiger of England; he was known by his tiger as Couture attracts
attention by his waistcoats. Thus he entered with
facility into the confederation of the club called
to-day De Grammont. He did not disturb any ambition after having renounced the diplomatic career;
he had not a dangerous spirit, he was well received
by everybody. We others, we would be offended
in our self-love if we encountered only smiling faces.
We are pleased to see the bitter grimace of the envious. Godefroid did not love to be hated. Everyone to his taste! Let us get to the solid facts, to the
material life. His apartment, in which I have discussed more than one déjeuner, recommended itself
by a mysterious dressing-room, well ornamented,

full of comfortable things, with a fire-place, with
a bath-tub; opening on a little stairway, fold-
ing-doors that made no noise, easy locks, discreet
hinges, windows of ground glass with impassable
curtains.   If the chamber offered and should have
offered the very finest disorder that the most exacting water-color painter could have desired, if everything in it exhaled the Bohemian charm of the life
of an elegant young man, the dressing-room was
like a sanctuary,—white, clean, well-ordered, warm,
no draughts, a carpet made for alighting on in
naked feet, in one's chemise, affrighted.   There
could be found the signature of the young man, a
real beau and one who knows life! for there during
several minutes he may reveal himself either
imbecile or great in those little details of existence
which betray character.   The marquise already
cited, no, it was the Marquise de Rochefide, issued
furious from this dressing-room and never returned
there; she found in it nothing *improper*.   Godefroid
had there a little cupboard full—"

"Of night-shirts?" said Finot.

"Come now, there you are, you gross Turcaret!
—I shall never be able to make anything of him!—
Not at all,—of cakes, of fruit, of pretty little flasks of
Malaga wine, of Lunel, a little refection à la Louis
XIV., all that could amuse delicate and well-educated
stomachs, the stomachs of sixteen quarterings.   A
malicious old domestic, very strong in the veter-
inary art, looked after the horses and waited on
Godefroid, for he had been in the service of the late

Monsieur Beaudenord, and had for Godefroid an
inveterate affection, that malady of the heart which
the savings banks have ended, by curing, for all
servants. All material happiness reposes on figures.
You, to whom Parisian life is known even to its
exostosis, you will understand that he required about
seventeen thousand francs of income, for he had
seventeen francs of imposts and a thousand écus of
fancies. Well, my dear infants, the day on which
he attained his majority the Marquis d'Aiglemont
presented him with the accounts of his stewardship,
such as we should not be able to render to our
nephews, and handed to him his statement of eighteen thousand francs of income from investments in
the public funds, the remnants of the paternal opulence, somewhat mauled by the great Republican
reduction and riddled by the arrears of the Empire.
This virtuous guardian put into his pupil's hands
some thirty thousand francs of savings placed in
the house of Nucingen, saying to him, with all the
courtesy of a grand seigneur and the easy freedom
of a soldier of the Empire, that he had saved this
sum for his youthful follies. 'If you will listen to
me, Godefroid,' he added, 'instead of expending this
sottishly, like so many others, practice some useful
follies, accept a post as attaché to the embassy at
Turin, from there go to Naples, from Naples to London, and for your money you will be amused,
instructed. Later, if you wish to adopt a career,
you will have lost neither your time nor your
money.' The late D'Aiglemont quite deserved his

3

reputation; no one will be able to say as much of us."

"A young man who starts life at twenty-one with eighteen thousand francs of income is a young man ruined," said Couture.

"If he is not avaricious, or very superior," said Blondet.

"Godefroid sojourned awhile in the four capitals of Italy," resumed Bixiou. "He saw Germany and England, a little of St. Petersburg, traversed Holland; but he separated himself from the aforesaid thirty thousand francs by living as if he had thirty thousand francs of income. He found everywhere 'the best part of the fowl, jellied meats,' and 'the wines of France,' heard French spoken everywhere, in fact he was not able to get out of Paris. He would have been quite willing to have depraved his heart, to have put it in a cuirass, to have lost his illusions, to have learned to hear everything without blushing, to talk without saying anything, to penetrate the secret interests of the powers.—Bah! it was scarcely worth his while to furnish himself with four languages, that is to say, to provide himself with four words for one idea. He returned widowed of several very tedious dowagers, called *good fortunes*, abroad, timid and scarcely formed, a good fellow, full of confidence, incapable of speaking evil of those who did him the honor to admit him to their houses, having too much good faith to be a diplomat, in short, what we call an honest fellow."

"In short, a *brat* who held his eighteen thousand francs of income for the first investment that should come along," said Couture.

"This devil of a Couture is so much in the habit of anticipating his dividends that he anticipates the dénouement of my history. Where was I? At Beaudenord's return. When he was installed in the Quay Malaquais, he found that a thousand francs above his needs were insufficient for his box at the Italiens and at the Opera. When he lost twenty-five or thirty louis at play in betting, naturally he paid; then, he spent them when he won, which always happens to us if we are stupid enough to allow ourselves to take to betting. Beaudenord, cramped in his eighteen thousand francs of income, felt the necessity of creating that which we call to-day *funds for running expenses*. He was quite resolved *not to get himself in too deep*. He went to consult his guardian: 'My dear child,' said D'Aiglemont to him, 'Rentes are at par, sell your Rentes; I have sold mine and those of my wife. Nucingen has all my capital, and gives me for it six per cent; do like me, you will have one per cent the more, and this one per cent will permit you to be perfectly comfortable.' In three days our Godefroid was quite comfortable. His revenues were in a state of perfect equilibrium with his superfluousness, his material happiness was complete. If it were possible to interrogate all the young people of Paris with one glance, as it appears will be done at the time of the last judgment for the billions of

generations which have splashed about on all the
worlds, as National Guards or as savages, and to
demand of them if the happiness of a young man
of twenty-six did not consist in being able to go
out on horseback, in a tilbury, or in a cabriolet
with a tiger as big as your fist, fresh and rosy as
Toby, Joby, Paddy; to have in the evening for
twelve francs a very convenient coupé to hire; to
show oneself elegantly gotten up according to the
laws of apparel which regulate eight o'clock, noon,
four o'clock, and the evening; to be well received
in all the embassies, and to gather there the ephem-
eral flowers of cosmopolitan and superficial friendships; to be of a supportable beauty, and to carry
well one's name, one's coat and one's head; to live
in a charming little entresol arranged as I have told
you was the entresol of the Quay Malaquais; to be
able to invite your friends to accompany you to the
Rocher de Cancale without having to previously interrogate one's pocket, and not to be arrested in
every reasonable movement by this word, 'but how
about the money?' to be able to renew the pink
tufts which ornament the ears of one's three thor-
oughbred horses, and to have always a new lining
to one's hat? Everybody, ourselves, superior persons, all would reply that this happiness is incomplete, that it is the Madeleine without an altar, that
it is necessary to love and be loved, or to love without being loved, or to be loved without loving, or to
be able to love through thick and thin. We will
arrive at the moral happiness. When, in January,

1823, he found himself comfortably settled in all his enjoyments, after having established his footing in all the different Parisian societies in which it pleased him to go, he felt the necessity of putting himself under the shelter of a parasol, of being able to complain to some woman *comme il faut*, of not having to chew the stem of a rose bought for ten sous from Madame Prévost, after the fashion of the little young people who cluck in the corridors of the Opera House, like pullets in a chicken-house. In short, he resolved to carry all his sentiments, his ideas, his affections to a woman, *a woman!* LA PHAMME! Ah! —He conceived at first the absurd idea of having an unhappy passion, he hovered for some time around his charming cousin, Madame d'Aiglemont, without perceiving that a diplomatist had already danced the waltz of 'Faust' with her. The year '25 passed in essays, in researches, in useless flirtations. The loving object demanded did not present itself. Passions are extremely rare. At this epoch, there were set up as many barricades in manners as in the streets! Verily, my brethren, I say to you the *improper* is overcoming us! As we have been reproached with imitating the method of the painters of portraits, of the auctioneers and of the dressmakers, I will not make you undergo the description of the person in whom Godefroid recognized his female. Aged nineteen years; stature one metre fifty centimetres; blond hair, eyebrows *idem*, eyes blue, forehead medium, nose arched, mouth small, chin short and high, visage oval; particular

indications, none. Such was the passport of the loved
object. Do not be more hard to please than the
police, than Messieurs the mayors of all the towns
and communes of France, than the gendarmes and
other constituted authorities. Moreover, this is the
block of the Venus de Medici, word of honor. The
first time that Godefroid went to the house of
Madame de Nucingen, who had invited him to one of
those balls by which she acquired, at a reasonable
price, a certain reputation, he perceived there, in a
quadrille, the person to love and was astonished
by this figure of a metre and fifty centimetres.
These blond locks flowed in rippling cascades on a
little head ingenuous and fresh as that of a naiad
who had put her nose out of the crystalline window
of her stream to see the flowers of Spring.—This is
our new style, phrases which spin themselves out
as our macaroni did just now.—The *idem* of the
eyebrows, without offence to the prefecture of
police, might have demanded six verses from the
amiable Parny; that playful poet would have compared them very agreeably to Cupid's bow, observing that the dart was below, but a dart without
force, a blunted dart, for there reigns there still to-
day the sheep-like softness which the chimney-
panels attribute to Mademoiselle de la Vallière, at the
moment when she bore witness to her tenderness before God, through lack of being able to bear witness
before a notary. You know the effect of these
blond locks and blue eyes, in combination with a
dance, soft, voluptuous, and decent? Such a young

person does not strike you at first audaciously to the heart, like those brunettes who by their glance have the air of saying to you, like Spanish beggars: 'Your purse or your life! Five francs or I scorn you.' These insolent beauties—and somewhat dangerous!—may be able to please many men; but according to me, the blond who has the happiness of appearing excessively tender and yielding, without losing her right of remonstrance, of teasing, of immoderate discourses, of unfounded jealousy and all that which renders woman adorable, will be always more certain of marriage than the ardent brunette. Wood is dear. Isaure, white as an Alsatian—she had first seen the day at Strasbourg and spoke German with a very agreeable little French accent—, danced marvelously. Her feet, which the police employé had not mentioned and which, however, might find their place under the rubric *particular indications*, were remarkable for their smallness, for that peculiar action which the old masters denominated *flic flac*, and comparable to the agreeable recitative of Mademoiselle Mars, for all Muses are sisters, the dancer and the poet alike have their feet on the earth. The feet of Isaure conversed with a clearness, a precision, a lightness, a rapidity of excellent augury for the things of the heart. 'She has the *flic flac*,' was the supreme eulogy of Marcel, the only dancing-master who has merited the title of great. He was called the great Marcel, like the great Frederick, and of the times of Frederick."

"Did he compose ballets?" asked Finot.

"Yes, something like 'The Four Elements,' 'Gallant Europe.' "

"What a period," said Finot; "like the times in which the grand seigneurs dressed the danseuses."

"*Improper!*" resumed Bixiou. "Isaure did not raise herself on her toes, she remained upon the earth, she balanced herself without shaking, neither more nor less voluptuously than a young person should balance herself. Marcel said, with profound philosophy, that each state had its peculiar dance, —a married woman should dance in a different fashion from a young person, a limb of the law otherwise than a financier, and a military man otherwise than a page; he went so far as to pretend that a foot soldier should dance in a different way than a cavalryman: and from this he set out to analyze the whole of society. All these fine shades are quite out of our line."

"Ah!" said Blondet, "you put your finger on a great misfortune. If Marcel had been comprehended, the French Revolution would never have taken place."

"Godefroid," resumed Bixiou, "had not had the advantage of traversing Europe without observing foreign dances closely. Without that profound knowledge of choregraphy, which is qualified as futile, perhaps he would not have loved this young person; but of the three hundred guests who crowded the handsome salons of the Rue Saint-Lazare, he was the only one to comprehend the unpublished love which is betrayed by a talkative dance. There were many who noticed the manner of Isaure d'Aldrigger; but, in that century in which everyone cries: 'Slide, do not bear on!' one said: 'there is a young girl who dances famously well' —this was a notary's clerk—; another, 'there is a young person who dances ravishingly'—this was a lady in a turban—; the third, a woman of thirty: 'there is a young person who does not dance badly!' Let us return to the great Marcel, and say, parodying his most famous saying: 'how many things in a forward-two!' "

"And let us get on a little faster!" said Blondet. "You are sentimentalizing."

"Isaure," resumed Bixiou, who looked at Blondet askance, "had a simple dress of white crêpe ornamented with green ribbons, a camelia in her hair, a camelia at her waist, another camelia at the bottom of her dress, and a camelia—"

"Oh! come on; here are the three hundred goats of Sancho!"

"It is like all literature, my dear fellow. 'Clarissa' is a masterpiece, there are fourteen volumes, and the dullest vaudevillist will recount it to you in an act. So long as I amuse you, of what do you complain? This toilet had a delicious effect. Do you not love camelias? would you like to have dahlias? No. Well, then, a chestnut, here!" said Bixiou, who doubtless threw a chestnut at Blondet, for we heard the noise on a plate.

"Go on, I was wrong; continue!" said Blondet.

"I resume," said Bixiou. "'Would it not be nice to marry?' said Rastignac to Beaudenord, indicating to him the little one with the white camelias, pure and without a leaf missing. Rastignac was one of the intimate friends of Godefroid. 'Eh! well, I was thinking of it,' replied Godefroid in his ear. 'I was saying to myself that, instead of trembling at each moment in his happiness, of only being able to utter occasionally a word in an inattentive ear, of looking, at the Italiens, to see if there were a red or a white flower in a coiffure, if there were at the Bois a gloved hand on the panel of a carriage, as is done at Milan, on the Corso; that instead of stealing a mouthful of sweetness behind a door, like a lackey who finishes a bottle; of using all his intelligence to give and to receive a letter, like a postman; that instead of receiving infinite tendernesses in two lines, of having five volumes in folio to read to-day, to-morrow a pamphlet of two pages, which is fatiguing; that instead of dragging one's self along the ruts and behind the hedges, it would be much better to give one's self up to the adorable passion envied by Jean-Jacques Rousseau, to love quite honestly a young person like Isaure, with the intention of making her his wife if, during the exchange of feelings, the hearts should come to an agreement, in short, to be Werther happy!'--'That is just as absurd as anything else,' said Rastignac, without laughing. 'In your place, perhaps, I would throw myself into the infinite delights of this asceticism; it is new, original and not costly. Your Mona Lisa

is sweet and soft, but simple as ballet music, I fore-
warn you.' The manner in which Rastignac uttered
this last phrase suggested to Beaudenord that his
friend had some interest in disenchanting him, and
he believed him his rival in his quality of a former
diplomat. The professions that have failed often color
a whole lifetime. Godefroid became so enamored
of Mademoiselle Isaure d'Aldrigger, that Rastignac
went in search of a tall girl who was conversing in
the card-room, and whispered to her: 'Malvina,
your sister has just caught in her net a fish that
weighs eighteen thousand francs of income; he has
a name, a certain place in the world and very good
style; watch over them; if they should spin out the
perfect love, have a care to be Isaure's confidante in
order that she may not reply a single word which
you have not corrected.' Toward two o'clock in
the morning the valet de chambre came to say to a
little Alpine shepherdess, forty years old, coquettish as the Zerlina of the opera of 'Don Juan,' and
under whose charge was Isaure: 'the carriage of
Madame la Baronne is at the door.' Godefroid then
saw his beauty of the German ballad conducting her
fantastic mother into the salon of departure, where
these two ladies were followed by Malvina. Godefroid, who pretended—the infant!—to be going to see
in what pot of jam Joby had lost himself, had the
happiness of perceiving Isaure and Malvina envel-
oping their sprightly mamma in her pelisse, rendering her all those little cares of the toilet required for
a nocturnal journey in Paris. The two sisters

examined him out of the corners of their eyes like well-trained cats, who watch a mouse without appearing to pay any attention to it. He experienced a certain satisfaction in seeing the style, the appearance, the manners, of the big Alsatian in livery, very well gloved, who brought the comfortable furred slippers to his three mistresses. Never were two sisters more unlike than were Isaure and Malvina. The elder, tall and brunette, Isaure petite and blonde; this one with fine and delicate features; the other much more vigorous and pronounced; Isaure was the woman who rules by her lack of strength and whom a lyceum student would have felt himself called upon to protect; Malvina was the woman of '*Avez-vous vu dans Barcelone?*' By the side of her sister, Isaure had the effect of a miniature in contrast with a portrait in oil. 'She is rich!' said Godefroid to Rastignac returning to the ball.—'Who?'—'That young person.'—'Ah! Isaure d'Aldrigger! Why, yes. The mother is a widow; her husband had employed Nucingen in his offices at Strasbourg. Should you like to see her again, turn off a compliment to Madame de Restaud, who gives a ball the day after to-morrow; the Baronne d'Aldrigger and her two daughters will be there; you will get an invitation!' For three days, in the camera obscura of his brain, Godefroid saw *his* Isaure and the white camelias, and the little movements of her head, just as when, after having long contemplated an object brilliantly lighted, we see it again when our eyes are shut, in a smaller form, radiant and colored, sparkling in the midst of the obscurity."

"Bixiou, you are falling into phenomena; pull your picture together more!" said Couture.

"Here you are!" resumed Bixiou, assuming doubtless, the attitude of a waiter, "here, messieurs, is your picture! Attention, Finot! you will have to pull at your mouth as a cab-driver does at that of his old horse! Madame Théodora-Marguerite-Wilhelmine Adolphus—of the house of Adolphus & Co., Mannheim—widow of the Baron d'Aldrigger, was not a good, fat German woman, compact and deliberate, fair-skinned, with a face gilded like the froth of a pot of beer, enriched with all the patriarchal virtues which Germany possesses, romantically speaking. Her cheeks were still fresh, colored on the cheek-bones like those of a Nuremburg doll, very sprightly corkscrew curls at her temples, enticing eyes, not a single white hair, a slender figure whose pretensions were set forth by tight-fitting dresses. She had on the forehead and on the temples some involuntary wrinkles which she would have very willingly, like Ninon, banished to her heels; but the wrinkles persisted in designing their zigzags in the most visible localities. The outline of her nose was drooping a little and the end reddening, which was all the more embarrassing that the nose thus came into harmony with the color of the cheeks. In her quality of sole heiress, spoiled by her parents, spoiled by her husband, spoiled by the city of Strasbourg, and always spoiled by her two daughters, who adored her, the baroness favored pink, wore short skirts, and the bow at the point of the corset which defined her figure. When a Parisian saw this baroness passing on the Boulevard, he smiled; he condemned her without admitting, as the jury always does, the extenuating circumstances in a fratricide! The scoffer is always a superficial being and consequently a cruel one; the knave never takes into account that for which society is responsible in the absurdity at which he laughs, for nature only made beasts; we owe the dolt to the social state."

"That which I find so fine in Bixiou," said Blondet, "is that he is complete; when he is not railing at others, he is laughing at himself."

"Blondet, I will be even with you for that," said Bixiou, in a shrewd tone. "If this baroness was giddy, careless, egotistical, incapable of reflection, the responsibility of her defects all fell upon the house of Adolphus & Co., of Mannheim, on the blind love of the Baron d'Aldrigger. Soft as a lamb, this baroness had a tender heart, easy to move, but, unluckily the emotion was of short duration and consequently was often renewed. When the baron died, this shepherdess all but followed him, so violent and real was her grief; but—the next day, at déjeuner, she was served with French peas, which she loved, and these delicious *petits pois* calmed the crisis. She was so blindly loved by her two daughters, by her servants, that all the household was happy at a circumstance which enabled them to prevent her from seeing the dolorous spectacle of the funeral. Isaure and Malvina hid their tears from this adored mother, and occupied her in selecting her mourning, in ordering it whilst the *Requiem* was sung. When a coffin is placed under that great catafalque black and white, spotted with wax drippings, which served for three thousand corpses of well-to-do people before being renewed, according to the estimate of a philosophic undertaker's man whom I consulted on this point, between two glasses of *petit blanc;* when the inferior clergy, very indifferent, bawl the *Dies iræ,* when the superior clergy, equally indifferent, sing the Office, do you know what the friends in mourning, seated or standing about in the church, say to each other?—Here is your picture.—Well, would you like to see? 'How much do you think Papa d'Aldrigger left?' said Desroches to Taillefer, who gave us, before his death, the very finest orgie known—''

"Was Desroches an attorney at that time?"

"He was admitted in 1822," said Couture. "And it was a good deal for the son of a poor employé who had never had more than eighteen hundred francs, and whose mother conducted an establishment for the sale of stamped paper. But he worked hard from 1818 to 1822. Entered as a fourth clerk in the office of Derville, he was second clerk in 1819!"

"Desroches?"

"Yes," said Bixiou. "Desroches rolled along,

like us, on the dung-hills of favoritism. Tired of wearing coats too small and sleeves too short, he ate up his fee in despair and secured a bare title. An attorney without a sou, without any clients, without any other friends than us, he had to pay the interest on a commission and on his securities."

"He looked to me then like a tiger from the Jardin des Plantes," said Couture. "Thin, with reddish hair, his eyes the color of Spanish tobacco, a harsh skin, a cold and phlegmatic air, but harsh for the widow, merciless for the orphan, a hard worker, the terror of his clerks, who did not dare to waste their time, learned, shrewd, two-sided, with a honeyed elocution, never excited, hateful after the manner of a judicial man."

"And there was some good in him," cried Finot; "he was devoted to his friends, and his first care was to take Godeschal, the brother of Mariette, for head clerk."

"At Paris," said Blondet, "advocates are of only two kinds,—there is the advocate who is an honest man, who keeps within the terms of the law, pushes his suits, does not run after business, neglects nothing, gives his clients good advice, comes to an agreement with them on all doubtful points, a Derville, in short. Then, there is the starveling advocate, for whom everything is good, provided only that his fees are assured; who would bring into action not the mountains, he would sell them, but the planets; who would interest himself in the triumph of a rascal over an honest man if by chance the honest man did not have the best case. When one of these advocates has done a trick, after the manner of Master Gonin, a little too strong, the Chamber compels him to sell out. Desroches, our friend Desroches, understood this trade, so badly managed by the sorry fellows; he took charge of the cases of those persons who feared to lose them; he threw himself eagerly into chicanery like a man determined to get out of his poverty. He was right; he followed his trade very honestly. He found protectors in men of political affairs by straightening out their embarrassed transactions, as in the case of our dear des Lupeaulx, whose position was so compromised. It required all this to get him into a good position, for Desroches had commenced by being very badly considered by the court, he who rectified with so much trouble the errors of his clients!—Well, Bixiou, to return—. How did Desroches come to be in the church?"

" 'D'Aldrigger left seven or eight hundred thousand francs!" answered Taillefer to Desroches. 'Ah, bah! there is only one person who knows what *their* fortune is,' said Werbrust, a friend of the deceased.—'Who?'—'That big scamp of a Nucingen; he will go to the cemetery; d'Aldrigger was his patron, and through gratitude he will appraise the property of the worthy man.' 'His widow will find a very great difference!' 'What do you mean?' 'But d'Aldrigger loved his wife so much! Don't laugh, people are looking at us.' 'Well, here is Du Tillet; he is very late; he gets here in time to hear

4

the epistle.' 'He will doubtless marry the elder.'
'Is it possible?' said Desroches. 'He is more than
ever engaged with Madame Roguin.' 'He! Engaged?—you do not know him.' 'Do you know the
position of Nucingen and of Du Tillet?' asked Desroches. 'Here it is,' said Taillefer,—'Nucingen is
a man to eat up the capital of his former patron and
to give it back to him.' 'Heu! Heu!' said Werbrust. 'It is devilishly damp in the churches, heu!
heu!' 'How give it up again?'—'Well, Nucingen
knows that Du Tillet has a great fortune, he wants
to marry him to Malvina; but Du Tillet mistrusts
Nucingen. For those who watch the play, this
game is amusing.' 'How,' said Werbrust, 'is she
already old enough to marry? How fast we grow
old!' 'Malvina d'Aldrigger is more than twenty,
my dear fellow. The goodman d'Aldrigger was
married in 1800! He gave us some very good fêtes
at Strasbourg on the occasion of his marriage and
at the birth of Malvina. That was in 1801, at the
Peace of Amiens, and we are now in 1823, Papa
Werbrust. In those times, everything was Ossi-
anized! he named his daughter Malvina. Six years
later, under the Empire, there was for some time a
fury for chivalric things, it was all *Partant pour la
Syrie*,—a heap of foolishnesses. He named his
second daughter Isaure; she is seventeen. There
are two marriageable girls!' 'Those women will
not have a sou in ten years,' said Werbrust, confi-
dentially, to Desroches. 'There is,' replied Taillefer, 'the valet de chambre of d'Aldrigger, that old

fellow who bellows at the back of the church; he
has seen the two demoiselles brought up; he is capable of doing everything to preserve them their
property.' The chanters: *Dies iræ!* The children
of the choir: *Dies illa!* Taillefer: 'Adieu, Werbrust; when I hear the *Dies iræ, it* reminds me too
strongly of my poor son.' 'I am going too, it is too
damp here,' said Werbrust.—*In favilla.*—The beggars at the door: 'A few pennies, my dear gentlemen!' The beadle: 'Pan! Pan! *for the needs of
the church.*' The chanters: '*Amen!*' A friend:
'What did he die of?' An inquisitive joker: 'Of
a broken blood-vessel in the heel.' A passer-by:
'Do you know who is the personage who has died?'
A relative: 'The President de Montesquieu.' The
sacristan to the beggars: 'Get away from here;
they have given to us for you. Don't ask any
more!'"

"What *verve!*" said Couture.

—In fact, it seemed to us that we heard everything
that happened in the church. Bixiou imitated
everything, even to the noise of those who went
away with the body, by a shuffling of his feet on
the floor.—

"There are poets, romancers, writers, who say a
great many pretty things about Parisian manners,"
resumed Bixiou, "but this is the truth about funer-
als. Of a hundred persons who render the last
duties to a poor devil of a dead man, ninety-nine talk
of business and of pleasure openly in the church.
In order to see some poor little real grief, it requires

impossible circumstances.   Further! is there a
grief without selfishness?—"

"Heu! Heu!" said Blondet.   "There is nothing
in the world less respected than death, perhaps
because there is nothing less respectable?"—

"It is so common!" resumed Bixiou.   "When the
service was over, Nucingen and Du Tillet accompanied the body to the cemetery.   The old valet de
chambre followed on foot.   The coachman drove
the carriage behind that of the clergy.   'Vel, my
gude vrent,' said Nucingen to Du Tillet, as they
turned the corner of the Boulevard, 'dis is a gude
zhance to marry Malvina; you vil be de prodecdor ov
dat boor vamily veeping, you vould haf a family,
a home; you vould find a house alretty vurnished,
und Malvina for zure is a real dresure.' "

"It is just like hearing him speak, that old Robert
Macaire of a Nucingen!" said Finot.

" 'A charming young woman,' " said Ferdinand du
Tillet, with enthusiasm, and without exciting himself,' " resumed Bixiou.

"It is all of Du Tillet in one word!" cried Couture.

" 'She might seem ugly to those who do not know
her, but, I am sure of it, she has a fine soul,' said
Du Tillet. 'And a hart, dat is de best ov it, my tear
vellow; zhe vould haf tefotion und indelligence.
In our tog ov a drade, you nefer know who vil life
und who vil tie; it is a great habbiness do be able
do drust in the hart of your vife. I vould sed
off Telvine, who, you know, brought me more dan

a million, against Malvina, who has nod so gread a
dod.' 'But how much has she?' 'I do nod know
schust,' said the Baron de Nucingen, 'but zhe has
somedings.' 'She has a mother who likes to wear
pink!' said Du Tillet. This speech put an end to
the attempts of Nucingen. After dinner, the baron
informed Wilhelmine Adolphus that there remained
in his keeping scarcely four hundred thousand
francs. The daughter of the Adolphuses of Mannheim, reduced to twenty-four thousand francs of
income, lost herself in calculations which bewildered her. 'What!' said she to Malvina, 'what! I
have always had six thousand francs for us to spend
at the dressmakers! but where did your father get
the money? We shall have nothing at all with
twenty-four thousand francs; we shall starve. Ah!
if my father should see me thus reduced he would
die of it, if he were not already dead! Poor
Wilhelmine!' And she wept. Malvina, not knowing how to console her mother, represented to
her that she was still young and pretty; that pink
was still becoming to her; that she would go to the
Opera, to the Bouffons in the box of Madame de
Nucingen. She lulled her mother to sleep in dreams
of fêtes, of balls, of music, of beautiful toilets and
of success, a dream which commenced under the curtains of a bed in blue silk, in an elegant chamber,
adjoining that in which had expired, two nights previously, Monsieur Jean-Baptiste Baron d'Aldrigger, whose history may be given in three words.
During his life-time, this respectable Alsatian,

a banker at Strasbourg, had acquired a fortune of about three millions. In 1800, at the age of thirty-six, at the climax of a fortune made during the Revolution, he had married, through ambition and by inclination, the heiress of all the Adolphuses of Mannheim, a young girl adored by a whole family, and naturally she received the ancestral fortune in the space of ten years. D'Aldrigger was then made a baron by His Majesty, the Emperor and King, for his fortune doubled itself. But he had a passion for the great man who had given him his title; therefore, between 1814 and 1815, he was ruined for having taken seriously the sun of Austerlitz. The honest Alsatian did not suspend payment, did not satisfy his creditors with values which he considered doubtful; he paid everything over the counter, retired from the bank and deserved the description of his former head clerk, Nucingen: 'Honest man, but a fool!' Everything included, there remained to him five hundred thousand francs and obligations due under the Empire, which no longer existed. 'See vat it is to haf beliefed too much in Nappolion,' said he, when he saw the result of his liquidation. When one has been one of the first citizens, what a descent to be one of the lesser ones!—The banker of Alsace did as do all the ruined provincials,—he came to Paris, he there wore courageously tri-colored suspenders on which were embroidered the imperial eagles, and he concentrated himself in Bonapartist society. He placed all his funds in the hand of the Baron de Nucingen, who gave him eight per cent for everything, accepting his imperial claims at sixty per cent only of loss, which was the cause of d'Aldrigger's clasping the hand of Nucingen and saying to him: 'I vas very zure to vind a hart in an Elzacien!' Nucingen secured payment in full from our friend, des Lupeaulx. Though much shorn, the Alsatian still had a working revenue of forty-four thousand francs. His chagrin was complicated with the *spleen* which affects those who are accustomed to live in the midst of affairs when they are separated from them. The banker gave himself for a duty the task of sacrificing himself, noble heart! to his wife, whose fortune had been made away with, and which she had allowed to be taken with the indifference of a young woman to whom monetary affairs were entirely unknown. The Baroness d'Aldrigger, then, was able to find again the pleasures to which she had been accustomed, the void which had been caused by the loss of the society of Strasbourg was filled by the pleasures of Paris. The house of Nucingen held then, as it still holds, the supremacy in financial society, and the clever baron made it a point of honor to treat well the honest baron. This fine virtue did good service in the Salon Nucingen. Each winter curtailed the capital of d'Aldrigger; but he did not dare to make the least reproach to the pearl of the Adolphuses; his tenderness was the most ingenuous and the most unintelligent that there is in this world. An honest man, but stupid! He died asking himself: 'What will become of them

without me?'   And during a moment in which he
was alone with his old valet de chambre, Wirth, the
good man, between two suffocations, commended
to him his wife and his two daughters, as if this
Caleb of Alsace was the only reasonable being that
there was in the house.   Three years later, in
1826, Isaure was twenty years old and Malvina was
not yet married.   In going out into the world, Malvina had ended by becoming convinced of the super-
ficiality of all its relations, of the extent to which
everything there is examined, defined.   Like the
greater number of young women said to be *well
brought-up*, Malvina was ignorant of the mechanism
of life, of the importance of a fortune, the difficulty
of acquiring the smallest amount of money, the price
of things.   Thus, during these six years, every
enlightenment had been to her like a wound.   The
four hundred thousand francs left by the late d'Aldrigger in the house of Nucingen were carried to
the credit of the baroness, for the estate of her husband was indebted to her in the sum of twelve
hundred thousand francs; and in times of need, the
shepherdess of the Alps drew from it as from an
inexhaustible treasury.   At the moment in which
our pigeon was advancing toward his turtle-dove,
Nucingen, knowing the character of his ancient
patroness, felt himself obliged to explain to Malvina
the financial situation in which the widow was
placed,—he had no more than three hundred thous-
and francs in his hands, the twenty-four thousand
francs of income were, therefore, reduced to eighteen

thousand.   Wirth had maintained the status during three years!   After the banker's revelation, the
horses were disposed of, the carriages sold and the
coachman dispensed with by Malvina, without her
mother's knowledge.   The furniture of the hotel,
which had been in use for ten years, could not be
renewed, but everything had faded in the same
time.   For those who love harmony, this was only
a semi-misfortune.   The baroness, this flower so
well preserved, had taken the aspect of a rose, cold
and shriveled which remains alone on the bush in
the middle of November.   I who speak to you, I
have seen this opulence vanishing by shades, by
demitones!   It was frightful, on my honor!   That
was my last grief.   After it I said to myself: 'It is
idiotic to take so much interest in others!'   While
I was an employé, I was stupid enough to interest
myself in all the houses in which I dined, I defended
them in case of scandal.   I did not calumniate them,
I—Oh! I was an infant!   When her daughter had
explained to her her position, the ci-devant pearl
exclaimed: 'My poor children!   Who will then
make my gowns!   I cannot then have any more
new bonnets, nor receive, nor go out in society!'—
In what way do you think love can be recognized
in a man?" said Bixiou, interrupting himself; "it
concerns us to know if Beaudenord was really in
love with this little blond."

"He neglects his affairs," replied Couture.

"He puts on three shirts in one day," said
Finot.

"A preliminary question," said Blondet,—"a superior man, can he and should he be in love?"

"My friends," resumed Bixiou, with a sentimental air, "beware, as you would of a venomous beast, of the man who, feeling himself taken with love for a woman, snaps his fingers or throws away his cigar, saying: 'Bah! there are others in the world!' But the government may employ this citizen in the Ministry of Foreign Affairs. Blondet, I'd have you note that this Godefroid had quit the diplomatic career."

"Well, he has been absorbed; love offers fools their only chance of growing," replied Blondet.

"Blondet, Blondet, why are we, then, so poor?" cried Bixiou.

"And why is Finot so rich?" replied Blondet; "I will tell you; come, my boy, we will understand each other. Just see, there is Finot, who pours out my wine as if I had carried up his fire-wood for him. But toward the end of the dinner you should *sip* your wine.—Well, then?"

"As you say, the absorbed Godefroid became very well acquainted with the tall Malvina, the fair baroness and the little danseuse. Ah! he fell into a state of servantism of the most detailed and the most astringent character. These remnants of a cadaverous opulence did not frighten him. Ah, bah! he became accustomed by degrees to all these rags. The green lampas of the salon, with its white ornaments, never appeared to this youth worn or old, nor spotted, nor in need of being renewed. The

curtains, the tea-table, the Chinese ornaments on
the chimney-piece, the rococo glass chandelier, the
carpet in imitation Cashmere worn threadbare, the
piano, the little flowered table service, the napkins
fringed and also open-worked in the Spanish style,
the Persian salon, which opened into the bed-chamber, in blue, of the baroness, with its accessories,
everything to him was saintly and sacred. Women
who are commonplace, and in whom beauty shines,
so as to throw into the shade wit, the heart and
the soul, alone can inspire such complete forgetfulness, for a spiritual woman never abuses her advantages; it is necessary to be petite and foolish thus
to carry a man away. Beaudenord, he told me so
himself, loved the old and solemn Wirth! This old
fellow respected his future master as a Catholic
believer respects the Eucharist. This honest
Wirth was a German Gaspard, one of those beer-
drinkers who conceal their shrewdness in their
good-nature, as a cardinal of the Middle Ages his
poniard in his sleeve. Wirth, seeing a husband for
Isaure, surrounded Godefroid with the ambages and
flowery circumlocutions of his Alsatian good-nature,
the most binding of all adhesive things. Madame
d'Aldrigger was profoundly *improper*, she found love
the most natural thing in the world. When Isaure
and Malvina went out together to the Tuileries or to
the Champs-Élysées, where they would meet the
young people of their society, the mother would say
to them: 'Amuse yourselves, my dear daughters.'
Their friends, the only persons who could speak

evil of the two sisters, defended them; for the great
liberty which reigned in the salon of the d'Aldriggers rendered it an unique locality in Paris. With
a fortune of millions, it would have been difficult to
have obtained such evenings, in which everything
was discussed with spirit, in which a careful partic-
ularity was not required, in which every one was
at his ease, even to the extent of asking for supper.
The two sisters wrote to whomsoever they pleased,
received peacefully their letters by their mother's
side, without the idea ever occurring to the baroness
to make any inquiries. This adorable mother gave
to her daughters all the benefits of her egoism, the
most amiable passion in the world, in this respect
that the egoists, not wishing to be interfered with,
interfere with no one, and do not in the least em-
barrass the life of those who surround them with
the brambles of good advice, with the thorns of
remonstrance, nor with the wasp-like teasing which
are permitted to those excessive friendships which
wish to know everything, to control everything.—"

"You go to my heart," said Blondet. "But, my
dear fellow, you are not telling your story, you are
hoaxing—"

"Blondet, if you were not drunk, you would give
me pain! Of us four, he is the only man who is
seriously literary! For his sake, I am doing you
the honor to treat you as epicures, I am distilling
to you my history, and he criticises me! My
friends, the greatest evidence of mental sterility
is the heaping up of fact. The sublime comedy of

the *Misanthrope* proves that art consists in build-
ing a palace on the point of a needle. The myth
of my idea is in the wand of the fairy which can
make of the plain of Sablons an Interlaken, in ten
seconds—the time to empty this glass!—Would
you have me make a recital to you that should go
like a cannon-ball, a report of the general-in-chief?
We are conversing, we are laughing, this newspaper man, bibliophobe fasting, wishes, when he
is drunk, that I should give to my language the sottish attraction of a book—he pretends to weep.—
Woe to the French imagination, the needles of its
pleasantry are to be blunted! *Dies iræ.* Weep,
Candide, and long live the *Critique de la raison
pure!* the *Symbolique*, and the systems in five
compact volumes, printed by the Germans, who
have not known at Paris since 1750, to put it neatly,
the diamonds of our national intelligence. Blondet
conducts the funeral train of its suicide, he who
utters in his journal the last words of all the great
men who have died for us without saying anything."

"Go your own gait," said Finot.

"I wish to explain to you in what consists the
happiness of a man who is not a shareholder—this
is a politeness to Couture!—Well, do you not see
now at what price Godefroid procured the greatest
happiness that a young man could dream of!—He
studied Isaure to be sure of being comprehended!—
Those things which comprehend each other should
be similar. Now, there are only like each other two
things, nothingness and the infinite; nothingness

is stupidity, genius is the infinite. These two
lovers wrote to each other the most stupid letters in
the world, sending them on paper perfumed with the
words then in the fashion: 'Angel! Æolian harp!
with thee I shall be complete! There is a heart in
my manly chest! Feeble woman! poor me!' all the
frippery of a modern heart. Godefroid scarcely
remained ten minutes in a salon, he talked with
women without any pretension, and they found him
very witty. He was of those who have no other
wit than that which is lent them. In short, you
may judge of his absorption,—Joby, his horses, his
carriages, became secondary things in his existence.
He was only happy when ensconced in her comfortable sofa before the baroness, at the corner of that
chimney-piece in verd-antique, occupied in watching Isaure, in drinking tea while conversing with a
little group of friends who came every evening, between eleven o'clock and midnight, to Rue Joubert,
and where one could always have a game of bouil-
lotte without fear:—I always won. When Isaure
had put out her pretty little foot, shod with a black
satin slipper and when Godefroid had looked at it
for a long time, he remained after all the others and
said to Isaure: 'Give me thy shoe'—Isaure raised
her foot, rested it on a chair, took off her shoe, gave
it to him, throwing upon him a look, one of those
looks—in short, you understand! Godefroid ended
by discovering a great mystery in Malvina. When
Du Tillet knocked at the door, the lively red which
colored the cheeks of Malvina said: 'Ferdinand!'

when looking at this tiger with two paws, the eyes of
the poor girl lit up like a brazier on which a current
of air is turned; she betrayed an infinite pleasure
when Ferdinand took her aside to tell her something
by a console or at the window. How very rare
and beautiful it is, a woman enough in love to become candid and to permit her heart to be read!
Mon Dieu, it is as scarce in Paris as is in the Indies
the flower that sings. Notwithstanding this friendship, commenced the day on which the d'Aldriggers appeared at the Nucingens, Ferdinand did not
marry Malvina. Our ferocious friend, Du Tillet, had
not seemed jealous of the assiduous court which
Desroches paid to Malvina, for, to finish paying for
his practice charges with a dot which appeared to
be not less than fifty thousand écus, he had feigned
love, he, a man of the law! Although profoundly
humiliated by the indifference of Du Tillet, Malvina
loved him too much to shut the door on him. In this
young woman, all soul, all sentiment, all expansion,
sometimes pride yielded to love, sometimes offended
love permitted pride to triumph. Calm and cold,
our friend Ferdinand accepted this tenderness, he
inhaled it with the tranquil satisfaction of a tiger
licking the blood which stains its jaws; he came to
get fresh proofs of it; he did not allow two days to
pass without presenting himself in the Rue Joubert.
The scamp possessed at this time about eighteen
hundred thousand francs; the question of fortune
should have been a secondary one in his eyes, and
he had resisted not only Malvina, but the Barons of

Nucingen and of Rastignac, who, both of them, had
made him do seventy-five leagues a day, with four
francs to the guides, the postilion in advance, and
with no clew! in the labyrinths of their shrewdness. Godefroid could not restrain himself from
speaking to his future sister-in-law of the unfortunate situation in which she was placed between a
banker and an advocate. 'You wish to sermonize
me on the subject of Ferdinand, to know the secret
which is between us,' she said frankly. 'Dear
Godefroid, do not speak of it again. The birth of
Ferdinand, his antecedents, his fortune, count for
nothing; therefore you may believe in something
extraordinary.' Nevertheless, a few days later,
Malvina took Beaudenord aside and said to him:
'I do not think Monsieur Desroches is an honest
man—such is the instinct of love!—he would like
to marry me, and is paying court to a grocer's
daughter. I should much like to know if I am a
make-shift, if marriage is for him only an affair
of money!' Despite his great intelligence, Desroches could not make out Du Tillet, and he
feared to see him marry Malvina. Thus the youth
had managed a retreat; his position was intolerable;
he gained with difficulty, all expenses paid, the
interest of his debt. Women never understand anything of these situations. For them, the heart is
always a millionaire!"

"But, as neither Desroches nor Du Tillet married
Malvina," said Finot, "explain to us Ferdinand's
secret."

"The secret, here it is," replied Bixiou. "General rule: A young person who has once given her slipper, if she should refuse it for ten years, is never married by him to whom—"

"Nonsense!" said Blondet, interrupting, "one loves also because one has loved. The secret, here it is. General rule: Do not marry as a sergeant, when you can become Duc de Dantzick and Marshal of France. Thus, see what an alliance Du Tillet did make! He married one of the daughters of the Comte de Granville, one of the oldest families of the French magistracy."

"The mother of Desroches had a friend," resumed Bixiou, "the wife of a druggist, which druggist had retired swollen with a fortune. These druggists have very absurd ideas,—in order to give his daughter a good education he had put her in a boarding-school!—This Matifat counted on marrying his daughter well, by virtue of two hundred thousand francs, in good and sound money which did not smell of drugs."

"The Matifat of Florine?" said Blondet.

"Well, yes, Lousteau's, ours, in short! These Matifats, then lost to us, had taken a house in the Rue du Cherche-Midi, the most opposite quarter to the Rue des Lombards, in which they had made their fortune. As for myself, I cultivated them, the Matifats! During my time in the ministerial galleys, in which I was locked up eight hours every day among dunces of twenty-two carats, I saw some originals which convinced me that shadows have

5

their asperities, and that in the greatest flatness one
may encounter angles! Yes, my dear fellow, one
bourgeois is to another as Raphaël is to Natoire.
The widow Desroches had brought about with all
her influence this marriage to her son, notwithstanding the enormous obstacle presented by a
certain Cochin, a son of the sleeping-partner of the
Matifats, a young man employed in the Ministry of
Finance. In the eyes of Monsieur and Madame
Matifat, the standing of an advocate appeared, as
they expressed it, to offer guarantees for the happiness of a wife. Desroches lent himself to his
mother's plans in order to have a certain choice. He
accordingly kept on good terms with the druggist of
the Rue du Cherche-Midi. To be able to understand
another species of happiness, it would be necessary
to describe for you these two trades-people, male and
female, enjoying a little garden, lodged in a fine
ground-floor, amusing themselves with watching a
little fountain, thin and long as a spike, which
played perpetually and sprang from a little round
table in freestone, in the middle of a basin six feet
in diameter; rising early to see if the flowers in
their garden had grown, unemployed and unquiet, dressing for the sake of dressing, boring
themselves at the theatre, and forever between
Paris and Luzarches, where they had a country-
house, and where I have dined. Blondet, one day
when they wished me to do something for them, I
related to them a story from nine o'clock in the
evening to midnight, an adventure of episodes. I

had arrived at the introduction of my twenty-ninth
personage—the serial novels stole it from me!—when
Father Matifat, who, in his character as head of the
house, had kept up a good appearance, fell to snoring
like the others, after having been winking for five
minutes. The next day everybody complimented
me on the ending of my story. These grocers had
for society Monsieur and Madame Cochin, Adolphe
Cochin, Madame Desroches, a little Popinot, a druggist exercising his profession, who brought them
the news of the Rue des Lombards—a man of your
acquaintance, Finot.—Madame Matifat, who loved
the arts, bought lithographs, chromo-lithographs,
colored designs, everything that was of the cheap-
est. The Sieur Matifat interested himself in
watching new enterprises and in endeavoring to
speculate with some funds in order to experience
some emotion—Florine had cured him of the styles
of the Regency.—A single word will enable you to
comprehend the profundity of my Matifat. The
good man bade his nieces good-night in these words:
'Go thou to bed, my nieces!' He was afraid, he
said, to hurt their feelings by saying *you* to them.
Their daughter was a young person without any
manners, with the appearance of a waiting-maid
in a good house, playing a sonata indifferently well,
with a pretty English hand-writing, knowing French
and orthography, in short, a complete bourgeois education. She was sufficiently impatient to be married,
in order to be able to leave the paternal mansion, in
which she was as much bored as a naval officer

during a night-watch; it must be said that the watch
here lasted the whole day.   Desroches or Cochin's
son, a notary or a Garde du Corps, an imitation
English lord, any husband would do for her.   As
she evidently knew nothing of life, I took pity on
her; I wished to reveal to her its great mystery.
Bah! the Matifats shut their door on me: the bourgeois and I, we shall never comprehend each other."

"She married General Gouraud," said Finot.

"In forty-eight hours, Godefroid de Beaudenord,
the ex-diplomat, had taken the measure of the Matifats and their intriguing corruption," resumed
Bixiou.   "As it happened, Rastignac was present in
the house of the light baroness, talking, at a corner of
the fire, while Godefroid made his report to Malvina.
Some words reached his ear, he guessed at the subject under discussion, especially because of the bit-
terly satisfied air of Malvina.   Rastignac remained
there until two o'clock in the morning,—and people
said that he was egotistical! Beaudenord left when
the baroness went to bed.   'Dear child,' said Rastignac to Malvina, in a good-humored and paternal tone,
when they were alone,'remember that a poor fellow
heavy with sleep has kept himself awake with tea
until two o'clock in the morning in order to be able
to say to you solemnly: *Get married.*   Do not
raise any difficulties, do not concern yourself with
feelings, do not think of the ignoble calculations of
men who have one foot here and one foot at the
Matifats, reflect on nothing: get married! For a
girl to get married, that is to impose herself on a

man who engages to support her in a position more
or less happy, but in which the material question
is assured. I know the world: young girls, mam-
mas and grandmothers are all hypocrites in making
so much ado about feelings when it is a question of
marriage. No one thinks of any other thing than
being well-established. When her daughter is well
married, a mother says that she has done an excellent thing.' And Rastignac proceeded to develop to
her his theory upon marriage, which, according to
him, is a commercial society instituted to support
life. 'I do not ask your secret,' said he, in conclusion, to Malvina, 'I know it. Men talk about everything among themselves, just as you do when you
go out after dinner. Well, then, this is my last
word: Get married. If you do not get married,
remember that I begged you here, this evening, to
get married!' Rastignac spoke with a certain
accent which commanded, not attention, but reflection. His insistence was of a nature to surprise.
Malvina was so much struck with it in her keenest
intelligence, which Rastignac wished to reach, that
she was still thinking of it the next day, and un-
availingly sought to discover the reason for this
advice.''

"I do not see in all these peg-tops which you set
off, anything which resembles the origin of Rastignac's fortune, and you take us for the Matifats
multiplied by six bottles of champagne!'' cried
Couture.

"We are there,'' replied Bixiou. "You have

followed the course of all the little streams which have made the forty thousand francs of income which so many people envy! Rastignac then held in his hands the thread of all these existences."

"Desroches, the Matifats, Beaudenord, the d'Aldriggers, d'Aiglemont?"

"And of a hundred others!—" said Bixiou.

"Well, now, how?" cried Finot. "I know a good many things, and I do not see the answer to this enigma."

"Blondet has described to you briefly the first two liquidations of Nucingen, here is the third in detail," resumed Bixiou. "At the Peace of 1815, Nucingen had comprehended that which we only understand to-day,—that money is a power only when it is in disproportionate quantities. He was secretly jealous of the brothers Rothschild. He possessed five millions, he wished to have ten! With ten millions he would know how to gain thirty, and with five he would only have fifteen. He had therefore resolved to bring about a third liquidation! This great man consequenty planned to pay his creditors with fictitious values while keeping their money. On the exchanges, an operation of this kind does not present itself in quite such a mathematical expression. A liquidation of this kind consists in giving a little pâté for a golden louis to big children, who, like the little children formerly, preferred the pâté to the coin, without knowing that for the coin they could have two hundred pâtés."

"What is it you are saying to us, Bixiou?" cried

Couture, "but nothing is more fair, there is not a week goes by nowadays without some one presenting pâtés to the public and demanding a louis for each. But is the public forced to give its money? has it not the right to inform itself?"

"You would like it better if compelled to buy its shares of stock," said Blondet.

"No," said Finot, "or where would be our smartness?"

"That is very good for Finot," said Bixiou.

"Who gave him that idea?" asked Couture.

"In short," resumed Bixiou, "Nucingen had had on two occasions the happinesses of giving, without intending it, a pâté which came to possess more value than he had received. This unlucky good fortune had caused him remorse. Happiness such as this, ends by killing a man. He waited during ten years for an occasion in which he would not deceive himself, in which to create values that should have the appearance of being worth something and which—"

"But," said Couture, "with this explanation of banking, no commerce is possible. More than one honest banker has persuaded, under the approval of a loyal government, the most able treasurers to accept funds which in the course of time have become depreciated. You have seen better than that! Have there not been issued, always with the advice, with the support of governments, securities with which to pay the interest of certain funds, in order to maintain their circulation and to enable them to be disposed of? These operations have more or less analogy with liquidation in the manner of Nucingen."

"In small affairs," said Blondet, "the transaction might appear singular; but on a great scale it is high financiering. There are certain arbitrary acts which are criminal between individuals, but which amount to nothing when they are expanded through any multitude whatever, like a drop of Prussic acid which becomes harmless in a tub of water. You kill a man and you are guillotined. But, with any governmental conviction whatever, you kill five hundred men, the political crime is respected. You take five thousand francs from my writing-desk, you go to the galleys. But, with the pimento of a profit to make, skilfully put in the mouths of a thousand purse-holders, you force them to take the stocks of I-know-not-what republic or monarchy in default, issued, as Couture says, to pay the interest of these same stocks,—no one can complain. These are the true principles of the age of gold in which we live!"

"The setting in operation of so vast a machine," resumed Bixiou, "required a great many punchinellos. In the first place, the house of Nucingen had knowingly, and with design, employed its five millions in an American enterprise, the profits of which had been calculated in such a manner as to come in too late. They had been put out of the way with premeditation. Every liquidation should be justified. The bank possessed in individual funds

and in values issued about six millions. Among the
individual funds were the three hundred thousand
francs of the Baroness d'Aldrigger, the four hundred
thousand of Beaudenord, a million belonging to
d'Aiglemont, three hundred thousand francs to
Matifat, a half million to Charles Grandet, the husband of Mademoiselle d'Aubrion, etc. If he had
created himself some industrial enterprise with the
shares of which he proposed to satisfy his creditors
by means of manœuvres more or less skilful,
Nucingen might have been suspected, but he went
about it with much more adroitness; he caused it to
be created by another!—that machine destined to
play the part which the Mississippi did in the system of Law. The peculiar quality of Nucingen
is to make the most able negotiators serve his
projects without communicating his own to them.
Nucingen accordingly let slip before Du Tillet a
suggestion of this pyramidal and victorious scheme
of getting up an enterprise by subscription with a
capital sufficiently large to pay very heavy interest
to the shareholders at first. If tried for the first
time, at a period when there was an abundance of
credulous capital, this combination should bring
about a rise in the shares, and consequently a benefit for the banker who issued them. Remember
that this was in 1826. Although struck with this
idea, fruitful as ingenious, Du Tillet naturally
reflected that, if the enterprise did not succeed, there
would be some blame laid somewhere. Therefore,
he would suggest putting forward some visible

director for this commercial machine.   You know
to-day the secret of the house of Claparon, founded
by Du Tillet, one of his finest inventions!—"

"Yes," said Blondet, "the responsible financial
editor, the agent that prepares the way, the scapegoat; but, to-day, we are more clever, we put out:
'Address the Management of the thing, such a street,
such a number,' where the public will find employés
in green caps, pretty as bailiff's men."

"Nucingen had supported the house of Charles
Claparon with all his credit," resumed Bixiou.   "A
million of the paper of Claparon could be issued
without any fear on some exchanges.   Du Tillet
proposed, therefore, to bring the house of Claparon
forward.   Adopted.   In 1825, the shareholder was
not spoiled in industrial enterprises.   The funds
destined to provide for *running expenses* were unknown!   The directors did not undertake to ever
issue their interest-bearing shares; they deposited
nothing in the Bank of France, they guaranteed
nothing.   The shareholder could not expect to have
the workings of the company explained to him when
informed that he was fortunate in not having more
than a thousand, or more than five hundred, or even
two hundred and fifty francs demanded of him!   It
was not published that the experience *in are publico*
would only endure for seven years, five years or
even three years, and that therefore the dénouement
would not have to be long waited for.   It was the
infancy of the art!   There had not even been called
in the publicity of those gigantic announcements by

which imaginations are now stimulated, by demanding money from everyone—"

"This happens when no one wishes to subscribe," said Couture.

"In short, the competition in this sort of enterprises did not exist," resumed Bixiou. "The manufacturers of papier-maché, of printed calicoes, the rollers of zinc, the theatres, the newspapers, did not throw themselves in like dogs of the chase at 'the death' of the expiring shareholder. The fine affairs by subscription, as Couture says, so ingenuously published, supported by the reports of experts—the princes of science!—were then transacted shamefacedly in the silence and in the obscurity of the Bourse. The monetary lynxes executed, financially speaking, the air of the Calumny of the *Barber of Seville*. They went *piano, piano,* proceeding by light cancans, on the good qualities of the enterprise, spoken from ear to ear. They did not exploit the patient, the shareholder, only at his house, at the Bourse, or in society, by that rumor skilfully created, and which increased to the *tutti* of a number of four figures—"

"But, since we are among ourselves and can say anything, I return to our subject," said Couture.

"You are a goldsmith, Monsieur Josse!" said Finot.

"Finot will remain classical, constitutional, and bewigged," said Blondet.

"Yes, I am a goldsmith," resumed Couture, "seeing that Cérizet has been condemned by the police tribunals. I maintain that the new method is infinitely less treacherous, more honest, less assassinating, than the old one. The publicity allows of reflection and examination. If any stockholder is gullible, he comes to it deliberately; he has not been made to purchase 'a pig in a poke.' Industry—"

"Ah! now we are coming to industry!" cried Bixiou.

"Industry would profit by it," said Couture, without paying any attention to the interruption. "Every government that interferes with commerce and does not leave it unrestricted, undertakes a costly folly; it brings about either the *maximum* or the monopoly. To my thinking, nothing is more conformable to the principles of the liberty of commerce than the societies of shareholders! To meddle with them, is to answer for both capital and profits, which is stupid. In every transaction, the profits are in proportion to the risks! What matters it to the state the manner in which is brought about the free circulation of money, provided that it be kept in perpetual activity? What matter who is rich, who is poor, if there is always the same quantity of taxable wealth? Moreover, for the last twenty years the societies of shareholders, stock-companies, premiums under all possible forms, have been in use in the most commercial country in the world, in England, where everything is disputed, where Parliament hatches out a thousand or twelve hundred laws each session, and

where a member of either House has never risen to
speak against the method—"

"Curative for full coffers, and a vegetarian one!"
said Bixiou; "carrots!" *

"Come now!" said Couture, excitedly.   "You
have ten thousand francs, you take ten shares of a
thousand each in ten different enterprises.   You are
robbed nine times—this is not so! the public is
wiser than any one person! but I make the suppo-
sition—one enterprise alone succeeds—by chance!—
agreed!—it has not been made expressly!—oh, go
ahead! talk nonsense!—Well, the *punter* who is
wise enough thus to divide up his forces will find a
superb investment, as did those who took the shares
of the mines of Wortschin.   Messieurs, let us admit
among ourselves that the people who cry out are the
hypocrites in despair at having neither the conception of an enterprise, nor the power to proclaim it,
nor the skill to exploit it.   The proof will not long
be waited for.   In a little while you will see the
aristocracy, the people of the Court, the ministeri-
alists, descending in solid columns into business
speculations, and reaching out hands more grasping
and finding more tortuous ideas than ours, without
having our superiority.   What a head it requires
to set on foot a good enterprise at an epoch in
which the avidity of the shareholder is equal to that
of the inventor!   What a great magnetizer must be
the man who creates a Claparon, who finds new
expedients!   Do you know the moral of all this?

* Carotte, a trick for obtaining money by skill or deception.

Our time is no better than we are! We live in an epoch of avidity in which no one concerns himself about the value of a thing, provided he can make something on it and pass it on to his neighbor; and it is passed on to the neighbor because the avidity of the shareholder, who hopes for a profit, is equal to that of the founder who proposed one to him!"

"Isn't he fine, Couture, isn't he fine!" said Bixiou to Blondet; "he is going to ask that statues be erected to him, as to a benefactor of humanity."

"It will be necessary to bring him to conclude that the money of fools is, by right divine, the patrimony of clever men," said Blondet.

"Messieurs," resumed Couture, "let us laugh here in return for the seriousness which we preserve elsewhere, when we hear uttered the respectable stupidities which consecrate the laws made without forethought."

"He is right. What a time, Messieurs," said Blondet, "is that in which as soon as the fire of intelligence appears it is quickly extinguished by the application of a circumstantial law! The legislators, nearly all of them come from little arrondissements where they have made their social studies in the newspapers, put the fire in the engine. When the engine blows up, then there are tears and grindings of teeth! A time in which the only laws made are fiscal and penal! The true word of all that happens, do you wish to know it! *There is no longer any religion in the state!*"

"Ah!" said Bixiou, "bravo, Blondet! you have

put your finger on the tender spot of France,—the code of fiscal laws, which has taken more conquests from our country than all the vexations of war. In the ministry where I served seven years at the galleys, yoked with the bourgeois, there was an employé, a man of talent, who had resolved to change the entire financial system—ah! well, we very soon dismissed him. France had been too happy, she would have amused herself by reconquering Europe, and we acted in the interest of the repose of nations. I killed Rabourdin by a caricature!"—See *The Civil Service*.

"When I said *religion*, I did not mean to say a stupid Capuchin's sermon; I understand the word in a grand political sense," resumed Blondet.

"Explain yourself," said Finot.

"In this way," continued Blondet. "There has been much talk of the affairs at Lyons, of the Republic cannonaded in the streets; no one has told the truth. The Republic took possession of the riot just as an insurgent grasps a gun. The real truth, I will give it to you, both absurd and profound. The commerce of Lyons is a commerce without any soul, which does not manufacture a yard of silk unless it is ordered and unless the payment is sure. When the orders cease, the workman dies of hunger; he earns with difficulty enough to live on when he works. The galley slaves are happier than he. After the Revolution of July, the misery reached such a point that the CANUTS* hoisted the flag,

* Canut, operative in the silk factories of Lyons.

'Bread or death!' one of those proclamations which
the government should study; it was produced by the
dearness of living at Lyons. Lyons wished to build
theatres and to become a capital, hence came sense-
less octroi duties.   The Republicans scented this
revolt in the cause of bread, and they organized the
Canuts, who fought in two parties.   Lyons has had
its three days, but everything has returned to order
and the Canut into his hole.   The Canut, honest up
to this period, returning in the woven stuff the silk
which was weighed out to him in hanks, has turned
his honesty out of the door, believing that the merchant had victimized him, and has put oil on his
fingers,—he has returned weight for weight, but he
had sold oil represented as silk, and the trade in
French silks has been infested with 'loaded silks,'
which may bring about the destruction of Lyons
and that of a branch of the commerce of France.
The manufacturers and the government, instead of
suppressing the cause of the evil, have, like certain
physicians, driven in the disease by a violent
topical remedy.   There should have been sent to
Lyons a skilful man, one of those who are called
immoral, an Abbé Terray, but the situation was
looked at only from the military point of view!
The troubles, therefore, have produced gros-grain at
forty sous the aune.   This gros-grain, it can be
said, is sold to-day, and the manufacturers have
doubtless invented I know not what system of veri-
fication.   This method of manufacture without forethought is naturally established in a country in

which RICHARD LENOIR, one of the greatest citizens
which France ever had, had ruined himself by giving
employment to six thousand workmen without
any orders, by supporting them, and had found
ministers stupid enough to let him succumb to the
revolution which 1814 brought about in the price of
stuffs. This is the only case in which a merchant
has merited a statue. Well, this man is to-day the
object of the subscription to which there are no subscribers, whilst a million has been raised for the
children of General Foy. Lyons is consistent; it
knows France; it is without any religious sentiment.
The story of Richard Lenoir is one of those faults
which Fouché found to be worse than a crime."

"If in the manner in which affairs present themselves," resumed Couture, going back to the point
where he was before the interruption, "there is a
tinge of charlatanism, a word which has become dishonoring and set astride the partition-wall between
the just and the unjust, I demand where commences, or where finishes, charlatanism, what is
charlatanism? Have the kindness to tell me who is
not a charlatan? Come, now, let us have a little
good faith, the rarest social ingredient! That commerce which should consist in going to seek at
night that which could be sold in the day would
be nonsense. A seller of matches has the instinct
of monopoly. To monopolize merchandise is the
idea of the shop-keeper of the Rue Saint-Denis,
called the most virtuous, as of the speculator *called*
the most shameless. When the stores are full, there

6

is a necessity to sell. To sell, it is necessary to *excite* the customer, hence the sign of the Middle Ages and the advertisement of to-day! Between calling in the customers and forcing them to enter, to purchase, I do not see the difference of a hair! It may happen, it should happen, it often does happen, that merchants get caught with damaged merchandise, for the seller is incessantly cheating the buyer. Well, consult the most honest people in Paris, the distinguished merchants, in short,—they will all relate to you triumphantly the trick which they have invented to get rid of their merchandise when it has been sold to them in a damaged condition. The famous House of Minard commenced by sales of this description. The Rue Saint-Denis will only sell you a dress of loaded silk; it has no other. The most virtuous merchant will repeat to you with the most candid air this phrase of the most brazen dishonesty: 'You get out of a bad bargain the best way you can.' Blondet has shown you the affair of Lyons in its causes and in its consequences; for my part, I will get to the application of my theory by an anecdote. A workman in wool, ambitious and overloaded with children by a wife too much loved, believes in the Republic. My fine fellow bought a lot of red wool and made these caps in knitted wool which you may have seen on the heads of all the gamins of Paris, and you will know why. The Republic was overcome. After the affair of Saint-Merri, the caps were unsalable. When a workman finds himself in his

household with a wife, children and ten thousand
red woolen caps which no hatter on any shore
wants, there come into his head as many ideas as
would present themselves to a banker loaded with
ten millions of shares to place in an enterprise which
he mistrusts. Do you know what he did, this workman, this Law of the Faubourgs, this Nucingen
of caps? He hunted up a dandy of the taverns,
one of those fellows who are the despair of the
police sergeants in the Bals Champêtres of the barriers, and requested him to play the part of an
American captain trading in colonial goods, stop-
ping at the Hôtel Meurice, to go and *inquire for* ten
thousand red woolen caps at the establishment of a
rich hatter who had still one of them in his stock.
The hatter foresaw a large transaction in America,
he hastened to the workman and eagerly took possession of all the caps, cash down.   You understand,
—no more American captain, but a great many caps.
To attack commercial liberty because of these in-
conveniences, would be to attack justice under
the pretext that there are delinquencies which it
does not punish, or to accuse society of being badly
organized because of the misfortunes to which it
gives rise! From caps and the Rue Saint-Denis to
shares of stock and the Bank of France, draw your
own conclusions!"

"Couture, a crown!" said Blondet, placing on his
head his twisted napkin. "I go farther, Messieurs.
If there be a vice in the actual theory, whose is the
fault? that of the law! the law considered in its

entire system, legislation! of those great men of the
arrondissements whom the provinces send puffed up
with moral ideas, ideas indispensable in the conduct
of life, at least to combat by the side of justice, but
stupid as soon as they prevent a man from lifting
himself to the height at which the legislator should
maintain himself. Though the laws may forbid to the
passions such or such a development—gambling, the
lottery, the Ninons of the barriers, whatever you
like,—they will never extirpate the passions. To
kill the passions, that would be to kill society,
which, if it does not engender them, at least develops them. Thus, if you fetter with restrictions
the desire to gamble which lurks at the bottom of
every heart, that of the young girl, that of the man
of the provinces, as in that of a diplomat, for all
the world sighs for a fortune *gratis*, gambling will
then display itself in other spheres. You suppress
the lottery stupidly; the cooks will not the less steal
from their masters, they will carry their thefts to
the savings-bank, and the stake is for them two
hundred and fifty francs instead of being forty sous,
for the shares in industrial enterprises, the stock-
companies, become the lottery, the play without the
green carpet, but with an invisible rake and with
a calculated success for the bank. The gambling
places are closed, the lottery no longer exists, behold
France much more moral, exclaim the imbeciles,
as if they had suppressed the *punters!* Gambling
still goes on, only the benefit no longer accrues to
the state, which replaces a tax paid with pleasure

by a vexatious tax, without diminishing the number of suicides, for the gambler does not die, but only his victim! I do not say anything about funds invested abroad, lost to France, nor of the lotteries of Frankfort, against the hawking about of which the Convention proclaimed the death penalty, and to which the *procureurs-syndics* themselves were addicted! Here you may see the sense of the silly philanthropy of our legislator. The encouragement given to the savings-bank is a gross political stupidity. Suppose any distrust whatever about the conduct of affairs, the government would have created *la queue* * *de l'argent* as they created during the Revolution, *la queue du pain.* So many savings-banks, so many riots. If, in a corner, three street boys set up a solitary flag, you will have a revolution. But this danger, however great it may be, seems to me less to be feared than that of the demoralization of the people. A savings-bank is the inoculation of all the vices engendered by interest, to those whom neither education nor reflection restrain in their tacitly criminal combinations. And there you have the effects of philanthropy. A great politician should be a blackguard in the abstract; without which societies are badly conducted. A politician who is an honest man is a steam-engine which has feelings, or a pilot who makes love while at the helm,—the vessel founders. A prime minister who takes a hundred millions and who renders France great and happy, is he not

* *Queue,* a long line of people waiting to be served.

to be preferred to a minister who has to be buried at the expense of the state, but who had ruined his country? Between Richelieu, Mazarin, Potemkin, all three of them possessed at certain epochs three hundred millions, and the virtuous Robert Lindet, who did not know enough to make anything either from the assignats, nor from the national property, or the virtuous imbeciles who ruined Louis XVI., would you hesitate? Go on with your story, Bixiou."

"I will not explain to you," resumed Bixiou, "the nature of the enterprise invented by the financial genius of Nucingen, it would be all the more inconvenient, as it is still existing to-day; its shares are quoted on the Bourse; the combinations were so real, the object of the enterprise so permanent, that, created with a nominal capital of a thousand francs, established by royal ordinance, fallen to three hundred francs, they went up again to seven hundred, and will arrive at par after having traversed the storms of the years '27, '30 and '32. The financial crisis of 1827 made them shrink, the Revolution of July brought them down, but the enterprise is sound at bottom—Nucingen would not know how to invent a bad affair—In short, as several first-class banking houses have participated in it, it would not be parliamentary to enter more into details. The nominal capital was fixed at ten millions, the real capital seven, three millions were to go to the originators and to the bankers who had charge of the issuing of the shares. Everything

was calculated so as to cause in the first six months
each share to gain two hundred francs by the distribution of a fictitious dividend. Hence, twenty
per cent on ten millions. The interest of Du
Tillet amounted to five hundred thousand francs.
In the financial vocabulary this gain is called the
glutton's part! Nucingen proposed to operate, with
his millions made from a quire of pink paper, with
the aid of a lithographic stone, some nice little
marketable shares, preciously preserved in his
cabinet. The real shares would go to help establish the enterprise, to buy a magnificent hôtel
and commence operations. Nucingen found still
other shares in I-know-not-what mines of silver-
bearing lead ore, in oil wells and in two canals,
interest-bearing shares issued to aid in the presentation of these four enterprises in full activity,
equipped in a superior manner and flourishing,
thanks to the dividend drawn on the capital.
Nucingen could count upon an *agio* if the shares
went up, but the baron left this out of his calculations; he allowed it to remain at its par value,
on the market, in order to attract the fish!
He had thus massed his funds, as Napoléon massed
his troops, in order to be able to liquidate during
the crisis which was revealing itself and which rev-
olutionized, in '26 and '27, the European markets.
If he had had his Prince de Wagram, he would have
been able to say, as did Napoléon on the heights of
Santon: 'Examine the locality well; on such a day,
at such an hour, there will funds be scattered!'

But in whom could he confide? Du Tillet did not
suspect his involuntary complicity. His first two
liquidations had demonstrated to our puissant baron
the necessity of attaching to himself a man who
could serve him as a piston to act on the creditor.
Nucingen had no nephew, did not dare to take a
confidant; he required a devoted man, an intelligent
Claparon, gifted with good manners, a veritable
diplomat, a man worthy of being a minister and
worthy of him. Such connections are not formed in
a day nor in a year. Rastignac had been so well
twisted up by the baron, that, like the Prince of
the Peace, who was loved as much by the king as by
the queen of Spain, he believed he had conquered
in Nucingen an invaluable dupe. After having
laughed at a man whose capacity was long unknown
to him, he had finished by vowing to him a grave
and serious worship in recognizing in him the
strength which he thought he alone possessed.
From the date of his début in Paris, Rastignac had
been led to despise society in its entirety. From
1820, he had thought, like the baron, that there
were only apparently honest men, and he regarded
the world as the reunion of all corruptions and of all
dishonesties. If he admitted exceptions, he condemned the mass; he did not believe in any virtue,
but in certain circumstances in which man is virtuous. This science was the result of a moment; it
was acquired at the top of Père-Lachaise, the day
on which he conducted there the funeral of a poor,
honest man, the father of his Delphine, who had

died the dupe of our society, of the truest feelings,
and abandoned by his daughters and by his sons-
in-law. He resolved to get the better of all this
world, and to maintain himself in a fine costume of
virtue, of probity, of beautiful manners. Egotism
armed this young noble cap-a-pie. When he met
Nucingen clothed with the same armor, he esteemed
him as, in the Middle Ages, in the tournament, a
knight in damascene steel from the feet to the head,
mounted on a war horse, would esteem his adversary
caparisoned and mounted like himself. But he
softened for a while in the delights of Capua. The
friendship of a woman like the Baroness de Nucingen is of a nature to banish all egotism. After having been deceived a first time in her affections by
meeting a piece of Birmingham mechanism, such
as was the late De Marsay, Delphine naturally felt
for a man young and full of the religious sentiment
of the provinces, an attachment without bounds.
This tenderness reacted on Rastignac. When
Nucingen had passed over to his wife's friend the
harness which every exploiter puts on his exploitee,
which happened precisely at the moment when he
was meditating his third liquidation, he confided to
him his position, presenting to him, as an obligation
growing out of his intimacy, as a reparation, the
rôle of accomplice to take up and to play. The
baron thought it dangerous to initiate his conjugal
collaborator into his plan. Rastignac feared a misfortune, and the baron let him believe that he might
save the shop. But, when a skein has so many

threads, there are sure to be knots.   Rastignac
trembled for the fortune of Delphine; he stipulated
for the independence of the baroness, requiring a
separation of property, swearing to himself to join
his account with hers and triple her fortune.   As
Eugène did not speak for himself, Nucingen begged
him to accept, in case of complete success, twenty-
five shares of a thousand francs each in the mines
of silver-bearing lead ore, which Rastignac took so
as not to offend him! Nucingen taught Rastignac
his tunes the evening before the day in which our
friend advised Malvina to get married.   At the
sight of the hundred happy families who came and
went in Paris tranquil in the possession of their fortunes, the Godefroid de Beaudenords, the d'Aldriggers, the d'Aiglemonts, etc., Rastignac was seized
with a shiver like a young general who for the first
time contemplates an army before the battle.   The
poor little Isaure and Godefroid, playing at love, did
they not represent Acis and Galatea under the rock
which the great Polyphemus is about to tumble on
them?—"

"This monkey of a Bixiou," said Blondet, "he
has almost a talent."

"Ah! I am not sentimentalizing, then, any
more?" said Bixiou, enjoying his success, and
looking at his surprised auditors.—"During two
months," he resumed, after this interruption,
"Godefroid gave himself up to all the little happinesses of a man who is about to marry.   He
resembles at this period those birds who make their

nests in springtime, come and go, pick up straws, carry them in their beaks, and line the domicile of their eggs. The future husband of Isaure had taken in the Rue de la Planche a little hôtel for a thousand écus, commodious, suitable, neither too large nor too small. He went every morning to see the workmen working and to inspect the painting. He had introduced comfort there, the only good thing that there is in England,—a heater to maintain an equal temperature in the house; furniture well chosen, neither too brilliant nor too elegant; colors fresh and pleasant to the eye, interior and exterior blinds to all the windows; silverware, new carriages. He had arranged the stable, the harness-house, the carriage-house, where Toby, Joby, Paddy agitated himself, fidgeting about like a marmot unchained, and apparently delighted to know that there would be women in the household and a *lady!* This passion of the man who sets up housekeeping, who selects clocks, who comes into the house of his betrothed with his pockets full of samples of stuffs, consults her on the furnishing of the bed-chamber, who goes, comes, trots, when he goes, comes, and trots animated by love, is one of those things which most rejoice an honest heart, and especially the furnishers. And, as nothing pleases the world more than the marriage of a pretty young man of twenty-seven with a charming girl of twenty who dances well, Godefroid, embarrassed by the bridegroom's gifts, invited Rastignac and Madame de Nucingen to déjeuner, in order to consult them on this capital affair.

He had the excellent idea of inviting his cousin d'Aiglemont and his wife, as well as Madame de Sérizy. Fashionable women like very well these little occasional dissipations in bachelor apartments, they like to breakfast there."

"It is their way of playing truant," said Blondet.

"Every one had to go and see in the Rue de la Planche the little hôtel of the future married pair," resumed Bixiou. "The women are for these little expeditions just like ogres for fresh flesh, they freshen up their own present with this young joy which has not yet begun to pall through enjoyment. The table was laid in the little salon, which, for the interment of this bachelor life, was adorned like a show horse in a cavalcade. The déjeuner had been selected so as to offer a variety of those pretty little dishes which the women love to eat, to craunch, to suck, in the mornings, a time of the day in which they have a frightful appetite, which they do not wish to admit, for it seems that they compromise themselves in saying: 'I am hungry!' 'And why are you all alone?' said Godefroid, seeing Rastignac arrive. 'Madame de Nucingen is indisposed, I will tell you all about it,' replied Rastignac, who had the appearance of a man much disturbed. 'Some dis- agreement?' cried Godefroid. 'No,' said Rastignac. At four o'clock, when the ladies had all flown away to the Bois de Boulogne, Rastignac remained in the salon, looking in a melancholy manner through the window at Toby, Joby, Paddy, who was posted audaciously before the horse harnessed to the tilbury, the arms folded like Napoléon; he could not keep him in check otherwise than by his clear, shrill voice, and the horse feared Joby, Toby. 'Well, what is the matter with you, my dear friend?' said Godefroid to Rastignac. 'You are sombre, disquieted; your gayety is not spontaneous. It is incomplete happiness which vexes your soul. It is, in fact, very unfortunate not to be married at the Mayor's office and at the church to the woman you love.' 'Have you courage, my dear fellow, to hear what I have to say to you, and will you know how to recognize to what a degree it is necessary to be attached to some one in order to commit the indiscretion of which I am about to be culpable?' said Rastignac to him in that tone which resembled a stroke of a whip. 'What?' said Godefroid, turning pale. 'I was grieved at your joy, and I have not the heart, in seeing all these preparations, this happiness in flower, to keep such a secret.' 'Tell me in three words.' 'Swear to me on your honor that you will be in this as silent as the tomb.' 'As the tomb.' 'That, if one of your nearest friends is interested in this secret, he shall not know it.' 'He shall not.' 'Well, Nucingen has gone off last night to Brussels; it will be necessary to go into bankruptcy if liquidation cannot be effected. Delphine has petitioned this very morning at the Palais for the separation of her property. You may yet save your fortune.' 'How?' said Godefroid, feeling an icy blood in his veins. 'Write simply to the Baron de Nucingen a letter antedated fifteen days, in which

you will give him the order to employ all your
funds in shares—and he named to him the Claparon
Company—You will have two weeks, a month,
three months, perhaps, to sell them above the present price; they will rise still higher.' 'But
d'Aiglemont, who breakfasted with us, d'Aiglemont, who has a million invested with Nucingen!'
'Listen, I do not know if there are enough of these
shares to cover him, and then I am not his friend.
I cannot betray the secrets of Nucingen; you
must not speak to him about it. If you say one
word, you will answer to me for the consequences.'
Godefroid remained for ten minutes perfectly
motionless. 'Do you accept, yes or no?' said Rastignac to him, pitilessly. Godefroid took pen and
ink, he wrote and signed the letter which Rastignac
dictated to him. 'My poor cousin!' he cried. 'Each
one for himself,' said Rastignac. 'And one saved
from the game,' he added, in leaving Godefroid.
While Rastignac was manœuvering in Paris, this
was the state of affairs on the Bourse. I have a
friend from the provinces, a stupid, who asked me,
when passing the Bourse, between four and five
o'clock, the reason for this assemblage of eager
talkers, who came and went, what they could be
saying to each other, and why they were thus going
about after the final settlement of the price of the
public funds. 'My friend,' I said to him, 'they
have eaten, they are digesting; during diges-
tion, they gossip about their neighbors; without
that, no commercial security in Paris.' There

enterprises are launched, and there is such and
such a man, Palma, for example, whose authority
is like that of Sinard at the Royal Academy of
Sciences. He says: 'Let there be speculation,' and
speculation there is."

"What a man, Messieurs," said Blondet, "is this
Jew, who possesses an education not of the Univer-
sities, but universal. In him, the universality does
not exclude profundity; what he knows, he knows
all the way to the bottom; his genius is intuitive in
business; he is the great referendary of the lynxes
who rule the Exchange of Paris, and who do not
undertake an enterprise until Palma has examined
it. He is grave, he listens, he studies, he reflects,
and says to his interlocutor, who, seeing his attention, believes him secured: 'That does not interest
me.' That which seems to me to be the most extraordinary, is, that after having been for ten years
the associate of Werbrust, there have never arisen
any differences between them."

"That only happens between those who are very
strong or very weak; all those who are between
these two extremes quarrel and speedily separate
enemies," said Couture.

"You understand," said Bixiou, "that Nucingen
had knowingly and with a skilful hand thrown
under the columns of the Bourse a little shell which
exploded about four o'clock. 'Do you know of a
grave piece of news?' said Du Tillet to Werbrust,
drawing him into a corner. 'Nucingen is in Brussels,
his wife has presented to the court a petition for

her separation of property.' 'Are you his accomplice in a liquidation?' said Werbrust, smiling. 'No nonsense, Werbrust,' said Du Tillet; 'you know the people who have his paper; listen to me, we have an affair to arrange. The shares of our new company earn twenty per cent, they will gain twenty-five at the end of the quarter; you know why. There will be a magnificent dividend.' 'You are sly,' said Werbrust, 'go on, go your way; you are a devil whose claws are long and pointed, and you plunge them in butter.' 'But let me tell you, or we will not have time in which to operate. I found my idea when I heard the news, and I have positively seen Madame de Nucingen in tears; she has fears for her fortune.' 'Poor little thing!' said Werbrust, with an ironical air. 'Well?' resumed this old Alsatian Jew, interrogating Du Tillet, who was silent. 'Well, there are in my office a thousand shares of a thousand francs which Nucingen delivered to me to put on the market, do you understand?' 'Good!' 'We will buy at ten, at twenty per cent discount, paper of the House of Nucingen for a million, we will gain a fine premium on this million, for we will be creditors and debtors, there will be uncertainty! But we must act carefully; the holders might believe that we are manœuvering in the interests of Nucingen.' Werbrust now comprehended the thing to be done and grasped Du Tillet's hand, throwing upon him the look of a woman who is playing a trick on her neighbor. 'Well, have you heard the news?' said Martin Falleix to them. 'The House of Nucingen

has suspended!' 'Bah!' replied Werbrust; 'Do
not noise that about, let the people who hold his
paper attend to their affairs.' 'Do you know the
cause of the disaster?—' said Claparon, intervening.
'You, you know nothing,' said Du Tillet to him;
'there will not be the least disaster, there will be
payment in full. Nucingen will resume and will
find all the funds he requires in my hands. I know
the cause of the suspension,—he has put all his
capital in Mexican investments, which repay him
in metals, in Spanish cannon so ridiculously cast
that there is gold in them, bells, church silver,
all the débris of the Spanish monarchy in the
Indies. The return of these values is delayed.
The dear baron is cramped, that is all.' 'That is
true,' said Werbrust, 'I take his paper at twenty
per cent discount. The news circulated thencefor-
ward with the rapidity of fire under a stack of
straw. The most contradictory things were said.
But there was so much confidence in the House of
Nucingen, always because of the two preceding
liquidations, that everybody kept its paper. 'It is
necessary that Palma give us a lift,' said Werbrust.
Palma was the oracle of the Kellers, who were gorged
with Nucingen securities. A word of alarm from
him would suffice. Werbrust persuaded Palma to
sound this tocsin. The next day, alarm pervaded
the Bourse. The Kellers, advised by Palma, disposed of their securities at ten per cent rebate, and
were accepted as authority at the Bourse; they
were known to be very shrewd. Taillefer then

7

disposed of three hundred thousand francs at twenty per cent, Martin Falleix two hundred thousand at fifteen per cent. Gigonnet guessed the trick! He encouraged the panic in order to be able to procure the Nucingen paper so as to gain some two or three per cent, by selling it to Werbrust. He perceived, in a corner of the Bourse, the poor Matifat, who had three hundred thousand francs in the hands of Nucingen. The druggist, pale and ghastly, did not see without a shudder the terrible Gigonnet, the discounter of his ancient quarter, coming to him to terrify him. 'That is bad, the crisis is at hand. Nucingen is making an arrangement! but that does not concern you, Father Matifat; you have retired from business.' 'Well, you are mistaken, Gigonnet, I am caught with three hundred thousand francs with which I wished to operate in Spanish funds.' 'They are saved; the Spanish funds would have entirely devoured you, whilst I will give you something like fifty per cent for your account with Nucingen.' 'I had rather see the liquidation,' replied Matifat; 'a banker has never given less than fifty per cent. Ah, if it were only a question of ten per cent loss,' said the former druggist. 'Well, will you have it at fifteen?' said Gigonnet. 'You seem to me very eager,' said Matifat. 'Good-evening,' said Gigonnet. 'Will you have it at twelve?' 'Agreed,' said Gigonnet. Two millions were bought up that evening and balanced at Nucingen's by Du Tillet, for the account of these three fortunate associates, who, the next day, received their premium. The old, pretty and little Baroness d'Aldrigger was breakfasting with her two daughters and Godefroid, when Rastignac came with a diplomatic air and engaged the conversation on the financial crisis. The Baron de Nucingen had a lively affection for the d'Aldrigger family; he had arranged in case of misfortune to cover the account of the baroness with his most valuable securities, shares in the mines of silver-bearing lead ore; but, for the security of the baroness, she should request him to employ her funds in this manner. 'That poor Nucingen,' said the baroness. 'And what has happened to him, then?' 'He is in Belgium; his wife has demanded a separation of her property; but he has gone to find other resources among the bankers.' *'Mon Dieu,* that reminds me of my poor husband! Dear Monsieur de Rastignac, how badly this must make you feel, you who are so attached to that house.' 'Provided that all the outsiders are protected, his friends will be recompensed later. He will get out of it; he is a clever man.' 'An honest man, above all,' cried the baroness. At the end of a month the liquidation of the liabilities of the House of Nucingen had been accomplished, without any other process than letters by which each one requested the employment of his money in certain designated securities, and without any other formalities on the part of the banking-houses than the transfer of the Nucingen securities to those stocks which were preferred. Whilst Du Tillet, Werbrust, Claparon, Gigonnet

and some others, who thought themselves clever,
brought back from abroad the paper of the House of
Nucingen with one per cent premium, for they made
a further profit in exchanging it against rising
stocks, the rumor was still more widely spread on the
Paris Exchange that no one had longer anything to
fear.   There was much talk about Nucingen.   He
was examined, he was judged; means were found to
calumniate him!   His luxury, his enterprises!
When a man carries on so, he will sink himself, etc.
In the midst of all this *tutti*, some persons were
much astonished to receive letters from Geneva,
Basle, from Milan, from Naples, from Genoa, from
Marseilles, from London, in which their correspon-
dents announced, not without astonishment, that
they were offered one per cent premium on Nucingen's paper, of whose failure they were advised.
'Something is going on,' said the financial lynxes.
The courts had pronounced separation of property
between Nucingen and his wife.   The affair became
still more complicated,—the newspapers announced
the return of Monsieur le Baron de Nucingen, who
had just concluded a negotiation with a well-known
Belgium manufacturer for the operation of some
ancient coal mines, then in difficulties, the pits of
the forests of Bossut.   The Baron reappeared on the
Bourse, without even taking the trouble to deny the
injurious rumors which had been in circulation concerning him.   He disdained to claim reparation
through the newspapers; he purchased for two millions a magnificent property at the gates of Paris.

Six weeks later the journals of Bordeaux announced the arrival of two vessels, consigned to the House of Nucingen, with cargoes of metals of the value of seven millions. Palma, Werbrust and Du Tillet comprehended that the operation was completed, but they were the only ones who comprehended it. These scholars studied the theatrical arrangement of this financial *puff*, recognized that it had been prepared eleven months previously, and proclaimed Nucingen the greatest European financier. Rastignac comprehended nothing of it, but he had gained thereby four hundred thousand francs which Nucingen had allowed him to shear from the Parisian lambs, and with which he had provided dots for his two sisters. D'Aiglemont, notified by his cousin Beaudenord, had come to entreat Rastignac to accept ten per cent of his million if he would obtain for him the employment of the million in shares of a canal which was yet to be made, for Nucingen had so well involved the government in this affair that the concessionaires of the canal were interested in not having it completed. Charles Grandet had implored Delphine's lover to permit him to exchange his money for shares. In short, Rastignac had played, during ten days, the rôle of Law, supplicated by the prettiest duchesses to give them shares, and to-day the scamp may have forty thousand francs of income, the origin of which might be traced to the shares in the mines of the silver-bearing lead ore."

"If everybody made money, who then lost?" said Finot.

"Conclusion," resumed Bixiou. "Allured by the pseudo-dividend which they had received some months after the exchange of their money for shares, the Marquis d'Aiglemont and Beaudenord kept theirs—I give you these to represent all the others— They had three per cent more than their capitals; they chanted the praises of Nucingen, and defended him at the very moment when he was suspected of suspending payment. Godefroid married his dear Isaure, and received a hundred thousand francs in shares in the mines. On the occasion of this marriage, the Nucingens gave a ball, the magnificence of which surpassed anything that can be conceived of it. Delphine offered to the young wife a charming set of rubies. Isaure danced, no longer as a young girl, but as a happy wife. The litttle baroness was more than ever shepherdess of the Alps. Malvina, the woman of *Avez-vous vu dans Barcelone?* heard, in the midst of the ball, Du Tillet dryly counselling her to become Madame Desroches. Desroches, excited by the Nucingens, by Rastignac, undertook to treat of pecuniary affairs; but, at the first words concerning mining stocks given in dowry, he broke off and returned to the Matifats. In the Rue du Cherche-Midi the lawyer found the damned canal shares with which Gigonnet had stuffed Matifat, instead of giving him money. So you see Desroches finding Nucingen's rake upon the two dots on which he had fixed his attention! The catastrophes were not delayed. The Claparon Company was engaged in too many affairs, there was a choking up; it ceased to pay interest and to declare dividends, although its operations were excellent. This misfortune happened in combination with the events of 1827. In 1829, Claparon was too well known to be the man of straw of these two colossi, and he fell from his pedestal to the earth. From twelve hundred and fifty francs, the shares fell to four hundred francs, although their intrinsic value was six hundred. Nucingen, who knew their real value, bought them in. The little Baroness d'Aldrigger had sold her shares in the mines which brought in nothing, and Godefroid sold his wife's for the same reason. Like the baroness, Beaudenord had exchanged his mining stock for shares of the Claparon Company. Their debts forced them to sell on a declining market. Of that which represented to them seven hundred thousand francs, they had two hundred and thirty thousand francs. They took their losses, and the remnant was prudently placed in the three per cents at seventy-five. Godefroid, that happy youth, without care, who had only to enjoy life, saw himself charged with a little wife stupid as a goose, incapable of supporting misfortune, for, at the end of six months, he perceived a transformation in the object so lightly loved; and, moreover, he was saddled with a mother-in-law without means who dreamed of toilets. The two families were living together in order to exist. Godefroid was obliged to call upon all his former influential connections, now chilled, to secure a situation of a thousand écus at the Ministry of Finance. His friends?—at the watering places. His relatives?—astonished, promising: '*What, my dear fellow, but count upon me! Poor boy!*' Clean forgotten a quarter of an hour afterwards, Beaudenord was indebted for his situation to the influence of Nucingen and of Vandenesse. These persons, so estimable and so unfortunate, live to-day in the Rue du Mont-Thabor, on the third floor above the entresol. The pearl of the daughter of the Adolphuses, Malvina, has nothing; she gives piano-lessons in order not to be a charge on her brother-in-law. Dark, tall, thin, dry, she resembles a mummy escaped from the museum of Passalacqua running about on foot through Paris. In 1830, Beaudenord lost his situation, and his wife presented him with a fourth child. Eight masters and two servants—Wirth and his wife—! money: eight thousand francs of income. The mines pay to-day such considerable dividends, that the thousand francs' share is worth a thousand francs of income. Rastignac and Madame de Nucingen have purchased the stocks sold by Godefroid and by the baroness. Nucingen was made peer of France by the Revolution of July, and Grand Officer of the Legion of Honor. Although he has not liquidated since 1830, he has, it is said, sixteen to eighteen millions. Foreseeing the Ordinance of July, he sold all his funds and replaced them courageously when the three per cents were at forty-five; he caused it to be believed at the Château that this was

through loyalty, and he has in this period gobbled
up, in concert with Du Tillet, three millions from
that great rogue of a Philippe Bridau! Recently,
passing through the Rue de Rivoli on his way to the
Bois de Boulogne, our baron perceived under the
arcades the Baroness d'Aldrigger. The little old
woman had a green capote lined with pink, a flowered dress, a mantilla; in short, she was still, and
more than ever, shepherdess of the Alps, for she no
more comprehended the causes of her misfortune
than the causes of her opulence. She was leaning
on the poor Malvina, that model of heroic devotion,
who had the air of being the old mother, while the
baroness had that of being the young daughter; and
Wirth followed them with an umbrella. 'Dere are
zome beebles,' said the baron to Monsieur Cointet,
a minister, with whom he was walking, 'whose
vortunes it was imbossible for me to make. De
vlurry of high brincibles is over, dake dis boor
Peautenord pack.' Beaudenord returned to the
finances through the care of Nucingen, whom the
d'Aldriggers praise as a hero of friendship, for he
always invites the little shepherdess of the Alps
and her daughters to his balls. It is impossible to
anyone, no matter whom, in the world to demonstrate how this man has, three times and without
breaking the law, wished to rob the public enriched
by him, despite him. Nobody had any reproaches
for him. Whoever would say that this great
banking is often throat-cutting would utter the
basest calumny. If stocks rise and fall, if values

augment and decrease, this flux and reflux is produced by some movement mutual, atmospheric, brought about by the influence of the moon, and the great Arago is culpable in not giving any scientific theory for this important phenomenon. The only result of all this is a pecuniary verity which I have never seen written anywhere—"

"Which one?"

"The debtor is stronger than the creditor."

"Oh!" said Blondet, "for myself, I see in what we have said the paraphrase of a saying of Montesquieu, in which he has concentrated all the *Ésprit des lois.*"

"What?" said Finot.

"Laws are spiders' webs through which the big flies pass and in which the little ones are caught."

"What do you want to arrive at?" said Finot to Blondet.

"An absolute government, the only one in which enterprises of the wits against the law can be repressed! Yes, the arbitrary power rescues the people in coming to the aid of justice, for the right of pardon has no reverse,—the king, who may pardon the fraudulent bankrupt, restores nothing to the plundered victim. Legality kills modern society."

"Make the electors comprehend that!" said Bixiou.

"There is some one who has taken charge of it."

"Who?"

"Time. As the bishop of Léon said: 'If liberty is ancient, royalty is eternal;' every nation of sound mind will return to it under one form or another."

"Look out, there is someone on the other side," said Finot, hearing us go out.

"There is always some one on the other side," replied Bixiou, who was probably by this time well wine-seasoned.

Paris, November, 1837.

THE SECRETS OF
LA PRINCESSE DE CADIGNAN

TO THÉOPHILE GAUTIER

LEAVING THE OPERA

"When coming out of the Opera, as out of the
_____, I saw him planted in the crowd, motionless
on his two legs,—he was _____, but he was not
moved. His eyes _____ _____ brilliant when he perceived me leaning on the _____ of some favorite. All
this time, not a word, not a letter, not a demonstration. You must admit that it was in good taste.
Sometimes, on returning home in the morning, I
found my man seated on one of the sides of my
porte-cochère. This loving one had very fine eyes."

∗

After the disasters of the Revolution of July,
which destroyed more than one of the aristocratic
fortunes sustained by the Court, Madame la Princesse de Cadignan had the cleverness to lay to the
account of the current political events the complete
ruin due to her extravagances. The prince had left
France with the royal family, leaving the princess
in Paris, inviolable through his absence,—for the
debts, for the satisfaction of which the sale of the
salable property could not suffice, weighed on him
only. The revenues of the entail had been seized.
In short, the affairs of this great family were in as
evil a state as those of the elder branch of the Bourbons. This woman, so well known under her first
name of the Duchesse de Maufrigneuse, then decided wisely to live in profound retirement,—she
wished to be forgotten. Paris was carried away by
a current of events so bewildering that very shortly
the Duchesse de Maufrigneuse, buried in the Princesse de Cadignan—a change of name unknown to
the greater number of the new actors in society
brought on the stage by the Revolution of July—
became like a stranger.

8 (113)

In France, the title of duke precedes all others, even that of prince, although in heraldic thesis, free from sophism, titles signify absolutely nothing and there should be perfect equality among gentlemen. This admirable equality was formerly carefully maintained by the Royal House of France; and, in our day, it still is, at least nominally, by the care which the kings take to give the simple title of count to their children.   It was in virtue of this system that Francis I. eclipsed the splendor of the titles which the pompous Charles V. gave himself by signing a reply to him: "François, Seigneur de Vanves." Louis XI. did better still, by marrying his daughter to an untitled gentleman, Pierre de Beaujeu. The feudal system was so well broken up by Louis XIV. that the title of duke became in his reign the highest honor of the aristocracy, and the one the most envied.   Nevertheless, there are two or three families in France of which the princedom, formerly richly possessed, is put before that of the duchy. The House of Cadignan, which possesses the title of Duc de Maufrigneuse for its eldest son, while all the others are entitled simply Chevaliers de Cadignan, is one of these exceptional families.   As was formerly the case with two princes of the House of Rohan, the princes de Cadignan were entitled to a throne amongst them; they were entitled to have pages and gentlemen in their service.   This explanation is necessary, as much to avoid the foolish criticisms of those who know nothing as to declare the important things of a world which, it is said, is

departing, and which so many people promote without comprehending it.   The Cadignans bore *d'or
with five fusils sable coupled and placed fesse*, with
the word "MEMINI" for device, and the closed
crown, without supporters or mantling.   To-day,
the great number of foreigners who throng to Paris,
and an almost general ignorance of the science of
heraldry, tend to bring the title of prince into
fashion.   There are no real princes excepting those
who have landed possessions and who are entitled
"Highness."   The disdain of the French nobility
for the title of prince and the reasons which induced
Louis XIV. to give supremacy to the title of duke,
have operated to prevent in France claims to
the title of Highness for the few princes who exist
in this nation, those of Napoléon excepted.   This
is the reason why the Princes de Cadignan found
themselves in an inferior position, nominally speaking, to the other Continental princes.

The princess was protected by that society called
"of the Faubourg Saint-Germain" through a respectful discretion due to hei name, which is one of those
always honored; to her misfortunes, which were not
discussed, and to her beauty, the only thing which
she had preserved of her lost opulence.   The
world, of which she was the ornament, was thank-
ful to her for having taken, as it were, the veil in
cloistering herself in her own house.   This good
taste was for her, more than for any other woman,
an immense sacrifice.   The great events are always
so keenly felt in France, that the princess regained

by her retirement all that she might have lost in
public opinion in the middle of her splendors. She
saw only one of her ancient friends, the Marquise
d'Espard; she went neither to the grand social
reunions nor to the festivities. The princess and
the marchioness visited each other in the early
morning, and, as it were, secretly. When the princess came to dine with her friend, the marchioness
closed her doors. Madame d'Espard was admirably
considerate for the princess; she changed her box at
the Italiens, and left the front row for a box on
the ground floor, so that Madame de Cadignan could
go to the theatre without being seen, and depart
incognito. Very few women would have been
capable of a delicacy which deprived them of the
pleasure of dragging in their suite a fallen former
rival, of proclaiming themselves her benefactress.
The princess, being thus able to dispense with the
ruinous extravagance of toilets, went privately in
the carriage of the marchioness, which she would
not have accepted publicly. No one has ever
known the reasons which induced Madame d'Espard
to act thus with the Princesse de Cadignan; but
her conduct was sublime, and permitted for a long
time a multitude of little things which, seen singly,
seem to be but sillinesses, but which, taken altogether, attain the gigantic. In 1832, the snows of
three years had drifted over the adventures of the
Duchesse de Maufrigneuse, and had so nearly
covered them that serious efforts of the memory
were required to recall the grave circumstances of

her previous life. Of this queen, adored by so many courtiers, and whose light adventures might have furnished material for several romances, there still remained a delightfully handsome woman, thirty-six years of age, but authorized to claim no more than thirty, although she was the mother of the Duc Georges de Maufrigneuse, a young man of nineteen, handsome as Antinous, poor as Job, who was entitled to the utmost success and whom his mother wished, before all, to make a rich marriage. Perhaps in this project might be found a secret of the intimacy which she preserved with the marchioness, whose salon enjoyed the reputation of being the first in Paris, and in which she might some day choose, among the heiresses, a wife for Georges. The princess foresaw five years yet to pass between the present moment and the epoch of her son's marriage; solitary and deserted years, for, in order to secure a good marriage, it would be necessary that her conduct should be marked with prudence.

The princess lived in the Rue de Miromesnil in a little hôtel, on the ground floor, at a moderate rent. She had brought thither a part of the remnants of her magnificence. Her elegance of the *grande dame* might still be felt there. She was still surrounded there by those things which announce a superior existence. On her chimney-piece might be seen a magnificent miniature, the portrait of Charles X., by Madame de Mirbel, under which were engraved these words: *"Presented by the king;"* and, as a companion, the portrait of MADAME, which was so

peculiarly excellent in her case.   On a table was a
resplendent album of the utmost costliness, which
not one of the bourgeois who enthrone themselves in
our industrial society, so shifting and uncertain,
would dare to display.   This audacity portrayed the
woman admirably.   The album contained a number
of portraits among which might be recognized some
thirty intimate friends whom the world had called
her lovers.   This number was a calumny; but, if
we were to say ten, perhaps that might be somewhat near it, as said the Marquise d'Espard, with
good honest scandal.   The portraits of Maxime de
Trailles, of De Marsay, of Rastignac, of the Marquis
d'Esgrignon, of General de Montriveau, of the two
Marquises, de Ronquerolles and d'Ajuda-Pinto, of the
Prince Galathionne, of the young Ducs de Grandlieu,
de Rhétoré, of the handsome Lucien de Rubempré,
of the young Vicomte de Sérizy, had, moreover,
been rendered with the greatest and most flattering
skill by the most celebrated artists.   As the princess no longer received more than two or three persons of this collection, she alluded to this book
pleasantly as "the collection of her errors."   Misfortune had made of this woman a good mother.
During the fifteen years of the Restoration she had
amused herself too constantly to think of her son;
but, when taking refuge in obscurity, this illustrious egotist reflected that the maternal sentiment
pushed to its extreme development might become
for her past life an absolution, confirmed by all right-
thinking people, who pardon everything to an

excellent mother. She loved her son all the more
that she no longer had any other thing to love.
Georges de Maufrigneuse is, moreover, one of those
children who might flatter all a mother's vanities;
and thus the princess made for him all kinds of sacrifices: she maintained for Georges a stable and a carriage-house, over which he lived in a little entresol
on the street, consisting of three apartments, beauti-
fully furnished; she had imposed upon herself some
privations that he might have a saddle-horse, a horse
for his cabriolet, and a small servant. She herself
kept no longer anything but her femme de chambre,
and, for cook, one of her former kitchen-maids. The
duke's tiger had at this period a somewhat exacting
service. Toby, the former tiger of the late Beaudenord—for such was the pleasant jest of the gay
world on this ruined dandy—this young tiger, who
at twenty-five was everywhere thought to be only
fourteen years old, was expected to take care of the
horses, clean the cabriolet or the tilbury, follow his
master, keep the apartments in order and be present
in the antechamber of the princess to announce her
guest if, by chance, she was receiving the visit of
some personage. When we reflect on that which
was, under the Restoration, the beautiful Duchesse
de Maufrigneuse, one of the queens of Paris, a
splendid queen, whose luxurious existence would
have been worthy of one of the richest women of
the world of London, there was something inde-
scribably touching to see her in a little shell of the
Rue de Miromesnil, a few steps only from her

immense hôtel, which no fortune was able to maintain and which the hammer of the speculators has
now demolished.   The woman who could scarcely
be served comfortably by thirty servants, who possessed the finest reception apartments in Paris, the
most charming little apartments, who gave in them
such admirable fêtes, now lived in a suite of five
rooms,—an antechamber, a dining-room, a salon,
a bed-chamber, and a dressing-room, with two
women for her only servants.

"Ah! she is admirable for her son," said that fine
gossip, the Marquise d'Espard, "and admirable
without affectation; she is happy.   One would
never have thought this woman, so light, capable
of resolutions followed so persistently; and our
good Archbishop has encouraged her, has shown
the greatest consideration for her, and has persuaded the old Comtesse de Cinq-Cygne to pay
her a visit."

Let us admit it, moreover, it is necessary to have
been a queen to know how to abdicate and to
descend nobly from an elevated position which,
however, is never entirely lost.   Those only who are
conscious in themselves of being nothing manifest
their regrets in thus falling, or murmur continually,
and go back in imagination to a past which will
never return, feeling sure, as they do, that they can
never attain it a second time.   Compelled to abandon
the rare flowers in the midst of which she had been
accustomed to live, and which so well set off her person, for it was impossible not to compare her to a

flower, the princess had skilfully chosen her ground-
floor apartment,—she there had the enjoyment of a
pretty little garden full of shrubs and bushes, and
of which the turf, always green, enlivened her
peaceful retreat.   She might have had at this period
about twelve thousand francs of income. This modest
revenue was composed of an annual stipend donated
by the old Duchesse de Navarreins, paternal aunt
of the young duke, which would be continued to the
day of his marriage, and of another stipend sent by
the Duchesse d'Uxelles, from her estate, where she
was economizing as the old duchesses know how to
economize, for, compared with them, Harpagon was
only a scholar.   The prince lived abroad, constantly
at the orders of his exiled masters, sharing their
evil fortune and serving them with a disinterested
devotion, the most intelligent perhaps of all those
who surrounded them.   The position of the Prince
de Cadignan still protected his wife at Paris.   It
was in the apartments of the princess that the marshal to whom we owe the conquest of Africa had,
at the period of the attempt of MADAME in La Vendée, conferences with the principal chiefs of the
Légitimistes,—so complete was the obscurity of the
princess, so little did her poverty excite the suspicion of the actual government!   In seeing the
approach of the terrible failure of love, that age
of forty years, beyond which there is so little for a
woman, the princess had thrown herself into the
kingdom of philosophy.   She read, she who had, for
sixteen years, manifested the greatest horror for

serious things.   Literature and politics are to-day
that which formerly devotion was for women, the
last refuge of their pretensions.   In the elegant circles of society, it was said that Diane would wish
to write a book.   Since the period when, from a
charming, from a beautiful woman, the princess had
passed into a clever woman, before she should pass
away altogether, she had made of a reception under
her roof a supreme honor which distinguished pro-
digiously the favored person.   Under cover of these
occupations she could deceive one of her first lovers,
De Marsay, the most influential personage in bourgeois politics, put into power July, 1830; she
received him sometimes in the evenings, while the
marshal and several Légitimistes were discussing,
with lowered voices, in her bed-chamber, the conquest of the kingdom, which could not be brought
about without the aid of ideas, the only element of
success which the conspirators forgot.   It was a
charming vengeance of a pretty woman, thus to
trick a Prime Minister by making him serve as a
screen for a conspiracy against his own government.
This adventure, worthy of the best days of the
Fronde, furnished a text for the most ingenious letter
in the world, in which the princess rendered an
account of the negotiations to MADAME.   The Duc
de Maufrigneuse went to La Vendée and was able to
return secretly, without being compromised, but not
without having shared the perils of MADAME, who,
unfortunately, sent him back when everything
appeared lost.   Perhaps the enthusiastic vigilance

of this young man might have baffled the treason. However great may have been the errors of the Duchesse de Maufrigneuse in the eyes of the bourgeois world, the conduct of her son has certainly effaced them in the eyes of the aristocratic world. There was something of nobility and of grandeur in thus risking the only son and the heir of an historical house.   There are those, reputed clever, who repair the errors of private life by political services, and reciprocally; but no sordid calculations entered into the actions of the Princesse de Cadignan. Perhaps there were none, either, in any of those who thus contributed.   Events count for at least half in these misconceptions.

On one of the first fine days of the month of May, 1833, the Marquise d'Espard and the princess were slowly promenading, it could not be called walking, in the only garden alley which surrounded the turf of the little enclosure, about two o'clock in the afternoon, in the declining sunlight.   The rays reflected by the walls made a warm atmosphere in this little space perfumed by the flowers, a present from the marchioness.

"We will soon lose De Marsay," said Madame d'Espard to the princess, "and with him will go your last hope of fortune for the Duc de Maufrigneuse; for, since you have tricked him so prettily, this great politician has again found his affection for you."

"My son will never yield to the younger branch," replied the princess, "should he die of hunger, should

I have to work for him.   But Berthe de Cinq-Cygne
does not hate him.''

"Children," said Madame d'Espard, "have not
the same engagements as their fathers—"

"Do not speak of it," said the princess.   "It will
be well enough, if I cannot bring the Marquise de
Cinq-Cygne to reason, to marry my son to some
blacksmith's daughter, as did that little d'Esgrignon!"

"Did you love him?" asked the marchioness.

"No," replied the princess gravely.   "The
naïvete of d'Esgrignon was a species of depart-
mental dulness of which I became aware a little too
late, or a little too early, if you prefer."

"And De Marsay?"

"De Marsay played with me as if I were a doll.
I was so young! We never fall in love with the
men who constitute themselves our instructors; they
ruffle too much our little vanities."

"And that little miserable who hanged himself?"

"Lucien?   That was an Antinous and a great
poet. I very sincerely loved him. I might have become happy.   But he loved a young girl, and I
yielded him to Madame de Sérizy—. If he had loved
me, would I have yielded him?"

"What a fantastical thing! you to come in conflict with an Esther!"

"She was more beautiful than I," said the princess.   "Here are now nearly three years which I
have passed in a complete solitude," she resumed
after a pause; "well, this calm has had in it nothing

painful. To you alone, I would dare to say that here I have found myself happy. I was weary of adoration, fatigued without pleasure, moved superficially without ever having my heart touched by emotion. I have found all the men whom I have known, little, mean, superficial; not one of them has ever caused me the slightest surprise; they were without innocence, without grandeur, without delicacy. I would have liked to have met someone who would have seemed imposing to me."

"Would you be, then, like me, my dear?" asked the marchioness; "would you have never encountered love in endeavoring to love?"

"Never," replied the princess, interrupting the marchioness, and laying her hand on her arm.

Both of them went and seated themselves on a rustic wooden bench, under a bush of flowering jessamine. Both of them had uttered one of those words so solemn for women of their age.

"Like you," resumed the princess, "perhaps I have been more loved than are other women; but through so many adventures, I feel it, I have not known happiness. I have committed many follies, but they all had an object, and the object recoiled in proportion as I advanced! In my heart grown old, I am conscious of an innocence which has not yet been touched. Yes, under so much experience still lies a first love which might be abused; just as, notwithstanding so much wear and fatigue, I still feel myself young and handsome. We can love without being happy, we can be happy and not love;

but to love and to have happiness, to bring together these two immense human enjoyments, that is
a prodigy.   This prodigy has not been accomplished
by me."

"Nor by me," said Madame d'Espard.

"I am pursued in my retreat by a frightful
regret,—I have amused myself, but I have never
loved."

"What an incredible secret!" cried the marchioness.

"Ah! my dear," replied the princess, "these
secrets, we can only confide them to ourselves: no
one in Paris would believe us."

"And," resumed the marchioness, "if we had not
both of us passed the age of thirty-six, we should
not, perhaps, make this avowal to ourselves—"

"Yes, when we are young we have some very
stupid fatuities!" said the princess. "We resemble at times those poor young people who play with
a tooth-pick to make believe that they have dined
well."

"In short, here we are," replied Madame d'Espard,
with a coquettish grace, making a charming gesture
of sapient innocence, "and we are, it seems to me,
still enough alive to take a revenge."

"When you told me, the other day, that Béatrix
had gone off with Conti, I thought about it all
night long," resumed the princess, after a pause.
"One must be very happy to sacrifice thus one's
position, one's future, and renounce the world
forever!"

"She is a little fool," said Madame d'Espard, gravely. "Mademoiselle de Touches was enchanted to be rid of Conti. Béatrix did not comprehend how much this abandonment, made by a superior woman, who has not for a single moment defended her pretended happiness, revealed the nothingness of Conti."

"She will then be unhappy?"

"She is so already," replied Madame d'Espard. "Of what good is it to leave your husband? In a woman, is not this an avowal of want of power?"

"Thus you believe that Madame de Rochefide was not influenced by the desire to enjoy in peace a real happiness, that happiness the enjoyment of which, for us two, is still a dream?"

"No; she mimicked Madame de Beauséant and Madame de Langeais, who, it may be said between us, in a century less vulgar than ours, would have been, like you, moreover, figures as great as those of the La Vallières, of the Montespans, of the Dianes de Poitiers, of the Duchesses d'Étampes and de Châteauroux."

"Oh! without the king, my dear. Ah! I would like to be able to evoke those women and ask them if—"

"But," said the marchioness, interrupting the princess, "it is not necessary to make the dead speak; we know some living women who are happy. There are more than twenty times that I have had lately, intimate conversations on such matters with the Comtesse de Montcornet, who, for

the last fifteen years, has been the happiest
woman in the world with that little Émile Blondet,
—not one infidelity, not one wandering thought;
they are to-day as on the very first day; but we
have always been interfered with, interrupted at
the most interesting moment. These long attachments, like those of Rastignac and of Madame de
Nucingen, of Madame de Camps, your cousin, for
her Octave, have a secret, and this secret we are
ignorant of, my dear. The world does us the extreme honor to take us for profligates worthy of
the Court of the Regent, and we are as innocent as
two little school-girls.''

"I should be still happy in that innocence,''
cried the princess, jestingly; "but ours is worse,
there is in it something humiliating. What would
you have! We will offer this mortification to
God in expiation of our fruitless researches; for,
my dear, it is not probable that we shall find, in the
late autumn, the fine flower which we have missed
during the spring and the summer.''

"That is not the question,'' resumed the marchioness after a pause full of retrospective medita-
tions. "We are still handsome enough to inspire
a passion; but we shall never convince anyone of
our innocence and of our virtue.''

"If it were a lie, it would be soon enough ornamented with commentaries, served up with pretty
preparations which would make it believable and
devoured like a delicious fruit; but to make a truth
believed! Ah! the greatest men have perished in

that attempt," added the princess, with one of those
fine smiles which the brush of Leonardo da Vinci
alone could render.

"The simpletons love well enough sometimes,"
said the marchioness.

"But," observed the princess, "for this, the simpletons themselves would not have sufficient credulity."

"You are right," said the marchioness, laughing.
"But it is neither a fool nor even a man of talent
that we should seek for. To solve such a problem
will require a man of genius. Genius alone has
the faith of childhood, the religion of love, and willingly lets its eyes be bandaged. Look at Canalis
and the Duchesse de Chaulieu. If, you and I, we
have met with men of genius, they were perhaps too
far from us, too much occupied, and we were too
frivolous, too much carried away, too much taken
up with other things."

"Ah, I would very much like, however, not to
quit this world without having known the pleasures
of a true love," cried the princess.

"It is nothing to inspire it only," said Madame
d'Espard; "it is a question of experiencing it. I
see many women who are only the pretext of a
passion, instead of being at once the cause and the
effect of it."

"The last passion which I inspired was a saintly
and beautiful thing," said the princess; "it had a
future. Fortune sent to me this time that man of
genius who is due to us, and who is so difficult to

9

take, for there are more pretty women than geniuses. But the devil interfered in the adventure."

"Tell me that, my dear; that is entirely new to
me."

"I only became aware of this fine passion in the
middle of the winter of 1829. Every Friday, at the
Opera, I saw in the orchestra seats a young man of
about thirty years of age, who came there for my
sake, always in the same seat, looking at me with
eyes of fire, but often saddened by the distance
which he found between us, or perhaps also by the
impossibility of succeeding."

"Poor boy! When one is in love, one becomes
very stupid," said the marchioness.

"Between each act he slipped into the corridor,"
resumed the princess, smiling at the friendly
epigram with which the marchioness had interrupted her; "then, once or twice, to see me or
to make himself seen, he showed his nose at the
glass of a box opposite mine. If I received a visit,
I perceived him flattened in my doorway; he could
then throw me a furtive glance; he had ended by
knowing by sight the persons of my society; he followed them when they came toward my box, in
order to have the benefit of the opening of my door.
The poor youth doubtless soon learned who I was,
for he knew by sight Monsieur de Maufrigneuse and
my father-in-law. I found, after that, my mysterious unknown at the Italiens, in a seat in which he
could admire me, directly opposite, in a simple
ecstasy :—it was very pretty. When coming out of

the Opera, as out of the Bouffons, I saw him planted in the crowd, motionless on his two legs,—he was elbowed, but he was not moved. His eyes became less brilliant when he perceived me leaning on the arm of some favorite. All this time, not a word, not a letter, not a demonstration. You must admit that it was in good taste. Sometimes, on returning home in the morning, I found my man seated on one of the sides of my porte-cochère. This loving one had very fine eyes, a thick and long beard cut fan-shaped, an imperial, a mustache and whiskers; you could only see two white cheeks and a handsome forehead; in short, a veritable antique head. The prince, as you know, defended the Tuileries on the side of the quays during the days of July. He returned in the evening to Saint-Cloud when everything was lost. 'My dear,' he said to me, 'I just escaped being killed about four o'clock. I was aimed at by one of the insurgents, when a young man with a long beard, whom I think I have seen at the Italiens and who led the attack, turned aside the barrel of the musket.' The ball struck I know not what man, a quartermaster in the regiment, and who was within two steps of my husband. This young man must then have been a Republican. In 1831, when I came back to live here, I encountered him leaning against the wall of this house; he seemed joyful because of my disasters, which, perhaps it seemed to him, would bring us nearer; but, since the affair of Saint-Merri I have no longer seen him: he perished in it. The evening of the funeral of General Lamarque, I went out on foot with my son, and my Republican followed us, sometimes behind, sometimes before us, from the Madeleine to the Passage des Panoramas, where I was going."

"Is that all?" said the marchioness.

"All," replied the princess. "Ah! the morning of the taking of Saint-Merri, a street boy wished to speak to me and handed me a letter, written on common paper, signed with the name of the unknown."

"Show it to me," said the marchioness.

"No, my dear. This love was too great and too holy in this man's heart for me to violate his secret. This letter, short and terrible, still moves me to the heart when I think of it. This dead man causes me more emotion than all the living ones whom I have distinguished, he returns again into my thoughts."

"His name?" asked the marchioness.

"Oh, a very common name, Michel Chrestien."

"You have done very well to tell it to me," replied Madame d'Espard, quickly, "I have often heard him spoken of. This Michel Chrestien was the friend of a celebrated man whom you have already wished to see, of Daniel d'Arthez, who comes once or twice a winter to my house. This Chrestien, who was really killed at Saint-Merri, did not lack for friends. I have heard it said that he was one of those great politicians to whom, as to De Marsay, it is only needful that the foot-ball of circumstances should come their way for them to become all at once what they should be."

"It is better, then, that he should be dead," said the princess, with a melancholy air under which she concealed her thoughts.

"Would you like to meet d'Arthez some evening at my house?" asked the marchioness; "you could talk of your apparition."

"Willingly, my dear."

Some days after this conversation, Blondet and Rastignac, who knew d'Arthez, promised Madame d'Espard to induce him to come and dine with her. This promise would without doubt have been imprudent were it not for the name of the princess, the meeting with whom could not be indifferent to this great writer.

Daniel d'Arthez, one of those rare men, who in our day, unite a fine character to a fine talent, had already obtained, not all the popularity which his works should have procured him, but a respectful esteem to which chosen souls could add nothing. His reputation would certainly increase still more, but it had already attained its full development in the eyes of connoisseurs,—he is of those authors who, sooner or later, find their true place, and retain it. A poor gentleman, he had comprehended his epoch in requiring everything from a personal illustration. He had combated for a long period in the Parisian arena, against the will of a rich uncle, who, through a contradiction which vanity endeavors to justify, after having left him a prey to the greatest poverty, had bequeathed to the celebrated man the fortune pitilessly refused to the

unknown writer.   This sudden change had changed
nothing in the manners of Daniel d'Arthez: he continued his labors with a simplicity worthy of antique
times, and imposed new ones on himself by accepting a seat in the Chamber of Deputies, where he
took a place on the Right.   Since his attainment
to fame he had gone out sometimes into society.
One of his old friends, a great physician, Horace
Bianchon, had made him acquainted with the Baron
de Rastignac, Under-Secretary of State to a minister, and friend of De Marsay.   These two men of
politics had with sufficient nobility lent their aid to
Daniel, Horace and some intimate friends of Michel
Chrestien, who wished to withdraw the body of this
Republican from the church of Saint-Merri and render it funeral honors.   Gratitude for a service
which contrasted so strongly with the administrative rigors displayed at this period in which political passions were so freely unchained, had bound, as
it were, d'Arthez to Rastignac.   The Under-Secretary of State and the illustrious minister were too
skilful not to profit by this circumstance ; they
thus gained over some friends of Michel Chrestien,
who, moreover, did not share his opinions, and who
henceforth attached themselves to the new government.   One of them, Léon Giraud, appointed at
first Maître des Requêtes, became Councillor of
State.   The existence of Daniel d'Arthez is entirely
consecrated to work, he only sees society in occasional glimpses ; it is for him like a dream.   His
house is a convent, in which he leads the life of a

Benedictine,—the same sobriety in the regimen, the
same regularity in the occupations.   His friends
know that up to the present time woman has only
been for him an accident always dreaded, he has
observed her too much not to fear her; but, by dint
of studying her, he has ended by no longer knowing
her, resembling in this those profound tacticians
who will always be beaten on unforeseen ground
where their scientific axioms are modified and con-
tradicted.   He has remained the most candid child,
while showing himself the most learned observer.
This contrast, apparently impossible, is easily
explicable for those who are able to measure the
depth which separates the faculties from the feelings: one proceeds from the head and the other from
the heart.   One can be a great man and a wicked
one, as one can be a fool and a sublime lover.
D'Arthez is one of those privileged beings in whom
the finesse of the intellect, the wide extent of the
qualities of the brain, exclude neither the strength
nor the grandeur of feeling.   He is, by a rare privilege, a man of action and a man of reflection, both
at once.   His private life is noble and pure.   If he
had carefully avoided love up to this time, he knew
himself well; he knew in advance what would be
the empire of a passion over him.   During a long
period, the heavy labors by which he prepared the
solid ground of his glorious works, and the cold of
poverty, had been a marvelous preservative.   When
he had attained to ease, he had the most vulgar and
the most incomprehensible liaison with a woman

sufficiently attractive, but who belonged to the lower
orders, without any instruction, without manners,
and carefully concealed from all observation.
Michel Chrestien conceded to men of genius the
power to transform the most massive creatures into
sylphids, the stupid ones into women of wit, the
peasant women into marchionesses: the more a
woman was accomplished, the more she lost in their
eyes; for, according to him, their imagination had no
part to play in this business. According to him also,
love, the simple craving of the senses in inferior
beings, was, in the superior beings, the most immense and the most attaching of all moral creations.
In order to justify d'Arthez, he fell back upon the
example given by Raphaël and the Fornarina. He
might have offered himself as a model in this
respect, he who saw an angel in the Duchesse
de Maufrigneuse. The curious whim of d'Arthez
might, moreover, be justified in various ways,—perhaps he had promptly and at once despaired of ever
encountering here below a woman who would
respond in any degree to that delightful chimera
which every man of intelligence creates for himself;
perhaps he was possessed of a heart too sensitive,
too delicate, to be yielded up to a woman of the
world; perhaps he thought it better to give to nature
her due merely and to keep his illusions intact by
cultivating his ideal; perhaps he had put aside love
as something incompatible with his work, with the
regularity of a monastic life in which passion would
have disarranged everything. For the last few

months d'Arthez had been the object of the jests of
Blondet and of Rastignac, who reproached him with
knowing neither the world nor women.   According
to them, his works were sufficiently numerous and
carried sufficiently far for him to permit himself
some distractions,—he had a fine fortune and he
lived like a poor scholar; he enjoyed nothing,
neither his gold nor his glory; he was ignorant of
the exquisite pleasure of that noble and delicate
passion which certain women well-born and well-
educated inspire in others or feel themselves; was
it not unworthy of himself to have never known
anything but the grossness of love?   Love, reduced
to that which nature makes of it, was in their eyes
the most sottish thing in the world.   One of the
glories of society, is to have created *the woman*
where nature had made a female; to have created
the perpetuity of desire where nature had thought
only of the perpetuity of the species; to have, in
short, invented love, the very finest human religion.   D'Arthez knew nothing of the charming
delicacies of language, nothing of those proofs of
affection incessantly given by soul and spirit, nothing of those desires ennobled by manners, nothing
of those angelic forms lent to the grossest things by
refined and charming women.   He was, perhaps,
acquainted with the woman, but he was ignorant of
the divinity.   It requires an extraordinary art, very
many beautiful toilets of the body and of the soul in
a woman to secure true love.   Finally, in lauding
the delightful depravations of the thought which

constitute the Parisian coquetry, these two cor-
ruptors pitied d'Arthez, whose diet was simple and
wholesome, and without any seasoning, for never
having tasted the delicacies of the finest Parisian
cooking, and they greatly stimulated his curiosity.
Doctor Bianchon, in whom d'Arthez confided, was
aware that this curiosity had been finally aroused.
The long liaison of this great writer with a common
woman, far from becoming satisfactory through
habit, had now become to him insupportable; but he
was restrained from breaking away by the excessive
timidity which takes possession of all solitary men.

"How," said Rastignac, "when one bears *party
per bend dexter gules and or to a bezant and a torteau
from one to the other,* why not make this old Picard
shield glitter on a carriage panel? You have thirty
thousand francs of income and the products of
your pen; you have justified your motto, which
makes the pun so much desired by our ancestors:
ARS, THES*aurusque virtus* and you do not promenade yourself in the Bois de Boulogne! We are in
a century in which virtue should show itself."

"If you read your works to that species of gross
Laforêt who makes your delights, I would pardon
you for keeping her," said Blondet. "But, my
dear fellow, if you are reduced to dry bread in material things, with respect to the spiritual you have
not even bread—"

This little friendly warfare had been going on
between Daniel and his friends for several months
when Madame d'Espard asked Rastignac and Blondet

to persuade d'Arthez to come and dine with her, saying to them that the Princesse de Cadignan had a very great desire to meet this celebrated man. These species of curiosity are, for certain women, what the magic lantern is for children, a pleasure for the eyes, a poor enough one, moreover, and full of disenchantments. The greater the curiosity and interest which a clever and distinguished man excites at a distance, the less satisfactory he is when brought near; the more brilliant he has been dreamed to be, the sooner he tarnishes. In this connection, the disappointed curiosity often goes to the extreme of injustice. Neither Blondet nor Rastignac could deceive d'Arthez, but they said to him laughingly that it would offer him the most seductive opportunity to clean up his heart and to become acquainted with the supreme delights which the love of a great Parisian lady might give. The princess was positively enamored of him; he had nothing to fear, he had everything to gain in this interview; it would be impossible for him to descend from the pedestal on which Madame de Cadignan had placed him. Neither Blondet nor Rastignac saw any impropriety in imputing this love to the princess; she could support this calumny, she had given rise to enough stories in the past. One and the other, they set to work to recount to d'Arthez the adventures of the Duchesse de Maufrigneuse,—her first indiscretions with De Marsay, her second inconsistency with d'Ajuda, whom she had turned away from his wife, thus avenging

Madame de Beauséant; her third liaison with the
young d'Esgrignon, who had accompanied her into
Italy and had horribly compromised himself for her;
then how she had been unhappy with a celebrated
ambassador, happy with a Russian general; how
she had been the Egeria of two Ministers of Foreign
Affairs, etc. D'Arthez informed them that he knew
more concerning her than they could tell him,
through their poor friend, Michel Chrestien, who
had adored her in secret for four years, and had
almost gone mad over it.

"I often went with my friend," said Daniel, "to
the Italiens, to the Opera. The unhappy man ran
with me through the streets, going as fast as the
horses, and admiring the princess through the windows of her coupé. It was to this love that the
Prince de Cadignan owed his life; Michel prevented
a gamin who would have killed him."

"Well, then, you will have a subject all ready,"
said Blondet, smiling. "There is the woman that
you require; she will only be cruel through delicacy,
and will initiate you very graciously into the
mysteries of elegance; but, beware, she has devoured
many fortunes! The beautiful Diane is one of those
dissipators who do not cost a centime, and for whom
millions are expended. Give yourself, body and
soul; but keep your money in your own hands, like
the old man in Girodet's 'Deluge.'"

According to this conversation, the princess had
all the profundity of an abyss, the grace of a queen,
the corruption of a diplomat, the mystery of an

initiation, the danger of a siren.   These two men of
wit, incapable of foreseeing the dénouement of this
pleasantry, had finished by making of Diane
d'Uxelles the most monstrous Parisian woman, the
most skilful coquette, the most intoxicating courtesan in the world.   Although they might have been
right, the woman whom they treated so lightly was
saintly and sacred for d'Arthez, whose curiosity had
no need of being excited; he consented to come
immediately, and the two friends wished nothing
better of him.

Madame d'Espard went to see the princess as soon
as she had a reply.

"My dear, do you feel yourself in the way to be
beautiful, coquettish?" she said to her; "come and
dine with me in a few days; I will serve up to you
d'Arthez.   Our man of genius is of a nature the
wildest; he fears women, and has never loved.   You
can prepare your theme on those lines.   He is
excessively intelligent, with a simplicity which gets
the better of you by depriving you of all suspicion.
His penetration, all retrospective, acts after the
stroke and deranges all calculations.   You have
surprised him to-day, to-morrow he will be no longer
dupe in anything."

"Ah!" said the princess, "if I were only thirty,
I would amuse myself greatly!   That which has
always failed me up to the present time has been a
man of wit to play with.   I have only had partners
and never adversaries.   Love was only a game instead of being a combat."

"Dear princess, admit that I am very generous, for, as you know, all well-regulated charity—"

The two women looked at each other laughingly and clasped each other's hands with friendship. Certainly, they knew important secrets of each other, not even excepting love affairs, and little service rendered; for, to have sincere and durable friendships between women, it is necessary that they should have been united by some little crimes. When two female friends are about to kill each other, and may be seen, poisoned dagger in hand, they offer a touching spectacle of a harmony which is only destroyed at the moment when one of them has, inadvertently, dropped her weapon. Therefore, a week later, there was in the house of the marchioness one of those evenings called *des petits jours*, reserved for intimate friends, to which no one comes without a verbal invitation, and during which the door is closed. This entertainment was given for five persons,—Émile Blondet and Madame de Montcornet, Daniel d'Arthez, Rastignac, and the Princesse de Cadignan. Including the mistress of the house, there were as many men as women. Never did fortune permit of more skilful preparations than these for the meeting of d'Arthez and Madame de Cadignan. The princess still enjoys to-day the reputation of being one of the most skilful women in all matters of the toilet, which is, for women, the first of all arts. She wore a gown of blue velvet with large white flowing sleeves, the bodice showing, in guimpe of tulle slightly gathered and bordered with blue, rising to within four finger breadths of the neck and covering the shoulders, as may be seen in some of Raphaël's portraits. Her maid had dressed her hair with some white heather skilfully arranged in the ripples of her blond tresses, one of those aids to beauty to which she owed her celebrity. Certainly Diane did not seem to be twenty-five years old. Four years of solitude and repose had restored the clearness to her skin. Are there not, moreover, moments in which the desire to please gives an increase of beauty to women? The will is not without influence on the variations of the countenance. If violent emotions have the power of yellowing the white tints in people of a sanguine temperament, or a melancholy one, of turning lymphatic countenances greenish, should there not be given to desire, to joy, to hope, the quality of clearing the skin, of illuminating the glance with a lively light, of animating beauty by a vivid illumination like that of a fine morning? The fairness of the princess, so celebrated, had taken a ripened tint which lent to her an august air. In this moment of her life, animated by so many self-reflections and by serious thoughts, her pensive and sublime forehead was in admirable accord with the slow and majestic glance of her blue eyes. It would have been impossible for the most skilful physiognomist to have discovered calculation and decision under this most unusual delicacy of feature. There are women's faces which deceive all science and vanquish observation

by their calm and by their fineness; it would
be necessary to be able to examine them when the
passions are speaking, which is difficult; or when
they have spoken, which serves for nothing,—then,
the woman is old and no longer dissimulates.   The
princess is one of those impenetrable women; she
is able to make herself whatever she wishes to be,
—playful, infantile, hopelessly innocent; or shrewd,
serious and profound to a disquieting extent.   She
came to the house of the marchioness with the
intention of being a woman sweet and simple, to
whom life was known by its deceptions only, a
woman full of spirit and sentiment and calumniated, but resigned; in short, an angel martyred.
She arrived early, so that she might be found posed
on a little sofa, at the corner of the fire, near to
Madame d'Espard, as she would wish to be seen, in
one of those attitudes in which science is carefully
concealed under an appearance of exquisite naturalness, one of those poses studied, thought out, which
bring into relief that beautiful serpentine line,
which, starting from the feet, mounts gracefully to
the hips and continues by admirable curves to the
shoulders, offering to the regard all the profile of the
body.   A woman nude would be less dangerous
than in a robe thus knowingly displayed, which
covers everything and reveals everything at the
same time.   By a refinement which very few women
would have invented, Diane, to the great stupefaction of the marchioness, was accompanied by the
Duc de Maufrigneuse.   After a moment of reflection,

Madame d'Espard grasped the hand of the princess with an air of intelligence:

"I understand you! In compelling d'Arthez to accept all the difficulties at the first outset, you will not have them to overcome later."

The Comtesse de Montcornet came with Blondet. Rastignac brought d'Arthez. The princess did not pay to the celebrated man any of those compliments with which the vulgar overwhelmed him; but she displayed those little attentions full of grace and of respect which seemed as though they might be the last limit of her concessions. She was doubtless thus with the King of France, with the princes. She seemed happy to see this great man and pleased with having sought him. Persons of good taste, like the princess, are distinguished above all by their manner of listening, by an affability without mockery, which is to politeness what practice is to virtue. When the celebrated man spoke, she had an attentive air a thousand times more flattering than the most skilful compliments. This mutual introduction was performed without any emphasis, and gracefully, by the marchioness. At dinner, d'Arthez was placed near the princess, who, far from imitating the little exaggerations of dieting which are permitted by affectation, ate with a very good appetite, and made it a point to show herself as a natural woman, without any strange fashions. Between two services, she profited by a moment during which the conversation became general to speak to d'Arthez aside.

10

"The secret of the pleasure which I have procured myself in meeting you," she said, "is the
desire of learning something of an unfortunate
friend of yours, Monsieur, who died for another
cause than ours, to whom I am under great obligation, without having been able to recognize them and
to acquit myself of them. The Prince de Cadignan
has shared my regrets. I have learned that you
were one of the best friends of this poor youth.
Your mutual friendship, pure and unaltered, was a
title to my consideration. You will not, then, find
it extraordinary that I have wished to know all that
you could tell me of this being who is so dear to
you. Though I am attached to the exiled family,
and held to entertain monarchical opinions, I am
not of the number of those who believe it to be
impossible to be at once Republican and noble of
heart. The Monarchy and the Republic are the only
two forms of government which do not suppress
elevated sentiments."

"Michel Chrestien was an angel, Madame,"
replied Daniel, in a voice of emotion. "I do not
know, among the heroes of antiquity, a man who
was superior to him. Avoid entertaining for one
of these Republicans those narrow ideas which
would set up again the Convention and the pretty
ways of the Committee of Public Safety; no.
Michel dreamed of the Swiss Federation applied to
the whole of Europe. Let us admit it, between
ourselves, after the admirable government of one
only, which, I believe, is more peculiarly adapted

to our country, the system of Michel is the suppression of war in the Old World and its reconstruction on bases other than those of conquest which formerly feudalized it. The Republicans were, in this respect, the nearest to his idea; this is why he lent them his aid in July and at Saint-Merri. Although entirely divided in opinion, we remained closely united."

"It is the finest eulogy of your two characters," said Madame de Cadignan, timidly.

"In the last four years of his life," resumed Daniel, "he confided to me only his love for you, and this confidence knit still tighter the already strong bonds of our fraternal friendship. He alone, Madame, would have loved you as you should be loved. How many times have I not endured the rain in accompanying your carriage to your house, in contending in speed with your horses, so as to keep at the same point on a parallel line in order to see you,—to admire you!"

"But, Monsieur," said the princess, "I am going to hold myself bound to indemnify you."

"Why is Michel not here?" replied Daniel, with an accent full of melancholy.

"He would perhaps have not loved me long," said the princess, shaking her head with a sorrowful movement. "The Republicans are even more absolute in their ideas than we other absolutists, who sin by indulgence. He doubtless dreamed of me as perfect; he would have been cruelly undeceived. We are pursued, we women, by as many calumnies

as you have to endure in a literary life, and we are
not able to defend ourselves, neither by glory, nor
by our works. We are not believed to be that
which we really are, but that which we are said to
be.   There are those who would have very soon
covered up for him the unknown woman which is
in me under the false portrait of the imaginary
woman, which is the true one for the world.   He
would have believed me unworthy of the noble sentiments which he entertained for me, incapable of
comprehending them."

Here, the princess shook her head, agitating her
beautiful blond tresses crowned with heather, by a
sublime gesture. That which she expressed of deso-
lating doubts, of hidden miseries, is unspeakable.
Daniel comprehended everything, and looked at the
princess with a lively emotion.

"However, the day on which I saw him again,
long after the revolt of July," she resumed, "I was
on the point of yielding to the desire which I felt, to
take him by the hand, to grasp it before all the
world, under the peristyle of the Théâtre-Italien,
in giving him my bouquet.   I thought that this testimony of gratitude would be misinterpreted, like so
many other noble things which to-day pass for the
follies of Madame de Maufrigneuse, and which I
could never explain, for there is only my son and
God who will ever know me."

These words, breathed into the listener's ear in
such a manner as to be unheard by all the other
guests, and with an accent worthy of the most skilful

comedienne, should have gone direct to the heart;
and they did attain to that of d'Arthez. It
did not concern the celebrated writer; this woman
sought to reëstablish herself in the favor of a dead
man. She might have been slandered, she wished
to know if nothing had tarnished her in the eyes
of him who loved her. Had he died with all his
illusions?

"Michel," replied d'Arthez, "was one of those
men who love absolutely, and who, if they choose
badly, know how to suffer for it without ever re-
nouncing her whom they have elected."

"Was I, then, loved in this manner?—" she cried,
with an air of exalted beatitude.

"Yes, Madame."

"I, then, made his happiness?"

"During four years."

"A woman never learns such a thing as this
without experiencing a proud satisfaction," she
said, turning her gentle and noble countenance
towards d'Arthez with a movement full of modest
confusion.

One of the most knowing manœuvres of these
comediennes is to veil their manners when the
words are too expressive, and to make the eyes
speak when the discourse is restrained. These
skilful dissonances, slipped into the music of their
love, false or true, bring about invincible seductions.

"Is it not," she resumed, lowering her voice still
more, and after assuring herself of having produced
the desired effect, "is it not to have accomplished

her destiny to have rendered happy, and without
crime, a great man?"

"Did he not write it to you?"

"Yes; but I wished to be very sure of it, for,
believe me, Monsieur, in setting me so high, he did
not deceive himself."

Women know how to give to their words a peculiar saintliness; they communicate to them I know
not what of vibration which extends the sense of
their ideas and lends them profundity; if, later, their
charmed auditor no longer recalls what they have
said, the object has been completely attained,
which is the proper quality of eloquence. The
princess might at this moment have worn the diadem
of France, her forehead would not have been more
imposing than it was under the beautiful diadem of
her tresses elevated in coils like a tower, and ornamented with the pretty heather. This woman
seemed to walk on the flood of calumny, like the
Saviour on the waves of the Lake of Tiberius, enveloped in the winding-sheet of this love, like an
angel in his nimbus. There was nothing in it
which suggested either the necessity of being thus,
or the desire to appear grand or loving,—it was
all simple and calm. A living man could never
have rendered to the princess the services which
she obtained of this dead one. D'Arthez, a solitary
worker, to whom the practices of the world were
unknown, and whom study had enveloped with its
protecting veils, was the dupe of this accent and of
these words. He was under the charm of these

exquisite manners; he admired this perfect beauty,
ripened by unhappiness, restored in retirement; he
adored the union, so rare, of a fine intelligence and
a beautiful soul.   Finally, he wished to obtain for
himself the heritage of Michel Chrestien.   The
commencement of this passion was, as it is among
most profound thinkers, an idea.   In seeing the
princess, in studying the shape of her head, the
disposition of her so gentle features, her figure, her
foot, her hands so finely modeled, so much more
closely than he had been able to do while accompanying his friend in his foolish courses through the
street, he remarked the surprising phenomenon of
the moral second sight which the man exalted by
love finds in himself.   With what lucidity had not
Michel Chrestien read this heart, this soul, lit up
by the fires of love?   The Federalist had then been
divined, he also! he would have doubtless been
happy.   The princess had thus in the eyes of
d'Arthez a great charm, she was surrounded by an
aureole of poesy.   During the dinner, the writer
recalled to himself the despairing confidences of the
Republican and his hopes when he thought himself
loved; the beautiful poem which a true feeling
inspires had been sung for him alone because of this
woman.   Unknowingly, Daniel was to profit by
these preparations due to chance.   It is but seldom
that a man passes without remorse from the position
of a confidant to that of a rival, and d'Arthez could
now do so without crime.   In a moment he perceived the enormous differences which exist between

superior women, these flowers of the great world,
and vulgar women, whom he knew, however, as yet,
by but one specimen; he was then assailed by the
most accessible sides, the most tender, of his soul
and of his genius.   Instigated by his simplicity, by
the impetuosity of his ideas, to take possession of this
woman, he found himself restrained by the world
and by the barrier which the manner, let us say the
word, which the majesty, of the princess put
between herself and him.   Thus, for this man, not
accustomed to respect that which he loved, there
was here something, I know not what, of irritating,
a charm all the more great, that he was forced to
conceal its effects upon himself and to guard his
attempts without betraying himself.   The conversation,   which   related   to   Michel   Chrestien
through the dinner to the dessert, furnished an
admirable pretext to Daniel, as to the princess, for
conversing with lowered voices,—love, sympathy,
divination; for her to pose as a woman misunderstood, calumniated; for him to slip his feet into the
shoes of the dead Republican.   Perhaps this ingenuous man was surprised to find himself regretting
his friend so little.   At the moment when the marvels of the dessert were resplendent on the table, in
the light of the candelabra, under the shelter of the
bouquets of natural flowers which separated the
guests by a brilliant hedge, richly colored with fruits
and with sweetmeats, the princess was pleased to
bring to a close this succession of confidences by a
delicious word, accompanied by one of those glances

by the aid of which blond women seem to be
brunettes, and in which she expressed finely this
idea that Daniel and Michel were two twin souls.
D'Arthez from this moment threw himself into the
general conversation, bringing to it an infantile joy
and a little fatuous air worthy of a scholar. The
princess took in the simplest manner his arm to
return into the little salon of the marchioness. In
traversing the grand salon, she walked slowly; and,
when she was separated from the marchioness, to
whom Blondet had given his arm, by a sufficiently
considerable interval, she halted d'Arthez.

"I do not desire to be inaccessible to the friend of
that poor Republican," she said to him. "And,
although I have made a law for myself to receive no
one, you alone of all the world should be able to
enter my house. Do not think that this is a favor.
A favor is always something for strangers only, and
it seems to me that we are old friends,—I would
wish to see in you the brother of Michel."

D'Arthez could only press the arm of the princess,
he found nothing to reply. When the coffee was
served, Diane de Cadignan enveloped herself, by a
coquettish movement, in a large shawl and rose.
Blondet and Rastignac were men too high in the
world of politics and too much accustomed to the
ways of society to utter the slightest bourgeois exclamation and endeavor to retain the princess; but
Madame d'Espard caused her friend to seat herself
again by taking her by the hand and saying in her
ear:

"Wait till the domestics have dined; the carriage is not ready."

And she made a sign to the valet de chambre, who carried away the coffee service. Madame de Montcornet understood that the princess and Madame d'Espard had something to say to each other, and engrossed the attention of d'Arthez, Rastignac and Blondet, whom she amused by one of those extravagant paradoxical attacks of which the Parisian women have such a marvelous understanding.

"Well," said the marchioness to Diane, "what do you make of him?"

"Why, he is an adorable child; he is just out of his swaddling-clothes. Truly, this time again, there will be, as always, a triumph without any contest."

"It is desperately discouraging," said Madame d'Espard, "but there is one resource."

"How?"

"Let me become your rival."

"As you like," replied the princess; "I have made up my mind. Genius is in a certain manner a being of the brain, I do not know what will touch its heart; we will talk about it later."

Hearing this last word, the meaning of which was impenetrable, Madame d'Espard took part in the general conversation and appeared neither hurt as to the "As you like," nor curious to know what this interview would lead to. The princess remained about an hour seated on the little sofa near the fire, in the attitude, full of nonchalance and abandonment, which Guérin has given to Didon,

listening with all the attention of one absorbed, and
looking at Daniel from time to time, without dis-
guising an admiration which, nevertheless, did not
exceed due bounds.   She made her escape when the
carriage was announced, after having exchanged a
clasp of the hand with the marchioness and an inclination of the head with Madame de Montcornet.

The evening came to a termination without further
reference to the princess.   The species of exaltation
experienced by d'Arthez was taken advantage of by
the others, and he displayed all the treasures of his
mind.   Certainly he had in Rastignac and in
Blondet two acolytes of the first quality in regard to
finesse of wit and extended intelligence.   As for the
two ladies, they have long been known as among
the most spirituelle of the higher society.   This
was then a halt in an oasis, an enjoyment rare and
perfectly appreciated by these personages habitually
possessed by the "Beware" of the world, of the salons
and of political life.   There are those who have the
privilege of being among men, as it were, the benefi-
cent stars whose light illumines all minds, whose
rays warm all hearts.   D'Arthez was one of those
fine souls.   A writer, who elevates himself to his
height, acquires the habit of reflecting on all things,
and forgets sometimes in the world that it is not
necessary to say everything; it is impossible for
him to have the restraint of those who live in it
continually; but, as his flights are nearly always
marked by a quality of originality, no one could
complain of him.   This savor so rare among talents,

this youthfulness full of simplicity, which rendered
d'Arthez so nobly original, made of this evening
something delightful.   He went away with the
Baron de Rastignac, who, in conducting him to his
own house, naturally spoke of the princess, asking
him what he had thought of her.

"Michel was right to love her," replied d'Arthez;
"she is an extraordinary woman."

"Very truly extraordinary," replied Rastignac, in
a tone of raillery. "By your accent, I see that you
love her already; you will be in her house before
three days, and I am too old an habitué of Paris not
to know what will come to pass between you. Well,
my dear Daniel, I entreat you to not allow your
personal interests to become involved in the least
confusion. Love the princess if you feel love for
her in your heart; but think of your fortune. She
has never taken nor demanded two farthings from
any one whatever, she is far too much a d'Uxelles
and Cadignan for that; but, from my certain knowledge, outside her own fortune, which was very
considerable, she has dissipated several millions.
How? why? by what means? no one knows; she
does not know herself.   I have seen her make away
with, thirteen years ago, the fortune of a charming
young man and that of an old notary in twenty
months."

"Thirteen years ago!" said d'Arthez; "why, how
old is she?"

"You did not then see," replied Rastignac, laughing, "at the table her son, the Duc de Maufrigneuse,

a young man of nineteen? Now, nineteen and seventeen make—"

"Thirty-six!" cried the author, in surprise; "I would have given her twenty years."

"She would have accepted them," said Rastignac; "but you need not worry on that subject, she will never be more than twenty for you. You are about to enter into the most fantastic world.—Goodnight, here you are at home," said the baron, seeing his carriage enter the Rue de Bellefond, in which d'Arthez lived in a pretty house of his own; "we will see each other during the week at Mademoiselle des Touches."

D'Arthez allowed love to penetrate into his heart after the manner of Uncle Toby, without making the least resistance; he proceeded by adoration without criticism, by pure admiration. The princess, this beautiful creature, one of the most remarkable creatures of this monstrous Paris, in which everything is possible in good as in evil, became—however common the misfortune of the times has rendered this word,—the angel dreamed of. In order to thoroughly comprehend the sudden transformation of this illustrious author, it would be necessary to know all that solitude and constant labor leave of innocence in the heart; all that love, reduced to mere need and become tedious by the side of an ignoble woman, develops of desires and of fancies, how much it excites regrets and gives birth to divine sentiment in the very highest regions of the soul. D'Arthez was indeed the child, the collegian whom

the tact of the princess had suddenly recognized.
An almost similar illumination had taken place in
the beautiful Diane.   She had then, at last, encountered that superior man whom all women desire, if
only to amuse themselves with him; that puissance
to which they consent to obey were it only for the
pleasure of mastering it; she had found, in short,
the great qualities of intelligence united to the simplicity of the heart, to a newness of passion; then
she saw, by an unheard-of good fortune, all these
riches contained in a form which pleased her.
D'Arthez seemed to her handsome, perhaps he was.
Although he had arrived at the serious age of man,
at thirty-eight years, he had preserved a flower of
youth due to the sober and chaste life which he had
led, and, like studious men, like men of the state,
he had acquired a reasonable *embonpoint*.   While
very young he had offered a slight resemblance to
General Bonaparte.   This resemblance was still
visible, as much so as a man with black eyes, with
thick brown hair, can resemble this sovereign with
blue eyes, with chestnut locks; but all that there
had been formerly of ardent and noble ambition in
the eyes of d'Arthez had been, as it were, made
tender by success.   The thoughts with which his
forehead had been burdened had flowered, the hollow
lines of his face had been filled out.   A happy
comfort had spread its golden tones where in
his youth poverty had mingled the yellowish tints
of the temperaments whose forces were banded together in order to sustain the crushing and continuous

combat. If you observe with care the fine faces
of the antique philosophers, you will perceive
in them always the deviations from the perfect type
of the human countenance to which each physiognomy owes its originality, rectified by the habit of
meditation, by the constant calm indispensable to
intellectual labor.   The most unquiet countenances,
like that of Socrates, become finally of a serenity
almost divine.   To this noble simplicity which
adorned his majestic head, d'Arthez joined a
candid expression, the naturalness of children,
and a touching benevolence. He had not that
politeness, always with a touch of falseness, by
which, in this world, those persons the best educated
and the most amiable assume qualities which are
often lacking to them, and which leave seriously
wounded those who recognize that they have been
duped.   He might fail to come up to the require-
ment of some of the worldly laws in consequence of
his isolation; but, as he never offended, this sort of
perfume of wildness rendered still more gracious the
affability peculiar to men of great talent, who know
how to leave their superiority at home in order to
let themselves down to the social level, in order to,
like Henry IV., lend their backs to the children and
their wit to the simpletons.

In returning home, the princess did not debate
with herself, any more than d'Arthez had defended
himself against the charm which she had thrown
over him.   Everything was now said for her: she
loved with her science and with her ignorance. If

she interrogated herself, it was to ask herself if she
merited so great a happiness, and what she had
done that Heaven had sent her such an angel.   She
wished to be worthy of this love, to perpetuate it,
to appropriate it to herself forever, and to finish
softly her life of a pretty woman in that paradise of
which she caught glimpses.   As for resistance, for
quibbling with herself, for coquetting, she did not
even think of it.   She was thinking of a very
different thing!   She had comprehended the grandeur of men of genius, she had divined that they do
not submit superior women to ordinary laws.   Thus,
by one of those rapid perceptions peculiar to these
great feminine spirits, she had promised herself to
be yielding at the very first desire.   From the
knowledge which she had gained, in one interview
only, of the character of d'Arthez, she had suspected that this desire would not be soon enough
expressed not to leave her the time in which to
make of herself that which she wished, that which
she should be in the eyes of this sublime lover.

Here commences one of those unknown comedies
played, in the interior tribunal of the conscience,
between two beings, of which one will be the dupe
of the other, and which push back the boundaries of
perversity, one of those black and comic dramas,
compared with which that of *Tartuffe* is a baga-
telle; but which are not of the scenic world, and
which, that everything in them may be extraordinary, are natural, conceivable and justified by
necessity, a horrible drama which should be named

the seamy side of vice. The princess commenced
by sending for the works of d'Arthez. She had not
read the first word of them; and, nevertheless, she
had sustained twenty minutes of eulogistic discussion with him, without *quid pro quo!* She read
them all. Then she wished to compare his books
with the best which contemporary literature had
produced. She had an indigestion of the mind the
day on which d'Arthez came to see her. Expecting
this visit, she had every day made a superior toilet,
one of those toilets which express an idea and cause
it to be accepted by the eyes, without knowing
how or why. She offered to the regard a harmonious combination of gray colors, a sort of half-mourn-
ing, a grace full of abandonment, the vestments
of a woman who no longer held to life but by
a few natural ties, her child perhaps, and who was
weary. She bore witness to an elegant disgust
which, however, would not go as far as suicide; she
would complete her term in the terrestrial bagnio.
She received d'Arthez like a woman who is waiting for him, and as if he had already been a hundred times in her house; she did him the honor to
treat him like an old acquaintance; she put him at
his ease by a single gesture indicating to him a sofa
on which to be seated, while she finished the letter
already commenced. The conversation began in
the commonest manner,—the weather, the ministry, the illness of De Marsay, the hopes of the
Legitimistes. D'Arthez was an Absolutist, the princess could not ignore the opinions of a man seated

11

in the Chamber among the fifteen or twenty persons
who represented the Legitimiste party; she found
an opportunity to relate to him how she had tricked
De Marsay; then, by a transition which was furnished her by the devotion of the Prince de Cadignan to the royal family and MADAME, she drew
the attention of d'Arthez to the prince.

"He has at least in his favor the love he bears
his masters and his devotion to them," said she.
"His public character consoles me for all the suffering which his private character has caused me.—
For," she went on, leaving the prince lightly aside,
"have you not remarked, you who know all, that
men have two characters,—they have one for their
household, for their wives, for their private life, and
which is the true one; there, no more mask, no
more dissimulation, they do not give themselves the
trouble to pretend, they are what they are, and are
often horrible; then the world, others, the salons,
the Court, the sovereign, politics, see them grand,
noble, generous, in a costume embroidered with
virtues, adorned with beautiful language, full of
exquisite qualities. What a horrible pleasantry!
And people are surprised sometimes at the smile of
certain women, at their air of superiority with their
husbands, at their indifference!—"

She let her hand fall on the arm of her chair,
without finishing her sentence, but this gesture completed her speech admirably. As she saw d'Arthez
occupied in studying her flexible figure, so well disposed in the depths of her cushioned arm-chair,

occupied with the fall of her skirts, and with
a pretty little gather which relieved the stiffness of
her corsage, one of those hardihoods of the toilet
which are only possible for figures sufficiently
slender to lose nothing by them, she resumed the
sequence of her thoughts as if she were speaking to
herself:

"I will not continue.   You have ended, you
writers, by rendering very ridiculous the women
who pretend to be misunderstood, who are unfortunately married, who make themselves dramatic,
interesting, which seems to me to the last degree
bourgeois.   One yields, and everything is said, or
one resists and you are amused.   In both cases,
silence should be kept.   It is true that I have neither
known how to yield altogether nor to resist altogether; but perhaps this is a still greater reason to
keep silence.   What foolishness it is in women to
complain!   If they have not been the strongest,
they have been wanting in wit, in tact, in finesse;
they deserve their fate.   Are they not the queens
in France?   They play with you as they wish,
when they wish, and as much as they wish."

She made her perfume flask dance with a marvelous movement of feminine impertinence and of
mocking gayety.

"I have often heard miserable little specimens
regret that they were women, wished that they were
men; I have always looked at them with pity," she
said, continuing.   "If I had to choose, I should still
prefer to be a woman.   A fine pleasure it is to owe

one's triumphs to strength, to all the powers which are given you by the laws made by you! But, when we see you at our feet, uttering and doing sillinesses, is it not then an intoxicating happiness to feel in one's self the weakness which triumphs? When we succeed, we are obliged to keep silent, under pain of losing our empire. Beaten, women are still obliged to keep silent through pride. The silence of the slave frightens the master."

This cackling was chirruped in a voice so softly mocking, so delicate, with such coquettish movements of the head, that d'Arthez, to whom this species of woman was totally unknown, remained exactly like the partridge charmed by the hunting dog.

"I pray you, Madame," said he, finally, "explain to me how a man has been able to make you suffer, and you may be sure that, even in that in which all women are common, you would be distinguished even though you might not have a manner of saying things which would render a cook-book interesting."

"You go quickly in friendship," said she with her grave voice, which rendered d'Arthez serious and disquieted.

The conversation changed, the hour advanced. The poor man of genius went away in a contrite frame of mind for having appeared curious, for having wounded this heart, and believing that this woman had strangely suffered. She had passed her life in amusing herself, she was a real female Don Juan, with this difference only, that it was not to supper that she would have invited the marble statue, and certainly she would have gotten the better of the statue.

It is impossible to continue this recital without saying a word of the Prince de Cadignan, better known under the name of the Duc de Maufrigneuse; otherwise, the salt in the miraculous inventions of the princess would disappear, and strangers would comprehend nothing of the frightful Parisian comedy which she was going to play for a man. Monsieur le Duc de Maufrigneuse, as a true son of the Prince de Cadignan, is a man long and dry, with a most elegant figure, full of graciousness, making charming speeches, who became colonel by the grace of God and good soldier by luck; moreover, brave as a Polander, on every occasion, without discernment, and hiding the void in his head under the jargon of the *grande compagnie.* From the age of thirty-six he was, by compulsion, of as complete an indifference to the fair sex as the King, Charles X., his master; punished, like his master, for having, like him, pleased too much in his youth. During eighteen years the idol of the Faubourg Saint-Germain, he had, like all the sons of families, led a dissipated life, filled only with pleasures. His father, ruined by the Revolution, had recovered his position on the return of the Bourbons, the government of a royal château, salaries, pensions; but this factitious fortune the old prince had very soon devoured, remaining the grand seigneur which he had been before the Restoration, so that, when the law of indemnity

arrived, the sums which he received were absorbed
by the luxury which he displayed in his immense
hôtel, the only property which he recovered, and
the largest part of which was occupied by his
daughter-in-law.   The Prince de Cadignan died
some time before the Revolution of July, at the age
of eighty-seven.   He had ruined his wife, and was
long in delicate relations with the Duc de Navarreins, who had married his daughter for his first
wife, and to whom he with difficulty rendered his
accounts.   The Duc de Maufrigneuse had had liai-
sons with the Duchesse d'Uxelles.   About 1814, at
the date when Monsieur de Maufrigneuse reached
his thirty-sixth birthday, the duchess, seeing him
poor, but very well received at Court, gave him her
daughter, who possessed about fifty or sixty thous-
and francs of income, in addition to that which she
might expect to receive from her.   Mademoiselle
d'Uxelles thus became also a duchess, and her
mother knew that she would have in all probability
the greatest liberty.   After having had the unhoped-for happiness of being presented with a son
and heir, the duke left his wife entirely free in her
actions, and went amusing himself from garrison to
garrison, passing the winters in Paris, contracting
debts which his father always paid, professing the
most complete conjugal indulgence, notifying the
duchess a week in advance of his return to Paris,
adored by his regiment, loved by the Dauphin, a
skilful courtier, something of a gambler, moreover
without any affectation; the duchess could never

persuade him to take an opera-dancer for appearance
sake and through regard for her, as she said pleasantly.   The duke, who had the succession of the
office of his father, knew how to please the two
kings, Louis XVIII. and Charles X., which went to
prove that he made a very good use of his nullity;
but this conduct, this life, were all covered with a
most beautiful varnish,—language, nobility of manners, appearance, all offered in him their perfection; in short, the Liberals loved him.   It was
impossible for him to continue the Cadignans who,
according to the old prince, were well known as
ruining their wives, for the duchess used up her
fortune herself.   These details became so public in
the circle of the Court and in the Faubourg Saint-
Germain, that during the last five years of the
Restoration, any one who would have spoken of
them would have been laughed at, as if he wished
to relate the death of Turenne or that of Henry IV.
Thus there was not one woman who spoke of this
charming duke without eulogy,—his conduct toward
his wife had been perfect, it would be difficult for a
man to show himself as considerate as Maufrigneuse
had been for the duchess; he had left her the free
disposition of her fortune, he had defended her and
sustained her on every occasion.   Whether it were
pride, or good nature, or chivalrousness, Monsieur
de Maufrigneuse had saved the duchess on more than
one occasion when any other woman would have
been lost, notwithstanding her connection, notwithstanding the credit of the old Duchesse d'Uxelles, of

the Duc de Navarreins, of her father-in-law and of her husband's aunt. To-day, the Prince de Cadignan passes for one of the finest characters of the aristocracy. Perhaps fidelity in need is one of the very finest victories which the courtiers can win over themselves. The Duchesse d'Uxelles was forty-five when she married her daughter to the Duc de Maufrigneuse; she had looked for a long time without jealousy and even with interest at the success of her former friend. At the time of her marriage of her daughter and the duke, she maintained a conduct of great nobility, and one which covered the immorality of this combination. Nevertheless, the malice of persons at Court found matter for jesting, and pretended that this fine conduct had not cost the duchess very dearly, though for about the last five years she had given herself up to the devotion and repentance of a woman who has much to be pardoned.

During several days, the princess showed herself more and more remarkable for her literary attainments. She took up with the greatest hardihood the most arduous questions, thanks to diurnal and nocturnal readings pursued with an intrepidity worthy of the highest eulogiums. D'Arthez, stupefied and incapable of suspecting that Diane d'Uxelles repeated in the evening what she had read in the morning, as do a great many writers, held her for a superior woman. These conversations increased the distance of Diane from her object, she endeavored to place herself again on the footing of

confidence from which her lover had prudently
retired; but it was not very easy to bring back to
this point a man of his temper who had once been
frightened off. Nevertheless, after a month of these
literary campaigns and fine Platonic discourses,
d'Arthez became more resolute and came every day
at three o'clock. He went away at six, and reappeared in the evening at nine, to remain until midnight or one o'clock in the morning, with the
regularity of a lover full of impatience. The princess was always dressed with more or less care at
the hour when d'Arthez presented himself. This
mutual fidelity, the care which they took of themselves, everything in them, expressed the sentiments
which they did not dare to avow, for the princess
divined marvelously well that this great child was
as much afraid of a contention as she was desirous
of it. Nevertheless, d'Arthez expressed in his constant, mute declarations a respect which pleased the
princess infinitely. Both of them felt themselves
each day so much more united that nothing conven-
tional nor direct and open would arrest them in the
flow of their ideas, as when, between lovers, there
are on one side formal demands, and on the other a
defense sincere or coquettish. Like all those men
who are younger than their age would entitle them
to be, d'Arthez was a prey to those agitating irres-
olutions caused by the power of desires and by the
terror of displeasing, a situation of which a young
woman comprehends nothing when she shares it, but
to which the princess had too often given occasion

not to appreciate all its pleasures. Thus Diane
enjoyed these delicious childishnesses with so much
the more charm that she knew perfectly well how to
make them cease. She resembled a great artist
pausing over the indecisive lines of a sketch,
certain of being able to finish in an hour of inspiration the masterpiece still floating in the limbo of
creation. How many times, seeing d'Arthez ready
to advance, had she not pleased herself by arresting
him by an imposing air! She suppressed the secret
storms of this young heart, she stirred them up
again, pacified them by a look, in giving her hand
to be kissed or by insignificant words uttered in a
moved and tender voice. This management, coldly
arranged, but divinely played, engraved her image
still deeper in the soul of this spiritual writer,
whom she was pleased to render childlike, confiding,
simple and almost silly beside her; but she had
also occasional returnings upon herself, and it was
then impossible for him not to admire so much
grandeur mingled with so much innocence. This
play of a great coquette attached her insensibly
to her slave. Finally, Diane became impatient with
this amorous Epictetus, and, when she thought she
had brought him to the most entire credulity, she
gave herself as a duty the task of applying over his
eyes the very thickest bandage.

One evening, Daniel found the princess pensive,
an elbow on her little table, her beautiful blond
head bathed in the light from the lamp; she was
trifling with a letter which she made dance on the

table-cloth. When d'Arthez had seen this paper sufficiently, she finished by folding it and putting it in her girdle.

"What troubles you?" said d'Arthez. "You appear disquieted."

"I have received a letter from Monsieur de Cadignan," she replied. "However grave may be his wrongs toward me, I reflected, after having read his letter, that he is exiled, without family, without his son, whom he loves."

These words, pronounced in a voice full of soul, revealed an angelic sensibility. D'Arthez was moved to the last degree. The curiosity of the lover became, so to speak, a curiosity almost psychological and literary. He wished to know up to what point this woman was grand, for what injuries her pardon was required, how much these women of the world, accused of frivolity, of hardness of heart, of selfishness, could be angelic. Remembering that he had been already repulsed when he wished to know better this celestial heart, he himself had something like a trembling in his voice when, taking the transparent and slender hand, with tapering fingers, of the beautiful Diane, he said to her:

"Are we now sufficiently good friends for you to tell me what you have suffered? Your former griefs should be of influence in this revery."

"Yes," said she, whispering this syllable like the very softest note that had ever been sighed by the flute of Tulou.

She fell back again in her revery, and her eyes
veiled themselves. Daniel remained waiting full of
anxiety, penetrated by the solemnity of this
moment. His poet's imagination caused him to see,
as it were, the clouds which were dissipated slowly
in discovering to him the sanctuary where he was
about to see at the feet of God the blessed lamb.

"Well?—" said he, in a voice soft and calm.

Diane looked at the tender suitor; then she
lowered her eyes slowly, displaying her eyelashes
by a movement which revealed the most noble modesty. No one but a monster would have been capable of imagining any hypocrisy in the graceful
undulation by which the malicious princess raised
her pretty little head to plunge once more her glance
in the desiring eyes of this great man.

"Can I? Should I?" she said, with an involuntary gesture of hesitation, looking at d'Arthez with
a sublime expression of dreamy tenderness. "Men
have so little faith in these things, they think themselves so little obliged to discretion!"

"Ah! if you doubt me, why am I here?" cried
d'Arthez.

"Ah! my friend," she replied, giving to her exclamation the gracefulness of an involuntary
avowal, "when she gives herself for life, does a
woman calculate? It is not a question of my refusal
—what can I refuse you?—but of the conception
which you will have of me, if I speak. I could
readily confide to you the strange situation in which
I am at my age; but what would you think of a

woman who discovered the secret wounds of marriage, who would betray the secret of another?
Turenne kept his word to the thieves; do I not owe
to my executioners the probity of Turenne?"

"Have you given your promise to anyone?"

"Monsieur de Cadignan did not think it necessary
to ask of me secrecy.   You wish, then, more than
my soul?   Tyrant! you wish, then, that I bury in
you my probity?" said she, throwing on d'Arthez
a look by which she set a higher value on this false
confidence than on her person.

"You make of me a man even less than common,
if from me you fear anything whatever evil," he
said, with a bitterness but thinly disguised.

"Forgive me, my friend," she replied, taking his
hand, looking at it, taking it between her own and
caressing it by drawing her fingers over it with a
movement of the greatest gentleness.   "I know all
that you are worth.   You have related to me your
whole life; it is noble, it is beautiful, it is sublime,
it is worthy of your name; perhaps, in return, I
owe you mine?   But I am afraid at this moment to
fall in your view by recounting to you secrets which
are not altogether mine.   Then, perhaps, you will
not believe, you, a man of solitude and of poetry,
in the horrors of the world.   Ah! you do not know
that in inventing your dramas, they are surpassed
by those which are really acted in families apparently the most united.   You are ignorant of the
extent of certain gilded misfortunes."

"I know all," he cried.

"No," she resumed, "you know nothing. Should a daughter ever deliver up her mother?"

In hearing this word, d'Arthez found himself like a man lost in a black night on the Alps, and who, at the first light of day, perceives that he is on the edge of a bottomless precipice. He looked at the princess with a bewildered air, he had a chill in his back ; Diane thought that this man of genius had a feeble spirit, but she saw a light in his eyes which reassured her.

"Finally, you have become for me almost a judge," she said, with a despairing air. "I can speak, in virtue of that right which everyone who has been slandered has to assert his innocence. I have been, I am still—so much so as anyone remembers a poor recluse forced by the world to renounce the world!—accused of so much lightness of conduct, of so many evil things, that it can be permitted to me to place myself in the heart in which I find an asylum in such a manner as not to be driven from it. I have always seen in self-justification a strong reflection on innocence, and for this reason have I always disdained to speak. To whom, moreover, could I address my speech? These cruel things can only be confided to God, or to some one who seems to us near to Him, a priest, or a second self. Well, if my secrets are not there," she said, placing her hand over d'Arthez's heart, "as they are here—" and the upper part of her corsage yielded to the pressure of her fingers—"you will not be the grand d'Arthez, I will have been deceived!"

A tear moistened the eye of d'Arthez, and Diane mastered this tear by a sidewise glance which did not cause the slightest movement of eyeball or eyelid. It was quick and neat as the stroke of a cat taking a mouse. D'Arthez, for the first time, after sixty days full of protocols, dared to take her warm and perfumed hand; he carried it to his lips, he impressed on it a long kiss trailed from the wrist to the nails with so delicate a voluptuousness that the princess inclined her head, auguring very favorably indeed of literature. She thought that men of genius might love with much more perfection than do the fops, the men of the world, the diplomats, and even the soldiers, who, however, have only that to do. She was a connoisseur, and knew that the amorous character signs itself in some way in nothings. An instructed woman can read her future in a simple gesture, as Cuvier could say, in seeing the fragment of a skeleton of a paw: "This belonged to an animal of such and such dimensions, with or without horns, carnivorous, herbivorous, amphibious, etc., so many thousand years old." Certain of encountering in d'Arthez as much imagination in love as he put in his literary style, she judged it necessary to make him arrive at the very highest degree of passion and of faith. She withdrew her hand quickly with a magnificent movement, full of emotions. She might have said: "Have done, you will make me die!" she would have spoken less energetically. She remained for a moment gazing at the eyes of d'Arthez, expressing all at once

happiness, prudishness, fear, confidence, languor,
a vague desire and the shame of a virgin.   She was
but twenty years old!   But, reflect that she had prepared for this hour of comic mendacity with an unheard-of art in her toilet; she was in her fauteuil
like a flower which is about to expand at the first
kiss of the sun.   Deceiving or true, she intoxicated
Daniel.

If I may be permitted to risk an individual opinion, let us admit that it would be delicious to be
thus deceived for a long time.   Certainly, Talma,
before the footlights, has often been more convinc-
ing than nature.   But was not the Princesse de
Cadignan the greatest comedienne of her time?
Nothing was lacking to this woman but an attentive
audience.   Unfortunately, in those epochs which
are ravaged by political storms, women disappear
like water-lilies which have need of a pure sky and
the mildest zephyrs to flower before our delighted
eyes.

The hour had come, Diane was about to enmesh
this distinguished man in the inextricable lianas of
a romance carefully prepared, and which he was
about to listen to as a neophyte in the best days of
the Christian faith would have listened to the epistle of an apostle.

"My friend, my mother, who is still living at
Uxelles, married me at seventeen years of age, in
1814—you see how old I am!—to Monsieur de Maufrigneuse, not for love of me, but for love of him.
She thus acquitted herself, with the only man whom

she had ever loved, for all the happiness which she
had received from him.   Oh! you need not be
astonished at this horrible combination; it often
takes place.   Very many women are more lovers
than mothers, as the greater number of them are
better mothers than wives.   These two sentiments,
love and maternity, developed as they are by our
customs, often come into conflict in the hearts of
women; one of them necessarily has to succumb
when they are not equal in strength, a fact which
makes of some exceptional women the glory of our
sex.   A man of your genius may readily comprehend these things, which astonish fools, but which
are none the less true, and, I will go still further,
which are justifiable by the differences of character,
of temperaments, of attachments, of situations.
Myself, for example, at this moment, after twenty
years of unhappinesses, of deceptions, of calumnies
endured, of heavy ennui, of hollow pleasures, would
I not be disposed to throw myself at the feet of a
man who would love me sincerely and forever?
Well, would I not be condemned by the world?
And yet, would not twenty years of suffering, would
they not furnish an excuse for giving to a holy and
pure love the dozen years which still remained to
me in which to be beautiful?   This will not be, I am
not foolish enough to diminish my merits in the eyes
of God.   I have borne the burden and heat of the
day unto the evening, I will finish my day's labor
and I shall have gained my reward—"

   "What an angel!" thought d'Arthez.
   12

"In short, I have never wished ill to the Duchesse d'Uxelles for having better loved Monsieur de Maufrigneuse than the poor Diane here present. My mother had seen very little of me, she had forgotten me; but she had behaved so badly towards me, as from one woman to another, that what is evil conduct from one woman to another becomes horrible from mother to daughter. Those mothers who lead a life like that of the Duchesse d'Uxelles keep their daughters at a distance from them, so that I only entered the world two weeks before my marriage. You may judge of my innocence! I knew nothing, I was incapable of suspecting the secret of this alliance. I had a fine fortune,—sixty thousand francs of income from forest land, in Nivernais, which the Revolution had forgotten to sell, or was not able to sell, and which appertained to the fine château d'Anzy; Monsieur de Maufrigneuse was riddled with debts. If, later, I learned what it is to have debts, I was then too completely ignorant of life to suspect it. The savings which had been effected on my fortune served to regulate the affairs of my husband. Monsieur de Maufrigneuse was thirty-eight years of age when I married him, but these years were like those of military campaigns, they should count double. Ah! he was indeed more than seventy-six. At forty, my mother still retained her pretensions, and I found myself between two jealousies. What a life did I lead during ten years! —Ah! if one knew what this poor little woman so much suspected had suffered! To be guarded by a

mother jealous of her daughter! God!—You, who
make dramas, you will never invent one as black,
as cruel, as this one.   Usually, from the little that
I know of literature, a drama is a sequence of
actions, of discourse, of movements which hurry
themselves towards a catastrophe; but that of which
I speak to you is the most horrible catastrophe in
action! It is the avalanche which fell on you in the
morning, which falls again in the evening, and
which will fall again to-morrow. I am chilled at
this moment in which I speak to you and in which
I show you the cavern without exit, cold and dark,
in which I lived. If it is necessary to tell you
everything, the birth of my poor child, who, moreover, is all myself,—you must have been struck
with his resemblance to me? he has my hair, my
eyes, the shape of my face, my mouth, my smile,
my chin, my teeth,—well, his birth was a chance
or the result of a convention between my mother
and my husband.   For a long time after my marriage I remained a young girl, all but abandoned the
next day, mother without being wife. The duchess
amused herself by prolonging my ignorance, and,
for this purpose, a mother has horrible advantages
over her daughter. I, poor little thing, brought up
in a convent like a *rose mystique,* knowing nothing
of marriage, developed very late, I found myself
very happy,—I took pleasure in the mutual understanding and the harmony of our family. In the
end I was entirely diverted from thinking of my
husband, who scarcely pleased me and who did

nothing to ingratiate himself, during my first joys of maternity,—they were, moreover, so much the more keen that I did not suspect that there were others. I had had so constantly dinned in my ears the respect that a mother owes to herself! And, moreover, a young girl always likes to 'play mamma.' At the age in which I then was, a child replaces the doll. I was so proud of this beautiful flower, for Georges was beautiful,—a marvel! How be able to think of the world outside when one has the happiness of nourishing and caring for a little angel! I adore children when they are very little, white and pink. I saw nothing but my son, I lived with my son, I would not let his nurse clothe him, unclothe him, change his linen. These cares, so wearying for mothers who have regiments of children, were nothing but pleasure for me. But, after three or four years, as I am not altogether stupid, notwithstanding the care which was taken to bandage my eyes, the light finally reached them. Do you see me undeceived, four years later, in 1819? *Les Deux Frères ennemis* is a rose-water tragedy compared with a mother and a daughter placed as we were, the duchess and I; I braved them then, her and my husband, by public coquetries which made the world talk—God knows how much! You understand, my friend, that the men with whom I was suspected of light conduct had for me the value of a dagger which one makes use of to stab his enemy. Absorbed in my vengeance, I was not conscious of the wounds which I was inflicting on myself.

Innocent as a child, I passed for a perverse woman, for the most wicked woman in the world, and I knew nothing of it. The world is very foolish, very blind, very ignorant; it only penetrates those secrets which amuse it, which serve its wickedness; the greatest things, the most noble, it puts its hand over its eyes not to see them. But it seems to me that, at that period, there must have been seen in me glances, attitudes, of innocence in revolt, movements of pride which would have made fortunes for the great painters. I should have lit up the balls by the tempests of my anger, by the torrents of my disdain. Poetry lost! these sublime poems are only written in that indignation which seizes us at twenty! Later, one no longer gets indignant, one is wearied; one is no longer astonished at vice, one is cowardly, one is afraid. I, I went on, oh! I went on finely. I played the part of the most foolish personage in the world,—I had all the costs of crime without having the benefits. I had so much pleasure in compromising myself! Ah! I was guilty of infantile malice. I went to Italy with a young scatterbrain whom I deposited there when he spoke to me of love; but when I learned that he had compromised himself for me—he had committed a forgery to obtain money—I hastened to save him. My mother and my husband, who knew all these secrets, restrained me like a prodigal woman. Oh! this time, I went to the king. Louis XVIII., that man without a heart, was touched—he gave me a hundred thousand francs from his privy purse. The

Marquis d'Esgrignon, this young man whom you
have perhaps met in society, and who finished by
making a very rich marriage, was saved from the
abyss into which he had plunged for me.   This adventure, caused by my recklessness, made me
reflect.   I perceived that I was the first victim of
my own vengeance.   My mother, my husband, my
father-in-law had the world on their side, they
seemed to be protecting my follies.   My mother,
who knew me too proud, too grand, too much a
d'Uxelles to be guilty of vulgar conduct, was then
frightened at the evil which she had done.   She
was fifty-two years of age; she left Paris, she has
gone to live at Uxelles.   She now repents of her
wrongs, she is expiating them by the most extravagant devotion and by a boundless affection for me.
But, in 1823, she left me alone and face to face with
Monsieur de Maufrigneuse. O, my friend, you other
men, you can never know what it is to be a man of
intrigues grown old.   What a household is that of a
man accustomed to the adoration of women of the
world, who finds neither incense nor censer in his
own house, when he is dead to everything, and all
the more jealous for that! I desired, when Monsieur de Maufrigneuse was left alone with me, I
desired to be a good wife; but I came into contact
with all the asperity of a bitter spirit, with all the
fantasies of impotence, with all the puerilities of
silliness, with all the vanities of self-sufficiency, with
a man who was, in short, the most wearying elegy in
the world, and who treated me like a little girl, who

pleased himself with humiliating my self-respect on every occasion, with crushing me under the weight of his experience, with proving to me that I was ignorant of everything. He wounded me every moment. In short, he did everything to cause me to hold him in detestation and to give me the right to betray him; but I was the dupe of my own heart and of my desire to do well during three or four years! Would you know the infamous word which caused me to commit further follies? Would you ever invent the most sublime slander in the world? 'The Duchesse de Maufrigneuse has returned to her husband,' it was said. 'Bah! it is mere depravity; it is a triumph to reanimate the dead; she had done everything but that,' answered my best friend, a relative in whose house I had the happiness of meeting you."

"Madame d'Espard!" cried Daniel, making a gesture of horror.

"Oh! I have pardoned her, my friend. In the first place, the speech is excessively witty, and perhaps I have myself uttered crueler epigrams on poor women who were quite as pure as I was."

D'Arthez kissed again the hand of this saintly woman, who, after having served up to him a mother cut to pieces, after having made of the Prince de Cadignan, whom you know, an Othello of triple watchfulness, had hashed up her own character and accused herself of wrongs, in order to cover herself in the eyes of this ingenuous writer with that virginity which the most stupid of women endeavors at any price to offer her lover.

"You understand, my friend, that I re-entered
society with a great display and in order to there
make a display. I there encountered new struggles;
it was necessary to conquer my independence and
to neutralize Monsieur de Maufrigneuse.   I accordingly led for other reasons a dissipated life.   To
distract myself, to forget real life in a fantastic life,
I gave fêtes, I played the princess, and I made debts.
For myself, I forgot everything in the sleep of
fatigue; I woke again beautiful, gay, crazy for the
world; but, in this melancholy combat of fancy
against reality, I devoured my fortune.   The revolt
of 1830 arrived just at the moment when I encountered, at the end of this existence of the *Thousand
and One Nights*, the pure and holy love which—I
am frank!—I desired to know.   Admit it, was it not
natural for a woman whose heart, suppressed by so
many causes and accidents, had re-awakened at the
age in which a woman feels herself deceived, and
at which I saw around me so many women happy
and loving? Ah! why was Michel Chrestien so
respectful?   There was in this still another mockery for me.   What would you have! in falling, I
have lost everything, I had no longer any illusions
whatever; I had tried everything excepting one fruit
only for which I had no longer either taste or teeth.
In short, I found myself disenchanted in the world
at the period when it was necessary for me to quit
the world.   There is in this something providen-
tial, as in those insensibilities which prepare us
for death."—She made a gesture full of religious

unction.—"Everything then served me," she resumed, "the disasters of the monarchy and its ruin
helped me to bury myself. My son consoles me for
very many things. Maternal love reimburses us for
all the other sentiments which have been deceived!
And the world is surprised at my retirement, but I
have here found happiness. Oh! if you could know
how happy here is the poor creature who is before
you! In sacrificing everything for my son, I forget
the happiness of which I am ignorant and of which
I shall always be ignorant. Who would be able to
believe that life has been, for the Princesse de Cadignan, only an evil marriage-night; and all the adventures that have been imputed to her only the
defiance of a young girl to two frightful passions?
No one. To-day, I have fear of everything. I
would repulse, doubtless, a true feeling, some true
and pure love, in remembering so many falsehoods,
so many misfortunes; just as the rich, imposed upon
by cheats who feign misfortune, repulse an honest
poverty, disgusted as they are with all benevolence.
All that is horrible, is it not? but, believe me, that
which I tell to you is the history of very many
women."

These last words were pronounced with the lightness and pleasantry of tone which recalled the elegant and mocking women of the world. D'Arthez
was stunned. In his eyes, those whom justice sends
to the galleys, for murder, for having stolen with ag-
gravating circumstances, for having made a mistake
of a signature on a note, are little saints compared

with the criminals of the great world. This atrocious elegy, forged in the arsenal of deceit and tempered in the waters of the Parisian Styx, had been pronounced with the inimitable accent of truth. The author contemplated for a moment this adorable woman, sunk in the depths of her fauteuil, and whose two hands hung over the two arms of her seat like two dew-drops on the edge of a flower, overwhelmed by this revelation, crushed in seeming to have felt all the sorrows of her life again in relating them; in short, an angel of melancholy.

"And you may judge," said she, sitting up suddenly, lifting one of her hands and darting a swift glance from her eyes in which twenty years of pretended chastity flamed, "you may judge what impression must have made on me the love of your friend; but, by an atrocious mockery of chance,— or of God, perhaps,—for at that time, I avow it, a man, that is a man worthy of me, would have found me feeble, so much was I thirsting for happiness! Well, he is dead, and dead in saving the life of whom?—of Monsieur de Cadignan! Are you astonished to find me thoughtful—"

This was the last stroke, and the poor d'Arthez no longer restrained himself,—he fell on his knees, he buried his head in the hands of the princess and there wept; he poured on them those soft tears which the angels shed,—if the angels weep. As Daniel had his head thus, Madame de Cadignan could allow to play around her lips a malicious smile of triumph, such a smile as that with which the monkeys might accompany a very superior trick,—if the monkeys laugh.

"Ah! I have him," she thought.

And she had him very much, in fact.

"But you are,—" said he, raising his handsome head and looking at her lovingly.

"—Virgin and martyr," she completed, smiling at the vulgarity of this old pleasantry, but giving it a charming meaning by this smile full of cruel gayety.

"If you see me smiling, it is that I think of the princess who knows the world so well, of this Duchesse de Maufrigneuse to whom they have given de Marsay, and the infamous de Trailles, a political ruffian, and that little fool d'Esgrignon, and Rastignac, Rubempré, ambassadors, ministers, Russian generals, who knows? Europe! They have put an evil meaning on this album which I had made, believing that those who admired me were my friends. Ah! it is frightful. I do not understand how I can permit a man at my feet: to scorn them all, such should be my religion."

She rose, went over to the window with a gait full of magnificent motifs.

D'Arthez remained on the chair where he had resumed his seat, not daring to follow the princess, but looking at her; he heard her wipe her pretty nose without blowing it. What can be said of the princess who blows her nose? Diane essayed the impossible in order to make her sensibility believed in. D'Arthez believed his angel in tears, he hastened to her, took her round the waist, pressed her against his heart.

"No, leave me," she said, in a feeble and murmuring voice, "I have too many doubts to be worthy of anything. To reconcile me with life is a task beyond a man's strength."

"Diane! I will love you, I myself, for your whole lost life."

"No, do not speak to me thus," she replied. "In this moment I am ashamed and trembling as if I had committed the greatest sins."

She had entirely returned to the innocence of a young girl, and showed herself, nevertheless, august, great, noble, as much so as a queen. It is impossible to describe the effect of this management, so very skilful that it attained to pure truth, on a soul as new and fresh as that of d'Arthez. The great writer remained mute with admiration, passive in this window embrasure, waiting for a word, while the princess was waiting for a kiss; but she was too sacred for him. When she became cold, the princess went back to her fauteuil, her feet were frozen.

"It will take a long while," she thought, looking at Daniel, her forehead high and her head sublime in virtue.

"Is it a woman?" this profound observer of the human heart asked himself. "How must one act with her?"

Until two o'clock in the morning, they occupied themselves in repeating to each other those stupidities which women of genius, such as the princess

is, know how to render adorable.   Diane pretended
to be too much destroyed, too old, too worn; d'Arthez proved to her, that of which she was well convinced, that she had the most delicate skin, the
most delicious to touch, the whitest to look at, the
most perfumed; she was young and in her flower.
They disputed beauty by beauty, detail by detail,
with the "Do you think so?—You are foolish!—It
is desire!—In two weeks, you will see me as I am.
—In fact, I am going on towards forty; can so old a
woman be loved?"   D'Arthez's eloquence was impetuous and like that of a young scholar larded
with the most exaggerated epithets.   When the
princess heard this witty and intelligent writer
uttering the sillinesses of an amorous sub-lieuten-
ant, she listened with an absorbed air, very tender,
but laughing inwardly.

When d'Arthez found himself in the street, he
asked himself if he might not have been a little less
respectful.   He went over in his memory those
strange confidences which naturally have been very
much abridged here; they would have required an
entire volume to be rendered in all their mellifluous
abundance and with all the manners with which
they were accompanied.   The retrospective per-
spicacity of this man, at once so natural and so profound, was deceived by the naturalness of this
romance, by its depth, by the accent of the princess.

"It is true," he said to himself, in his sleepless-
ness; "there are such dramas in the world; the

world covers such horrors under the flowers of its
elegance, under the embroidery of its slanders,
under the wit of its recitals. We never invent
anything but the truth. Poor Diane! Michel had
a presentiment of this enigma; he said that under
that layer of ice there were volcanoes! And Bianchon, Rastignac, were right,—when a man can be
able to combine the grandeurs of the ideal and the
pleasures of desire in loving a woman whose ways
are beautiful, full of wit, of delicacy, that should
indeed be a happiness without a name."

And he sounded in himself the depths of his love,
and he found it infinite.

The next day, about two o'clock, Madame d'Espard, who for more than a month had not seen the
princess, and had not received from her a single
traitorous word, came, drawn by an excessive curiosity. Nothing could have been more pleasant than
the conversation of these two fine adders during the
first half-hour. Diane d'Uxelles avoided speaking
of d'Arthez just as she would the wearing of a
yellow dress. The marchioness circled around this
question like a Bedouin around a rich caravan.
Diane was amusing herself, the marchioness was
becoming enraged. Diane waited; she wished to
utilize her friend and to make of her a hunting dog.
Of these two women so celebrated in the actual
world, one of them was stronger than the other.
The princess stood a head higher than the marchioness, and the marchioness recognized inwardly
this superiority. In this, perhaps, lay the secret of

this friendship. The most feeble waited, crouching in her false attachment, for the hour—so long waited for by all feeble things—in which to leap at the throat of the strong and to imprint upon it the mark of a joyous bite. Diane saw this clearly. The whole world was the dupe of the cajoleries of these two friends. At the moment when the princess perceived an interrogation on the lips of her friend, she said to her:

"Well, my dear, I owe to you a complete happiness, immense, infinite, celestial."

"What do you mean to say?"

"Do you remember what we were meditating on, some three months ago, in this little garden, on the bench in the sun, under the jessamine? Ah! it is only people of genius who know how to love. I would willingly apply to my grand Daniel d'Arthez the speech of the Duc d'Albe to Catherine de Medici: 'The head of one salmon is worth that of all these frogs.'"

"I am not surprised that I have not seen you," said Madame d'Espard.

"Promise me, if you see him, not to say to him one word about me, my angel," said the princess, taking the hand of the marchioness. "I am happy, oh! but happy beyond all expression, and you know how, in the world, a word, a pleasantry, will go a great way. A word kills, so well is it known how to put venom in a word! If you knew how, for the last week, I have desired that you might have a similar passion! In fine, it is sweet, it is a beautiful triumph for us women to complete our womanly life, to sink to rest in an ardent love, pure, devoted, complete, entire, above all when one has sought for it so long."

"Why do you ask me to be faithful to my best friend?" said Madame d'Espard. "You believe me, then, capable of playing you an evil trick?"

"When a woman possesses such a treasure, the fear of losing it arises so naturally that it makes one doubt everything. I am absurd; forgive me, my dear."

Some moments later the marchioness departed; and, as she saw her go, the princess said to herself:

"How she will serve me up! if she could but tell everything of me! But to spare her the trouble of drawing Daniel from here, I will send him to her."

At three o'clock, a few minutes later, d'Arthez came. In the midst of an interesting discourse, the princess cut his speech short and laid her handsome hand on his arm.

"Forgive me, my friend," she said, interrupting him, "but I will forget something which seems a foolishness, and yet which is of the utmost impor-tance. You have not set your foot in the house of Madame d'Espard since the day, a thousand times happy, on which I met you there; go there, not for yourself, not for politeness, but for me. Perhaps you have made of her an enemy for me, if she has by chance learned that, since her dinner, you have not, so to speak, left my house. Moreover, my

friend, I should not like to see you abandon your
relations in the world, nor your occupation and
your works.   I should be again strangely slandered.
What would they not say? 'I keep you in leash,
I absorb you, I fear comparisons, I wish to be talked
about again, I take good care to preserve my conquest, well knowing that it is the last!' Who could
guess that you are my only friend? If you love me
as much as you say you love me, you will make
it believed in the world that we are purely and simply brother and sister.   Continue."

D'Arthez was always disciplined by the ineffable
sweetness with which this graceful woman arranged
her robe so that it might fall in the most elegant
manner.   There was I know not what fineness and
delicacy, in this discourse which touched him to
tears.   The princess came outside of all the ignoble
and bourgeois conditions of women who disputed
with each other and who quibble over coin after
coin on the divans; she displayed an unheard-of
grandeur; she had no need to say it, this union was
nobly understood between them.   It was neither
yesterday, nor to-morrow, nor to-day; it would be
whenever they wished it, one and the other, without
the interminable fillets of that which common
women call "a sacrifice;" doubtless, they are aware
of all which they are likely to lose thus, whilst this
fête is a triumph for those women certain of gaining by it.   In this phrase, everything was vague
as a promise, soft as a hope, and, nevertheless, certain as a right.   Let us avow it, these sorts of

13

grandeurs appertain only to those illustrious and
sublime deceivers, who remain royal there were
other women become subjects. D'Arthez could then
measure the distance which exists between these
women and the others. The princess always
showed herself worthy and beautiful. The secret
of this nobility is perhaps in the art with which the
great ladies know how to remove their veils; they
succeed in being, in this situation, like antique
statues; if they preserved a rag, they would be
unchaste. The bourgeois women always endeavor
to wrap themselves up.

Equipped with tenderness, sustained by the most
splendid virtues, d'Arthez obeyed and went to call
on Madame d'Espard, who displayed for him her most
charming coquetry. The marchioness carefully
avoided saying a word to d'Arthez about the princess; only she asked him to come to dinner on a
near date.

D'Arthez met there a numerous company. The
marchioness had invited Rastignac, Blondet, the
Marquis d'Ajuda-Pinto, Maxime de Trailles, the
Marquis d'Esgrignon, the two Vandenesses, Du
Tillet, one of the richest bankers of Paris, the Baron
de Nucingen, Nathan, Lady Dudley, two of the most
perfidious attachés of embassies, and the Chevalier
d'Espard, one of the most profound personages of
this salon, the half of the politics of his sister-in-
law.

It was laughingly that Maxime de Trailles said
to d'Arthez:

"You see a great deal of the Princesse de Cadignan?"

D'Arthez answered this question only with a dry inclination of the head. Maxime de Trailles was a *bravo* of a superior order, without faith or law, capable of anything, ruining the women who were enamored of him, causing them to pawn their diamonds, but covering this conduct with a brilliant varnish, with charming manners and a wit that was satanic. He inspired in everyone a fear and a contempt that were equal; but, as no one was hardy enough to testify toward him any other sentiments than the most courteous ones, he could perceive nothing; or he lent himself to the general dissimulation. He owed to the Comte de Marsay the last degree of elevation to which he could arrive. De Marsay, who knew Maxime intimately, had judged him capable of filling certain secret and diplomatic functions which he gave him, and of which he acquitted himself marvelously. D'Arthez had been for some time sufficiently interested in political affairs to know this person to the bottom, and he alone perhaps had a sufficiently-elevated character to express openly that which everyone thought in secret.

"It ees toutless for her dat you neglegt la Jampre," said the Baron de Nucingen.

"Ah! the princess is one of the most dangerous women in whose house a man can put his foot," cried softly the Marquis d'Esgrignon; "I owe to her the infamy of my marriage."

"Dangerous?" said Madame d'Espard. "Do not speak thus of my best friend. I have never known nor seen anything in the princess which did not seem to me to partake of the most elevated sentiment."

"Let the Marquis speak," cried Rastignac. "When a man has been thrown by a fine horse, he finds him full of faults and he sells him."

Piqued at this speech, the Marquis d'Esgrignon looked at Daniel d'Arthez and said to him:

"Monsieur is not, I hope, on such terms with the princess as to prevent our speaking of her?"

D'Arthez kept silent. D'Esgrignon, who did not lack wit, made in reply to Rastignac an apologetic portrait of the princess, which put the table into good humor. As this jesting was excessively obscure for d'Arthez, he leaned over toward Madame de Montcornet, his neighbor, and asked of her the meaning of these pleasantries.

"But, excepting yourself only, to judge by the good opinion which you have of the princess, all the guests have been, it is said, in her good graces."

"I can assure you that there is nothing but what is false in that opinion," replied Daniel.

"However, there is Monsieur d'Esgrignon, a gentleman of Perche, who was completely ruined for her, some twelve years ago, and who, for her, nearly mounted the scaffold."

"I know all about that affair," said d'Arthez. "Madame de Cadignan saved Monsieur d'Esgrignon at the Court of Assizes, and we see how he rewards her to-day!"

Madame de Montcornet looked at d'Arthez with
an astonishment and a curiosity that were almost
stupid, then she turned her eyes on Madame d'Espard in indicating him to her, as if to say: "He is
bewitched!"

During this short conversation, Madame de Cadignan had been defended by Madame d'Espard,
whose protection resembled that of those lightning
conductors which attract the lightning.   When
d'Arthez returned to the general conversation, he
heard Maxime de Trailles launching this speech:

"In Diane, depravation is not an effect, it is a
cause; perhaps she owes to this cause her exquisite
naturalness; she does not seek, she invents nothing;
she offers to you the most refined elegances as if
they were an inspiration of the most naïve love,
and it is impossible for you not to believe it."

This phrase, which seemed to have been prepared
for a man of the capacity of d'Arthez, was so strong
that it was like a conclusion.   Every one left the
princess, she seemed to be overwhelmed.   D'Arthez
looked at De Trailles and d'Esgrignon with a mocking air.

"The greatest fault of this woman is to come in
competition with men," said he.   "She dissipates
like them all the wealth outside the jointures; she
sends her lovers to the usurers, she devours dowries,
she ruins orphans, she demolishes old châteaux, she
inspires and, perhaps, also commits crimes; but—"

Of the two personages to whom d'Arthez was
replying, neither had ever heard anything so strong.

With this *but*, the entire table was struck, each one remained with his fork in the air, his eyes fixed alternately on the courageous writer and on the assassins of the princess, waiting for the conclusion in a horrible silence.

"But," said d'Arthez, with a mocking lightness, "Madame la Princesse de Cadignan has over men an advantage,—when you have put yourself in danger for her, she saves you and speaks evil of none. Why, among them all, can there not be found a woman who will amuse herself with the men, as the men amuse themselves with the women? Why is it that the fair sex does not occasionally take its revenge?—"

"Genius is stronger than wit," said Blondet to Nathan.

This avalanche of epigrams was in fact like the fire of a battery of cannon opposed to a fusillade of musketry. Every one hastened to change the conversation. Neither the Comte de Trailles nor the Marquis d'Esgrignon seemed disposed to quarrel with d'Arthez. When the coffee was served, Blondet and Nathan came up to the writer with an air of earnestness which no one would dare to imitate, so difficult was it to reconcile the admiration inspired by his conduct and the fear of making two powerful enemies.

"It is not to-day for the first time that we have been convinced that your character is equal in grandeur to your talent," said Blondet to him. "You have conducted yourself, just now, not like a man, but in a god-like fashion. Not to have allowed yourself to have been carried away, neither by your heart nor by your imagination; not to have taken up the defense of a loved woman, a fault which was expected of you, and which would have given a great triumph to this world so devoured with jealousy of literary celebrities—. Ah! permit me to say to you, this is to touch the sublime of private politics."

"Ah! you are a statesman," said Nathan. "It requires as much skill, as it is difficult to avenge a woman without defending her."

"The princess is one of the heroines of the Legitimiste party; is it not a duty for every man with a heart to protect her *in any case?* replied d'Arthez, coldly. "That which she has done for the cause of her masters would excuse the most frivolous life."

"He plays a close game," said Nathan to Blondet.

"Absolutely as if the princess were worth the trouble," replied Rastignac, who had joined them.

D'Arthez went to see the princess, who was waiting for him, a prey to the liveliest anxiety. The result of this experiment which Diane had brought about might be fatal to her. For the first time in her life, this woman felt a real suffering in her heart and a cold perspiration under her dress. She did not know what course to take in case d'Arthez should believe the world, which told the truth, instead of believing her, she who lied: for never had so fine a character, so complete a man, a soul so pure, a conscience so ingenuous, come

within her acquaintance. If she had concocted such
cruel falsehoods, she had been driven to it by the
desire of knowing veritable love. This love, she
felt it dawning in her heart, she loved d'Arthez;
she was condemned to deceive him, for she wished
to remain for him all that he thought the sublime
actress who had played her comedy before him.
When she heard Daniel's step in the dining-room,
she experienced a commotion, a thrill which agitated
her in the very principles of her life. This movement, which she had never before experienced during an existence the most adventurous known for a
woman of her rank, made her aware at this moment
that she had gambled for her happiness. Her eyes,
which looked into space, embraced d'Arthez in his
entirety; she saw through his flesh, she read in his
soul,—suspicion had not, then, even touched him
with its bat's wing! The terrible *movement* of
this fear was followed by its reaction, joy all but
suffocated the happy Diane; for there is no creature
which has not more strength to support trouble than
to resist extreme happiness.

"Daniel, they have slandered me and thou hast
avenged me!" she cried, rising and opening to him
her arms.

In the profound astonishment produced in him by
this word, the roots of which were invisible to him,
Daniel permitted his head to be taken between two
beautiful hands, and the princess kissed him in
saintly fashion on the forehead.

"How did you know?—"

"Oh! illustrious ninny! seest thou not that I love thee foolishly?"

Since that day, there has no longer been any question of the Princesse de Cadignan nor of d'Arthez. The princess has inherited something of a fortune from her mother; she passes her summers at Geneva, in a villa, with the great writer, and returns to Paris for some months during the winter. D'Arthez only shows himself in the Chamber of Deputies. Finally, his publications have become excessively rare. Is this a dénouement? Yes, for the intelligent; no, for those who wish to know everything.

Aux Jardies, June, 1839.

SARRASINE

(205)

SARRASINE

*

I was plunged in one of those profound reveries to which everybody is liable, even a frivolous man, in the midst of the most tumultuous festivals. Midnight had just sounded from the clock of the Élysée-Bourbon. Seated in the embrasure of a window and hidden behind the undulating folds of a curtain of moire, I was able to contemplate at my ease the garden of the hôtel in which I was passing the evening. The trees, partially covered with snow, detached themselves faintly against the grayish background formed by a cloudy sky, slightly whitened by the moon. Seen in the midst of this fantastic atmosphere, they bore a vague resemblance to spectres partially enveloped in their shrouds, a gigantic image of the famous *Dance of Death*. Then, turning toward the other side, I could admire the dance of the living! a splendid salon, with walls of silver and of gold, with sparkling candelabra, brilliant with tapers. There, crowded together, agitated and fluttered the most beautiful women in Paris, the richest, the highest-titled, splendid, pompous, blazing with diamonds! with flowers on their heads, on their breasts, in

their hair, scattered on their dresses, or in garlands
at their feet. There were light shudderings, voluptuous steps which made the laces, the blonds, the
gauze and the silk swirl around their delicate flanks.
Here and there sparkled brilliant glances, eclipsing
the lights, the fire of the diamonds, and which lent
a new animation to hearts already too much on fire.
There might be surprised also little attitudes of the
head significant for the lovers, and negative attitudes for the husbands. The sudden outbursts of
the voices of the players, at each unforeseen stroke,
the clinking of gold, mingled with the music, with
the murmur of the conversations; to complete the
transport of this multitude—inebriated by all that
the world can offer of seductions—a vapor of perfume and a general intoxication acted upon all these
wandering imaginations. Thus, on my right, the
sombre and silent image of death; on my left, the
decent bacchanalians of life: here, nature cold, dull,
in mourning; there, men in enjoyment. I myself,
on the border of these two pictures so incongruous,
which, a thousand times repeated in various manners, render Paris the most amusing city in the
world and the most philosophical, I made for myself
a sort of moral medley, half pleasant, half funereal.
With the left foot I beat time to the music, and I
seemed to have the other in a coffin. My leg was in
fact chilled by one of those draughts of air which
freeze one-half of your body whilst the other half
feels the moist heat of the salons, an accident frequent enough at balls.

"It is not very long that Monsieur de Lanty has owned this hôtel?"

"Oh! yes. It is nearly ten years since the Maréchal de Carigliano sold it to him—"

"Ah!"

"These people must have an immense fortune?"

"I should say so."

"What a fête! It is of an insolent luxury."

"Do you think them as rich as Monsieur de Nucingen or Monsieur de Gondreville?"

"But you do not then know?—"

I put out my head and recognized the two interlocutors as belonging to that inquisitive class who, in Paris, occupy themselves exclusively with the *Whys? The Hows? Where did it come from? Who are they? What is there? What has she done?* They were talking in a low tone of voice, and went away to converse more at their ease on some solitary sofa. Never had a richer mine been opened to the searchers of mysteries. No one knew from what country came the family Lanty, nor from what commerce, from what spoliation, from what piracy, or from what inheritance proceeded a fortune estimated at several millions. All the members of this family spoke Italian, French, Spanish, English and German with such perfection as to make it seem probable that they had lived for a long time in these different countries. Were they Bohemians? Were they filibusters?

"If they were the devil!" said the young politicians, "they know how to receive marvelously well."

14

"Had the Comte de Lanty plundered some *Casbah*, I would marry his daughter all the same!" cried a philosopher.

Who would not have married Marianina, a young girl of sixteen, whose beauty realized the fabulous conception of the Oriental poets! Like the daughter of the Sultan in the tale of *The Wonderful Lamp*, she should have been kept veiled. Her singing made to pale their incomplete talents the Malibrans, the Sontags, the Fodors, in whom some dominant quality has always impaired the perfection of the ensemble; whilst Marianina knew how to unite in the same degree the purity of sound, the feeling, the justness of the movement and of the intonation, the soul and the science, the correctness and the sentiment. This girl was the type of that secret poetry, common bond of all the arts, and which always flies from those who seek it. Gentle and modest, learned and spirituelle, nothing could eclipse Marianina unless it were her mother.

Have you ever encountered one of those women whose overpowering beauty defies the attacks of age, and who seem, at thirty-six, more desirable than they could have been fifteen years earlier? Their countenance is a passionate soul, it sparkles; each feature is illuminated with intelligence; every detail possesses a particular brilliancy, especially in the light. Their seductive eyes attract, refuse, speak or keep silent; their gait is innocently knowing; their voice displays the melodious richness of tones, the most coquettishly soft and tender. Their praises, by comparison, flatter the self-love of those most hard to please. A movement of their eyebrows, the least glance of the eye, their lip, which grows stern, all impress a sort of terror on those whose life and whose happiness depends on them. Inexperienced in love and docile to persuasion, a young girl may allow herself to be seduced; but for these women, a man should know how, like Monsieur de Jaucourt, not to cry out when, hiding himself in the back of a wardrobe, the femme de chambre crushes two of his fingers in the crack of a door. To love these puissant sirens, is it not to gamble with one's life? And this is why perhaps we love them so passionately! Such was the Comtesse de Lanty.

Filippo, the brother of Marianina, partook, like his sister, of the marvelous beauty of the countess. To say all in one word, this young man was a living image of the Antinous, with a form more slender. But how well these thin and delicate proportions accord with youth when an olive skin, strong eyebrows and the fire of a velvety eye, promise for the future male passions, generous thoughts! If Filippo lived in the hearts of all the young girls as a type, he lived equally in the regard of all the mothers as the best *parti* in France.

The beauty, the fortune, the wit, the graces of these two children came altogether from their mother. The Comte de Lanty was short, ugly, and pock-marked; sombre as a Spaniard, wearisome as a banker. He passed moreover for a profound politician, perhaps because he laughed but seldom, and

was always quoting Monsieur de Metternich or
Wellington.

This mysterious family had all the attraction of a
poem by Lord Byron, the difficulties of which were
translated in a different manner by each person of
the fashionable world,—a chant obscure and sublime
from strophe to strophe. The reserve which Monsieur and Madame de Lanty preserved respecting
their origin, their past existence and their relation
with the four corners of the globe, was not for any
great length of time a subject of astonishment in
Paris. In no country perhaps is the axiom of Ves-
pasian better comprehended. There, the écus, even
though spotted with blood or with mud, betray
nothing and represent everything. Provided that
the upper classes of society know the figure of your
fortune, you are classed among the sums which are
equal to yours, and no one asks to see your parch-
ments, because everybody knows how little they
cost. In a city in which social problems are solved
by algebraic equations, the adventurers have excellent chances in their favor. Even supposing that
this family had been Bohemian in its origin, it was
so rich, so attractive, that the upper circles of
society could well afford to pardon it its little mysteries. But, unfortunately, the enigmatic history
of the house of Lanty offered a perpetual interest of
curiosity, similar enough to that of the romances
of Anne Radcliffe.

The observers, those persons who make it a point
to know in what shop you buy your candelabra, or

who ask you the amount of your rent when your apartment pleases them, had remarked, from time to time, in the midst of the fêtes, the concerts, the balls, the routs given by the countess, the appearance of a strange personage. This was a man. The first time that he showed himself in the hôtel, was during a concert, where he seemed to have been attracted to the salon by the enchanting voice of Marianina.

"Within the last minute I have felt cold," said a lady standing near the door, to her neighbor.

The unknown, who was near this lady, went away.

"Here is something curious! I am too warm," said this woman after the departure of the stranger. "And you will accuse me, perhaps, of being crazy, but I cannot avoid the impression that my neighbor, that gentleman in black, who had just gone away, made me cold."

Very soon, the exaggeration natural to people in high society originated and accumulated the most amusing ideas, the oddest expressions, the most ridiculous stories concerning this mysterious personage. Without being precisely a vampire, a ghoul, an artificial man, a species of Faust or of Robin des Bois, he partook, according to these friends of the fantastic, of all these anthropomorphic natures. There were to be met with here and there certain Germans who took for truths these ingenious mockeries of the Parisian slander. The stranger was simply an *ancient man*. Several of these young men, who were in the habit of deciding the future of Europe every morning in a few elegant phrases, determined to see in the unknown some great criminal, the possessor of immense riches. The romancers related the life of this old man, and gave you truly remarkable details of the atrocities committed by him during the time he was in the service of the prince of Mysore. The bankers, a more positive class, set up a plausible fable.

"Bah!" said they, shrugging their great shoulders with a movement of pity, "this little old man is a *tête génoise!*"

"Monsieur, if it is not an indiscretion, would you have the kindness to explain to me what you mean by a Genoese head?"

"Monsieur, it is a man upon the duration of whose life repose enormous sums, and on his good health depend doubtless the revenues of this family. I remember to have heard at Madame d'Espard's a magnetizer proving, by very specious historical considerations, that this old man, kept under glass, was the famous Balsamo, called Cagliostro. According to this modern alchemist, the Sicilian adventurer had escaped death, and amused himself by making gold for his grandchildren. And, finally, the bailiff of Ferette pretended to have recognized in this singular personage the Comte de Saint-Germain."

These sillinesses, uttered in the light tone, with the mocking air which, in our days, characterizes a society without any faiths, gave rise to vague suspicions concerning the house of Lanty. Finally, by a singular combination of circumstances, the members of this family justified the conjectures of the world by a line of conduct sufficiently mysterious toward this old man, whose life was in some sort concealed from all investigation.

Should this personage cross the threshold of the apartment which he was reputed to occupy in the Hôtel Lanty, his appearance always caused a great sensation in the family. It could have been said to be an event of the highest importance. Filippo, Marianina, Madame de Lanty and an old domestic alone had the privilege of aiding the unknown to walk, to rise, to seat himself. Each one watched solicitously his slightest movements. It seemed as though this was an enchanted person on whom depended the happiness, the life or the fortunes of all. Was it fear or affection? The society people could not discover any indication which would aid them to solve this problem. Hidden for entire months in the depths of an unknown sanctuary, this familiar genius issued suddenly and, as it were, furtively, without being expected, and appeared in the midst of the salons like those fairies of other times who descended from their flying dragons to come and trouble those solemnities to which they had not been bidden. The most skilful observers could alone at these periods divine the inquietude of the masters of the household, who knew how to conceal their feeling with a singular skill. But, sometimes, even while dancing in a quadrille, the too candid Marianina cast a glance of terror on the old man, whom she followed through the multitude. Or else Filippo hastened, slipping through the crowd, to join him, and remained near him, tender and attentive, as if the contact of men or the least breath would destroy this curious creature. The countess endeavored to approach him, without appearing to have the intention of rejoining him; then, in assuming a manner and a countenance as expressive of servility as of tenderness, of submission as of despotism, she said two or three words to which the old man nearly always deferred: he disappeared, led away, or, to speak more clearly, carried away, by her. If Madame de Lanty were not there, the count employed a thousand stratagems to reach him; but he had the appearance of making himself heard with difficulty and treated him like a spoiled child whose mother satisfies its caprices or dreads its unruliness. Some indiscreet persons have ventured to question rashly the Comte de Lanty, but this cold and reserved man had never appeared to be able to comprehend the interrogation of these curious ones. Thus, after a great many attempts, which the circumspection of all the members of this family had rendered fruitless, no one sought any longer to discover a secret so well guarded. The spies of good society, the open-mouthed and the politic ones, had finished, weary of the contest, by no longer occupying themselves with this mystery.

But, in this moment, there were perhaps in the

midst of these resplendent salons certain philosophers who, even while taking an ice, a sorbet, or in
setting down on a console their empty punch glass,
said to each other:

"I should not be surprised to learn that these people are sharpers. This old fellow, who hides himself and only appears at the equinoxes or at the
solstices, has to me quite the air of an assassin—"

"Or of a bankrupt—"

"It is very nearly the same thing. To kill a
man's fortune is sometimes worse than to kill him
himself."

"Monsieur, I have bet twenty louis; there are
forty coming to me."

"Faith, Monsieur, there are only thirty left on
the table."

"Well, there, you see how society is mixed here!
No one can play."

"That is true.—But here are now six months that
we have not seen the Spirit. Do you believe that
it is a living being?"

"Eh! eh! at the very most—"

These last words were uttered, near me, by unknown persons who went away at the moment in
which I resumed, in the last train of thought, my
reflections mingled with white and black, with life
and death. My fantastic imagination, as well as
my eyes, contemplated alternately the festivity
which had now reached its highest degree of splendor and the sombre picture of the gardens. I do not
know how long I had been meditating on these two

sides of the human medal; but suddenly the smothered laughter of a young woman recalled me to myself. I remained stupefied at the appearance of the
figure which presented itself before my eyes. By
one of the rarest caprices of nature, the half funereal thought which had been traversing my brain
had issued forth, it was there before me, personified,
living; it had sprung, like Minerva, from the head of
Jupiter, grand and strong; it had at once a hundred
years of age and twenty-two, it was living and dead.
Escaped from his chamber, like a maniac from his
cell, the little old man had doubtless slipped skilfully behind a hedge of persons listening to the
voice of Marianina, who was finishing the cavatina
of *Tancred*. He seemed to have issued from underground, pushed up by some theatrical mechanism. Motionless and sombre, he remained a
moment looking at this festival, the murmur of
which had perhaps reached his ears. His preoccu-
pation, almost somnambulic, was so concentrated on
certain things, that he found himself in the midst
of the world without seeing the world. He had
surged up without ceremony close to one of the
most ravishing women in Paris, a dancer elegant
and youthful, with delicate forms, one of those figures as fresh as that of a child, white and pink, and
so frail, so transparent, that it would seem as
though a man's glance could penetrate them, as the
rays of the sun traverse pure ice. They were
there, before me, both of them together, united and
so close together that the stranger touched the dress

of gauze and the garlands of flowers and the lightly
crimped hair and the floating girdle.

I had brought this young woman to Madame de
Lanty's ball. As this was the first time that she
had been in this house, I forgave her her smothered
laugh; but I made to her quickly some imperious
sign, I do not know what, which filled her with confusion and inspired her with respect for her neighbor. She seated herself near me. The old man did
not wish to quit this delicious creature, to whom he
attached himself wilfully with that obstinacy, mute
and without apparent cause, which is characteristic
of the extremely aged, and which causes them to
resemble children. In order to seat himself near the
young lady, he was obliged to take a folding-chair.
His least movements were marked by that cold
heaviness, that stupid indecision which characterizes the gestures of a paralytic. He sat down
slowly on his seat, with circumspection, and in
mumbling some unintelligible words. His broken
voice resembled the noise which a stone makes in
falling into a well. The young woman pressed my
hand closely, as if she sought to save herself from a
precipice, and shuddered when this man, whom she
was looking at, turned upon her two eyes without
warmth, two glaucous eyes which could only be
compared to tarnished mother-of-pearl.

"I am afraid," she said to me, leaning toward my
ear.

"You can speak," I replied; "he hears with great
difficulty."

"You know him, then?"

"Yes."

At this she took courage sufficiently to examine for a moment this creature without a name in human language, form without substance, being without life, or life without action. She was under the influence of that fearful curiosity which impels women to procure for themselves dangerous emotions, to see tigers chained, to look at boa-constrictors, while frightening themselves at being separated from them only by feeble barriers. Although the little old man was stoop-shouldered, like a laboring man, it could readily be seen that his figure must have been of ordinary height. His excessive meagreness, the delicacy of his limbs, proved that his proportions had always remained slender. He wore small-clothes of black silk which floated around his fleshless thighs in folds, like a furled sail. An anatomist could have promptly recognized the symptoms of a frightful phthisis on seeing the slight legs which served to sustain this strange body. You would have said they were two bones crossed on a tomb. A sentiment of profound horror for mankind seized the heart when a fatal attention had revealed to you the signs impressed by decrepitude on this fragile machine. The unknown wore a white waistcoat, embroidered with gold, in the ancient style, and his linen was of a dazzling whiteness. A jabot of English lace sufficiently yellowed, the richness of which would have been envied by a queen, formed yellow ruches on his chest; but, on

him, this lace was rather a rag than an adornment.
In the midst of this jabot a diamond of an incalcula-
ble value glittered, like the sun. This superannu-
ated luxury, this material richness without taste,
served to set off in still stronger fashion the countenance of this strange being. The frame was
worthy of the portrait. This dark visage was
angular and hollowed in every sense,—the chin
was hollow, the temples were hollow, the eyes were
lost in yellowish orbits. The maxillary bones,
rendered prominent by an indescribable meagreness, designed cavities in the middle of each cheek.
These gibbosities, more or less revealed by the
lights, produced curious shadows and reflections
which completed the want of resemblance between
this visage and the human countenance. Moreover,
the years had so closely fastened to the bone the
yellowish and fine skin of this visage that they had
there described everywhere a multitude of wrinkles,
either circular, like the ripples of water caused by a
stone thrown by a child, or star-shaped, like the
fracture of a window-pane, but always deep and as
close together as the edges of the leaves of a book.
There are old men who present to us more hideous
portraits; but that which contributed the most to
give the appearance of an artificial creation to the
spectre risen before us was the red and the white
with which he shone. The eyebrows of his mask
received from the lights a lustre which revealed a
painting very well executed. Happily for the sight
saddened by so many ruins, his cadaverous cranium

was concealed under a blond peruque, the innumerable curls of which betrayed an extraordinary pretension. For the rest, the feminine coquetry of this phantasmagoric personage was emphatically enough announced by the gold rings which hung in his ears, by the rings of which the wonderful stones glittered on his ossified fingers, and by a watch chain which scintillated like the brilliants of a necklace at the throat of a woman. Finally, this species of Japanese idol preserved on his bluish lips a fixed and arrested smile, a smile implacable and bantering, like that of a death's-head. Silent, motionless as a statue, it exhaled the musky odor of those old gowns which the heirs of a duchess exhume from her drawers during an inventory. If the old man turned his eyes toward the assembly, it seemed as though the movement of those globes, incapable of reflecting a light, were accomplished by an imperceptible artifice; and, when the eyes arrested themselves, he who examined them ended by doubting if they had moved. To see, near to this human débris, a young woman whose neck, whose arms and whose chest were naked and white; whose lines were full and redolent of beauty, whose hair rising admirably from an alabaster forehead inspired love, whose eyes did not receive but gave out light, who was soft, fresh, and whose vaporous curls, whose balmy breath, seemed too heavy, too hard, too powerful for this shadow, for this man in dust,—ah! it was certainly death and life, my revery, an imaginary arabesque, a chimera half hideous, divinely female from the waist up.

"There are, however, such marriages, which take place with sufficient frequency in the world," I said to myself.

"He smells of the cemetery!" cried the terrified young woman, who pressed against me as if to assure herself of my protection, and whose tumultuous movements revealed to me the extremity of her fear.—"It is a horrible vision," she resumed.

"I cannot stay here any longer. If I look at it again I shall believe that death itself has come to seek me. But does it live?"

She put out her hand and touched the phenomenon with that hardihood of which women are capable in the violence of their desires; but a cold sweat broke out on her skin, for, as soon as she touched the old man, she heard a cry like that of a rattle. This sharp voice, if it were a voice, issued from a throat almost dried up. Then to this clamor succeeded quickly a little cough like a child's, convulsive and of a peculiar sonorousness. At this noise, Marianina, Filippo, and Madame de Lanty turned their looks upon us, and their glances were like lightning. The young woman could have wished herself at the bottom of the Seine. She took my arm, drew me off toward a boudoir. Men and women, everybody, made way for us. When we reached the end of the reception apartments, we entered a little semicircular cabinet. My companion threw herself on a divan, palpitating with terror, without knowing where she was.

"Madame, you are distracted," I said to her.

"But," she answered, after a moment of silence during which I admired her, "is it my fault? Why does Madame de Lanty permit ghosts to wander about in her hôtel?"

"Come," I replied, "you imitate the silly ones. You take a little old man for a spectre."

"Keep silent," she replied, with that mocking and imposing air which all women know so well how to assume when they are determined to be right.— "What a pretty boudoir!" she cried, looking around her. "Blue satin always makes an admirable effect for hangings. How fresh it is! Ah! the beautiful picture!" she added, rising and going to take her stand before a magnificently framed canvas.

We remained for a moment contemplating this marvel, which seemed due to some supernatural brush. The picture represented Adonis reclining on a lion skin. The lamp suspended in the middle of the boudoir, and contained in an alabaster vase, illuminated this canvas with a soft light which permitted us to see all the beauties of the painting.

"Can so perfect a being exist?" she asked me, after having examined, not without a soft smile of contentment, the exquisite grace of the contours, the attitude, the color, the hair, everything in fact.

"He is too beautiful for a man," she added, after such a scrutiny as she would have given a rival.

Oh! how I then experienced the attacks of that

jealousy in which a poet had vainly endeavored to make me believe! the jealousy of engravings, of paintings, of statues, in which the artists exaggerate human beauty, carrying out the doctrine which leads them to idealize everything.

"It is a portrait," I replied to her. "It is a product of the talent of Vien. But this great painter never saw the original, and your admiration will be less lively, perhaps, when you learn that this academical study was painted from a statue of a woman."

"But who is it?"

I hesitated.

"I wish to know," she added, quickly.

"I think," I said to her, "that this *Adonis* represents a—a—a relative of Madame de Lanty."

I had the pain of seeing her absorbed in the contemplation of this figure. She seated herself in silence. I placed myself beside her and took her hand without her perceiving it! Forgotten for a portrait! At this moment, the slight sound of the step of a woman whose dress rustled was heard in the silence. We saw the young Marianina enter, still more brilliant by her expression of innocence than by her grace and by her fresh toilet; she was walking slowly, and leading with a maternal care, with a filial solicitude, the clothed spectre which had caused us to fly from the music-room; she conducted him, watching with a species of inquietude, the slow march of his debilitated feet. They both arrived with sufficient difficulty at a door

15

hidden in the tapestry. There Marianina knocked softly. There immediately appeared, as if by magic, a tall, dry man, a species of familiar genius. Before confiding the old man to this mysterious guardian, the beautiful child kissed respectfully the walking skeleton, and her chaste caress was not exempt from that graceful cajolery the secret of which belongs to some privileged women.

"*Addio, addio!*" she said, with the most charming inflections of her young voice.

She even added to the last syllable a roulade admirably executed, but in a low voice, and as if to paint by a poetic expression the effusion of her heart. The old man, suddenly struck by some souvenir, remained on the threshold of this secret retreat. We then heard, owing to a profound silence, the heavy sigh which issued from his chest; he drew off the richest of the rings with which his skeleton fingers were loaded and placed it in Marianina's breast. The young girl commenced to laugh, took the ring, slipped it over one of her gloved fingers, and turned swiftly toward the salon, from which might be heard at this moment the preludes of a contradance. She perceived us.

"Ah! you were there!" she said, blushing.

After having looked at us as if to interrogate us, she hastened to her partner with the careless petulance of her age.

"What does it all mean?" asked of me my young companion. "Is it her husband? I think I am dreaming. Where am I?"

"You," I replied, "you, Madame, who are exalted, and who, comprehending so well the most imperceptible emotions, know how to cultivate in a man's heart the most delicate sentiments, without blighting them, without bruising them from the very first day; you who have pity for all the pains of the heart, and who, to the wit of a Parisienne, join a passionate soul worthy of Italy or of Spain—"

She saw clearly that my language was that of bitter irony; and, without appearing to pay any attention to it, she interrupted me:

"Oh! you make me according to your own ideas. What a singular tyranny! You would so have me that I should not be myself."

"Oh! I wish nothing," I cried, terrified at her severe attitude. "At least, is it true that you like to hear the recital of the histories of those vivid passions awakened in our hearts by the ravishing women of the South?"

"Yes. Well, then?"

"Well, then, I will come to see you to-morrow evening about nine o'clock, and I will reveal to you this mystery."

"No," she replied, with a mutinous air, "I wish to learn it immediately."

"You have not yet given me the right to obey you when you say: 'I wish.'"

"At present," she replied, with a coquetry that would drive a man to despair, "I have the greatest desire to know this secret. To-morrow I will not listen to you, perhaps—"

She smiled, and we separated, she even more proud, more forbidding, and I even more ridiculous at this moment than ever. She had the audacity to waltz with a young aide-de-camp, and I remained alternately vexed, pouting, admiring, loving and jealous.

"Till to-morrow," she said to me, near two o'clock in the morning, when she left the ball.

"I will not go," thought I, "and I abandon thee. Thou art more capricious, more fantastic a thousand times, perhaps—than my imagination."

The next evening, we were before a good fire, in an elegant little salon, seated both of us, she on a low sofa, I on a cushion, almost at her feet, and my eye under hers. The street was silent. The lamp shed a soft light. It was one of those evenings delightful to the soul, one of those moments which are never forgotten, one of those hours passed in peace and in desire,—and the charm of which is later always a subject of regret, even when we are more happy. What can efface the vivid impression of the first solicitations of love?

"Go on," she said, "I am listening."

"But I dare not commence. The adventure has some passages dangerous for the narrator. If I become enthusiastic, you will silence me."

"Speak."

"I obey."

"Ernest-Jean Sarrasine was the only son of a procurator of Franche-Comté," I resumed, after a pause. "His father had acquired with sufficient honesty

from six to eight thousand francs of income, a practitioner's fortune, which, formerly, in the provinces,
was considered colossal.   The old Maître Sarrasine,
having but one child, resolved to neglect nothing
for his education: he hoped to make of him a mag-
istrate, and to live long enough to see, in his old
days, the grandson of Mathieu Sarrasine, laborer in
the country of Saint-Dié, seated on his fleur-de-lys
and sleeping through the hearing for the greater
glory of justice; but Heaven did not reserve this joy
for the procurator.   The young Sarrasine, confided
at an early age to the Jesuits, gave proofs of an
uncommon turbulence.   He had the childhood of a
man of talent.   He would not study save as he
chose, was often in revolt, and remained sometimes
for hours plunged into confused meditation, occupied
sometimes in contemplating his comrades at their
play, sometimes in representing to himself the heroes
of Homer.   Then, when he did choose to divert
himself, he brought into his plays an extraordinary
ardor.   When a quarrel occurred between himself
and one of his comrades, it was but seldom that the
combat ended without bloodshed.   If he were the
weaker of the two, he bit.   Alternately acting or
passive, without aptitude or being too intelligent, his
singular character caused him to be feared by his
masters as much as by his comrades.   Instead of
acquiring the elements of the Greek language, he
made a drawing of the reverend father who
explained to them a passage of Thucydides; he
sketched the master of mathematics, the prefect, the

valets, the corrector, and covered all the walls with
shapeless outlines.   Instead of chanting the praises
of the Lord in the church, he amused himself, during the service, with carving a bench; or, when
he had stolen a piece of wood, he sculptured some
figure of a saint.   If he had no wood, nor stone, nor
crayon, he gave form to his ideas with soft bread.
Whether he was copying the figures in the paintings
which ornamented the choir, or whether he was
originating, he left always behind him gross
sketches, the licentious character of which filled
with horror the younger fathers; and the slanderers
pretended that the old Jesuits smiled over them.
Finally, if the chronicle of the college may be
believed, he was expelled for having, while waiting
his turn at the confessional on a Good Friday,
carved a large billet into the shape of Christ.   The
impiety of this statue was too great not to draw
down chastisement on the artist.   Had he not even
had the audacity to place on top of the tabernacle
this sufficiently cynical figure!   Sarrasine came to
seek at Paris a refuge against the menaces of the
paternal malediction.   Having one of those strong
wills which know no obstacles, he followed the
commands of his genius and entered the atelier of
Bouchardon.   He worked throughout the day, and
in the evening begged for his livelihood.   Bouchardon, surprised at the progress and at the intelligence
of the young artist, soon became aware of the poverty in which his pupil was living; he aided him,
took him into his affections and treated him as his

own child. Then, when the genius of Sarrasine had revealed itself by one of those works in which the dawning talent struggles against the effervescence of youth, the generous Bouchardon endeavored to restore him to the good graces of the old procurator. Before the authority of the celebrated sculptor the parental anger was appeased. All Besançon congratulated itself on having given birth to a future great man. In the first moments of ecstasy which his flattered vanity brought him, the avaricious practitioner enabled his son to again appear with advantage before the world. The long and laborious studies required by the art of sculpture kept for a long time in subjection the impetuous character and the wild genius of Sarrasine. Bouchardon, foreseeing the violence with which the passions would be unchained in this young soul, perhaps as vigorously constituted as that of Michael Angelo, smothered the energy under continual labors. He succeeded in maintaining within reasonable bounds the extraordinary impetuosity of Sarrasine, in forbidding him to work, in proposing some distraction when he saw him carried away by the fury of an idea or in confiding important works to him at the moment when he was about to deliver himself up to dissipation. But, upon this passionate soul, gentleness was always the most powerful of arms, and the master only assumed a great empire over his pupil when he excited his gratitude by a paternal kindness.

"At the age of twenty-two, Sarrasine was forcibly withdrawn from the salutary influence which

Bouchardon exercised over his manners and his habits. He carried off the fruits of his genius in gaining the prize in sculpture founded by the Marquis de Marigny, the brother of Madame de Pompadour, who did so much for the arts. Diderot extolled as a masterpiece the statue of Bouchardon's pupil. It was not without deep grief that the sculptor to the king saw depart for Italy a young man in whom, through principle, he had inculcated profound ignorance of the things of life. Sarrasine had been for six years of the household of Bouchardon. Fanatical in his art, as Canova was later, he rose at day-break, entered his atelier, from which he did not issue till night, and lived only with his Muse. If he went to the Comédie-Française, he was dragged there by his master. He felt himself so awkward in the house of Madame Geoffrin and in the great world in which Bouchardon endeavored to introduce him, that he preferred to remain alone, and repudiated the pleasures of this licentious epoch. He had no other mistresses than sculpture and Clotilde, one of the celebrities of the opera. But this intrigue did not last long. Sarrasine was sufficiently ugly, always badly dressed, and naturally so free, so little regular in his private life that the illustrious nymph, fearing some catastrophe, very soon returned the sculptor to the love of art. Sophie Arnould said a good thing on this subject that I have forgotten. She was astonished, I believe, that her comrade had been able to drag him away from the statues. Sarrasine departed for Italy in 1758.

During the journey, his ardent imagination took fire
under a glowing sky and at the sight of the marvelous monuments with which the country of the arts
is sown.   He admired the statues, the frescoes, the
paintings; and, full of emulation, he came to Rome
a prey to the desire to inscribe his name between
those of Michael Angelo and of Bouchardon; thus,
during the first days, he divided his time between
his work in the atelier and the examination of the
works of art which abound in Rome.   He had
already passed two weeks in that state of ecstasy
which seizes all young imaginations at the aspect
of the queen of ruins, when, one evening, he entered
the theatre of Argentina, before which a great
crowd was gathered.   He inquired the cause of this
multitude and everybody answered him with two
names:

"'Zambinella!   Jomelli!'

"He entered and took a seat in the parterre,
crowded by two *abbati* notably fat; but he was fortunately placed near the stage.   The curtain went
up.   For the first time in his life he heard that
music of which Monsieur Jean-Jacques Rousseau
had so eloquently praised the delights to him, during
a soirée of the Baron d'Holbach.   The senses of the
young sculptor were, so to speak, lubricated by the
accents of the sublime harmony of Jomelli.   The
languorous originalities of these Italian voices, skilfully commingled, plunged him into a ravishing
ecstasy.   He remained mute, motionless, not even
feeling himself crowded by the two priests.   His

soul passed into his ears and into his eyes. He
thought he listened by every one of his pores. All
at once, an outbreak of applause sufficient to bring
down the house welcomed the appearance on the
scene of the *prima donna*. She advanced coquettishly to the front of the scene and saluted the
public with an infinite grace. The lights, the enthusiasm of a whole audience, the illusion of the
scene, the attraction of her costume, which at that
period was sufficiently distinguished, all conspired
in favor of this woman. Sarrasine uttered cries of
pleasure. At that moment he was able to admire
that ideal beauty the perfections of which he had,
up to that moment, sought in vain throughout
nature, compelled to require from a model, often
ignoble, the roundness of a perfect leg; from such
another, the contours of a breast; from this one, her
white shoulders; reduced, in fact, to take the neck of
a young girl, and the hands of this woman, and the
polished knees of that infant, without ever finding
under the cold sky of Paris the rich and suave creations of antique Greece. These, La Zambinella
displayed to him all united in one figure, truly
living and delicate, those exquisite proportions of
feminine nature so ardently desired, of which a
sculptor is at once the judge the most severe and
the most enthusiastic. There was an expressive
mouth, loving eyes, skin of a dazzling whiteness.
And join to these details, which would have ravished
a painter, all the marvels of that Venus revered
and rendered by the chisel of the Greek. The

artist was never weary of admiring the inimitable
grace with which the arms were joined to the
chest, the bewitching roundness of the neck, the
harmonious lines described by the eyebrows, by
the nose; then the perfect oval of the visage, the
purity of its living contour, and the effect of the
heavy eyelashes, curled upward, which terminated
the heavy and voluptuous eyelids. It was more
than a woman, it was a *chef-d'œuvre*. There were
to be found in this unhoped-for creation, love to
ravish all men, and beauty worthy to satisfy a
critic. Sarrasine devoured with his eyes the statue
of Pygmalion, for him descended from its pedestal.
When La Zambinella sang, it was a delirium. The
artist grew cold; then he was conscious of a fire
which sparkled suddenly in the depths of his in-
most being, of that which we call the heart for
want of a word! He did not applaud, he said nothing; he experienced a sensation of madness, a species of frenzy which only agitates us at that age in
which desire has, I know not what, of terrible and of
infernal. Sarrasine longed to spring upon the stage
and to take possession of this woman. His strength,
increased a hundred-fold by a moral depression
impossible to explain, since these phenomena take
place in a sphere inaccessible to human observation,
had a tendency to project him forward with an unhappy violence. To see him, you would have taken
him for a cold and stupid man. Glory, science,
future, existence, crowns, everything crumbled.

" 'To be loved by her, or to die!' Such was the

judgment which Sarrasine pronounced upon himself.

"He was so completely intoxicated that he saw no longer either the theatre, or the spectators, or the actors; he heard no longer the music. Still more, no distance existed between him and La Zambinella; he possessed her, his eyes, fastened on her, took her for his own. A power almost diabolical permitted him to feel the breath of this voice, to respire the balmy powder with which her hair was impregnated, to see the details of this countenance, to count upon it the blue veins which marked the satin skin. And finally this voice, active, fresh and of a silvery tone, delicate as a thread to which the least breath of air gives a form, which it rolls and unrolls, develops and disperses, this voice attacked his soul so vividly, that he uttered more than once involuntary cries torn from him by the convulsive delights too rarely given by human passion. Presently he was obliged to leave the theatre. His trembling legs almost refused to sustain him. He was overwhelmed, weak as a nervous man who had delivered himself to some frightful anger. He had experienced so much pleasure, or perhaps he had suffered so much, that his life had flowed away from him like the water of a vase overturned by a shock. He felt within him a void, a swooning similar to those debilities which are the despair of convalescents recovering from a grave malady. A prey to an inexplicable sadness, he went and seated himself on the steps of a church.

There, his back against a column, he lost himself in
a meditation confused as a dream. Passion had
overwhelmed him. On his return to his lodging,
he fell into one of those paroxysms of activity which
reveal to us the presence of entirely new principles
in our existence. A prey to this first fever of love
which is connected as closely with pleasure as with
sorrow; he wished to deceive his impatience and
his delirium by designing La Zambinella from memory. It was a sort of material meditation. On
this sheet of paper, La Zambinella was seen in that
attitude, apparently calm and cold, favored by
Raphaël, by Giorgione and by all the great painters.
On such another, she turned her head with an
appreciative delicacy, terminating a roulade, and
seemed to be listening to herself. Sarrasine cray-
oned his mistress in all poses : he made her unveiled,
seated, upright, lying, or chaste, or amorous, in
realizing, thanks to the delirium of his crayon,
all the capricious ideas which solicit our imagination when we think strongly of a mistress. But
his furious thought went farther than his designing.
He saw La Zambinella, he spoke to her, supplicated
her, exhausted a thousand years of life and of happiness with her, placing her in all imaginable situations, in essaying—so to speak—the future with
her. The next day, he sent his lackey to hire for
the whole season a box near the stage. Then, like
all young people in whom the soul is powerful, he
exaggerated to himself the difficulties of his enterprise, and gave for first food to his passion the

happiness of being able to admire his mistress without obstacles. This golden age of love, during which we draw enjoyment from our own feeling and in which we find ourselves happy almost by ourselves, was not destined to endure long in the case of Sarrasine. Nevertheless, he was surprised by events while he was still under the charm of this springtime hallucination, as naive as it was voluptuous. During a week he lived a whole life, occupying his mornings with modeling the clay by the aid of which he succeeded in copying La Zambinella, despite the veils, the petticoats, the corsets and the knots of ribbon which hid her from him. In the evening, installed at an early hour in his box, alone, reclining on a sofa, he procured for himself, after the manner of a Turk intoxicated with opium, a happiness as fruitful, as prodigal as he could wish. At first, he familiarized himself gradually with the too vivid emotions which the song of his mistress occasioned him; then he subdued his eyes to see her, and finished by contemplating her without fearing the explosion of that dumb rage by which he had been animated on the first day. His passion became more profound as it became more tranquil. For the rest, the ferocious sculptor would not permit that his solitude, peopled with images, adorned with the fantasies of hope and full of happiness, should be troubled by his comrades. He loved with so much strength, and so ingenuously, that he had to submit to the innocent scruples with which we are assailed when we love for the first time. In

commencing to perceive that it would be necessary
very soon to act, to intrigue, to ask where La Zambinella lived, to know if she had a mother, an uncle,
a guardian, a family; in thinking, in short, on the
methods of seeing her, of speaking to her, he felt
his heart swell so strongly with such ambitious
ideas, that he put off all these cares till the morrow,
happy because of his physical sufferings as much as
of his intellectual pleasures."

"But," said Madame de Rochefide to me, interrupting me, "I do not see anything yet, either of
Marianina or of her little old man."

"You see nothing but him," I cried, impatient as
an author who had been compelled to spoil the effect
of his theatrical demonstration.

"For several days," I resumed after a pause,
"Sarrasine had come so faithfully to take his place
in his box, and his looks expressed so much love,
that his passion for the voice of Zambinella would
have been the news of all Paris if this adventure
had happened there; but, in Italy, Madame, at the
theatre each one is present on his own account,
with his own passions, with an interest of the heart
which excludes the spying of the lorgnettes. However, the frenzy of the sculptor was not destined to
long escape the observation of the singers and the
cantatrices. One evening, the Frenchman perceived that they were laughing at him in the side-
scenes. It would have been difficult to know to
what extremity he might not have been carried if
La Zambinella had not entered on the scene. She

threw upon Sarrasine one of those eloquent looks which often say much more than the women wish them to. This look was a complete revelation. Sarrasine was loved!

"'If it is only a caprice,' thought he, already accusing his mistress of too much ardor, 'she does not know the domination under which she is going to fall. Her caprice will endure, I hope, as long as my life.'

"At this moment, three blows lightly struck on the door of his box attracted the attention of the artist. He opened the door. An old woman entered mysteriously.

"'Young man,' said she, 'if you wish to be happy, have prudence. Wrap yourself up in a cape, pull down over your eyes a broad hat; then, about ten o'clock in the evening, place yourself in the Rue du Corso, before the Hôtel de *Spagna*.'

"'I will be there,' he replied, putting two louis in the withered hand of the duenna.

"He slipped out of his box, after having made a sign of intelligence to La Zambinella, who lowered timidly her voluptuous eyelids like a woman happy in being finally comprehended. Then he hastened home, in order to borrow from his toilet all the seductions which it could lend him. As he came out of the theatre, an unknown arrested him by the arm.

"'Take care of yourself, Seigneur Frenchman,' he said in his ear. 'It is a question of life or death. Cardinal Cicognara is her protector, and does not permit any frolics.'

"Though a demon should have opened between Sarrasine and La Zambinella the profundities of hell, in this moment he would have traversed them all with one stride. Like the horses of the immortals, described by Homer, the love of the sculptor had passed over in the twinkling of an eye immense spaces.

" 'Though death waited for me on coming out of the house, I would go still quicker,' he replied.

" '*Poverino!*' cried the unknown, as he disappeared.

"To speak of danger to a lover, is it not to sell him pleasures? Never had Sarrasine's lackey seen his master so particular in matters of the toilet. His finest sword, a present from Bouchardon, the tie which Clotilde had given him, his gold embroidered coat, his waistcoat of silver brocade, his snuff-box, his jeweled watches, all were drawn from his coffers, and he adorned himself like a young girl who is about to present herself before her first lover. At the appointed hour, drunk with love and boiling with hope, Sarrasine, his nose buried in his mantle, hastened to the rendezvous given by the old woman. The duenna was waiting for him.

" 'You are very late!' she said to him. 'Come.'

"She led the Frenchman through a number of little streets and stopped before a palace of a sufficiently handsome appearance. She knocked, the door opened. She conducted Sarrasine through a labyrinth of staircases, of galleries, and of apartments which were only lighted by the uncertain
16

gleams of the moon, and arrived presently at a door, between the wings of which escaped a bright light, through which issued the joyful sounds of several voices.   Suddenly, Sarrasine was dazzled when, on a word from the old woman, he was admitted into this mysterious apartment and found himself in a salon as brilliantly lighted as it was sumptuously furnished, in the middle of which was placed a well-served table, charged with doubly-sacred bottles, with laughing flasks, the ruby facets of which sparkled in the light. He recognized the singers and the cantatrices of the theatre, mingled with charming women, all of them ready to commence an artistes' orgie which waited only for him.   Sarrasine suppressed a movement of displeasure, and put on a good countenance.   He had hoped for a chamber dimly lit, his mistress over a brazier, some jealous one within two steps, death and love, confidences exchanged in an undertone, heart-to-heart, perilous kisses, and the faces so close that the hair of La Zambinella should caress his forehead charged with desire, burning with happiness.

" '*Vive la folie!*' he cried.—'*Signori e belle donne,* you will permit me to take my revenge later, and to testify to you my gratitude for the manner in which you welcome a poor sculptor.'

"After having received the compliments, sufficiently hearty, of most of the persons present, whom he knew by sight, he endeavored to approach the couch on which La Zambinella was nonchalantly reclining.   Oh! how his heart beat when he perceived a delicate foot, shod in one of those slippers which, permit me to say it, Madame, gave formerly to the women's feet an expression so coquettish, so voluptuous, that I do not know how the men were able to resist. The white stockings, well fitting and with green clocks, the short skirts, the pointed slippers and the high heels of the reign of Louis XV. have perhaps contributed a little to demoralize Europe and the clergy.''

"A little,'' said the marchioness. "You have not, then, read anything?''

"La Zambinella,'' I resumed, smiling, "had saucily crossed her legs, swinging the one which was on top, the attitude of a duchess, which suited very well her species of capricious beauty, full of a certain engaging softness. She had discarded her theatre costume, and wore a bodice which outlined a slender figure and gave style to paniers and a skirt of satin embroidered with blue flowers. Her bust, whose treasures were hidden by lace with a luxurious coquetry, shone with whiteness. Her hair was dressed almost like that of Madame du Barry, her face, although overshadowed by a large bonnet, appeared none the less delicate, and the powder suited her well. To see her thus, was to adore her. She smiled graciously on the sculptor. Sarrasine, quite discontented at being able to speak to her only before witnesses, seated himself politely near her, and conversed with her of music, praising her extraordinary talent; but his voice trembled with love, with fear and with hope.

"'What are you afraid of?' Vitagliani, the most celebrated singer of the troupe, asked him. 'Go ahead; you have not a single rival to fear here.'

"After having spoken, the tenor smiled silently. The lips of all the guests repeated this smile, the expression of which had a hidden malice probably unperceived by a lover. The publicity of his love was like a dagger stroke which Sarrasine had suddenly received in his heart. Although endowed with a certain force of character, and though certainly no circumstances could master the violence of his passion, he had not yet, perhaps, reflected that Zambinella was almost a courtesan, and that he could not have in one being the pure delights which render the love of a young girl so delicious and the tempestuous transports by which a woman of the theatre causes to be purchased her perilous possession. He reflected and resigned himself. The supper was served. Sarrasine and La Zambinella placed themselves without ceremony by the side of each other. During half of the festival the artistes preserved some decorum, and the sculptor could converse with the cantatrice. He found in her wit and finesse; but she was of a surprising ignorance, and showed herself to be feeble and superstitious. The delicacy of her organs was reproduced in her intellectual apprehension. When Vitagliani uncorked the first bottle of champagne, Sarrasine read in the eyes of his neighbor a sufficiently lively fear of the little explosion produced by the release of the gas. The involuntary shudder of this feminine organization was interpreted by the amorous artist as the indication of an excessive sensibility. This weakness charmed the Frenchman. There is so much protection in the love of a man!

" 'You will dispose of my power as of a shield!'

"Is not this phrase written at the bottom of all the declarations of love? Sarrasine, too passionate to retail gallantries to the beautiful Italian, was, like all lovers, alternately grave, laughing, or thoughtful. Although he apppeared to listen to the guests, he did not hear a word of what they said, so much did he give himself up to the pleasure of finding himself near her, of touching her hand, of serving her. He was swimming in a secret joy. Notwithstanding the eloquence of a few mutual glances, he was astonished at the reserve which La Zambinella maintained with him. She had indeed been the first to commence to press his foot and to incite him with the malice of a woman free and amorous; but suddenly she enveloped herself in the modesty of a young girl after having heard Sarrasine relate an incident which depicted the excessive violence of his character. When the supper became an orgie, the guests began to sing, inspired by the peralta and the pedro-ximénes. There were ravishing duets, airs of Calabria, Spanish seguidillas, Neapolitan canzonettes. Intoxication was in all eyes, in the music, in the hearts and in the voices. There broke out all at once an enchanting vivacity, a cordial unreservedness, an Italian good nature, of which nothing can give an idea to those who

know only the assemblies of Paris, the routs of
London, or the circles of Vienna. Jests and words
of love crossed each other, like balls in a battle,
through the laughter, the impieties, the invocations
to the Holy Virgin or *al Bambino*.   A man lay
down on a sofa and went to sleep.   A young girl
listened to a declaration without knowing that she
was spilling sherry on the table-cloth.   In the middle of this disorder, La Zambinella, as if struck
with terror, remained thoughtful.   She refused to
drink, ate perhaps a little too much; but gormandiz-
ing is, it is said, a grace in women.   While admiring the modesty of his mistress, Sarrasine was
making serious reflections upon the future.

"'She doubtless wishes to be married,' said he to
himself.

"Then he gave himself up to the delights of this
marriage.   His entire life seemed to him to be not
long enough to exhaust the spring of happiness
which he found in the bottom of his soul.   Vitagliani, his neighbor, filled his glass so often that,
towards three o'clock in the morning, without being
completely drunken, Sarrasine found himself unable
to resist his delirium.   In a moment of impetuosity
he seized and carried off this woman, taking refuge
in a sort of boudoir which communicated with the
salon, and to the door of which he had more than
once turned his eyes.   The Italian was armed with
a poniard.

"'If you approach,' she said, 'I shall be forced to
plunge this weapon in your heart.   Go!   You would

despise me. I have conceived too much respect for your character to deliver myself thus. I do not wish to destroy the sentiment which you have for me.'

"'Ah! ah!' said Sarrasine, 'it is a bad way to extinguish a passion by exciting it. Are you already corrupted to such a point that, old in heart, you would act like a young courtesan, who sharpens the emotions of which she makes a commerce?'

"'But it is Friday to-day,' she replied, frightened at the violence of the Frenchman.

"Sarrasine, who was not devout, commenced to laugh. La Zambinella leaped like a young roebuck and fled into the supper room. When Sarrasine appeared running after her, he was welcomed by a laughter truly infernal. He saw La Zambinella fainting on a sofa. She was pale and as if exhausted by the extraordinary effort which she had just made. Although Sarrasine knew very little Italian, he heard his mistress saying in a low voice to Vitagliani:

"'But he will kill me!'

"This strange scene had the effect of quite confusing the sculptor. His reason returned to him. He remained at first motionless; then he recovered his speech, seated himself near his mistress and protested his respect for her. He found strength to transform his passion in proffering to this woman the most exalted discourse; and, to paint his love, he displayed the treasures of that magic eloquence, serviceable interpreter which women rarely refuse to believe. At the moment when the first gleams of morning came to surprise the guests, a woman proposed to go to Frascati. Everybody welcomed with lively acclamations the idea of passing the day at the Villa Ludovisi. Vitagliani went down to hire some coaches. Sarrasine had the happiness of accompanying La Zambinella in a phaëton. Once out of Rome, the gayety, suppressed for a moment by the combats which each one had waged with sleep, suddenly reawakened. Men and women, all appeared accustomed to this strange life, to these continued pleasures, to this enthusiasm of the artiste which makes of life a perpetual festival, in which one laughs without any after-thought. The companion of the sculptor was the only one who appeared depressed.

"'Are you unwell?' said Sarrasine to her. 'Would you rather return to your own house?'

"'I am not strong enough to support all these excesses,' she replied. 'I am obliged to take great care of myself; but, by your side, I feel so well! Without you, I would not have stayed for that supper; a wasted night makes me lose all my freshness.'

"'You are so delicate!' resumed Sarrasine, contemplating the refined features of this charming creature.

"'The orgies ruin my voice.'

"'Now that we are alone,' cried the artist, 'and that you have no longer to fear the effervescence of my passion, say to me that you love me.'

"'Wherefore?' she replied; 'for what purpose? I

"'If you approach,' she said, 'I shall be forced to plunge this weapon in your heart. Go! You would despise me. I have conceived too much respect for your character to deliver myself thus. I do not wish to destroy the sentiment which you have for me.'

"'Ah! ah!' said Sarrasine, 'it is a bad way to extinguish a passion by exciting it.'

seem to you pretty. But you are French, and your
feeling will pass away. Oh! you would not love
me as I would like to be loved.'

" 'How ?'

" 'Without any purpose of vulgar passion, purely.
I abhor men still more perhaps than I hate women.
I have need to take refuge in friendship. The world
is a desert for me. I am an accursed creature, condemned to comprehend happiness, to feel it, to desire
it, and, like so many others, obliged to see it flee
away from me every hour. Remember, seigneur,
that I would not have deceived you. I forbid you
to love me. I can be a devoted friend for you, for I
admire your strength and your character. I have
need of a brother, of a protector. Be all that for
me, but nothing more.'

" 'Not love you!' cried Sarrasine; 'but, dear angel,
thou art my life, my happiness!'

" 'If I said one word, you would repulse me with
horror.'

" 'Coquette! nothing can frighten me. Say to
me that thou wilt cost me my future, that in two
months i shall die, that I shall be damned for only
having embraced thee—'

"He embraced her notwithstanding the efforts
which La Zambinella made to avoid this passionate
kiss.

" 'Say to me that thou art a demon, that thou
wilt require my fortune, my name, all my celebrity! Wilt thou that I should not be a sculptor?
Speak.'

" 'If I were not a woman?' asked La Zambinella, timidly, in a silvery and soft voice.

" 'What a fine pleasantry!' cried Sarrasine. 'Thinkest thou to deceive the eye of an artist? Have I not, for the last ten days, devoured, scrutinized, admired thy perfections? Only a woman could have this round and soft arm, these elegant contours. Ah! thou desirest compliments!'

"She smiled sadly, and said in a murmuring voice :

" 'Fatal beauty!'

"She lifted her eyes to Heaven. At that moment her look had an unnamable expression of horror so powerful, so vivid, that Sarrasine shuddered at it.

" 'Seigneur Frenchman,' she resumed, 'forget forever an instant of madness. I esteem you; but, as to love, do not ask it of me; this feeling is smothered in my heart. I have no heart!' she cried, weeping. 'The theatre on which you have seen me, that applause, that music, that glory, to which I have been condemned, that is my life; I have no other. Within a few hours, you will no longer see me with the same eyes, the woman whom you love will be dead.'

"The sculptor did not reply. He was a prey to a dumb rage which oppressed his heart. He could only look at this extraordinary woman with ardent eyes which burned. This voice so full of weakness, the attitude, the manner, and the gestures of Zambinella, so expressive of sadness, of melancholy, and of discouragement, reawakened in his soul all the wealth of passion. Each word was another goad. At that moment they arrived at Frascati. When the artist offered his arm to his mistress to help her to descend, he felt her shuddering all over.

" 'What is the matter with you? You will cause me to die,' he cried, in seeing her turn pale, 'if you should have the least sorrow of which I am the cause, even innocently.'

" 'A snake!' she said, indicating an adder which was sliding along the bottom of a ditch. 'I am afraid of those odious beasts.'

"Sarrasine crushed the head of the adder with his heel.

" 'How can you have so much courage?' exclaimed La Zambinella, looking with a visible terror at the dead reptile.

" 'Well,' said the artist, smiling, 'would you dare to pretend that you are not a woman?'

"They rejoined their companions and walked about in the woods of the Villa Ludovisi, which was then the property of Cardinal Cicognara. This morning passed away too quickly for the amorous sculptor, but it was filled with a crowd of incidents which revealed to him the coquetry, the weakness, the prettiness and delicacy of this soul soft and without energy. It was all the woman, with her sudden fears, her unreasonable caprices, her instinctive troubles, her audacities without cause, her bravadoes and her delicious nicety of sentiment. At one time, straying out into the country, the little company of joyful singers saw at a distance some men armed to the teeth and whose costume was in no ways reassuring. At the exclamation: 'See! the brigands!' each one hurried his steps to seek refuge in the enclosure of the cardinal's villa. At that critical moment Sarrasine perceived by the pallor of La Zambinella that she no longer had strength to walk; he took her in his arms and carried her, running for some distance. When he was within a short distance of a neighboring vineyard, he set his mistress on her feet again.

" 'Explain to me,' he said to her, 'how this extreme weakness, which, in any other woman, would displease me, would seem odious, and the least proof of which would almost suffice to extinguish my love, pleases me in you, charms me?—Oh, how I love you!' he resumed. 'All your defects, your terrors, your littlenesses, add an indescribable grace to your soul. I feel that I should detest a strong woman, a Sappho, courageous, full of energy, of passion. O! frail and soft creature! how couldst thou be otherwise? That voice of an angel, that delicate voice, would be a contradiction if it issued from any other body than thine.'

" 'I cannot,' she said, 'give you any hope. Cease to speak to me thus, for you are mocked. It is impossible for me to forbid you the entrance to the theatre; but, if you love me or if you are wise, you will come there no more. Listen, Monsieur,—' she said, in a grave voice.

" 'Oh! be silent,' said the intoxicated artist. 'Obstacles only increase the love in my heart.'

"La Zambinella remained in a graceful and

modest attitude; but she was silent, as if a terrible
thought had revealed to her some misfortune. When
it was time for them to return to Rome, she took her
place in a four-seated berlin, and ordered the sculptor, with an imperiously cruel air, to return alone
in the phaëton. On the road, Sarrasine resolved
to carry off La Zambinella. He passed the whole day
in forming plans, each one more extravagant than
the other. At nightfall, as he left his house to inquire of someone the situation of the palace inhab-
ited by his mistress, he encountered one of his
comrades on the threshold of the door.

"'My dear fellow,' said the latter to him, 'I am
requested by our ambassador to invite you to come
to his house this evening. He is giving a magnificent concert, and, when you know that Zambinella will be there—'

"'Zambinella!' cried Sarrasine, in a delirium at
this name; 'I am crazy for her!'

"'You are like all the rest of the world,' replied
his comrade.

"'But, if you are my friends, you, Vien, Lauter-
bourg, and Allegrain, you will lend me your assistance for a fine stroke after the fête?' asked Sarrasine.

"'There is not some cardinal to be killed?—
some—?'

"'No, no,' said Sarrasine, 'I ask nothing of you
which honest people cannot do.'

"In a short time, the sculptor had arranged everything for the success of his enterprise. He was one
of the last to arrive at the ambassador's, but he

came in a traveling carriage drawn by vigorous
horses driven by one of the most enterprising *vet-
turini* of Rome.   The palace of the ambassador was
crowded; it was not without difficulty that the
sculptor, unknown to all the domestics, reached the
salon in which at that moment Zambinella was
singing.

"'It is doubtless in consideration of the cardinals,
the bishops and the abbés who are here,' asked Sarrasine, 'that *she* is dressed like a man, that *she* has
her hair in a bag and frizzled and wears a sword?'

"'She!   What she?' replied the old seigneur to
whom Sarrasine spoke.

"'La Zambinella.'

"'La Zambinella!' replied the Roman prince.   'Of
what are you talking?   Where do you come from?
Has there ever been a woman on the stage in the
theatres of Rome?   And do you not know by what
kind of creatures the female parts are filled in the
States of the Pope?   It is I, Monsieur, who gave
Zambinella his voice.   I have paid everything for
that scamp, even his singing-master.   Well, he has
so little gratitude for the service which I have rendered him, that he is never willing to set foot inside
my door.   And yet, if he makes his fortune, he will
owe it to me entirely.'

"The Prince Chigi could certainly have spoken a
long time, Sarrasine did not hear him.   A frightful
truth had penetrated his soul.   He was struck as if
by a thunderbolt.   He remained motionless, his eyes
fastened on this dubious singer.   His flaming regard

had a sort of magnetic influence on Zambinella, for the *musico* finally turned his eyes toward Sarrasine, and then his celestial voice faltered. He trembled! An involuntary murmur escaped the audience, which he held spell-bound by his lips, and completed his trouble; he discontinued his air and sat down. The Cardinal Cicognara, who had seen out of the corner of his eye the direction of the glance of his protégé, perceived the Frenchman; he leaned over toward one of his ecclesiastical aides-de-camp, and seemed to demand the name of the sculptor. When he had obtained the desired response, he looked very attentively at the artist and gave his order to an abbé, who disappeared rapidly. However, Zambinella, having recovered himself, recommenced the piece which he had interrupted so capriciously; but he executed it badly, and refused, notwithstanding all the insistence with which he was surrounded, to sing any more. This was the first time that he exercised this capricious tyranny which, later, rendered him not less celebrated than his talent and his immense fortune, due, it was said, not less to his voice than to his beauty.

" 'It is a woman,' said Sarrasine, thinking himself alone. 'There is underneath all this some secret intrigue. The Cardinal Cicognara deceives the Pope and the whole city of Rome!'

"Whereupon, the sculptor left the salon, reassembled his friends and ambuscaded them in the courtyard of the palace. When Zambinella was assured of the departure of Sarrasine, he seemed to recover some tranquillity. Toward midnight, after having wandered through the salon like a man who is seeking an enemy, the *musico* left the assembly. At the moment when he passed the door of the palace, he was adroitly seized by men who gagged him with a handkerchief and put him into the carriage hired by Sarrasine. Frozen with horror, Zambinella remained in a corner without daring to make a movement. He saw before him the terrible figure of the artist, who preserved the silence of death. The journey was but short. Zambinella, carried up by Sarrasine, soon found himself in an atelier, sombre and bare. The singer, half dead, remained in a chair, without daring to look at the statue of a woman, in which he had recognized his own features. He did not offer a word, but his teeth chattered; he was paralyzed with fear. Sarrasine walked up and down with great strides. Suddenly he stopped before Zambinella.

"'Tell me the truth,' he demanded, in a dull and changed voice. 'Thou art a woman? The Cardinal Cicognara—'

"Zambinella fell on his knees, and replied only by bowing his head.

"'Ah! thou art a woman,' cried the artist, in delirium; 'for even a—'

"He did not finish.

"'No,' he resumed, '*he* would not have such baseness.'

"'Ah! do not kill me!' cried Zambinella, melting into tears. 'I only consented to deceive you in order to please my comrades, who wished to laugh.'

"'To laugh!' replied the sculptor, in a voice which had an infernal explosion. 'To laugh! to laugh! Thou hast dared to play with a man's passion, thou?'

"'Oh, mercy!' replied Zambinella.

"'I should put thee to death!' cried Sarrasine, drawing his sword with a violent movement. 'But,' he resumed, with a cold disdain, 'in searching all thy being with this blade, would I find in it a single sentiment to extinguish, one vengeance to satisfy? Thou art nothing. Man or woman, I would kill thee! but—'

"Sarrasine made a gesture of disgust which obliged him to turn his head, and then he looked at the statue.

"'And that is an illusion!' he cried.

"Then, turning toward Zambinella:

"'A woman's heart would be for me an asylum, a country. Hast thou sisters who resemble thee? No. Well, then, die!—But no, thou shalt live. To leave thee alive, is it not to devote thee to something worse than death? It is not my blood nor my existence that I regret, but the future and my heart's fortune. Thy debilitated hand has overthrown my happiness. What hope can I ravish from thee for all those which thou hast blighted? Thou hast dragged me down even to thy level. *To love, to be loved!* are henceforth words empty of meaning for me, as for thee. Without ceasing I

17

shall think of this imaginary woman in seeing a real woman.'

"He indicated the statue with a gesture of despair.

"'I shall always have in memory a celestial harpy who will come to bury its claws in all my manhood sentiments, and who will stamp all other women with the seal of imperfection. Monster! thou who canst give life to nothing, thou hast unpeopled the earth of all its women.'

"Sarrasine seated himself in front of the terrified singer. Two great tears issued from his dry eyes, rolled down his manly cheeks and fell to the floor,— two tears of rage, two tears bitter and burning.

"'No more love! I am dead to all pleasure, to all human emotions.'

"With these words, he seized a hammer and threw it at the statue with such extravagant force that he missed it. He thought he had destroyed this monument of his folly, and he then grasped his sword and brandished it to kill the singer. Zambinella uttered piercing cries. At this moment, three men entered, and the sculptor fell suddenly, pierced with three stiletto thrusts.

"'From the Cardinal Cicognara,' said one of them.

"'It is a good turn worthy of a Christian,' replied the Frenchman, as he expired.

"These sombre emissaries informed Zambinella of the uneasiness of his protector, who was waiting at the door, in a closed carriage, in order to carry him away as soon as he should be rescued."

"But," said Madame de Rochefide to me, "what connection is there between this history and the little old man whom we have seen at the Lantys?"

"Madame, Cardinal Cicognara took possession of the statue of Zambinella and caused it to be executed in marble; it is to-day in the Museum Albani. It was there that, in 1791, the Lanty family found it again, and requested Vien to copy it. The portrait which showed to you Zambinella at twenty, a moment after having seen him a centenarian, served later for the *Endymion* of Girodet; you have been able to recognize its type in the *Adonis.*"

"But this he or she Zambinella?"

"Can be no other, Madame, than the great-uncle of Marianina. You may readily conceive now the interest which Madame de Lanty may have in concealing the origin of a fortune which comes from—"

"Enough!" she said, making to me an imperious gesture.

We remained for a moment plunged in the most profound silence.

"Well?" I said to her.

"Ah!—" she cried, rising and walking rapidly about the chamber.

She came up to look at me, and said in a changed voice:

"You have disgusted me with life and with passions for a long time. With the exception of monsters, all human sentiments—do they not unravel themselves thus, by atrocious deceptions? Mothers, our infants assassinate us either by their evil conduct

or by their thanklessness. Wives, we are betrayed.
Lovers, we are forsaken, abandoned. Friendship!
does it exist? I would turn nun to-morrow if I did
not know how to remain like an inaccessible rock in
the midst of the storms of life. If the future state of
the Christian is also an illusion, at least it is not
proved so till after death. Leave me alone."

"Ah!" I said to her, "you know how to punish."

"Should I be wrong?"

"Yes," I replied, with a sort of courage. "In relating this story, sufficiently well known in Italy, I
have been able to give you a striking proof of the
actual progress made by civilization. There are no
longer made any of these unfortunate creatures."

"Paris," said she, "is a very hospitable soil: it
welcomes everything, the shameful fortunes and the
blood-stained fortunes. Crime and infamy there
have right of asylum; virtue alone is there without
altars. But the pure souls have a country in heaven!
No one will ever have recognized me! I am proud
of it."

And the marchioness remained thoughtful.

Paris, November, 1830.

FACINO CANE

(261)

FACINO CANE

*

I lived at that time in a little street which you doubtless know, the Rue de Lesdiguiéres: it commences at the Rue Saint-Antoine, opposite a fountain near to the Place de la Bastille, and comes out on the Rue de la Cerisaie. Love of science had lodged me in a garret, where I worked during the night, and I spent the day in a neighboring library, that of MONSIEUR. I lived frugally, I had accepted all the conditions of the monastic life, so necessary to workers. When the weather was fine, I permitted myself rarely to take a walk on the Boulevard Bourdon. One passion only drew me out of my studious habits; but was not this also study? I was interested in observing the manners and customs of the faubourg, its inhabitants and their characters. As poorly dressed as the workmen themselves, indifferent to the proprieties, I did not put them on their guard against me; I was able to mingle with them, to see them concluding their bargains, and quarreling amongst themselves at the hour when they left their work. In me, the faculty of observation had already become intuitive, it penetrated the soul without neglecting the body; or, rather, it seized so promptly the exterior details, that it immediately went beyond them; it gave me the faculty of living the life of the individual on whom it was directed, in permitting me to substitute myself for him as the dervish of the *Thousand and One Nights* assumed the body and the soul of those persons over whom he pronounced certain words.

When, between eleven o'clock and midnight, I encountered a laborer and his wife returning together from the Ambigu-Comique, I amused myself by following them from the Boulevard du Pont-aux-Choux to the Boulevard Beaumarchais. These honest people talked at first of the piece which they had just seen; then they passed insensibly to their own affairs; the mother dragged her child along by the hand, without hearing either its complaints or its questions; the couple counted the money which would be paid to them the next day, they expended it in twenty different ways. Then there would be household details, lamentations over the excessive price of potatoes, or on the length of the winter and the dearness of fuel, energetic observations on the sum due to the baker; finally, discussions which became venomous, and in which each of them displayed his or her character in picturesque words. In hearing these poor folk, I was able to assume their life, I felt their rags on my back, I walked with my feet in their worn shoes; their desires, their needs, all passed into my soul, or my soul passed into theirs. It was the dream of a waking man. I grew

indignant, with them, at the overseers of the work-
shops who tyrannized over them, or against the bad
arrangements which made them return several times
for their money. To quit one's daily habits, to
become a being outside of yourself by the intoxica-
tions of the moral faculties, and to play this game at
will, such was my distraction. To whom did I owe
this gift? Is it a second sight? is it one of those
qualities the abuse of which leads to madness? I
had never sought for the causes of this power; I
possess it and make use of it, that is all. Know
only that, since that time, I have decomposed the
elements of that heterogeneous mass called the people, that I have analyzed it in such a manner as to
be able to value its good or its evil qualities. I
knew already of what utility this faubourg could be
made, this seminary of revolutions which encloses
heroes, inventors, knowing practitioners, cheats,
blackguards, virtues and vices all crowded together
by poverty, smothered by necessity, drowned in
wine, worn out by strong liquors. You could not
possibly imagine how many lost adventures, how
many forgotten dramas there are in this city of
sorrow! How many horrible and beautiful things!
Imagination will never discover the full truth which
is hidden there and which no one can set out to
discover; it is necessary to descend too low to find
these admirable scenes, tragic or comic, master-
pieces given birth to by chance. I do not know how
I have so long kept untold the story which I am about
to relate to you; it is one of those curious recitals

left in the sack from which memory draws them capriciously like the numbers of the lottery: I have many others quite as singular as this one, equally hidden; but they will have their turn, believe me.

One day, my housekeeper, the wife of a workman, came to ask me to honor with my presence the wedding of one of her sisters. In order that you may comprehend what this wedding could be, it is necessary to tell you that I gave forty sous a month to this poor creature, who came every morning to make my bed, clean my shoes, brush my clothes, sweep the chamber and prepare my déjeuner; the rest of her time she spent in turning the handle of a machine, and earned by this hard trade ten sous a day. Her husband, a cabinet-maker, earned four francs. But, as this household had three children, it could with difficulty manage honestly to have bread to eat. I have never encountered more solid honesty than that of this man and this woman. Whenever I left the quarter, during five years, the Mère Vaillant came to congratulate me on my fête, bringing me a bouquet and some oranges, she who never had ten sous of savings. Poverty had brought us close together. I was never able to give her anything more than ten francs, often borrowed for this purpose. This may explain my promise to go to the wedding, I counted on being able to envelop myself in the happiness of these poor people.

The festival, the ball, all took place in the establishment of a wine merchant in the Rue de Charenton, on the first floor, in a large room lit by lamps with tin reflectors, ornamented with a dirty wall-paper up to the height of the tables, and along the walls of which there were wooden benches. In this chamber, eighty persons in their best clothes, set off with bouquets and ribbons, all of them animated by the spirit of that lively quarter, la Courtille, with flushed faces, danced as if the world were about to end. The newly-married couple embraced each other to the general satisfaction, and there were the "Eh! eh!" the "Ah! ah!" very facetious, but really less indecent than are the timid eye-glances of well-bred young girls. All this company expressed a brutal contentment which had in it something inexpressibly contagious.

But neither the physiognomies of this assembly, nor the wedding, nor anything of this company has any relation to my story. Remember only the oddness of the scene. Figure to yourself the ignoble shop painted in red, smell the odor of the wine, listen to the roarings of this joy, place yourself in this faubourg, in the middle of these workpeople, of these old men, of these poor women given over to the pleasures of a night!

The orchestra was composed of three blind men from the hospital of the Quinze-Vingts,—the first was a violin, the second a clarionet, and the third a flageolet. All three were paid a lump sum of seven francs for the night. For that price, certainly, they gave neither Rossini nor Beethoven; they played what they would and what they could; no one addressed them any reproaches, a charming

delicacy! Their music attacked the tympanum so
roughly, that after having looked at the general
assembly, I directed my observation to this blind
trio, and was immediately disposed to be indulgent
in recognizing their uniform. These artists were
placed in the embrasure of a window; to distinguish
their countenances it was necessary to be near
them.—I did not place myself there immediately,
but when I approached them, I do not know why,
everything was said, the wedding and its music
disappeared, my curiosity was excited to the highest
degree, for my soul passed into the body of the clarionet player. The violin and the flageolet had both
of them commonplace faces, the well-known countenance of the blind, full of intenseness, attentive
and grave; but that of the clarionet was one of
those phenomena which arrest suddenly the artist
and the philosopher.

Imagine to yourself the plaster mask of Dante, lit
up by the red light of the argand lamp, and sur-
mounted by a forest of hair of a silvery whiteness.
The bitter and dolorous expression of this magnificent head was increased by the blindness, for the
extinguished eyes were restored to life by thought;
it revealed itself in them like a burning light, produced by an unique and incessant desire, vigorously
inscribed on the arched forehead which was traversed by wrinkles like the courses on an old wall.
This old man blew in his instrument at hazard, without paying the least attention to the measure or the
air, his fingers were raised or lowered, manipulating

the old keys, mechanically; he did not give himself any trouble to make what is called in the language
of the orchestra the *canards*, the dancers did not perceive it any more than did the two acolytes of my
Italian; for I wished that he should be an Italian, and
he was an Italian. Something of grand and the des-
potic was to be encountered in this old Homer who
guarded in himself an Odyssey condemned to forgetfulness. It was a grandeur so real, that it
triumphed still over his abjection; it was a despotism so vivid that it dominated poverty. Not one of
the violent passions which conduct man to good as
to evil, which make of him a convict or a hero, was
lacking to this visage nobly modeled, of an Italian
lividness, shaded by grayish brows which projected
their shadows over profound cavities in which one
feared to see reappear the light of thought, as one
fears to see come to the mouth of a cavern brigands
armed with torches and poniards. There existed a
lion in that cage of flesh, a lion whose rage had
been uselessly exhausted against the iron of his barriers. The fire of despair was extinct in its cinders,
the lava had grown cold; but the furrows, the over-
turnings, a little smoke, still bore witness to the
violence of the eruption, the ravages of flame.
These ideas, called up by the aspect of this man,
were as heated in my soul as they were cold on his
countenance.

Between each contradance the violin and the
flageolet, seriously occupied with their glasses and
their bottle, hung their instruments to certain

buttons of their rusty coats, put out their hands to a little table placed in the embrasure of a window in which was their supply, and offered each time to the Italian a full glass, which he could not take himself, for the table was behind his chair; each time the clarionet thanked them by a friendly sign of the head. Their movements were performed with that precision which is always so surprising among the blind of the Quinze-Vingts, and which makes it seem as though they saw. I approached the three blind men to listen to them, but when I was near them, they studied me, failing to recognize doubtless one of the working-class, and kept silent.

"From what country are you, you who play the clarionet?"

"From Venice," replied the blind man, with a slight Italian accent.

"Were you born blind, or did you lose your sight by—?"

"By accident," he replied quickly, "a cursed *gutta serena*."

"Venice is a beautiful city; I have always desired to go there."

The countenance of the old man became animated, his wrinkles were agitated, he was violently moved.

"If I were to go there with you, you would not lose your time," he said to me.

"Do not speak to him of Venice," said the violin to me, "or our Doge will go off again; all the more so that he already has put two bottles away, the prince!"

"Come, forward march, Père Canard," said the flageolet.

All three of them commenced to play; but, during the time which they took to execute the four parts of the contradance, the Venetian scented me; he guessed at the excessive interest which I took in him. His physiognomy lost its cold expression of sadness; I do not know what hope lit up his features, spread like a blue flame in his wrinkles; he smiled and wiped his forehead, that audacious and terrible forehead; in short, he became gay like a man who mounts his hobby-horse.

"How old are you?" I asked him.

"Eighty-two years."

"How long have you been blind?"

"For nearly fifty years," he replied, with an accent which revealed that his regrets were not only for the loss of his sight, but for some great power of which he had been deprived.

"Why do they, then, call you the Doge?" I asked him.

"Ah! a farce," said he: "I am a patrician of Venice, and I might have been Doge as well as any other."

"What is your name, then?"

"Here," he said to me, "the Père Canet. My name could never be inscribed in any other way on the registers; but, in Italian, it is *Marco Facino Cane, principe de Varese.*"

"How! you are descended from the famous condottiere, Facino Cane, whose conquests passed to the Dukes of Milan?"

"*E vero*," said he. "In those times, in order not
to be killed by the Visconti, the son of Cane took
refuge in Venice and caused his name to be inscribed on the Golden Book. But there is now no
longer any Cane nor any Book!"

And he made a terrifying gesture of extinguished patriotism and of disgust for all things
human.

"But, if you were Senator of Venice, you should
be rich; how have you been able to lose all your fortune?"

At this question, he raised his head toward me as
if to contemplate me with a movement truly tragic,
and replied to me:

"In misfortunes!"

He no longer cared to drink; he refused by a gesture a glass of wine which the old flageolet offered
him at this moment, then he lowered his head.
These details were not of a nature to extinguish
my curiosity. During the contradance which was
played by these three machines, I contemplated the
noble old Venetian with those sentiments which
take possession of a young man of twenty. I saw
Venice and the Adriatic, I saw it in ruins in this
ruined figure. I walked about in this city so dear
to its inhabitants; I went from the Rialto to the
Grand Canal, from the quay of the Schiavoni to the
Lido, I returned to its cathedral, so originally sublime, I looked at the windows of the Casa d'Oro,
the ornaments of each of which are different; I contemplated its old palaces so rich in marble, in short

all those marvels with which he who is wise sympathizes all the more that he colors them at his own will, and does not deprive his dreams of their poetry by the spectacle of reality. I followed up the course of the life of this scion of the greatest of the condottieri, searching in it the traces of his misfortunes and the causes of that profound degradation, physical and moral, which rendered finer still the sparks of grandeur and of nobility reanimated in this moment. Our thoughts were doubtless reciprocal, for I believe that blindness renders the intellectual communications much more rapid in prohibiting the attention from scattering itself on exterior objects. The proof of our sympathy was not long in manifesting itself. Facino Cane ceased to play, rose, came to me and said to me "Let us go!" which produced on me the effect of an electric shock. I gave him my arm and we went out.

When we were in the street, he said to me:

"Will you take me to Venice, conduct me there? Will you have faith in me? You will be richer than are the ten richest houses of Amsterdam or of London, richer than the Rothschilds; in short, rich as the *Thousand and One Nights.*"

I thought that this man was mad; but he had in his voice a power which I obeyed. I let him conduct me and he led me toward the ditches of the Bastille as if he had eyes. He seated himself on a stone, in a very solitary locality, where since has been built the bridge by which the Canal Saint-Martin communicates with the Seine. I placed

18

myself on another stone before this old man, whose white hair shone like silver threads in the light of the moon. The silence which was scarcely troubled by the stormy noise of the boulevard which reached us, the purity of the night, everything, contributed to render this scene truly fantastic.

"You speak of millions to a young man, and you think that he would hesitate to endure a thousand evils to possess them! Are you not mocking me?"

"May I die unconfessed," he said to me, violently, "if that which I am going to say to you is not true. I was twenty years of age, as you are at this moment. I was rich, I was handsome, I was noble; I commenced by the first of follies, love. I have loved as one no longer loves, even to the point of putting myself in a chest and risking being poniarded without having received anything but the promise of a kiss. To die for *her* seemed to me a whole life. In 1760, I fell in love with a Vendramini, a woman of eighteen, married to a Sagredo, one of the richest senators, a man of thirty, madly loving his wife. My mistress and I, we were as innocent as two cherubim, when the *sposo* surprised us talking love; I was without arms, he was armed, but he missed me; I sprang upon him, I strangled him with my two hands, twisting his neck like that of a pullet. I wished to depart with Bianca; she would not follow me. Such are women! I went away alone. I was condemned, my goods were sequestered for the benefit of my heirs; but I had carried off my diamonds, five pictures by Titian rolled up, and all my gold. I went to Milan, where I was not disturbed: my affair did not interest the state.—A little observation before continuing," he said after a pause. "Whether the fancies of a woman have any influence or not on her child while she carries it or when she conceives it, it is certain that my mother had a passion for gold during her pregnancy. I have for gold a monomania, the satisfaction of which is so necessary to my life that, in all the situations in which I have found myself, I have never been without gold about me; I handle gold constantly; when young I always wore jewels and I had always about me two or three hundred ducats."

In saying these words, he drew two ducats from his pocket and showed them to me.

"I am sensitive to gold. Although blind, I stop before the jewelers' windows. This passion ruined me; I have become a gambler to play with gold. I was not a cheat; I was cheated, I was ruined. When I no longer had any fortune, I passionately longed to see Bianca again,—I returned secretly to Venice, I found her again; I was happy during six months, hidden by her, nourished by her. I thought deliciously to finish my life thus. She was sought by the Proveditor; he suspected a rival; in Italy, they smell them,—he spied on us, he surprised us in bed, the coward! Judge how fierce was our struggle: I did not kill him, I wounded him grievously. This adventure destroyed my happiness. Since that day, I have never found again a Bianca. I have had great pleasures, I have lived at the

Court of Louis XV., among the most celebrated
women; nowhere have I found the qualities, the
graces, the love of my dear Venetian.   The Proveditor had his servants; he summoned them, the
palace was surrounded, invaded; I defended myself
so as to be able to die under the eye of Bianca, who
aided me in killing the Proveditor.   This woman
had once not been willing to fly with me; but, after
six months of happiness, she wished to die with me,
and did receive several strokes.   Taken in a great
cloak which was thrown over me, I was rolled
in it, carried to a gondola and transported to a
dungeon in the Wells.   I was twenty-two years
of age; I held on so well to a fragment of my
sword that, to have taken it, it would have been
necessary to cut off my hand.   By a singular chance,
or rather by a wise precaution, I hid this piece of
steel in a corner, as though it might be of use to
me.   I was cared for.   None of my wounds were
mortal.   At twenty-two, one recovers from anything.   As I was doomed to die decapitated, I pretended illness in order to gain time.   I believed
myself in a dungeon near the canal; my project was
to escape by digging a hole through the wall and
swimming the canal, at the risk of drowning.

"These were the reasonings on which my hope
was founded.

"Every time that the jailer brought me food, I
read the indications written on the walls, such as
'To the Palace,' 'To the Canal,' 'To the Crypts,' and
I finally made out a plan the meaning of which

disquieted me but little, but which was explicable
by the actual condition of the ducal palace, not then
completed. With that inspiration which the desire
of regaining liberty gives, I succeeded in decipher-
ing, by feeling with the ends of my fingers, the
surface of a stone, an Arab inscription by which the
author of this work notified his successors that he
had detached two stones of the last course and exca-
vated eleven feet underground. To continue his
work, it would be necessary to spread on the floor
of the dungeon itself the pieces of stone and mortar
produced by the work of excavation. Even if the
guardians or the inquisitors had not been reassured
by the construction of the edifice, which required
only an exterior surveillance, the disposition of the
Wells, in which it was necessary to descend by several steps, permitted the gradual raising of the soil
without the guardians perceiving it. This immense
labor had been profitless, at least for the one who
had undertaken it, for its incompletion announced
the death of the unknown. In order that his devotion should not be forever lost, it was necessary
that a prisoner should understand Arabic, but I had
studied the Oriental languages at the Convent of
the Armenians. A phrase written behind the stone
revealed the destiny of this unfortunate, who had
died a victim to his immense wealth, which Venice
had coveted and of which she had taken possession.
A month's time was required to enable me to arrive
at a result. While I worked, and in those moments
in which fatigue overwhelmed me, I heard the sound

of gold, I saw gold before me, I was dazzled by diamonds!—Oh! wait.

"One night, my worn steel blade encountered
wood. I sharpened my bit of sword, and made a
hole in this wood. In order to work, I extended
myself like a serpent on my stomach; I stripped
myself naked to work like a mole, extending my
hands in front of me and making of the stone itself
a point of support. Two days before that in which
I was to appear before my judges, during the night,
I wished to make a last effort; I pierced the wood,
and my steel encountered nothing beyond.

"Judge of my surprise when I applied my eye to
this hole! I was in the roof of a cave in which a
feeble light permitted me to perceive a mountain of
gold. The Doge and one of the Ten were in this
cavern; I heard their voices; their conversation informed me that this was the secret treasure of the
Republic, the gifts of the Doges and a portion of
booty called the *denier* of Venice, and taken from
the product of expeditions.

"I was saved!

"When the jailer came, I proposed to him to aid
me in my flight and to go with me, carrying off all
that we could take. There was no question of hesitation; he accepted. A vessel was about to sail for
the Levant, all precautions were taken. Bianca
favored the plan which I dictated to my confederate.
In order not to excite suspicion, Bianca was to rejoin
us at Smyrna. In one night the hole was enlarged
and we descended into the secret treasury of Venice.

What a night! I saw four casks full of gold. In the preceding room, the silver was also piled up in two heaps which left a path in the middle to traverse the chamber, where the coins in sloping piles rose to the height of five feet against the walls. I thought that the jailer would go crazy: he sang, he leaped about, he laughed, he gamboled in the gold; I threatened to strangle him if he wasted time or if he made a noise. In his joy, he did not see at first a table on which were the diamonds. I threw myself upon it cleverly enough to fill my sailor's jacket and the pockets of my pantaloons. My God! I did not take a third of them. Under this table were the ingots of gold. I persuaded my companion to fill with gold as many sacks as we could carry, telling him that this was the only means of avoiding detection in foreign countries.

" 'Pearls, jewels and diamonds would cause us to be recognized,' I said to him.

"With all our greediness we could only take two thousand pounds of gold, which necessitated six journeys through the prison to the gondola. The sentinel at the water-gate had been bribed by a sack of ten pounds of gold. As to the two gondoliers, they believed themselves serving the Republic. At day-break we departed. When we were in the open sea, and when I thought of this night; when I recalled to myself all the sensations which I had experienced, when I saw again this immense treasure, where, according to my valuation, I had left thirty millions in silver and twenty millions in gold,

several millions in pearls, diamonds and rubies, I
felt in myself something like a sensation of madness.   I had the fever of gold.

"We disembarked at Smyrna, and we took ship
again immediately for France.   As we went on board
the French vessel, God did me the favor to relieve
me of my confederate.   At that moment I did not
think of all the consequences of this chance evil, at
which I so rejoiced.   We were so completely un-
nerved that we remained stupefied, saying nothing
to each other, while waiting till we should be in
safety to enjoy ourselves at our ease.   It is not surprising that this scamp lost his head.   You will see
how God punished me!

"I did not feel easy until I had sold two-thirds
of my diamonds in London and in Amsterdam, and
converted my gold-dust into commercial obligations.
During five years I hid myself in Madrid; then, in
1770, I came to Paris under a Spanish name and led
a most brilliant life.   Bianca was dead.   In the
midst of my pleasures, while I was enjoying a fortune of six millions, I was struck with blindness.   I
do not doubt that this infirmity was the result of my
sojourn in the cell, of my working in the stone, if,
however, my faculty of seeing gold had not carried
with it an abuse of the visual power which predes-
tined me to lose my sight.

"At this time, I was in love with a woman to
whom I thought to unite my fate. I had revealed to
her the secret of my name: she belonged to a powerful family.   I had great hopes in the favor which

Louis XV. accorded me; I had put all my confidence
in this woman, who was the friend of Madame du
Barry; she advised me to consult a famous oculist
in London; but after some months spent in that
city, I was abandoned there by this woman in Hyde
Park. She had stripped me of all my fortune without
leaving me any resource; for, obliged to conceal my
name, which would have delivered me to the vengeance of Venice, I could not invoke the assistance
of any one; I feared Venice. My infirmity was made
the most of by the spies with whom this woman had
surrounded me. I spare you the recital of adventures worthy of Gil Blas. Your Revolution arrived.
I was obliged to become an inmate of the Quinze-
Vingts, to which this creature caused me to be admitted after having kept me for two years at the
Bicêtre as a lunatic. I have never been able to kill
her. I could not see, and I was too poor to buy an
arm. If, before losing Benedetto Carpi, my jailer,
I had consulted him on the situation of my cell, I
would have been able to find again the treasury and
would have returned to Venice when the Republic was abolished by Napoléon—

"Nevertheless, notwithstanding my blindness, let
us go to Venice! I will find again the door of the
prison; I will see the gold through the walls, I will
smell it under the waters in which it is buried; for
the events which have overthrown the power of
Venice are such that the secret of this treasure must
have died with Vendramino, the brother of Bianca,
a Doge, who, I hoped, would have made my peace

with the Ten. I sent letters to the First Consul, I
proposed a treaty to the Emperor of Austria; everywhere have I been refused as a madman! Come, let
us set out for Venice; we will depart beggars, we
will come back millionaires; we will re-purchase
my property and you shall be my heir, you shall be
Prince de Varese!"

Stupefied by this confidence, which in my imaginations took the proportions of a poem, at the aspect
of this whitened head, and before the black water
of the moat of the Bastille, a water as still as that
of the canals of Venice, I did not reply. Facino
Cane thought, doubtless, that I judged him like all
the others, with a scornful pity; he made a gesture
which expressed all the philosophy of despair.

This recital had carried him back, perhaps, to his
happy days at Venice: he seized his clarionet and
began to play in a melancholy manner a Venetian
ballad, a barcarolle for which he found his early
skill, his talent of the amorous patrician. It was
something like the *Super flumina Babylonis*. My eyes
filled with tears. If some belated passers-by happened to pass along the Boulevard Bourdon, doubtless they lingered to hear this last prayer of the
banished, the last regret of a lost name, in which
was mingled the memory of Bianca. But the gold
soon regained the ascendancy, and the fatal passion
extinguished the light of youth.

"This treasure," he said to me, "I see it everywhere, awakened as in a dream; I walk there, the
diamonds glitter before me; I am not so blind as you

think; the gold and the diamonds light up my night, the night of the last Facino Cane, for my title passes to the Memmi. My God! the punishment of the murderer commenced early! *Ave Maria*—"

He recited some prayers which I did not hear.

"We will go to Venice!" I said to him when he rose.

"I have then found a man!" he cried, his face lighting up.

I conducted him home, giving him my arm; he grasped my hand at the door of the Quinze-Vingts, at the moment when some of the guests at the wedding were returning and making a noise sufficient to waken the dead.

"Shall we set out to-morrow?" said the old man.

"As soon as we have a little money."

"But we can go on foot, I will ask alms.—I am robust, and one is young when one sees gold before him."

Facino Cane died during the winter, after having languished for two months. The poor man had a catarrh.

Paris, March, 1836.

A MAN OF BUSINESS

.

TO MONSIEUR LE BARON JAMES DE ROTHSCHILD,

CONSUL-GENERAL OF AUSTRIA AT PARIS, BANKER

(287)

.

published 1890 by

With this word, the narrator obtained the most profound silence.

"'Monsieur le Comte,' said Cérizet, 'I am sent by one Monsieur Charles Claparon, formerly a banker.'

"'Ah! what does he want with me, the poor devil?—'

"'Well, he has become your creditor for a sum of three thousand two hundred francs seventy-five centimes, in capital, interest, and costs—'

"'The Coutelier claim,' said Maxime, who knew all about his affairs as a pilot knows his coasts.

Lorette is a decent word invented to express the
state of a young girl or the young girl of a state
difficult to indicate, and which, in its modesty, the
French Academy has neglected to define, in consideration of the age of its forty members. When a
new name is applicable to a social case which cannot be otherwise expressed without periphrase, the
fortune of that word is made. Thus *la lorette* has
passed into all classes of society, even into those in
which a lorette herself will never pass. The word
was only made in 1840, doubtless owing to the
accumulation of these nests of swallows around the
church dedicated to Notre-Dame de Lorette. This
is only written for the etymologists. These gentlemen would not be so much embarrassed if the
writers of the Middle Ages had taken the pains to
describe manners and customs, as we do in these
times of analysis and of description. Mademoiselle
Turquet, or Malaga, for she is much better known
under her nom de guerre—see *The Pretended Mistress*
—is one of the first parishioners of this charming
church. This joyful and spirituelle young woman,
possessing as her fortune only her beauty, furnished,

19 (289)

at the moment of which this history relates, the
happiness of a notary who had in his notaress a
wife a trifle too devout, a trifle too stiff, a trifle too
dry to find happiness at home. Now, on an evening
of the Carnival, Maître Cardot had regaled, at
Mademoiselle Turquet's, Desroches the advocate,
Bixiou the caricaturist, Lousteau the feuilletonist,
and Nathan, whose illustrious names in LA COMÉDIE
HUMAINE render superfluous any kind of portrait.
The young La Palférine, notwithstanding his title
of *comte de vieille roche,* rock, alas! without any
vein of metal in it, had honored with his presence
the illegitimate domicile of the notary. If one does
not dine in the house of a lorette in order to eat
there the patriarchal beef, the meagre chicken of
the conjugal table and the family salad, neither is
one expected to hold there the hypocritical discourses
which take place in a salon furnished by virtuous
female bourgeoises. Ah! when will good manners
be attractive? when will the women of the fashionable world show a little less of their shoulders and a
little more of good humor or of wit? Marguerite
Turquet, the Aspasia of the Cirque-Olympique, is
one of those fresh and lively natures to whom everything is forgiven because of their candor in the fault
and their spirit in the repentance, to whom you say,
as did Cardot, clever enough, although a notary, to
say to her: "Cheat me cleverly!" Do not believe,
however, in any enormity. Desroches and Cardot
were two too good fellows and too old in the trade not
to be on a level with Bixiou, Lousteau, Nathan and

the young count. And these gentlemen, having often had recourse to the two officers of the law, knew them too intimately to, in lorette phrase, "*make them pose.*" The conversation, perfumed by the fragrance of seven cigars, fantastic at first as a goat at liberty, concentrated finally on that strategy which creates at Paris the incessant battle waged between the creditors and the debtors. Now, if you will give yourself the trouble to remember the life and the antecedents of the guests, you will recognize that it would have been difficult to have found in Paris persons better instructed in this matter, — some *emeritus*, the others artists, they resembled magistrates joking with the accused. A series of designs sketched by Bixiou on Clichy had been the cause of the direction which the discourse had taken. It was midnight. These personages, variously grouped in the salon around the table and before the fire, were discoursing in turns that not only are comprehensible and possible only in Paris, but which, still more, are only made and can only be understood in the zone described by the Faubourg Montmartre and by the Rue de la Chaussée-d'Antin, between the heights of the Rue de Navarin and the line of the boulevards.

In ten minutes, the profound reflections, the great and the little moral, all the quibbles, were exhausted on this subject, already exhausted about 1500 by Rabelais. It was not of small merit to renounce this display of fireworks terminated by this last squib contributed by Malaga:

"All this turns to the profit of the bootmaker," said she. "I have left a milliner who failed me in two hats. She came raging twenty-seven times to demand of me twenty francs. She did not know that we never have twenty francs. One has a thousand francs, one sends to one's notary for five hundred francs; but twenty francs, I have never had them. My cook or my femme de chambre have perhaps twenty francs between them. For myself, I have only credit, and I should lose that in borrowing twenty francs. If I should ask for twenty francs, nothing would any longer distinguish me from my *confrères* who promenade along the boulevard."

"Has the milliner been paid?" said La Palférine.

"Ah, there! are you getting stupid, you there?" she said to La Palférine, winking at him; "she came this morning for the twenty-seventh time; that is why I tell you about it."

"What did you do?" said Desroches.

"I took pity on her, and—I ordered of her the little hat which I have ended by inventing in order to get away from commonplace style. If Mademoiselle Amanda succeeds, she will ask nothing more of me; her fortune is made."

"That which I have seen of the finest in this species of contest," said Maitre Desroches, "paints, it seems to me, Paris, for those who practice it, much better than all the pictures which they are forever painting of a fantastic Paris. You think yourselves pretty strong, you others," he said, looking at Nathan and Lousteau, Bixiou and La

Palférine; "but the king in this respect is a certain
count who, at the present time, is occupying himself
with coming to an end, and who, in his time, has
passed for the most skilful, the most adroit, the most
foxy, the most instructed, the most daring, the most
subtle, the firmest, the most foreseeing of all the
corsairs in yellow gloves, in cabriolets, with beautiful manners, who have navigated, navigate and will
navigate on the stormy sea of Paris. Without faith
or law, his private politics have been directed by the
principles which direct those of the English cabinet.
Up to the time of his marriage, his life was a continual warfare like that of—Lousteau," he said.
"I have been and I am still his advocate."

"And the first letter of his name is Maxime de
Trailles," said La Palférine.

"He has, moreover, always paid, has never
wronged anyone," resumed Desroches; "but, as
our friend Bixiou had just remarked, to pay in
March that which you do not wish to pay till Octo-
ber is an attack on personal liberty. By virtue of
an article of his particular code, Maxime considered
as a swindling the means which one of his creditors
employed to be paid immediately. For a long time
the bill of exchange had been comprehended by him
in all its consequences, immediate and mediate. A
young man spoke of the bill of exchange in my
place before him as: '*The Asses' Bridge!*' 'No,'
said he, 'it is The Bridge of Sighs; one never
returns.' Thus his science in matters of commercial
jurisprudence was so complete that a procurator

could have taught him nothing. You know that at that time he possessed nothing; his carriage, his horses were hired; he lived with his valet de chambre, for whom, it is said, he will always be a great man, even after the marriage which he will make! A member of three clubs, he dined at one of them when he had no invitation out. Generally, he used his domicile so little—"

"He said to me, to me," cried La Palférine, interrupting Desroches: "'my only fatuity is to pretend that I live in the Rue Pigalle.'"

"There is one of the two combatants," resumed Desroches; "now, then, here is the other. You have heard more or less spoken of a certain Claparon."

"He wears his hair in this way," cried Bixiou, making his hair stand on end.

And, gifted with the same talent that Chopin, the pianist, possessed in so high a degree, that of counterfeiting people, he represented the personage on the instant with a frightful truthfulness.

"He rolls his head this way in speaking; he has been a traveling salesman, he has tried all trades—"

"Well, he was born for traveling, for he is, at this moment while I am talking to you, on his way to America," said Desroches. "There is no other chance for him but that, for he will probably be condemned by contumacy for fraudulent bankruptcy at the coming Session."

"A man overboard," cried Malaga.

"This Claparon," resumed Desroches, "was during six or seven years the screen, the man of straw, the scapegoat, of two of our friends, Du Tillet and Nucingen; but, in 1829, his part was so well known that—"

"Our friends dropped him," said Bixiou.

"In short, they abandoned him to his destiny; and," resumed Desroches, "he rolled in the mud. In 1833, he associated himself to carry on business with a man named Cérizet—"

"What! he who in the matter of stock companies got up one with such a pretty combination that the sixth chamber knocked him over with two years in prison?" asked the lorette.

"The same," replied Desroches. "Under the Restoration, the trade of this Cérizet consisted, from 1823 to 1827, in signing intrepidly articles pursued inveterately by the public minister, and in going to prison. A man rendered himself illustrious cheaply at that time. The Liberal Party called its department champion THE COURAGEOUS CERIZET. This zeal was recompensed about 1828 by *the general interest.* The general interest is a species of civic crown awarded by the newspapers. Cérizet wished to discount the general interest; he came to Paris, where, under the patronage of the bankers of the Left, he made his debut by a business agency, combined with banking operations, with funds loaned by a man who had banished himself, a player too skilful, whose funds, in July, 1830, had foundered in company with the Ship of State—"

"Eh! it is that which we have surnamed the Method of the cards!—" cried Bixiou.

"Do not speak evil of that poor fellow," cried Malaga. "D'Estourny was a good boy!"

"You can understand the rôle which a ruined man might be expected to play in 1830 who was known, politically speaking, as the courageous Cérizet! He was sent into a very pretty sub-prefecture," resumed Desroches. "Unfortunately for Cérizet, authority has not as much ingenuity as have the parties, who, during the fight, make projectiles of everything. Cérizet was obliged to send in his resignation after three months of service. Had he not taken it into his head to wish to be popular! As he had not yet done anything to lose his title of nobility—the courageous Cérizet!—the government proposed to him, as an indemnity, to become director of an opposition journal which should be ministerial *in petto*. Thus it was the government who perverted this fine character. Cérizet, finding himself a little too much in his directorship like a bird on a rotten bough, launched himself into that pretty stock-company where he unluckily, as you have just said, caught two years in prison,—but in which the sharpest of them entrapped the public."

"We know the sharpest of them," said Bixiou; "do not slander that poor fellow, he is trapped! Couture let his cash be caught there; who would ever have thought it!"

"Cérizet is, moreover, an ignoble man, and one whom the evils of vulgar debauch have disfigured,"

resumed Desroches. "Let us return to the promised
duel! Then, never did two traders of the worst
species, of the worst manners, more ignoble in
aspect, associate themselves together to carry on a
dirtier business. For funds to provide for the running expenses, they counted on that species of slang
which is given by the knowledge of Paris, the
hardihood which is given by poverty, the trickery
which is given by the habits of business, the
science which is given by the knowledge of Parisian fortunes, of their origin, of their relations, the
acquaintances and intrinsic values of each one.
This association of two *carotteurs*, excuse the word,
the only one which can, in the slang of the Bourse,
describe them to you, was of short duration. Like
two famished dogs, they fought over each bit of car-
rion. The first speculations of the house of Cérizet
and Claparon were, however, sufficiently well con-
trived. These two rogues associated themselves
with the Barbets, the Chaboisseaus, the Samanons
and other usurers from whom they bought doubtful claims. The Claparon agency was then situated in a little entresol of the Rue Chabannais,
composed of five rooms, and the rent of which did
not amount to more than seven hundred francs.
Each partner slept in a little chamber which,
through prudence, was kept so carefully closed that
my master clerk was never able to penetrate them.
The offices consisted of an antechamber, a salon,
and a cabinet of which the furniture would not have
brought three hundred francs at the auctioneers'.

You know Paris well enough to be able to see the
arrangement of the two offices: haircloth chairs,
a table with a green cloth, a mean clock between
two candlesticks under glass which bored to look
at, before a little mirror with a gilded frame,
on a chimney-piece the fire-brands in which
were, according to my master clerk, two years old!
As to the cabinet, you can guess it: many paste-
board boxes and little business!—a common portfolio
for each partner; then in the middle the cylin-
drical desk empty as the cash-box! two working
chairs on each side of a chimney-piece with a coal
fire. On the floor was laid a carpet, second-hand,
like the credits. In short, it was that stuff
mahogany which is sold in our offices during
fifty years from predecessor to successor. You are
now acquainted with each of the two adversaries.
Well, in the first three months of their association,
which was liquidated by blows of the fist at the end
of seven months, Cérizet and Claparon bought two
thousand francs' worth of paper signed Maxime—
since Maxime there is—and stuffed the two portfol-
ios full—judgment, appeal, decree, execution, report,
—in short, a credit of three thousand two hundred
francs and some centimes which they had for five
hundred francs by a conveyance under private signature, with special power of attorney to act in
order to avoid the costs.—At that time, Maxime,
already ripe, had one of those caprices peculiar to
men of fifty—"

"Antonia!" cried La Palférine, "that Antonia

whose fortune had been made by a letter in which I reclaimed a tooth brush from her!"

"Her real name is Chocardelle," said Malaga, whom this pretentious name vexed.

"That's the one," resumed Desroches.

"Maxime had committed this fault only this once in all his life; but, what would you have, vice is not perfect!" said Bixiou.

"Maxime was still ignorant of the life which one leads with a little girl of eighteen who wishes to throw herself, head first, out of her honest garret to fall into a sumptuous equipage," resumed Desroches, "and statesmen should know everything. At this epoch, De Marsay had just employed his friend, our friend, in the high comedy of politics. A man of great conquests, Maxime had known only titled women; and, at fifty, he certainly had the right to bite into a little fruit said to be wild, like a hunter who stops in a peasant's field under an apple tree. The count found for Mademoiselle Chocardelle a little literary establishment sufficiently elegant, a great opportunity, as always—"

"Bah! she did not stay there six months," said Nathan; "she was too handsome to keep a literary establishment."

"Are you the father of her child?—" said the lorette to Nathan.

"One morning," resumed Desroches, "Cérizet, who, since the purchase of Maxime's notes, had arrived by degrees at the style of the first clerk of a bailiff, was introduced, after seven unavailing

attempts, into the count's apartments. Suzon, the
old valet de chambre, though expert, had come to
take Cérizet for a solicitor who arrived to propose a
thousand écus to Maxime if he would obtain for a
young woman a shop for stamped paper. Suzon,
without any suspicion of this little scamp, a real
gamin of Paris with prudence drubbed into him by
his condemnation by the correctional police, persuaded his master to receive him. Do you see this
man of business, with an uneasy glance, thin hair,
a bald forehead, with a little dry black coat, in
muddy boots—"

"What an image of Credit!" cried Lousteau.

"—Before the count," resumed Desroches, "the
image of the Debt insolent, in a dressing-gown of
white flannel, in slippers embroidered by some marchioness, in pantaloons of beautiful white wool
having on his black dyed hair a magnificent cap,
displaying a dazzling shirt front, and playing with
the tassels of his girdle?—"

"It is a Genre painting," said Nathan, "for those
who know the pretty little waiting-room in which
Maxime breakfasted, full of pictures of great value,
hung with silk, in which one walked on a Smyrna
carpet, whilst admiring cabinets full of curiosities,
of rarities that would fill with envy a king of
Saxony—"

"That is the scene," said Desroches.

With this word, the narrator obtained the most
profound silence.

"'Monsieur le Comte,' said Cérizet, 'I am sent

by one Monsieur Charles Claparon, formerly a banker.'

" 'Ah! what does he want with me, the poor devil?—'

" 'Well, he has become your creditor for a sum of three thousand two hundred francs seventy-five centimes, in capital, interest, and costs—'

" 'The Coutelier claim,' said Maxime, who knew all about his affairs as a pilot knows his coasts.

" 'Yes, Monsieur le Comte,' replied Cérizet bowing. 'I have come to know what are your intentions?'

" 'I shall not settle this obligation until it pleases me,' replied Maxime, ringing for Suzon. 'Claparon is very daring to buy a credit on me without consulting me! I am vexed on his account, he who for so long had so well conducted himself as a *man of straw* for my friends. I said of him 'Truly, he must be an imbecile to serve for so little gain, and with so much fidelity, men who are stuffed with millions.' Well, he gives me here a proof of his stupidity.— Yes, men merit their fate! One is fitted with a crown or a bullet! one is millionaire or porter, and everything is just. What would you have, my dear fellow! I—I am not a king, I maintain my principles. I am without pity for those who make costs for me or who do not know their business of creditors.—Suzon, my tea!—You see, monsieur?' he said to the valet de chambre. 'Well, you have let yourself be taken in, you poor old thing. Monsieur is a creditor; you should have recognized it by his boots.

Neither my friends, nor the strangers who have
need of me, nor my enemies, come to see me on foot.
—My dear Monsieur Cérizet, you understand? You
will not wipe your boots on my carpet any more,'
said he, looking at the mud which whitened the
soles of his adversary. 'You will make my compliments to this poor boniface of a Claparon, for I
will put this affair in the Z.'

"All this was said in a tone of benevolence that
would have given the colic to a virtuous bourgeois.

"'You are wrong, Monsieur le Comte,' replied
Cérizet, taking a little peremptory tone; 'we will
be paid in full and in a manner which may be somewhat inconvenient to you. Therefore I have come
to see you amicably, as should be done by well-
bred people.'

"'Ah! you understand it that way?—' answered
Maxime, whom this last pretension of Cérizet
angered.

"In this insolence there was some of Talleyrand's
spirit, if you see clearly the contrast between the
two costumes and the two men. Maxime knit his
brows and fastened his looks upon the Cérizet,
who not only sustained this jet of cold rage but,
still more, who responded to it by that glacial
malice which distils from the fixed eyes of a cat.

"'Very well, monsieur, go—'

"'Very well; adieu, Monsieur le Comte. Before
the end of six months, we shall be even with each
other.'

"'If you can *steal* from me the amount of your

credit, which I recognize is legitimate, I shall be
obliged to you, Monsieur,' replied Maxime; 'you
will have taught me some new precaution to take. —
I am truly your servant.'

" 'Monsieur le Comte,' said Cérizet, 'it is I who
am yours.'

"This was neat, full of strength and of security
on both sides. Two tigers who regard each other
before fighting, over some prey, would not be finer
nor more wily than were these two natures as
crafty one as the other, one in his impertinent
elegance, the other in his filthy harness. —Which
will you bet on?—" said Desroches, who looked
at his audience surprised to find themselves so
deeply interested.

"Well, that is one, that is a story!—" said Malaga. "Oh! go on, I beg you, my dear; that goes to
my heart."

"Between two *dogs* of that strength, nothing
common should have happened," said La Palférine.

"Bah! I will bet my furniture-maker's bill, and
he worries me to death, that the little toad downed
Maxime," cried Malaga.

"I will bet on Maxime," said Cardot; "no one
ever took him napping."

Desroches made a pause while emptying a little
glass which was presented to him by the lorette.

"The reading-room of Mademoiselle Chocardelle,"
he resumed, "was situated in the Rue Coquenard,
two steps from the Rue Pigalle, in which Maxime lived. The aforesaid Demoiselle Chocardelle

occupied a little apartment opening on a garden and
separated from her shop by a large dark place in
which she kept her books.   Antonia had this establishment kept by her aunt—"

"She already had her aunt?—" cried Malaga.
"The devil! Maxime managed things well."

"It was, alas! a real aunt," resumed Desroches,
"whose name was—wait a moment—"

"Ida Bonamy—," said Bixiou.

"Thus, Antonia relieved of a great deal of trouble
by her aunt, rose late, went to bed late, and only
appeared at her counter between two and four
o'clock," resumed Desroches.   "From the very
first, her presence sufficed to bring customers to her
reading-room; thither came several old gentlemen of
the quarter, among others a former coach-maker
named Croizeau.   After having seen this miracle
of feminine beauty through a window, the former
coach-maker concluded to read the newspapers
every day in this salon, an example which was followed by a former custom-house officer, named
Denisart, a man with a decoration, in whom the
Croizeau concluded to see a rival and to whom later
he said: 'Môsieur, *you have certainly given me
a practical lesson.*"

"This word should enable you to perceive the
personage.   The Sieur Croizeau belonged to that
species of little old men who, since Henry Monnier, have been known as the species Coquerel, so
well has he rendered the little voice, the little manners, the little queue, the little powder in the hair,

the little step, the little movements of the head, the little dry tone, in his character of Coquerel of *La Famille Improvisée.* This Croizeau said: 'Here, fair lady!' in passing his two sous to Antonia with a pretentious gesture. Madame Ida Bonamy, aunt of Mademoiselle Chocardelle, soon learned through the cook that the former coach-maker, a man of excessive ugliness, was taxed at forty thousand francs income in the quarter where he lived, Rue de Buffault. A week after the installation of the handsome circulator of romances, he was delivered of this pun:

"'You lend me *livres*, but I return you many francs—'

"Some days later he assumed a knowing little air to say:

"'I know that you are engaged, but my day will come: I am a widower.'

"Croizeau always appeared with beautiful linen, with a blue-bottle colored coat, a waistcoat in that silk known as *pou-de-soie*, black pantaloons, double-soled shoes tied with ribbons of black silk and creaking like those of an abbé. He carried always in his hand his fourteen-franc silk hat.

"'I am old and without children,' he said to the young person some days after the visit of Cérizet to Maxime. 'I have a horror of my collateral heirs. They are all peasants, made to cultivate the earth! Just imagine that I came from my village with six francs, and that I made my fortune here. I am not proud—. A pretty woman is my equal. Would it

20

not be better to be Madame Croizeau for some time
than to be the servant of a count during a year?—
You will be left, some day or other. And you
will then think of me. Your servant, fair lady!'

"All this was managed very quietly. The very
slightest gallantries are uttered secretly. No one
in the world knew that this spruce little old man
loved Antonia, for the prudent countenance of this
lover in the reading-room would have conveyed
nothing to a rival. Croizeau was suspicious for a
couple of months of the retired director of customs.
But towards the middle of the third month he had
grounds for recognizing the very slight foundations
of the suspicions. Croizeau exercised his ingenuity in keeping near to Denisart when in his company, then, taking his opportunity, he said to him:
  "'It is fine weather, Môsieur:—'

"To which the former functionary replied:

  "'The weather of Austerlitz, Monsieur: I was
there—, I was even wounded there; my cross is
because of my conduct on that fine day—'

"And, insensibly, from one thing to another,
step by step, through little confidences, an intimacy was developed between these two relics
of the Empire. The little Croizeau was connected with the Empire by his intimacy with the
sisters of Napoléon,—he had been their carriage-
maker, and he had often tormented them by his bills.
He therefore gave himself out as *having had relations
with the imperial family*. Maxime, informed by
Antonia of the propositions offered by the *agreeable*

old man, for such was the title given by the
aunt to the *rentier*, wished to see him. The declaration of war made by Cérizet had had the effect of
making this fine gentleman in yellow gloves study
his position on his chess-board and observe the least
important pieces. Now, apropos of this agreeable
old gentleman, he received the understanding that
stroke of the clock which announces to you a misfortune. One evening, Maxime placed himself in the
second dusky apartment, around which were arranged the shelves of the library. After having
examined by an opening between two green curtains
the seven or eight habitués of the salon, he gauged
with a look the soul of the little carriage-maker; he
appraised his passion, and was very well satisfied
to know that, at the moment when his fancy should
be over, a sufficiently sumptuous future would open
at command its varnished portals to Antonia.

"'And that one,' he said, indicating the fine, large
old man decorated with the Legion of Honor; 'who
is he?'

"'A former director of customs.'

"'He has a disquieting appearance!' said Maxime,
admiring the style of the Sieur Denisart.

"In fact, this old soldier held himself straight as
a steeple; his head attracted attention by its pow-
dered and pomaded arrangement, almost similar to
that of the *postillons* of a masked ball. Under this
species of felt, modeled on an oblong head was
presented an old countenance, administrative and
military both at once, marked by a proud air, similar

enough to that which caricature has lent to the
Constitutionnel. This former administrator, of an
age, of a quality, of a curve of the back which permitted him to read nothing without glasses, maintained his respectable abdomen with all the pride
of an old man with a mistress, and wore in his ears
gold rings which recalled those of the old General
Montcornet, the habitué of the Vaudeville. Denisart
held blue in favor,—his pantaloons and his old
frock-coat, very full, were of blue cloth.

"'How long has that old fellow been coming
here?' asked Maxime, to whom the glasses appeared
to have a suspicious aspect.

"'Oh! from the commencement,' replied Antonia. 'It is now nearly two months—'

"'Good; Cérizet came only about a month ago,'
said Maxime to himself.—'Make him speak,' he
said in Antonia's ear; 'I wish to hear his voice.'

"'Bah!' she replied, 'that would be difficult; he
never says anything to me.'

"'Why does he come, then?—' asked Maxime.

"'For a queer enough reason,' replied the beautiful Antonia. 'In the first place, he has a passion,
notwithstanding his sixty-nine years; but, because
of his sixty-nine years, he is regulated like a clock-
dial. This good man there goes to dine with his
passion, Rue de la Victoire, at five o'clock every
day.—There is an unlucky woman! He leaves her
house at six o'clock, comes to read the newspapers
for four hours, and returns there at ten o'clock.
The papa Croizeau says he is acquainted with the

motives of Monsieur's conduct; he approves them; and, in his place, he would act the same way. Thus, I know my future! If ever I become Madame Croizeau, from six to ten o'clock I shall be free.'

"Maxime consulted the *Almanach des 25,000 adresses;* he found there this reassuring line:

"'DENISART *, former director of customs, Rue de la Victoire.

"There was no further uneasiness. By degrees, there were established between Monsieur Denisart and the Sieur Croizeau certain confidences. Nothing unites men more than a certain conformity of views respecting women. Papa Croizeau dined in the house of her whom he called *La Belle de Monsieur Denisart.* Here I should insert a sufficiently important observation. The reading-room had been purchased by the count for a sum, half cash down and half in notes signed by the aforesaid Demoiselle Chocardelle. Rabelais' *quart d'heure* arrived, the count found himself without funds. Whereupon, the first of the three notes of a thousand francs was paid in full by the agreeable coach-maker, whom the old scoundrel of a Denisart counseled to secure his loan by establishing for himself certain advantages of a privileged creditor upon the reading-room.

"'I,' said Denisart, 'I have seen some beauties among the fair sex!—Thus, in every case, even when I have no longer my head about me, I always take my precautions with women. This

creature for whom I am so crazy, well, she is not in
her own furniture; she is in mine. The lease of the
apartment is in my name—'

"You know Maxime; he thought that the coach-
maker was very young! The Croizeau could pay
the three thousand francs without having anything
to show for it for a long time, for Maxime found
himself more enamored than ever of Antonia—"

"I can well believe it," said La Palférine; "she
is the *Belle Imperia* of the Middle Ages."

"A woman who has a rough skin!" cried the lorette, "and so rough that she ruins herself in bran
baths."

"Croizeau spoke with a coach-maker's admiration
of the sumptuous furnishing which the amorous
Denisart had given for a setting-off to his Belle; he
described it with a satanic complacency to the ambitious Antonia," resumed Desroches. "There
were coffers of ebony inlaid with mother-of-pearl
and gold wire, Belgian carpets, a mediæval bed of
the value of a thousand écus, a clock by Boulle; then,
in the dining-room, candelabra at the four corners,
curtains of China silk on which Chinese patience
had painted birds, and portières suspended from
cross-pieces much more valuable than the divided
portières.

"'See what you should have, fair lady—, and
what I should be willing to offer you—,' said he in
conclusion. 'I know very well that you would love
me tolerably well; but, at my age, one is reasonable. You may judge how much I love you, since

I have lent you a thousand francs. I can admit it to you: in all my life nor in my days have I ever lent so much!'

"And he tendered the two sous of his sitting with the importance which a scientist attaches to a demonstration.

"That evening, Antonia said to the count, at the Variétés:

" 'It is pretty stupid all the same, a reading-room. I don't feel any inclination for that sort of a business; I don't see any chance of fortune in that. That is something for a widow who just wishes to keep life together, or for a young woman who is atrociously ugly and who thinks she may catch a man by dressing a little.'

" 'That is what you asked of me,' replied the count.

"At this moment, Nucingen, whom, from the evening before, the king of the Lions, for the yellow gloves had then become lions, had won a thousand écus, came in to give them to him, and seeing the astonishment of Maxime, he said to him:

" 'I haf receivet a brotest at the reguest of dat tevil of a Glabaron—'

" 'Ah! that's their method!' cried Maxime; 'they are not very clever, that lot—'

" 'All de zame,' replied the banker, 'bay dem, for dey can attress demselves to others dan myself and but you in de wrong—. I dake for widness dis preddy voman dat I have baid you dis morning, even bevore de brotest—'

"Queen of the spring-board," said La Palférine, smiling. "You will lose—"

"It has long happened," resumed Desroches, "that, in a similar case, but where the too honest debtor, frightened at having to make an affirmation in the courts of justice, did not wish to pay Maxime, we had roughly dragged in the protesting creditor by opposing protests *en masse*, so as to absorb the whole amount in expenses of contribution—"

"What's all that?"—cried Malaga. "Here are a lot of words which sound to me like gibberish. Since you have found the sturgeon excellent, pay me the value of the sauce in lessons in trickery."

"Well," said Desroches, "the amount which one of your creditors covers with a protest in the hands of one of your debtors may become the object of a similar protest on the part of all your other creditors. What, then, does the court, of whom all the creditors demand the authorization to be paid?—It divides legally the sum seized among them all. This division, made under the eye of justice, is called a contribution. If you owe ten thousand francs, and if your creditors seize by protest a thousand francs, they have each so much per cent of their claim, by means of a repartition *au marc le franc*, according to the terms of the Palais, that is to say, in a distribution pro rata of their amounts; but they only receive this by means of a legal paper called an *Extrait du Bordereau de Collocation*, which is delivered by the clerk of the court. You can imagine this work accomplished by a judge and prepared by the advocates? it involves a great deal of stamped paper covered with empty and scattered lines, in which the figures are lost in columns of entire emptiness. The first thing to do is to deduct the cost. Now, the cost being the same for a sum of a thousand francs seized and for a sum of a million, it is not difficult to eat up a thousand écus, for instance, in costs, especially if one succeeds in stirring up contestants."

"An advocate always succeeds," said Cardot; "how many times has one of yours asked me: 'How much is there to get?'"

"They succeed above all," resumed Desroches, "when the debtor provokes you to eat up the sum in costs. Thus the count's creditors got nothing; they had only their running about to the advocates and their efforts. In order to be paid by a debtor as clever as the count, a creditor would be obliged to put himself in a legal situation excessively difficult to establish,—he would have to be at once his debtor and his creditor, for then one has the right, according to the law, to bring about the confusion—"

"Of the debtor?" said the lorette, who lent an attentive ear to this discourse.

"No, of the two qualities of creditor and debtor, and pay one's self by his hands," resumed Desroches. "The innocence of Claparon, who had only invented protests, had therefore the effect of tranquillizing the count. In taking Antonia home from the Variétés, he adopted the more readily the

idea of selling the reading-room in order to pay off
the last two thousand francs of the price, for he
feared the ridicule of being known as the silent
partner in such an enterprise. He therefore accepted
the plan of Antonia, who wished to enter the upper
sphere of her profession, to have a magnificent
apartment, a femme de chambre, a carriage, and to
enter the lists with our beautiful amphitryon, for
example—"

"She is not well enough made for that," cried the
illustrious beauty of the Cirque; "but she well
rinsed out the little d'Esgrignon all the same!"

"Ten days later, the little Croizeau, perched upon
his dignity, used something like this language to the
beautiful Antonia," resumed Desroches:

"'My child, your literary shop is a hole, you are
becoming yellow in it, the gas will ruin your eyes;
you should get out of it, and here, now! let us profit
by the occasion. I have found for you a young
woman who asks nothing better than to purchase
your reading-room. She is a little woman, quite
ruined, who has nothing left but to throw herself in
the river; but she has four thousand francs in cash,
and it would be better to make use of them to nour-
ish and bring up two children—'

"'Well, you are very amiable, Papa Croizeau'"
said Antonia.

"'Oh! I shall be much more amiable presently,'
replied the old coach-maker. 'Just imagine, that
that poor Monsieur Denisart has been so upset that it
has given him the jaundice—. Yes, that has

affected his liver, as is always the case with sensitive old men. He was wrong to be so sensitive. I
said to him: 'Be passionate if you like, good!
but sensitive,—stop there! one kills one's self—.'
I did not expect it, really, such an upsetting in a
man sufficiently strong, sufficiently wise to absent
himself while he was digesting from the house
of —'

"'But who is it?'—asked Mademoiselle Chocardelle.

"'That little creature with whom I dined left him
in the lurch, clean—. Yes, she forsook him without
notifying him in any other way than by a letter
without any spelling in it.'

"'See what it is, Papa Croizeau, to bore the
women!—'

"'It is a lesson! fair lady,' replied the affection-
ate Croizeau. '*Meanwhile*, I have never seen a man
in such a state of despair,' said he. 'Our friend
Denisart can no longer tell his right hand from his
left; he no longer wishes to see that which he calls
the theatre of his happiness—. He has so completely lost his senses, that he proposed to me to
buy for four thousand francs all the furniture of
Hortense—. Her name is Hortense!'

"'A pretty name,' said Antonia.

"'Yes, it was that of the step-daughter of Napoléon. I furnished her her equipages, as you know.'

"'Well, come, I will see,' said the clever Antonia;
'begin by sending me your young woman—'

"Antonia hastened to see the furniture, returned

fascinated, and captivated Maxime by an enthusiasm
worthy of an antiquary.   That very evening the
count consented to the sale of the reading-room.
The establishment, you understand, was in the
name of Mademoiselle Chocardelle.   Maxime laughed
at the little Croizeau, who found him a pur-
chaser.   The firm of Maxime and Chocardelle lost
two thousand francs, it is true, but what was this loss
in presence of four beautiful notes of a thousand
francs each?—as the count said to me:

"'Four thousand francs cash in hand!—there are
moments when one would sign eight thousand francs
of notes to have them!'

"The count went to see the furniture himself, on
the third day, having the four thousand francs about
him.   The sale had been consummated, thanks to
the diligence of the little Croizeau, who pushed at
the wheel; he had *enclaudé* the widow, as he said.
Concerning himself but little with this agreeable
old gentleman, who was going to lose a thousand
francs, Maxime wished to have all the furniture
carried immediately to an apartment taken in the
name of Madame Ida Bonamy, Rue Tronchet, in a
new house.   Thus he had furnished himself in advance with several large furniture vans.   Maxime,
enamored anew of the beauty of the furniture, which,
for an upholsterer, would have been worth six thous-
and francs, found the unhappy old man, yellow
with his jaundice, at the corner of the fire, his head
enveloped in two handkerchiefs and a cotton night-
cap over all, muffled up like a chandelier; collapsed,

not able to speak, in short, so dilapidated that the count was forced to negotiate with the valet de chambre. After having paid over the four thousand francs to the valet de chambre, who carried them to his master so that he might give a receipt for them, Maxime was about to order his people to bring up the furniture vans; but he heard at that moment a voice which sounded in his ears like a rattle, and which cried to him:

"'It is unnecessary, Monsieur le Comte; we are even; I have six hundred and thirty francs and fifteen centimes to hand over to you!'

"And he was quite aghast to see Cérizet issue from his wrappings, like a butterfly from his larva, offering to him his cursed bundle of papers, and adding:

"'In my misfortune I learned to play comedy, and I can equal Bouffé in the old men.'

"'I am in the forest of Bondy!' cried Maxime.

"'No, Monsieur le Comte, you are in the house of Mademoiselle Hortense, the friend of the old Lord Dudley, who concealed her from everybody; but she has the bad taste to love your servant.'

"'If ever,' said the count to me, 'I had a desire to kill a man, it was at that moment; but what would you have! Hortense showed me her pretty head; it was necessary to laugh, and to preserve my superiority. I said to him, throwing him the six hundred francs: 'This is for the lady.'

"'That is just like Maxime!' cried La Palférine.

A Robida.

Gazonal gave his hand to the actress down to the closed carriage which was waiting for her, and he pressed it so tenderly that Jennie Cadine replied, shaking her fingers:

"Eh, I have no spare ones!"

When they were in the carriage, Gazonal undertook to take Bixiou by the waist, exclaiming

"She has bitten!— You are a fine scoundrel—"

TO MONSIEUR LE COMTE JULES DE CASTELLANE

*

Léon de Lora, our celebrated landscape painter, is a member of one of the most noble families of Roussillon, Spanish in origin, and which, admirable as it is by the antiquity of the race, has for the last hundred years been devoted to the proverbial poverty of the Hidalgoes. Arrived light-footed in Paris from the department of the Pyrénées-Orientales, with the sum of eleven francs for his entire viaticum, he had there, in some measure, forgotten the sorrows of his childhood and of his family in the midst of the miseries which are never lacking to the struggling students of painting, whose entire fortune consists in an intrepid vocation. Then the cares of glory and those of success furnished additional causes for forgetfulness.

If you have followed the sinuous and capricious course of these Studies, perhaps you will remember Mistigris, pupil of Schinner, one of the heroes of *A Start in Life*—SCENES OF PRIVATE LIFE—and his appearances in some other Scenes. In 1845, the landscape painter, emulous of the Hobbemas, of the Ruysdaels, of the Lorrains, no longer resembles the denuded and brisk *rapin* whom you have seen above. An illustrious man, he now possesses a charming house in the Rue de Berlin, not far from the Hôtel de *Brambourg,* in which dwells his friend Bridau, and near the house of Schinner, his first master.   He is a member of the Institute and an officer of the Legion of Honor; he is thirty-nine, he has an income of twenty thousand francs, his canvases are purchased at their weight in gold, and, that which seems to him more extraordinary than to be invited some- times to the Court balls, his name, thrown so often for the last sixteen years by the press to the winds of all Europe, has finally penetrated into the valley of the Pyrénées-Orientales, where vegetate three veritable Loras, his eldest brother, his father and an old paternal aunt, Mademoiselle Urraca y Lora.

In the maternal line, there remained to the painter only a cousin, a nephew of his mother, of the age of fifty, the inhabitant of a little manufacturing city of the department.   This cousin was the first to remember Léon. In 1840, for the first time, Léon de Lora received a letter from Monsieur Sylvestre Palafox-Castel Gazonal, known simply as Gazonal, to which he replied that it was indeed he, that is to say, the son of the late Léonie Gazonal, wife of the Comte Fernand Didas y Lora.

The cousin, Sylvestre Gazonal, went in the fine season of 1841 to inform the illustrious unknown family of the Loras that the little Léon had not departed for the Rio de la Plata, as they believed; that he was not dead, as they believed, and that he was one of the finest geniuses of the French School, which they did not believe. The eldest son, Don Juan de Lora, said to his cousin Gazonal that he was the victim of some joker in Paris.

Now, the said Gazonal proposing to go to Paris in order to follow up a legal process which, through a contest, the prefect of the Pyrénées-Orientales had wrested from the ordinary jurisdiction of the province to carry it up to the Council of State, the provincial promised himself to clear up the matter and *to demand a reason* for his impertinence from the Parisian painter. It happened that Monsieur Gazonal, putting up in *a poor lodging* in the Rue Croix-des-Petits-Champs, was astonished to see the palace in the Rue de Berlin. When he learned that the master was traveling in Italy, he renounced for the moment his *demanding reason,* and doubted if his maternal relationship would be recognized by the celebrated man.

From 1843 to 1844 Gazonal followed his lawsuit. This contest, which related to a question of the course and of the height of the water, of the erection of a dam, in which the administration was interested, sustained by the dwellers on the banks of the river, menaced the very existence of the manufactory. In 1845, Gazonal considered this case as entirely lost, the secretary of the Maitre des Requêtes charged with making the report having confided to him that this report would be opposed to his contentions, and his advocate having confirmed it to him. Gazonal, though commandant in the National

Guard of his city and one of the most skilful manufacturers of his department, found so little in Paris,
he was so dismayed at the dearness of living and at
the least trifles, that he kept himself secluded in his
poor little hôtel. This Southerner, deprived of his
sun, execrated Paris, which he denominated a manufactory of rheumatisms. In counting up the
expenses of his lawsuit and of his sojourn, he promised himself that, when he returned, he would either
poison the prefect or he would make a cuckold of
him! In his moments of sadness he killed the prefect; in his moments of gayety, he contented himself with *minotaurising* him.

One morning, at the end of his déjeuner, fuming
and swearing, he took up furiously his newspaper.
These lines, which terminated an article, "Our
great landscape painter, Léon de Lora, who returned
from Italy a month ago, will exhibit several canvases
at the Salon; thus the exposition will be, as may
be seen, very brilliant,—" struck Gazonal as if that
voice which speaks to gamblers when they win had
sounded in his ear. With that promptness of action
which distinguishes the people of the South, Gazonal leaped from the hôtel into the street, from the
street into a cabriolet, and went to the Rue de Berlin, to see his cousin.

Léon de Lora sent word to his cousin Gazonal
that he invited him to déjeuner at the Café de *Paris*
for the next day, for he was at that moment occupied in such a manner that it would be impossible
for him to receive him. Gazonal, like a true man

of the South, related all his troubles to the valet de chambre.

The next morning, at ten o'clock, Gazonal, too well arrayed for the occasion—he had put on his blue-bottle coat with gilded buttons, a shirt with a jabot, a white vest and yellow gloves—waited for his amphitryon while walking up and down for an hour on the boulevard, after having learned from the *cafetier*—title of the café proprietors in the provinces—that these messieurs usually breakfasted between eleven o'clock and noon.

"About half-past eleven, two Parisians, like simple priests," he said, when he afterwards related his adventures to those of his locality, "and who had a general air of nothing at all, exclaimed on seeing me on the boulevard: 'Behold thy Gazonal!—'"

This speaker was Bixiou, with whom Léon de Lora had provided himself to mystify his cousin.

"'Do not disturb yourself, my dear cousin! I am yours,' cried the little Léon, clasping me in his arms," said Gazonal to his friends on his return. "The déjeuner was splendid. And I thought I saw double when I saw the number of gold pieces that it took to pay the bill. Those people must make their weight in gold, for my cousin gave thirty sols to the waiter, a day's wages."

During this monstrous breakfast, seeing that there were then consumed six dozen Ostende oysters, six cutlets à la Soubise, a chicken à la Marengo, a lobster mayonnaise, fresh peas, a croute aux champignons, washed down with three bottles of Bordeaux, three bottles of champagne, plus the black coffee, the liqueurs, without counting the horsd'œuvre, Gazonal was magnificent in his fury against Paris. The noble manufacturer complained of the length of the four-pound loaves, of the height of the houses, of the indifference of the passers-by for each other, of the cold and of the rain, of the dearness of the hackney-coaches, and all that so cleverly, that the two artists conceived a lively friendship for Gazonal and got him to describe his lawsuit.

"My suit," said he, using his r's thickly and accenting everything provincially, "is something very simple: they want my manufactory. I find here a beast of an advocate to whom I give twenty francs each time to keep his eye open, and I always find him asleep.—It is a snail which rolls in its carrriage and I go on foot. They trrick me shamefully; I do nothing but run from one to the other, and I see that I shall have to take a carrriage—. No one pays attention here but to the people who hide themselves in their carrriages!—On the other hand, the Council of State is a pile of drones who let their work be done by some little scamps who are bribed by our prrefect—. There is my case!—They want to get it, my manufactory; very well, they shall have it!—and they may come to terms with my workmen, of whom there are a hundred, and who will make them change their mind with a cudgel—"

"Come, cousin," said the landscapist, "how long hast thou been here?"

"Since two years!—Ah! this business of the prefect; he will pay dear for it; I will take his life and I will give mine at the Court of Assizes—"

"Who is the Councilor of State who presides in that section?"

"A former journalist, who is not worth ten sols, and who calls himself Massol!"

The two Parisians looked at each other.

"The Rapporteur?—"

"Still bigger rogue! he is a Maître des Requêtes, prrofessor of something or other at the Sorbonne, who has written something in a review, and for whom I prrofess a disesteem the most prrofound—"

"Claude Vignon?" said Bixiou.

"That is he,—" replied the Southerner; "Massol and Vignon; there you have the social rright, without rright, the Trestaillons of my prrefect."

"There is some remedy," said Léon de Lora. "Seest thou, cousin, everything is possible in Paris, in good as in evil, just and unjust. Everything is done there, everything is undone there, everything is done over again there."

"To the devil if I stay ten seconds longer—; it is the most tedious place in Frrance."

At this moment the two cousins and Bixiou were promenading from one end to the other of that patch of asphalt on which, between one and two o'clock, it is difficult not to see passing some of those personages for whom Fame puts to her mouth one or the other of her trumpets. Formerly, it was the Place Royale, then the Pont Neuf, which enjoyed

this privilege, acquired to-day by the Boulevard des
Italiens.

"Paris," said the landscape painter to his cousin,
"is an instrument on which it is necessary to know
how to play; and, if we remain here ten minutes I
will give you a lesson. There, now, look," said he
to him, lifting his cane, designating a couple who
came out of the Passage de l'Opéra.

"What is that?" asked Gazonal.

That was an old woman with a bonnet which had
remained six months in stock, with a very pretentious gown, a shawl in faded plaid, who had evidently lived for twenty years in a damp lodge,
whose greatly dilated *cabas* announced a social
position no higher than that of an ex-portress; next
a young girl, slender and thin, whose eyes, edged
with black lashes, no longer showed innocence,
whose complexion betrayed much weariness, but
whose face, of a pretty outline, was fresh, and
whose hair should be abundant; the forehead charming and audacious, the corsage thin; in two words,
a green fruit.

"That," replied Bixiou to him, "is a rat ornamented with its mother."

"A rat?—what is that?"

"This rat," said Léon, who nodded in a friendly
manner to Mademoiselle Ninette, "can gain for thee
thy suit."

Gazonal started, but Bixiou held him by the arm
since leaving the café, for he considered his face a
trifle too much inclined to redness.

"This rat, which is coming out from a rehearsal at the Opera, goes home to get a thin dinner and will come back in three hours to dress itself, if it appears this evening in the ballet, for to-day is Monday. This rat is thirteen years old; it is a rat already old. In two years from now, this creature will be worth sixty thousand francs on the Exchange; she will be nothing or everything, a great danseuse or a *marcheuse*, a famous name or a common courtesan. She has been working since she was eight years old. Such as you see her, she is worn out with fatigue, she has broken her body this morning in the dancing-class; she is coming out from a rehearsal in which evolutions are as difficult as the combinations of a Chinese puzzle; she will come back this evening. The rat is one of the elements of the Opera, for she is to the première danseuse what the little clerk is to the notary. The rat, it is hope."

"Who produces the rat?" asked Gazonal.

"The porters, the poor, the actors, the dancers," replied Bixiou. "It is only the very deepest poverty which will advise a child of eight years to deliver her feet and her joints to the hardest torment, to remain virtuous till sixteen or eighteen, entirely through speculation, and to keep at her side a horrible old woman, as you put manure around a pretty flower. You are going to see file out, one after the other, all the talent little and great, artists in blade and in flower, who elevate, to the glory of France, that monument of all time called the Opera, a reunion of the powers, the wills, the geniuses which are only found in Paris—"

"I have already seen the Opera," replied Gazonal, with a sufficient air.

"From the top of your bench at three francs, sixty centimes," replied the landscapist, "as you have seen Paris in the Rue Croix-des-Petits-Champs,—without knowing anything about it.—-What were they giving at the Opera when you went there?"

"*William Tell*."

"Good," returned the painter; "the grand duet of Matilda should have given you pleasure. Well, what, according to your ideas, would be the first thing the cantatrice would do on leaving the stage?"

"She would—, what?—"

"Sit down to eat two mutton cutlets nearly raw, which her servant kept ready—"

"Ah! *Bouffre!*"

"La Malibran sustained herself with brandy, and it was that which killed her.—Another thing! You have seen the ballet; you are going to see it go by here, in simple morning costume, without knowing that your suit depends on some of those legs?"

"My suit?—"

"There, cousin, see, what they call a *marcheuse*."

Léon pointed out one of those superb creatures who, at twenty-five, have already lived sixty years, of a beauty so real and so sure to be cultivated, that they do not make it obvious. She was tall, walked well, had the assured look of a dandy and her toilet recommended itself by a ruinous simplicity.

"It is Carabine," said Bixiou, who made, as did the painter, a slight salutation with his head, to which Carabine replied with a smile.

"There is another who can shipwreck your prefect."

"A *marcheuzze!* but what is that?"

"The *marcheuse* is a rat of great beauty whom her mother, false or true, has sold the day on which she could not become either the first or the second or the third figure of the dance, and when she has preferred the state of coryphée to any other, for the great reason that after having employed her youth in it she could not take any other; she would be rejected at the little theatres where dancers are required; she would not have succeeded in the three cities of France in which ballets are given; she would not have had the money or the desire to go abroad, for, know it, the great Parisian school of the dance furnishes the entire world with dancers and danseuses. Thus, for a rat to become a *marcheuse*, that is to say, *figurante* of the dance, it is necessary that she should have had some solid attachment which detained her in Paris, a rich man whom she did not love, a poor youth whom she loved too much. This one whom you have just seen pass, who will change her costume perhaps three times this evening, as a princess, as a peasant woman, as a Tyrolean, etc., has some two hundred francs a month."

"She is better dressed than our prefect's wife—"

"If you go to see her," said Bixiou, "you will

find there a femme de chambre, cook and domestic; she occupies a magnificent apartment in the Rue Saint-Georges; in short, she is, in the proportions of the French fortunes of to-day with the ancient ones, the successor to the *fille d'Opéra* of the eighteenth century. Carabine is a power, she governs at this moment Du Tillet, a banker who is very influential in the Chambers—"

"And above these two steps of the ballet what else is there?" asked Gazonal.

"Look!" said his cousin to him, showing him an elegant calash which was passing at the end of the boulevard, in the Rue de la Grange-Batelière, "there is one of the *premiers sujets* of the dance, whose name on the poster attracts all Paris, who earns sixty thousand francs a year, and who lives like a princess: the price of your manufactory would not be enough to buy the right to say good-day to her thirty times."

"Eh! well, I can say it to myself; that will not be so dear!"

"Do you see," said Bixiou to him, "on the front of the calash that handsome young man? it is a viscount who bears a fine name; it is her first gentleman of the chamber, he who conducts her business with the newspapers, who carries the words of peace or war each morning to the director of the Opera, or who occupies himself with the applause which salutes her when she comes on the stage or when she leaves it."

"This, my dear Messieurs, is the final stroke; I knew nothing at all of Paris."

"Well, at least know all that can be seen in ten minutes, in the Passage de l'Opéra.   Look!" said Bixiou.

Two persons came out from the passage at this moment, a man and a woman.   The woman was neither pretty nor ugly, her dress had that distinction of form, of cut and of color which reveals an artist, and the man had sufficiently the air of a singer.

"There," said Bixiou to him, "is a baritone and a *second premier sujet* of the dance.   The baritone is a man of immense talent, but being only an accessory to the score, he scarcely earns as much as the dancer earns.   Famous before Taglioni and the Elssler appeared, the *second sujet* has preserved for us the character dance, the Mimic; if the two others had not revealed in the dance a poetry unperceived up to that time, this one would be a talent of the first order; but she is in the second rank to-day; nevertheless, she fingers her thirty thousand francs, and has for a faithful friend a peer of France, very influential in the Chamber.   Ah! see, there is a danseuse of the third order, a danseuse who would not exist were it not for the all-powerfulness of a journal.   If her engagement were not renewed, the Minister would have one enemy more on his back.   The corps de ballet is to the Opera the great power,—therefore, is it of the very highest tone in the higher spheres of dandyism and of politics to have relations with the dance rather than with the singing.   In the orchestra, where the

habitués of the Opera congregate, these words:
'Monsieur is for the singing,' are a sort of jest.''

A little man, with a commonplace face, dressed
simply, passed by.

"Finally, see there the second half of the Opera's
receipts passing; it is the tenor.   There is no longer
any poem or any music or any theatrical representation possible without a celebrated tenor, whose
voice reaches a certain note.   The tenor, it is love,
it is the voice which touches the heart, which
vibrates in the soul, and which figures for a salary
more considerable than that of a minister.   A hundred thousand francs for a throat, a hundred thousand francs for a pair of heels, these are the two
financial burdens of the Opera.''

"I am stupefied,'' said Gazonal, "at all the hundred thousand francs which promenade themselves
around here.''

"You are going to be still more so, my dear
cousin; follow us.—We are going to take Paris as
an artist takes a violoncello, and make you see how
one performs on it; in short, how one amuses one's
self in Paris.''

"It is a kaleidoscope seven leagues around!''
cried Gazonal.

"Before piloting Monsieur, I ought to see Gaillard,'' said Bixiou.

"But Gaillard may be useful to us for the cousin.''

"What is this other machine?'' asked Gazonal.

"It is not a machine! it is a machinist. Gaillard
is one of our friends who has ended by becoming

the director of a newspaper, and of whom the character, as well as the cash, recommends itself by movements comparable to those of the tides. Gaillard can contribute to help you gain your suit."

"It is lost—"

"That is just the time to gain it!" replied Bixiou.

In the house of Théodore Gaillard, then lodged in the Rue de Ménars, the valet de chambre caused the three friends to wait in a boudoir, saying to them that Monsieur was in secret conference—

"With whom?" asked Bixiou.

"With a man who is selling to him the incarceration of an unseizable debtor," replied a magnificent woman who appeared in a delicious morning toilet.

"In that case, dear Suzanne," said Bixiou, "we can enter, we—"

"Oh! the beautiful creature!" cried Gazonal.

"It is Madame Gaillard," said Léon de Lora to him, speaking in his cousin's ear. "You see, my dear fellow, the most modest woman in Paris: she had all the public; she contents herself with her husband."

"*What would you have, messeigneurs?*" said the facetious director, seeing his two friends, and imitating Frédérick Lemaître.

Théodore Gaillard, formerly a man of wit, had ended by becoming stupid and in remaining in the same surroundings, a moral phenomenon which may be observed in Paris. His principal accomplishment consisted at this time in sprinkling his conversation with quotations taken from the theatrical

22

pieces then in favor and pronounced with the accent which was given them by the celebrated actors.

"We have come to humbug," replied Léon.

"*Again, young man!*"—Odry in *Les Saltimbanques*—.

"Finally, surely, we shall have him," said Gaillard's interlocutor, summing up.

"Are you very sure of it, Père Fromenteau?" asked Gaillard; "here are eleven times that we have had him in the evening and that you have missed him in the morning."

"What would you have! I have never seen a debtor like that one; he is a locomotive; he goes to sleep in Paris and wakes up in Seine-et-Oise. He is a *combination lock*."

Seeing a smile on the lips of Gaillard, he added:

"That is said also in our *partie*. To *pinch* a man, to *lock* a man, that is to arrest him. In the judiciary police, they speak otherwise. Vidocq said to his customer: '*You are served.*' That is droller, for it means the guillotine."

Under the jog with the elbow which Bixiou gave him, Gazonal became all eyes and all ears.

"Does Monsieur grease the palm?" asked Fromenteau, in a menacing tone, although a cold one.

"It is a question of *fifty centimes*"—Odry in *Les Saltimbanques*,—replied the director, taking a hundred sous and offering them to Fromenteau.

"And for the canaille?—" replied the man.

"Which?" asked Gaillard.

"Those whom I employ," replied Fromenteau, tranquilly.

"Are there any below?" asked Bixiou.

"Yes, Monsieur," replied the spy. "There are those who give information without knowing it and without being paid for it. I put the fools and the simpletons below the canaille."

"It is often fine and clever, the canaille!" cried Léon.

"You belong, then, to the police?" asked Gazonal, looking with an unquiet curiosity at this little dry man, impassible and dressed like the third clerk of a bailiff.

"Of which do you speak?" asked Fromenteau.

"There are, then, several of them?"

"There are as many as five of them," replied Fromenteau. "The judiciary police, the chief of which was Vidocq! The secret police, the chief of which is always unknown. The political police, that of Fouché. Then that of Foreign Affairs, and that of the Château—the Emperor, Louis XVIII., etc.,—which squabbled with that of the Quay Malaquais. That finished with Monsieur Decazes. I belonged to that of Louis XVIII. ; I was with it since 1793, with that poor Contenson."

Léon de Lora, Bixiou, Gazonal and Gaillard looked at each other, all expressing the same thought: "How many men's necks has he cut?"

"Nowadays, they want to go on without us, a stupidity!" resumed, after a pause, this little man, become so terrible in a moment. "At the Prefecture,

since 1830, they want honest people; I resigned and
I have made for myself a little *tran-tran* with
arrests for debt."

"It is the right arm of the guardians of commerce," said Gaillard in Bixiou's ear; "but you can
never know which pays it the most, the debtor or
the creditor."

"The more contemptible a trade is, the more it
must be honest," said Fromenteau, sententiously:
"I am for that one who pays me the most. You wish
to recover fifty thousand francs and you come to an
agreement with the means of action.   Give me five
hundred francs, and to-morrow morning your man
is *arrested*, for we have him *spotted* since yesterday."

"Five hundred francs for you alone?" cried Théodore Gaillard.

"Lisette has no shawl," replied the spy, without
a muscle of his face moving; "I call her Lisette
because of Béranger."

"You have a Lisette and you remain in your vocation," cried the virtuous Gazonal.

"It is so amusing!   You may talk about the
charms of fishing and the chase; to hunt men in
Paris is a much more interesting occupation."

"In fact," said Gazonal, speaking aloud to himself, "they must have great talent—"

"If I were to enumerate to you the qualities which
make a man remarkable in our *partie*," said Fromenteau to him, his rapid glance having enabled him
to take in the whole of Gazonal, "you would think

that I was speaking of a man of genius. Do we
not have to have the eyes of the lynx!—Audacity!
—to enter like bombs into the houses, to accost people as if one knew them, to propose villainies
which are always accepted, etc.—Memory.—Sa-
gacity.—Invention—to find schemes rapidly conceived, never the same, for the espionage is
modified according to the character and the habits of
each one; it is a heavenly gift.—Finally, agility,
strength, etc. All these qualities, Messieurs, are
inscribed on the door of the Gymnasium Amoros as
being virtues! We have to possess all these under
penalty of losing the allowance of a hundred francs
a month which is given to us by the state, the Rue
de Jérusalem, or the Garde de Commerce."

"And you seem to me to be a remarkable man,"
said Gazonal to him.

Fromenteau looked at the provincial without
replying to him, without giving any sign of emotion, and went out without saluting anybody. A
trait of true genius!

"Well, cousin, you have seen the police incar-
nated," said Léon to Gazonal.

"It has had on me the effect of a digestive,"
replied the honest manufacturer, while Gaillard and
Bixiou were conversing with lowered voices.

"I will give you an answer this evening at Carabine's," said Gaillard aloud, reseating himself at his
desk, without seeing or saluting Gazonal.

"He is an impertinent!" exclaimed the Southerner on the threshold of the door.

"His paper has twenty-two thousand subscribers," said Léon de Lora. "It is one of the five great powers of the day, and he has not in the morning the time to be polite.—"

"If we are going to the Chamber, there to arrange his lawsuit, let us take the longest road," said Léon to Bixiou.

"Words said by great men are like spoons of silver-gilt which lose their gold by use: through being repeated they lose all their brilliancy," replied Bixiou; "but where are we going?"

"Near here, to our hatter's," replied Léon.

"Bravo," cried Bixiou. "If we continue thus, perhaps we shall have an amusing day."

"Gazonal," resumed Léon, "I am going to make him *pose* for you; only, be as serious as the king on a hundred-sou piece, for you are going to see gratis a proud original, a man whose importance has made him lose his head. To-day, my dear fellow, all the world wishes to cover itself with glory, and a great many cover themselves with ridicule; from thence come living caricatures entirely new—"

"When all the world shall have glory, how can anyone be distinguished?" asked Gazonal.

"Glory?—that would be to be a fool," replied Bixiou to him. "Your cousin is decorated, I am well dressed; it is I whom people look at—"

With this observation, which may explain why the orators and other great men of politics put nothing in the button-holes of their coats in Paris, Léon

caused Gazonal to read in letters of gold the illustrious name of VITAL, SUCCESSEUR DE FINOT,
FABRICANT DE CHAPEAUX—and not *Chapelier* as
formerly—whose advertisements bring as much
money to the newspapers as those of three sellers
of pills or of burnt almonds, and who, moreover,
is the author of a little brochure on the hat."

"My dear fellow," said Bixiou to Gazonal, who
was showing him the splendor of the front of the
shop, "Vital has forty thousand francs income."

"And he remains a hatter!" cried the Southerner,
twisting Bixiou's arm with a sudden movement.

"You are going to see the man," replied Léon.
"You need a hat; you are going to have one gratis."

"Monsieur Vital is not in?" asked Bixiou, who did
not see anyone at the counter.

"Monsieur is correcting his proofs in his office,"
replied a first salesman.

"Hein! what style!" said Léon to his cousin.

Then, addressing the first salesman:

"May we speak to him without injuring his
inspirations?"

"Permit those gentlemen to enter," said a voice.

It was a bourgeois voice, a voice of an eligible, a
powerful voice and one with a good income.

And Vital deigned to show himself, clothed all in
black, decorated with a magnificent shirt, frilled
and ornamented with a diamond. The three friends
perceived a young and pretty woman seated in the
office, working at embroidery.

Vital is a man of from thirty to forty years of

age, of a primitive joviality restrained under the
pressure of his ambitious ideas. He enjoys a medium stature, a privilege of fine organizations.
Sufficiently stout, he is careful of his person; his
forehead is losing its hair, but he contributes to his
baldness in order to give himself the air of a man
devoured by thought. You may see, by the manner in which his wife looks at him and listens to
him that she believes in the genius and in the fame
of her husband. Vital loves the artists, not that he
has any taste for the arts, but through confrater-
nity; for he believes himself an artist and causes
this to be made evident while protesting against his
title of nobility, in placing himself with a constant
premeditation at an enormous distance from the arts,
in order that it may be said to him: "But you have
elevated the hat to the height of a science."

"Have you at last found me a hat?" said the
landscape-painter.

"How, monsieur, in two weeks?" replied Vital,
"and for you!—But would it be enough to find the
form which would be in consonance with your
physiognomy in two months? See your lithograph,
there it is; I have already studied you well! I
would not give myself so much trouble for a prince;
but you are more, you are an artist! and you comprehend me, my dear monsieur."

"Here is one of our greatest inventors, a man who
would be as grand as Jacquart if he would let himself die a little," said Bixiou, presenting Gazonal.
"Our friend, a cloth manufacturer, has discovered

a means of restoring the indigo of old blue coats, and he has wished to see you as a great phenomenon, for you have said: '*The hat, it is the man.*' This saying has delighted Monsieur. Ah! Vital, you have faith! you believe in something, you have an enthusiasm for your work."

Vital listened with difficulty; he had become pale with pleasure.

"Rise, wife!—Monsieur is a prince of science."

Madame Vital rose at her husband's gesture, Gazonal bowed to her.

"Shall I have the honor to serve you?" resumed Vital, with a joyous obsequiousness.

"The same price as for me," said Bixiou.

"Certainly; I ask no other honorarium than the pleasure of being occasionally quoted by you, Messieurs! Monsieur requires a picturesque hat, in the style of that of Monsieur Lousteau," said he, looking at Bixiou with a magisterial air. "I will reflect upon it."

"You give yourself a great deal of trouble," said Gazonal to the Parisian manufacturer.

"Oh! for some persons only, for those who know how to appreciate the cost of my cares. Why, in the aristocracy there is only one man who has comprehended the hat, that is the Prince de Béthune. How is it that men do not reflect, like women, that the hat is the first thing which attracts attention in the dress, and why do they not think to change the actual system, which, let us say it, is ignoble? But the Frenchman is, of all people, the one who

persists the longest in a stupidity! I know well the
difficulties, Messieurs! I do not speak of my writ-
ings on this subject, in which I believe I have approached it in the spirit of philosophy, but merely
as a hat-maker. I alone have discovered the means
of giving a character to the infamous head-piece
which France possesses until the moment when I
shall succeed in overthrowing it."

He showed the frightful hat worn to-day.

"Here is the enemy, Messieurs," he resumed.
" 'To say that the most brilliant people on the earth
consent to wear on their head this piece of stove-
pipe!' has said one of our writers—. See all the
inflections which I have been able to give to these
frightful lines," he added, designating one by one
his creations. "But, although I may know how to
make them appropriate to the character of each one,
as you see, for here is the hat of a physician, of a
grocer, of a dandy, that of an artist, of a fat man,
of a thin man, it is always horrible! Hold, grasp
well all my thought!"

He took a hat, low in form and with a large
rim.

"Here is the former hat of Claude Vignon, a great
critic, a liberal man and a good liver.—He rallied to
the support of the ministry; he is appointed professor,
librarian; he works only for the *Débats,* he has
been made *Maître des Requêtes;* he has sixteen
thousand francs allowance, he earns four thousand
francs on his journal; he is decorated.—Well, then,
see his new hat!"

And Vital showed a hat of a cut and of a design veritably justly moderate.

"You should have made for him a Punchinello's hat!" cried Gazonal.

"You are a man of genius ahead of all others, Monsieur Vital," said Léon.

Vital bowed, without suspecting the pun.

"Could you tell me why your stores remain open in the evening, in Paris, later than all others, even after the cafés and the wine-shops? Truly, that has puzzled me," asked Gazonal.

"In the first place, our establishments are much handsomer to see lit up than they are during the day; then for ten hats that we sell during the day fifty are sold in the evening."

"Everything is odd at Paris," said Léon.

"Well, notwithstanding my efforts and my successes," resumed Vital, pursuing the course of his eulogium, "it is necessary to arrive at the hat with a round calotte. It is to that that I tend!"

"What is the obstacle to it?" asked Gazonal of him.

"The low price, monsieur! In the first place, they would set up for you beautiful silk hats for fifteen francs, which would kill our commerce, for at Paris one never has fifteen francs to invest in a new hat. If the beaver costs thirty francs, it is still the same problem. When I say beaver, there are not sold ten pounds of beaver fur in France. This article costs three hundred and fifty francs a pound; it requires an ounce for a hat; moreover, the

beaver hat is not worth anything,—this fur takes
the dye badly, reddens in ten minutes in the sun,
and the hat gets warped in the heat.   That which
we call *beaver* is nothing more than the fur of the
hare.   The best qualities are made with the back
of the animal, the second with the sides, the third
with the belly.   I give to you the secret of the
trade, you are honorable gentlemen.   But whether
we have hareskin or silk on the head, fifteen or
thirty francs, the problem is always unsolvable.   It
is always necessary to pay for the hat; that is why
the hat remains what it is.   The honor of France
vestimental will be saved the day on which the
gray hat with the round calotte will cost a hundred
francs!   We shall then be able, like the tailors, to
give credit.   To arrive at this result, it will be
necessary to decide to wear the buckle and the ribbon of gold, the feather, the reveres of satin as
under Louis XIII. and Louis XIV.   Our business,
thus becoming inventive, will increase tenfold.
The market of the world will belong to France as
do the fashions for women to which Paris will
always give the style; while our present hat can
be made anywhere.   Ten millions of foreign money
annually for our country are involved in this question—."

"It is a revolution!" said Bixiou to him, professing enthusiasm.

"Yes, radical, for it will be necessary to change
the form."

"You are happy after the fashion of Luther," said

Léon, who was always cultivating puns, "you dream a reform."

"Yes, Monsieur.   Ah! if twelve or fifteen artists, capitalists or dandies, who set the style, would have the courage during twenty-four hours, France would gain a fine commercial battle! Why, I say to my wife: 'To succeed, I would give my fortune!' Yes, all my ambition is to regenerate the thing and to disappear!—"

"That man is colossal," said Gazonal, as they went out, "but I assure you that all your originals have something southern—"

"Let us go that way," said Bixiou, designating the Rue Saint-Marc.

"We are going to see something else?—"

"You are going to see the usurer of the rats, of the *marcheuses,* a woman who possesses as many frightful secrets as you will see gowns hung behind her shop window," said Bixiou.

And he pointed out one of those shops whose neglect makes a spot in the midst of the dazzling modern establishments.   It was a shop with a front painted in 1820 and which a bankruptcy had undoubtedly left on the hands of the proprietor of the house in a doubtful state; the color had disappeared under a double layer imposed by use and greatly thickened by dust; the windows were dirty, the door latch turned by itself, as in all those places from which one issues still more promptly than one enters.

"What do you say to that, is it not the first

cousin of Death?" said the artist in the ear of
Gazonal, in showing him at the counter a terrible
companion. "Well, she calls herself Madame Nourrisson."

"Madame, how much for this guipure lace?"
asked the manufacturer, who wished to contest in
enterprise with the two artists.

"For you who come from afar, Monsieur, it will
be only a hundred écus," she replied.

And, remarking a little movement peculiar to
Southerners, she added, with a penetrating air:

"That comes from the poor Princesse de Lamballe."

"Why! so near to the Château?" cried Bixiou.

"Monsieur, they do not believe in it," she replied.

"Madame, we did not come here to buy," said
Bixiou, gravely.

"I know that well enough, Monsieur," replied
Madame Nourrisson.

"We have several things to sell," said the illustrious caricaturist, continuing. "I live in the Rue
de Richelieu, 112, on the sixth floor. If you would
stop in there a moment, you might make an excellent bargain?—"

"Monsieur would like perhaps a few yards of very
superior muslin?" she asked, smiling.

"No, it is about a wedding dress," replied Léon
de Lora, gravely.

A quarter of an hour later Madame Nourrisson did
in fact come to the apartments of Bixiou, who, to

carry out this pleasantry, had brought home with him Léon and Gazonal; Madame Nourrisson found them as serious as authors whose collaboration *does not obtain all the success that it merits.*

"Madame," said the intrepid mystifier to her, showing her a pair of women's slippers, "here is something that belonged to the Empress Joséphine."

It was quite necessary to return to Madame Nourrisson the change for her guipure lace of the Princesse de Lamballe.

"That?—" she said. "Those were made this year; see this stamp on the soles?"

"Do you not guess that these slippers are a preface," replied Léon, "although they are usually the conclusion of a romance?"

"My friend, who is here," resumed Bixiou, designating the Southerner, "in some very important family interests wishes to learn if a young person, of a good, of a wealthy house, and whom he desires to marry, has committed a fault?"

"How much will Monsieur give?" she asked, looking at Gazonal, who was no longer surprised at anything.

"A hundred francs," replied the manufacturer.

"Thanks!" said she, embellishing her refusal with a grimace that might make a baboon despair.

"What is it you want, my little Madame Nourrisson?" asked Bixiou, taking her by the waist.

"In the first place, my dear Messieurs, since I have worked for my living I have never seen anyone, either man or woman, bargaining over happiness!

And, then, see here, you are three jokers," she
went on, permitting a smile to play around her
cold lips and reinforcing it with a look chilled by
a cat-like mistrust. "If it is not a question of your
happiness, it is one of your fortune; and, in the
high station in which you are placed, there is still
less bargaining over a dot.—Come, now," said she,
assuming an affected air, "what is it all about, my
lambs?"

"Of the house of Beunier & Co.," replied Bixiou,
well content to acquire some information concerning a person who interested him.

"Oh! for that," she answered, "a louis; that is
enough—"

"And why?"

"I have all the mother's jewels; and from one
three months to another she is mighty uncomfortable, I should say so! She has all she can do to pay
me the interest on that which I have lent her. You
wish to get married over there, ninny!—" said she.
"Give me forty francs, and I will talk for more than
a hundred écus."

Gazonal showed a forty-franc piece and Madame
Nourrisson launched herself into frightful details on
the secret poverty of certain women reputed *comme
il faut.* The dealer in old clothes, enlivened by the
conversation, revealed herself. Without betraying
any name, any secret, she made the two artists
shudder in demonstrating to them that there was
very little happiness in Paris which was not established on the vacillating basis of borrowing. She

held in her secret drawers souvenirs of late grandmothers, of living children, of deceased husbands,
of dead granddaughters, framed in gold and in brilliants! She learned frightful histories in setting her
customers to talk of each other, in wresting their
secrets from them in moments of passion, of quarreling, of anger, and in those soothing preparations
which lead up to a loan for a conclusion.

"How did you come to engage in this business?"
asked Gazonal.

"For my son," said she ingenuously.

Nearly always, these dealers in second-hand
clothes justify their commerce by reasons full of
fine motives. Madame Nourrisson pretended to
have lost several suitors, three daughters who had
taken to evil, all her illusions, in fact! She displayed as being among her most valuable effects,
tickets from the pawnshops to prove how many
evil chances there were in her business. She gave
out that she would be much embarrassed on the
thirtieth proximo. There was a great deal *stolen*
from her, she said.

The two artists looked at each other on hearing
this word, a little too strong.

"See here, my dears, I will show you how they
do us over again! This is not my case, but that of
my opposite neighbor, Madame Mahuchet, the
ladies' shoemaker. I had lent some money to a
countess, a woman who has too many passions con-
sidering her income. It is all putting on airs among
beautiful furniture, in a magnificent apartment! It

23

is giving receptions, it is making, as we say, a
devil of a spread. She owes, then, three hundred
francs to her shoemaker, and there is a dinner
given, a soirée, no later than the day before yesterday.   The shoemaker, who learned this through
the cook, came to see me ; we got excited, she wished
to make a scandal; I, I said to her: 'My little
Mother Mahuchet, what good will that do? to get
yourself hated. It would be much better to obtain
good security. *To a liar, a liar and a half!* and you
only save your bile—.'   She insisted upon going
there; asked me to back her up; we went there.
'Madame is not at home.'   'We know it!'   'We will
wait for her,' said Mother Mahuchet, 'if I have to
stay here till midnight.'   And we settled ourselves
in the antechamber and went to talking.   Ah! you
should have heard the doors which opened and shut,
the little footsteps, the hushed voices—.   For myself, that made me uncomfortable.   The guests
began to arrive for dinner.   You can judge of the
state of affairs which this made.   The countess sent
her femme de chambre to wheedle the Mahuchet.
'You shall be paid to-morrow!'   In short, all the
humbugs!—Nothing would work.   The countess,
fine as a Sunday, arrived at the dining-room.   My
Mahuchet, who heard her, opened the door and presented herself.   Bless me! on seeing a table glitter-
ing with silver—the chafing-dishes, the chandeliers,
everything shining like a jewel-box—she went off
like a *sodavatre* and threw her bomb-shell: 'When
one spends the money of others, one should be

temperate, and not give dinner parties! To be a
countess and to owe a hundred écus to a poor woman-
shoemaker who has seven children!—' You can
imagine what a volley she poured forth, this woman
has so little education. At a word of excuse—'No
funds!'—of the countess, my Mahuchet cried: 'Eh!
Madame, see the silver-ware, pawn your spoons and
pay me!' 'Take them yourself,' said the countess,
gathering up six covers and thrusting them into her
hand. We tumbled down the stairs—ah, bah! like
a success!—No, in the street, the Mahuchet began to
cry, for she is a good woman; she took back the
covers, making her excuses: she had understood the
misery of this countess, they were in white
metal!—"

"She remained *uncovered*," said Léon de Lora, in
whom the ancient Mistigris often reappeared.

"Ah! my dear Monsieur," said Madame Nourrisson, enlightened by this pun, "you are an artist,
you make the theatre pieces; you live in the Rue
du Helder, and you were with Madame Antonia;
you have the knacks that I know—. Come, now, you
wish to have some rarity in the grand style, Carabine, or Mousqueton, Malaga or Jenny Cadine?"

"Malaga, Carabine! it is we who have made
them what they are!—" cried Léon de Lora.

"I swear to you, my dear Madame Nourrisson, that
we wished solely to have the pleasure of making
your acquaintance and that we desire some information as to your antecedents, to know by what
descent you slipped into your trade," said Bixiou.

"I was a confidential woman in the house of a marshal of France, the Prince d'Ysembourg," she said, taking a Dorine attitude. "One morning, there came one of the most topping countesses of the Imperial Court; she wished to speak to the marshal, and secretly. I, I placed myself immediately so that I could hear. My lady melted into tears, she confided to this booby of a marshal—the Prince d'Ysembourg, this Condé of the Republic, a booby!—that her husband, who was serving in Spain, had left her without a thousand-franc note; that, if she did not have one or two immediately, her children would be without bread, she would have nothing to eat to-morrow—. My marshal, sufficiently generous at that time, drew two thousand-franc notes from his secretary. I watched this fine countess from the stairway without her being able to see me; she was laughing with a contentment that seemed so little maternal that I slipped out under the peristyle, and I heard her say in a very low voice to her footman: 'To Leroy's!' I hastened there. My materfamilias entered the shop of this famous merchant, in the Rue de Richelieu, you know—. She ordered and paid for a dress fifteen hundred francs; at that time a dress was settled for when it was ordered. Two days later she was able to appear at an ambassador's ball, adorned as a woman should be to please at the same time all the world and some one in particular. From that day, I said to myself: 'I have a business! When I shall be no longer young, I will lend money on their apparel to the great ladies, for passion does not calculate and pays blindly.' If it is subjects for vaudeville that you are seeking, I will sell them to you—"

She went off on this tirade, in which each of the phases of her previous life had left its color, leaving Gazonal as much aghast at this confidence as at five yellow teeth which she had shown in endeavoring to smile.

"And what are we going to do?" asked Gazonal.

"Notes!—" said Bixiou, who whistled for his porter, "for I have need of money, and I will let you see what the porters are for; you think that they are to pull the cords of the front door,—they are to pull out of embarrassment vagabond people like myself, artists whom they take under their protection; thus some day, mine will have the prize Montyon."

Gazonal opened his eyes in such a manner as to make comprehendable this phrase,—an *œil-de-bœuf*.

A middle-aged man, half lackey and half office-boy, but more oily and more oiled, the hair greasy, the stomach plump, the complexion pale and damp like that of the Superior of a convent, shod with cloth slippers, clothed in a vest of blue cloth and grayish pantaloons, suddenly appeared.

"What will you have, Monsieur?—" said he, with an air which partook at once of the protector and of the subordinate.

"Ravenouillet—, his name is Ravenouillet," said Bixiou, turning toward Gazonal, "have you our bill-book?"

Ravenouillet drew from his side pocket the most glutinous note-book that Gazonal had ever seen.

"Write in it, at three months, these two notes for five hundred francs each which you will sign for me."

And Bixiou presented two notes already drawn to his order by Ravenouillet, which Ravenouillet signed on the spot, and which he put down in the greasy note-book in which his wife recorded the debts of the lodgers.

"Thanks, Ravenouillet," said Bixiou.   "Well, now, here is a box for the Vaudeville."

"Oh! my daughter will have a good time this evening," said Ravenouillet, going away.

"We are here seventy-one tenants," said Bixiou; "the average of what is owed to Ravenouillet is about six thousand francs a month, eighteen thousand francs every three months, for advances and carrying letters, without counting the rents due. It is a Providence—at thirty per cent, which we give to him without his ever having asked for anything—"

"Oh! Paris, Paris—" cried Gazonal.

"When we go away," said Bixiou, who pocketed the notes, "for I am going to take you, cousin Gazonal, to see again a comedian who is going to play gratuitously a charming scene—"

"Where?" interrupted Gazonal.

"At a usurer's—.   As we go, I will relate to you the début of friend Ravenouillet in Paris."

As they passed before the porter's lodge, Gazonal

saw Mademoiselle Lucienne Ravenouillet, who was studying a solfeggio; she was a pupil of the Conservatoire; the father was reading a newspaper, and Madame Ravenouillet held in her hand letters to be sent up to the lodgers.

"Thanks, Monsieur Bixiou," said the little one.

"It is not a rat," said Léon to his cousin, "it is a chrysalis of a grasshopper."

"It appears," said Gazonal, "that the friendship of the lodge is obtained, like that of all the rest of the world, by *les loges*—the lodges—"

"Which is developed in our society!" cried Léon, charmed with the pun.

"This is the history of Ravenouillet," resumed Bixiou when the three friends found themselves on the boulevard. "In 1831, Massol, your Councilor of State, was a journalist-advocate who wished at that time only to be Keeper of the Seals, he deigned to leave Louis-Philippe on the throne; but his ambition will have to be forgiven, he was from Carcassonne. One morning he saw a young countryman enter, who said to him: 'You know me very well, *Monsu* Massol, I am the little one of your neighbor, the grocer; I have just come from down there, for they say to us that in coming here each one will find his place—' On hearing these words Massol was taken with a shudder, and said to himself that, if he had the misfortune to oblige this compatriot, who was otherwise perfectly unknown to him, the whole department would come tumbling in upon him; that he would lose a great many bell-actions,

eleven bell-cords, his carpets; that his only valet
would leave him; that he would have difficulties
with his landlord concerning the stairway, and
that the other tenants would complain of the odor of
garlic and of the commotion caused throughout the
house.   Therefore, he looked at this solicitor as a
butcher looks at his sheep before cutting its throat;
but although the peasant had received this glance
or this knife-thrust, he went on in this way, as
Massol told us: 'I am ambitious just like any other,
and I do not wish to return to the country in any
other way but rich, if I do return; for Paris is the
antechamber of paradise.   It is said that you who
write in the journals, you make here rain and fair
weather; that it is enough for you to ask to obtain
no matter what from the government; but, if I have
any abilities, like all of us, I know myself, I have
no education; even if I had the means I would not
know how to write, and that is a misfortune, for I
have ideas; I do not, then, think to rival you; I judge
myself, I would not succeeed; but, as you can manage anything, and as we are almost brothers, having played together during our childhood, I count on
your giving me a start and your protecting me—.
Oh! it is necessary; I want a situation, a place
which is suitable to my means, to what I am, and
where I can make my fortune—.'   Massol was about
to put his *pays* out of the door brutally, throwing in
his face some brutal phrase, when the countryman
concluded thus: 'I do not ask, then, to enter the
administration, where one gets on like tortoises,

where your cousin has remained traveling comptroller for twenty years—. No, I wish only to come out—.' 'At the theatre?—' said Massol to him, happy at this termination. 'No, I have, well enough, the gesture, the face, the memory; but there is too much pulling; I wish to make my début in the career—of a porter.' Massol kept his gravity and said to him: 'There will be still more pulling in that, but at least you will see the lodges full.' And he obtained for him, as Ravenouillet says, his first cordon.''

"I am the first," Léon said, "who has seriously occupied himself with the species *portier*. There are sharpers of morality, buffoons of vanity, modern sycophants, *septembriseurs* * caparisoned with gravity, inventors of questions palpitating with actuality which preach the emancipation of the negroes, the amelioration of petty thieves, benevolence toward liberated convicts, and who leave their porters in a state worse than that of the Irish, in prisons more frightful than dungeons, and who give them less money to live on than the state gives for a convict—. I have only done one good action in my life, that is the lodge of my porter."

"If," continued Bixiou, "a man having built great cages, divided into a thousand apartments like the cells of a bee-hive or the cages of a menagerie, and destined to receive creatures of every species and of every avocation, if this animal in the figure of an

* *Septembriseurs*—the name given to those who took part in the massacre of September, 1792.

owner should come to consult a scientist and say to
him: 'I want an individual of the genus *bimana*
who can live in a sink full of old shoes, pestiferous
with rags, and ten feet square; I want him to live
there all his life, to sleep there, to be happy there,
to have children as pretty as Loves; that he shall
work there; that he shall do his cooking there; that
he shall promenade himself there; that he shall cultivate flowers there; that he shall sing there, and
that he shall not go out; that he shall not see clearly
there, and that he shall perceive everything that
goes on outside!—' assuredly, the scientist would
not have been able to invent the porter; it required
Paris to create him, or, if you like, the devil—"

"Parisian industry has gone still farther into the
impossible," said Gazonal, "there are the workpeople—. You do not know all the products of industry, you who display them. Our industry combats that of the continent by misfortunes as, under
the Empire, Napoléon combated Europe with regiments."

"Here we are at the house of my friend Vauvinet,
the usurer," said Bixiou. "One of the greatest
faults committed by the people who depict our manners is to repeat the old portraits. To-day, every
profession has been renewed. The grocers become
peers of France, the artists capitalize, the vaude-
villistes have incomes in Rentes. If some rare
figures remain that which they formerly were, in
general, the professions no longer have their special
costume, nor their ancient manner. If we have had

Gobseck, Gigonnet, Chaboisseau, Samanou, the last of the Romans, we are in the enjoyment to-day of Vauvinet, the good-fellow usurer, little fop who haunts the side-scenes, the lorettes, and who takes the air in a little low coupé with one horse—. Observe my man well, friend Gazonal, you are going to see the comedy of money, the cold man who wishes to give nothing, the hot man who suspects a profit; listen to him, above all."

And, all three of them entered the second story of a house of a very fine appearance situated on the Boulevard des Italiens, and there found themselves surrounded by all the luxuries then in fashion. A young man of about twenty-eight came to meet them with an almost laughing air, for he saw Léon de Lora first. Vauvinet gave a hand-clasp, in appearance the most friendly, to Bixiou, saluted Gazonal with a cold air, and caused them to enter into a cabinet, where all the tastes of the bourgeois might be divined under the artistic appearance of the furnishing, and, despite the statuettes *à la mode*, the thousand little things appropriated to our little apartments by the modern art, which has made itself as little as the consumer. Vauvinet was gotten up, like the young people who occupy themselves with business, with an excessive care, which, for very many of them, is a species of prospectus.

"I have come to you to get some money," said Bixiou, laughing, presenting his note.

Vauvinet assumed a serious air which made Gazonal smile, so much difference was there between the smiling visage and that of a discounter officially occupied.

"My dear fellow," said Vauvinet, looking at Bixiou, "I would oblige you with the greatest pleasure, but at this moment I have no money."

"Ah, bah!"

"Yes, I've given everything, you know to whom. —That poor Lousteau has associated himself for the management of a theatre with an old vaudevilliste very much protected by the minister—, Ridal; and they had to have thirty thousand francs yesterday. I am cleaned out, and so cleaned out that I have sent for some money to Cérizet to pay a hundred louis lost at lansquenet this morning, at Jenny Cadine's—"

"It must be that you are very much cleaned out not to oblige this poor Bixiou," said Léon de Lora, "for he has a very short tongue when he finds himself *by the side*—"

"But—" said Bixiou, "I cannot say anything but good of Vauvinet; he is full of good—"

"My dear fellow," resumed Vauvinet, "it would be impossible for me, even if I had the money, to discount for you, were it at fifty per cent, notes signed by your porter.—The Ravenouillet is not in demand. It is not like the Rothschild. I warn you that this endorsement is quite worn out; it will be necessary for you to invent another banking-house. Look out for an uncle! for, the friend who signs notes for us, that is no longer to be had, the positivism of the century makes horrible progress."

"I have," said Bixiou, indicating Léon's cousin, "I have Monsieur,—one of our most illustrious cloth manufacturers of the Midi, named Gazonal.—He is not very well *coiffé*," he resumed, looking at the luxuriant and upright head of hair of the provincial; "but I am going to take him to Marius, who will relieve him of this resemblance to a poodle, so injurious to his consideration and to ours."

"I do not believe much in the securities of the Midi, be it said without offence to Monsieur," replied Vauvinet, who rendered Gazonal very well content, for he was not in the least vexed at this insolence.

Gazonal, in his character of an excessively shrewd man, believed that the painter and Bixiou intended, in order to make him acquainted with Paris, to make him pay a thousand francs for the *déjeuner* of the *Café de Paris;* for the son of the Roussillon had not abandoned that prodigious suspicion which in Paris fortifies the man from the provinces.

"How would you have me have business relations at two hundred and fifty leagues from Paris, in the Pyrenees?" added Vauvinet.

"Then that is all?" replied Bixiou.

"I have twenty francs about me," said the young discounter.

"I am sorry for you," replied the joker. "I thought that you were worth a thousand francs," he added, dryly.

"You are worth a hundred thousand francs,"

replied Vauvinet, "sometimes even you are inesti-
mable,—but I am cleaned out."

"Well," replied Bixiou, "let us say no more
about it—. I would have arranged for you this evening, at the Carabine's, the best affair that you
could have wished,—you know?"

Vauvinet winked in looking at Bixiou, a grimace
of the horse dealers which says between themselves:
"Let us not play sharp with each other."

"You no longer remember having taken me around
the waist, exactly like a pretty woman, and wheedling me with looks and with words," replied Bixiou,
"when you said to me: 'I will do anything for you
if you can procure me at par shares of the railroad
which Du Tillet and Nucingen put on the market.'
Well, my dear fellow, Maxime and Nucingen are
coming to Carabine's, who is receiving this evening
a great many men in political life. You are losing
there, my old fellow, a beautiful opportunity.
Come, good day, dabbler!"

And Bixiou arose, leaving Vauvinet sufficiently
unmoved in appearance, but really dissatisfied, like
a man who is conscious of having committed a folly.

"My dear fellow, a moment,—" said the discounter; "if I have no money, I have credit.—If your
notes are worth nothing I can keep them and give
you in exchange securities in bills—. Afterwards,
we can come to an arrangement about the railway
shares; we will divide, in a certain proportion, the
profits of this operation, and I will then make you a
remittance on account of the prof—"

"No, no," replied Bixiou, "I must have some money; it is necessary that I should use my Raven-ouillet—"

"Ravenouillet is otherwise very good," said Vauvinet; "he deposits in the savings-bank, he is excellent—"

"He is better than you," said Léon to him, "for he does not keep a lorette; he has no rent to pay; he does not embark in speculations fearing all the time the rise or the fall—"

"You think to amuse, great man?" replied Vauvinet, suddenly become jovial and caressing; "you have got out the quintessence of La Fontaine's fable, *The Oak and the Reed.*—Come, *Gubetta, my old confederate*," said Vauvinet, taking Bixiou by the waist, "you must have some money? very well, I can just as well borrow three thousand francs from my friend Cérizet, instead of two thousand.— And *we will be friends, Cinna!*— Give me your two giant cabbage-leaves. If I refused you, it was because it was very hard for a man who can only carry on his poor business by depositing his securities with the Bank, to keep your Ravenouillet in his bureau drawer,—it is hard, it is very hard.—"

"And what will you take for discount?" asked Bixiou.

"Almost nothing," replied Vauvinet. "That will cost you, at three months, fifty unhappy francs—."

"As Émile Blondet said formerly, you will be my benefactor," replied Bixiou.

"Twenty per cent and interest!" said Gazonal in

Bixiou's ear, who replied to him by a great poke with his elbow in the region of the œsophagus.

"Wait," said Vauvinet, opening the drawer of his bureau; "I see here, my good fellow, an old note of five hundred which has stuck to the band and I did not know myself so rich, for I find for you a bill receivable due very soon, of four hundred and fifty. Cérizet will lend it to you without much *rebate,* and there is your sum made up. But no joking, Bixiou?—. Hein! this evening, I will go to Carabine's—you swear to me"

"Are we not *re*-friends?" said Bixiou, who took the five-hundred-franc bill and the note for four hundred and fifty francs; "I give you my word of honor that you will see this evening Du Tillet and a number of other people who wish to make their way, —railway, with Carabine."

Vauvinet conducted the three friends as far as the landing, wheedling Bixiou. Bixiou remained serious until upon the threshold of the door; he was listening to Gazonal, who endeavored to enlighten him upon this operation and who proved to him that, if the confederate of Vauvinet, this Cérizet, lent him at twenty francs of discount on a note of four hundred and fifty francs it was money at forty per cent. —On the asphalt of the pavement, Bixiou froze Gazonal by the laugh of the Parisian mystifier, this silent and cold laugh, a sort of labial north-easter.

"The adjudication of the railway will be positively adjourned in the Chamber," he said; "we know it since yesterday through that *marcheuse* at whom

we have smiled.—And, if I gain this evening five
or six thousand francs at lansquenet, what are
seventy francs of loss for having the wherewithal to
stake!"—

"Lansquenet is still one of the thousand facets of
Paris as it is," resumed Léon. "Thus, cousin, we
count on presenting you in the house of a duchess
of the Rue Saint-Georges, where you will see the
aristocracy of the lorettes and where you can gain
your lawsuit. Now, it is impossible to show you
with your Pyrenean hair; you have the appearance
of a hedgehog; we are going to conduct you near
here in the Place de la Bourse, to Marius, another
of our actors—"

"Who is this new actor?"

"Here is the anecdote," replied Bixiou. "In
1800, a Toulousian named Cabot, a young peruke-
maker devoured with ambition, came to Paris, and
there *lifted* a shop—I adopt your slang.—This
man of genius—he enjoys twenty-four thousand
francs income at Libourne, where he has retired—
comprehended that this common and ignoble name
would never attain to fame. Monsieur de Parny,
whom he served, gave him the name of Marius, infinitely superior to the Christian names of Armand
and of Hippolyte, under which hid themselves the
patronymic names attacked with the Cabot-disease.
All the successors of Cabot are called Marius. The
present Marius is Marius V.; his name is Mougin.
This is the custom in many trades, as for the eau
de Botot, for the ink de la Petite-Vertu. At Paris,

24

a name becomes a commercial property and ends by
constituting a sort of sign of nobility. Marius,
who moreover has pupils, has created, he says, the
first school of coiffure in the world."

"I have already seen, in traveling through
France," said Gazonal, "a number of signs on
which might be read these words: 'SUCH A ONE,
Pupil of Marius.'"

"These pupils must wash their hands after each
curling and dressing," replied Bixiou; "but Marius
does not admit them indiscriminately; they must
have handsome hands and not be ugly. The most
remarkable in address, in appearance, serve their
customers in their own houses; they return very
much fatigued. Marius himself only leaves his
establishment for women with titles; he has a cabriolet and a groom."

"But this is after all only a *merlan!* (journeyman
hair-dresser)," cried Gazonal, indignantly.

"*Merlan!*" replied Bixiou; "remember that he is
a captain in the National Guard and that he is decorated for having been the first to leap a barricade in
1832."

"Take care; this is neither a coiffure nor a
perruquier, this is a director of salons of coiffure,"
said Léon, as they mounted a stairway with a
crystal balustrade, with a mahogany rail, and the
steps of which were covered with a sumptuous
carpet.

"Ah, there! do not go and compromise us," said
Bixiou to Gazonal: "In the antechamber, you will

find lackeys who will relieve you of your coat, your
hat, to brush them, and who will accompany you to
the door of one of the salons de coiffure, to open
and shut it.   It is well to tell you this, my friend
Gazonal," added Bixiou, slyly, "for you might cry
out: 'Help, thieves!'"

"These salons," said Léon, "are three boudoirs
in which the director has assembled all the inventions of modern luxury.   At the windows are lam-
brequins; everywhere are jardinières, luxurious
divans, on which you can await your turn while
reading the papers, when all the attendants are occupied.   When you enter you may feel for your
purse, thinking that at least five francs will be
demanded of you; but there is extracted from every
species of pocket only ten sous for a *frisure*, and
twenty sous for a *coiffure* with cutting the hair.
Elegant dressing-tables are interspersed among the
jardinières, and the water flows from them through
brass taps.   Everywhere enormous mirrors reflect
the figures.   Therefore, do not show any astonishment.   When the *client*—such is the elegant word
substituted by Marius for the ignoble word *customer*
—when the client appears on the threshold, Marius
gives him a glance and he is gauged,—for him,
you are *a head* more or less worthy of his attention.
For Marius, there are no longer any men, there are
only *heads.*"

"We are going to let you hear Marius in all the
tones of his gamut," said Bixiou, "if you know how
to imitate our methods."

As soon as Gazonal appeared, the rapid glance of
Marius was favorable to him, and he exclaimed:

"Regulus! that head for you! clip it first with the
little scissors."

"Pardon," said Gazonal to the pupil, at a gesture
from Bixiou, "I desire to have my head dressed by
Monsieur Marius himself."

Marius, very much flattered by this preference,
came forward, leaving the head on which he was
operating.

"I am at your service; I am finishing, do not be
uneasy; my pupil will prepare you; I alone, I will
decide on the cut."

Marius, a little pock-marked man, the hair frizzled like that of Rubini, black as jet, and dressed
all in black with ruffles, the jabot of his shirt
ornamented with a diamond, then recognized
Bixiou, whom he saluted as a power equal to
his own.

"It is an ordinary head," he said to Léon, indicating the gentleman with whom he was then occupied, "a grocer!—. What will you have! if one
were occupied with nothing but art, one would die
in the Bicêtre, mad!—"

And he returned with an inimitable gesture to his
client, after having said to Regulus:

"Attend to Monsieur; he is evidently an artist."

"A journalist," said Bixiou.

At this word, Marius gave two or three touches
with the comb to the commonplace head, and threw
himself on Gazonal, taking Regulus by the arm at

the moment when he was about to commence operations with his little scissors.

"I will take charge of Monsieur.—See, Monsieur," said he to the grocer, "look at yourself in the large mirror, if the mirror will permit.—Ossian!"

The lackey entered and took possession of the client to dress him.

"You will pay the cashier, Monsieur," said Marius to the stupefied customer, who had already produced his purse.

"Is it very advantageous, my dear fellow, to proceed with this operation of the little scissors?" said Bixiou.

"No head comes to me until it has been cleansed," replied the illustrious coiffeur; "but for you, I will do that of Monsieur altogether. My pupils make the preliminary sketch, for I do not attend to that. The phrase of all the world is yours: 'To be *coiffé* by Marius!' I can only give the finishing touch.—On what journal is Monsieur engaged?"

"In your place, I would have three or four Mariuses," said Gazonal.

"Ah! Monsieur, I see, is a feuilletonist?" said Marius. "Alas! in hairdressing, in which one is obliged to act personally, it is impossible—. Pardon!"

He left Gazonal to go and oversee Régulus, who was preparing a newly-arrived head. By striking his tongue against the palate he produced a little disapproving sound which might be translated by "titt titt, titt!"

"Come, bon Dieu! that is not square enough;
your scissors are cutting jaggedly—. Wait—see!
Régulus, it is not a question of clipping poodles, but
of men who have their own character; and, if you
continue to look at the ceiling instead of dividing
yourself between the mirror and the face, you will
dishonor *my house.*"

"You are severe, Monsieur Marius."

"I owe to them the secrets of the art—"

"It is, then, an art?" said Gazonal.

Marius, indignant, looked at Gazonal in the mirror
and stood motionless, the comb in one hand, the
scissors in the other.

"Monsieur, you speak about it like a—child! and
yet, by your accent, you appear to be of the South,
the land of men of genius."

"Yes, I know that it requires a sort of taste,"
replied Gazonal.

"Oh! keep silent, Monsieur! I expected better
things of you. That is to say that a coiffeur, I do
not say a good coiffeur, for one is or one is not a
coiffeur,—a coiffeur,—it is more difficult to find—
than—, what is it that I can best say?—than a, I do
not know what, a minister—keep your place—no,
for one cannot judge of the value of a minister, the
streets are full of ministers—. A Paganini?—no,
that is not enough!—A coiffeur, Monsieur, a man
who divines your soul and your habits in order to
arrange your hair according to your physiognomy,
it is necessary for him to have that which constitutes a philosopher. And the women, then!—. Ah!

the women appreciate us; they know what we are
worth to them,—it is we who bring the conquest
which they wish to make the day on which they
have their hair arranged to carry off a victory;—
that it to say that a coiffeur, one does not know
what he is. Hold, I who speak to you, I am nearly
that which might be found of—, without praising
myself, I am known—. Eh! well, no, I find that
there should be something better—. The execution, that is the thing! Ah! if the women would
only give me *carte blanche*, if I could execute all
the ideas that come to me!—for I have, do you see,
an infernal imagination!—but the women do not
lend themselves to it; they have their plans, they
will stick you their fingers or their comb, when you
have gone, into our delicious edifices, which should
remain grave and reserved, for our works, Monsieur,
only endure for a few hours—. A great coiffeur,
eh! that would be something like Carême and Ves-
tris, in their parts—. The head this way, there,
if you please, *I am doing the faces;* good.—Our profession is spoiled by the bunglers who comprehend
neither their epoch nor their art—. There are
dealers in wigs and in washes to make the hair
grow,—they see in it only so many bottles to sell
you!—that is pitiful!—that is business. These
miserables cut the hair or they dress it anyway
they can!—. I, when I arrived here from Toulouse,
I entertained the ambition to succeed to the great
Marius, to be a true Marius, and to illustrate the
name, in myself alone, more than the four others.

I said to myself, 'To conquer or die'—There, hold
yourself straight, I am about to finish you off.—
It was I who, first, employed elegance. I have rendered my salons an object of curiosity. I disdain
advertising, and that which advertising costs, I
will put it, Monsieur, in comfort, in embellishment.
Next year, I will have in a little salon a quartette;
they will furnish music, and of the best. Yes, it
is necessary to charm the weariness of those who
are having their hair dressed. I do not conceal
from myself the discomforts of the operation.—Look
at yourself.—To have one's hair dressed, it is
fatiguing, perhaps as much so as to *pose* for one's
portrait; and Monsieur knows perhaps that the
famous Monsieur de Humboldt—I knew how to
make the most of the little hair that America had
left him; science has this in common with the
savage, that it scalps its man very well—this illustrious scientist has said that after the pain of being
hanged—*se faire pendre*—, there was that of going
to be painted—*se faire peindre;*—but, according to
certain women, I should place that of having the
hair dressed before that of being painted. Well,
Monsieur, I wish that people might come to have
their hair dressed for pleasure.—You have a lock of
hair which should be kept in place.—A Jew proposed to me Italian cantatrices who, between the
acts, should attend to the hair of the young men of
forty; but they are all to be found in the condition
of young girls at the Conservatoire, of teachers of
the piano in the Rue Montmartre. There you are,

Monsieur, dressed as a man of talent should be. —
Ossian," said he to his lackey in livery, "brush
Monsieur and show him out. — Whose turn next?"
he added with pride, looking at the persons who
were waiting.

"Do not laugh, Gazonal," said Léon to his cousin
as they reached the bottom of the stairway, from
which his eye wandered over the Place de la
Bourse, "I see down there one of our great men, — you
will be able to compare his speech with that of this
workman, and you can tell me, after having heard
him, which of these two is the more original."

"Do not laugh, Gazonal," said Bixiou, repeating
facetiously Léon's intonation.   "In what do you
think Marius is occupied?"

"In hair-dressing."

"He has acquired," replied Bixiou, "the monopoly of the sale of hair in bulk, as any dealer in pro-
visions who comes to sell us a dish for an écu
claims for himself that of the sale of truffles; he dis-
counts the paper of his business; he lends on security to his clients when they are embarrassed; he
deals in annuities, he gambles at the Bourse; he is
a shareholder in all the fashion journals; finally, he
sells, through a druggist, an infamous remedy
which, for his share, gives him thirty thousand
francs a year, and which costs a hundred thousand
francs in advertising."

"Is it possible?" cried Gazonal.

"Retain this in your memory," said Bixiou,
gravely.   "In Paris, there is no small business;

everything enlarges itself, from the sale of rags up
to that of matches.   The lemonade-seller who, with
a napkin under his arm, sees you enter his shop, may
have an income of fifty thousand francs; a waiter
in a restaurant is an eligible elector, and such a man
whom you would take for a very poor one, to see
him passing in the street, carries in his waistcoat a
hundred thousand francs' worth of diamonds to have
them mounted, and does not steal them—''

The three inseparables, for this day at least, went
along under the direction of the landscape-painter
in such a manner that they ran against a man of
about forty, wearing a decoration, who came from
the boulevard by the Rue Neuve-Vivienne.

"Well," said Léon, "what are you dreaming of,
my dear Dubourdieu? of what fine symbolic composition?—My dear cousin, I have the pleasure
of presenting to you our illustrious painter
Dubourdieu, not less celebrated by his talent than
by his humanitarian convictions.—Dubourdieu, my
cousin Palafox!''

Dubourdieu, a little man with a pale complexion,
with a melancholy blue eye, slightly saluted Gazonal, who bowed before the man of genius.

"You have then nominated Stidmann in the place
of—?''

"What would you have! I was not in it," replied
the great landscapist.

"You bring the Academy into disesteem," replied
the painter.   "To choose such a man, I do not
wish to speak evil of him, but he makes it a

trade!—. To what point would you conduct the
first of the arts, that of which the works are the
most durable, which portrays the nations after the
world has lost all trace of them, even their memory,
—which consecrates the great men? It is a priest-
hood, sculpture; it resumes the thoughts of an epoch,
and you want to recruit it with a maker of images
and of chimneys, an ornamentalist, one of the
hawkers in the Temple! Ah! as Chamfort said, it
is necessary to commence the day by swallowing
a viper every morning in order to support life in
Paris.—At least, art remains to us; we cannot be
hindered from cultivating it."

"And then, my dear fellow, you have a consola-
tion which few artists possess, the future is yours,"
said Bixiou. "When the world shall be converted
to our doctrine, you will be at the head of your art,
for you bring to it ideas which will be comprehended
when they shall have been generalized! In fifty
years from now you will be for all the world what
you are now only for a few, a great man! Only, it
is a question of going that far!"

"I am going," replied the artist, whose countenance dilated as does that of a man whose hobby is
flattered, "to finish the allegorical figure of Harmony, and if you will come to see it you will readily comprehend how it is that I have been able to
spend two years upon it. There is in it everything! At the very first glance, you will perceive
the destiny of the globe. The queen holds a pas-
toral staff in one hand, symbol of the aggrandizement

of the races useful to mankind; she wears on her head the liberty cap, her breasts are sextuple in the Egyptian fashion, for the Egyptians anticipated Fourier; her feet rest upon two joined hands which embrace the globe as the sign of the fraternity of the human races; she tramples upon cannon, broken to signify the abolition of war, and I have endeavored to make her express the serenity of triumphant agriculture.—I have, moreover, placed near her an enormous curled colewort which, according to our master, is the image of concord.   Oh! it is not one of the least of Fourier's titles to veneration that he has restored meanings to plants, he has re-united all things in creation by the reciprocal signification of things and also by their special language.   In a hundred years, the world will be much greater than it is—"

"And how, Monsieur, will that be done?" said Gazonal, stupefied to hear a man speak in this manner outside of an insane asylum.

"By the extent of production.   If one were willing to apply THE SYSTEM, it would not be impossible to react upon the stars—"

"And what would then become of painting?" asked Gazonal.

"It would be greater."

"And would we have greater eyes?" said Gazonal, looking at his two friends with a significant air.

"Man would become that which he was before his degeneracy; our men of six feet would then be dwarfs—"

"Your picture," said Léon, "is it finished?"

"Entirely finished," replied Dubourdieu. "I have endeavored to see Hiclar to have him compose a symphony; I would that in seeing this composition one should hear music like Beethoven's which should develop the ideas expressed in it in order to bring them to the level of intelligent comprehension by two methods. Ah! if the government would lend me one of the halls of the Louvre—"

"But I will speak of it, if you wish, for nothing should be neglected to attract attention—"

"Oh! my friends are preparing some articles, but I am afraid that they will go too far—"

"Bah!" said Bixiou, "they will not go so far as the future—"

Dubourdieu looked at Bixiou askance, and continued on his way.

"But he is crazy," said Gazonal; "it is the moon that guides him."

"He has the hand, he has the knowledge,—" said Léon; "but Fourierism has killed him. You may see there, cousin, one of the effects of ambition on artists. Too often, at Paris, in the desire to arrive more quickly than by the natural way at that celebrity which is for them fortune, the artists borrow wings from circumstances; they think to make themselves greater in making themselves the men of one thing, in becoming the sustainers of a system, and they hope to change a clique into a public. Such a one is Republican, such another was Saint-Simonian, such a one is aristocratic, such a one is

Catholic, such a one just medium, such a one mediæval, or German, by deliberate choice.   But, if
the opinion does not give the talent, it always ruins
it; witness the poor fellow whom we have just seen.
The opinion of an artist should be the faith in his
works,—and his only means of success, work, when
nature has given him the sacred fire."

"Let us escape," said Bixiou, "Léon is moraliz-
ing."

"And this man acts in good faith?" exclaimed
Gazonal, still stupefied.

"In very good faith," replied Bixiou; "as sincere
as was just now the king of the *merlans.*"

"He is crazy!" said Gazonal.

"And he is not the only one whom Fourier's ideas
have rendered crazy," said Bixiou.   "You know
nothing of Paris.   Ask of it a hundred thousand
francs to realize the most useful idea for the human
species, to try something like the steam engine,
you will die there like Salomon de Caus, in the
Bicêtre; but, if it is a question of a paradox, you
will let yourself be killed for it, you and your
fortune.   Well, here, it is with systems as it is
with things.   The impossible publications brought
out here have devoured millions within the last
fifteen years.   That which renders your case so
difficult to gain is that you are right, and that
there are, according to you, secret reasons for the
prefect."

"Do you imagine that when he has once comprehended the moral aspect of Paris, a man of

intelligence could live elsewhere?" said Léon to his cousin.

"If we take Gazonal to the Mère Fontaine," said Bixiou, who made a sign to a closed public coach to come forward, "that would be to pass from the severe to the fantastic?—Coachman, Rue Vieille-du-Temple."

And they all three rolled away in the direction of the Marais.

"What are you going to show me?" asked Gazonal.

"The proof of that which Bixiou said to you," replied Léon, "by showing you a woman who makes twenty thousand francs a year by exploiting an idea."

"A fortune-teller!" said Bixiou, who could not refrain from interpreting as an interrogation the Southerner's air. "Madame Fontaine passes, among those who seek to know the future, for being wiser than was the late Mademoiselle Lenormand."

"She ought to be very rich!" exclaimed Gazonal.

"She has been the victim of her idea, as long as the lottery existed," replied Bixiou; "for, at Paris, there are no great receipts without great expenses. All the strong heads come to grief in this way, as if to give a safety-valve to their steam. All those who earn a great deal of money have vices or fancies, doubtless to establish an equilibrium."

"And now that the lottery is abolished?—" asked Gazonal.

"Well, she has a nephew for whom she saves."

Once arrived, the three friends perceived, in one of the oldest houses of this street, a staircase with shaky steps, having the upright of each step rough with mud, which conducted them, in the half-light and through an evil odor peculiar to houses in alleys, up to the third floor, to a door which a design alone could justly render; literature would lose too many nights in endeavoring to paint it suitably.

An old woman, in harmony with the door, and who, perhaps, was the door animated, introduced the three friends into a room serving as antechamber, where, notwithstanding the warm atmosphere which flooded the streets of Paris, they felt the icy cold of the most profound crypts. There came into it a damp air from an interior court-yard which resembled a vast breathing-hole of a dungeon, the daylight was gray, and on the sill of the window was a little garden full of unhealthy plants. In this room, plastered with a greasy and sooty substance, the chairs, the table, everything had a miserable air. The floor sweated like a water-cooler. In short, the least accessory was here in harmony with the frightful old woman with a hooked nose, a pale face, and clothed in decent rags, who told the consultors to seat themselves, informing them that only one at a time could go in to see MADAME.

Gazonal, affecting intrepidity, entered bravely and found himself before one of those women forgotten by Death, who, doubtless, forgets them purposely in order to leave some exemplars of himself among the living. It was a dried face, in which

glittered two gray eyes of a fatiguing immobility;
an indented nose, smeared with tobacco; with two
small bundles of bones very well covered by muscles
sufficiently like them and which, under the pretext
of being hands, were nonchalantly shuffling the
cards, like a machine, the movement of which is
about to stop.   The body, a species of broom-
handle, decently covered with a gown, enjoyed all
the advantages of still life; it did not move in the
least.   Over the forehead rose a head-dress of black
velvet.   Madame Fontaine, it was a real woman,
had a black hen at her right, and at her left an immense toad called Astaroth, which Gazonal did not
see at first.

The toad, of surprising dimensions, was less terrifying in himself than by two topazes, large as fifty-
centime pieces and which threw two lights like a
lamp.   It is impossible to sustain this look.   As
was said by the late Lassailly, who, lying out in the
country, wished to get the best of a toad by which
he was fascinated, the toad is an unexplained being.
Perhaps the animal creation, man included, is
summed up in him; for, said Lassailly, the toad lives
indefinitely; and, as is known, it is the one of all
created animals whose marriage endures the longest.

The black hen had her cage at two steps from the
table, which was covered with a green cloth, and
reached it by a board which served as a drawbridge
between the cage and the table.

When this woman, the most unreal of the creatures which furnished this Hoffmannesque den,

25

said to Gazonal "Cut!—" the honest manufacturer
felt an involuntary shudder. What renders these
creatures so formidable, is the importance of that
which we wish to know. One wishes to buy from
them hope, and they know it very well.

The grotto of this sibyl was much more sombre
than the antechamber, the color of the paper could
not be distinguished. The ceiling, blackened by
smoke, far from reflecting the little light which
came through the window obstructed by a meagre
and pale vegetation, absorbed the greater part of it;
but this half-light lit fully the table at which the
sorceress was seated. This table, the arm-chair of
the old woman and that in which Gazonal sat composed all the furniture of this little apartment, cut
in two by a loft, in which doubtless Madame Fontaine slept. Through a little door partly opened,
Gazonal heard a peculiar murmur of a pot boiling
over the fire. This sound of cooking, accompanied
with a composite odor in which preponderated that
of a sink, mingled incongruously the ideas of the
necessities of actual life with the ideas of a supernatural power. It was disgust in curiosity. Gazonal perceived a step of white wood, the last
doubtless of the interior stairway which led to the
loft. He took in all these details with one glance,
and he was nauseated. It was frightful in a very
different way from the recitals of the romancers and
the scenes in the German dramas; it was of a
suffocating veracity. A heaviness that induced
vertigo disengaged itself from the air, the obscurity

ended by irritating the nerves. When the Southerner, stimulated by a species of fatuity, looked at
the toad, he felt something like the heat of an
emetic in the pit of his stomach, in experiencing a
terror similar enough to that of a criminal before
the gendarme. He endeavored to recomfort himself
by examining Madame Fontaine, but he encountered
two eyes almost white, the motionless and freezing
eyeballs of which were to him insupportable. The
silence then became frightful.

"What will you have, Monsieur," said Madame
Fontaine to Gazonal, "the deal of five francs, the
deal of ten francs, or the grand deal?"

"The deal of five francs is already sufficiently
dear," replied the Southerner, who was making unheard-of efforts within himself not to allow himself
to be affected by his surroundings. At the moment
when Gazonal was endeavoring to gather himself
together, an infernal voice made him leap in his
chair: the black hen cackled.

"Go away, my daughter, go away; Monsieur
does not wish to expend more than five francs."

And the hen seemed to have comprehended her
mistress, for, after having come to within a step of
the cards, she returned gravely to her place.

"What flower do you like?" asked the old woman,
in a voice made hoarse by the humors which incessantly ascended and descended in her bronchial tubes.

"The rose."

"What color do you like the best?"

"Blue."

"What animal do you prefer?"

"The horse. Why these questions?" asked Gazonal in his turn.

"Man is connected with all forms by his anterior states," said she, sententiously; "from these come his instincts, and his instincts dominate his destiny. —What do you eat with the most pleasure? fish, game, cereals, butchers' meat, sweets, vegetables or fruits?"

"Game."

"In what month were you born?"

"September."

"Put out your hand."

Madame Fontaine studied very attentively the lines in the hand which was presented to her. All this was done seriously, without any premeditation of sorcery, and with a simplicity which a notary would have assumed in inquiring the intentions of a client before drawing up a deed. When the cards were sufficiently shuffled, she requested Gazonal to cut them, and to make himself three packs. She took the packs, spread them out one above the other, examined them as a player examines the thirty-six numbers of the roulette before risking his stake. Gazonal felt his bones chilled, he no longer knew where he was; but his astonishment mounted higher and higher as this frightful old woman in a green capote, greasy and flat, of which the false elevation showed much more of black ribbons than of hair, frizzled into points of interrogation, went on to retail to him in her voice charged with phlegm all the particulars, even the most secret, of his former life, recounted to him his tastes, his habits, his character, even the ideas of his childhood; all that could have had influence upon him, his intended marriage, why it had failed, with whom, the exact description of the woman whom he had loved, and finally, from what country he had come, his lawsuit, etc.

Gazonal believed at first in a mystification prepared by his cousin; but the absurdity of this conspiracy revealed itself to him as soon as the idea presented itself, and he rested open-mouthed before this power truly infernal, the incarnation of which borrows from humanity that which, in all times, the imagination of painters and poets has regarded as the most frightful thing,—an atrocious little old woman, short-winded, toothless, with cold lips, with a flat nose, with white eyes. The eyeball of Madame Fontaine had become animated, there passed into it a ray sprung from the profundities of the future or of hell. Gazonal asked mechanically, in interrupting the old woman, of what use were the toad and the hen.

"To be able to predict the future. The *consultor* himself throws some grains at hazard on the cards, Cleopatra comes to pick them up; Astaroth drags himself over to seek his nourishment which the client offers him, and these two admirable intelligences are never deceived: would you wish to see them at work, you will know your future? It is a hundred francs."

Gazonal, frightened at the look of Astaroth,

precipitated himself into the antechamber, after
having saluted the terrible Madame Fontaine. He
was all wet, and as if under the infernal incubation
of the evil spirit.

"Let us go!—" he said to the two artists. "Have
you ever consulted this sorceress?"

"I do nothing important without making Astaroth
speak," said Léon, "and I have always been recompensed."

"I am waiting for the honest fortune which Cleopatra has promised me," said Bixiou.

"I am in a fever," cried the Southerner; "if I
believe in what you tell me, I should then believe in
sorcery, in a supernatural power?"

"That can only be natural," replied Bixiou. "The
third of the lorettes, a quarter of the statesmen, half
the artists consult Madame Fontaine, and a minister
is known to whom she served as an Egeria."

"Did she tell you your future?" asked Léon.

"No, I had enough of it with my past. But, if
she can, with the aid of her frightful collaborators,
predict the future," said Gazonal, seized with an
idea, "how is it that she loses at the lottery?"

"Ah! there you put your finger upon one of the
greatest mysteries of the occult sciences," replied
Léon. "As soon as that species of interior mirror
in which is reflected for them the future or the past
becomes obscure under the breath of a personal sentiment, of any idea whatever foreign to the active
power which they exercise, sorcerers or sorceresses
no longer see anything, in the same way that an

artist who sullies art by a political or systematic
combination loses his talent.   It is not so long ago
that a man endowed with a gift of divination by the
cards, a rival of Madame Fontaine, and who was
addicted to criminal practices, was not able to cut
the cards for himself and to foresee that he would be
arrested, judged and condemned in the Court of Assizes.   Madame Fontaine, who predicts the future
eight times out of ten, has never been able to fore-
tell that she would lose her stake in the lottery."

"It is so in magnetism," observed Bixiou.   "No
one is able to magnetize himself."

"Good! now for magnetism!" cried Gazonal.
"Ah, there! you are then acquainted with everything?—"

"Friend Gazonal," replied Bixiou, gravely, "in
order to be able to laugh at everything, it is necessary to be acquainted with everything.   As for myself, I have been in Paris since my childhood, and
my pencil enables me to live here by ridicule, five
caricatures a month—.   I thus very often mock at
an idea in which I have faith!"

"Let us go on to other exercises," said Léon;
"let us go to the Chamber, and we will arrange the
cousin's affair."

"This," said Bixiou, imitating Odry and Gaillard,
"is in the realms of high comedy, for we will make
the first orator whom we meet in the audience-hall
pose for us, and you will recognize there as everywhere else the Parisian language, which has never
but two rhythms: interest and vanity."

As they took their carriage again, Léon perceived in a cabriolet which passed rapidly a man, to whom, with a sign of the hand, he communicated his desire to speak a word to him.

"It is Publicola Masson," said Léon to Bixiou; "I am going to ask him for a sitting this evening, at five o'clock, after the Chamber. The cousin will have the most curious of all the originals—"

"Who is it?" asked Gazonal while Léon was speaking to Publicola Masson.

"A pedicure, author of a treatise on *Corporistique*, who will treat your corns by subscription, and who, if the Republicans triumph in the next six months, will certainly become immortal."

"In a carriage?" cried Gazonal.

"But, friend Gazonal, it is only the millionaires who have sufficient leisure to go on foot in Paris."

"To the Chamber," cried Léon to the coachman.

"Which one, Monsieur?"

"Of Deputies," replied Léon, after exchanging a smile with Bixiou.

"Paris begins to confound me," said Gazonal.

"In order to make you acquainted with its immensity, moral, political and literary, we are doing at this moment like the Roman cicerone, who shows to you at St. Peter's the thumb of the statue which you thought of the size of life; you find it a foot long. You have not yet measured one of the great toes of Paris!—"

"And notice, Cousin Gazonal, that we take what we meet; we are not making a selection."

"This evening, you will sup as they used to feast with Belshazzar, and you will see our Paris, intimately, playing at lansquenet, and risking a hundred thousand francs on a stake, without winking."

A quarter of an hour later, the coach stopped at the foot of the steps to the Chamber of Deputies, at that end of the Pont de la Concorde which leads to discord.

"I thought the Chamber unattainable?—" said the Southerner, surprised to find himself in the middle of the great *Salle des Pas Perdus.*

"That is according to circumstances," replied Bixiou; "materially speaking, it costs thirty sous for carriage hire; politically, one expends something more. The swallows think, says a poet, that the Arc de Triomphe de l'Étoile was built for them; we think, we artists, that this monument here has been built to compensate us for the deficiencies of the Théâtre-Français and to make us laugh; but these comedians cost a much higher price, and do not always give us the worth of our money."

"Let us then see the Chamber!—" repeated Gazonal.

And he strode around the hall, in which there happened to be at this moment some ten persons, looking at everything with an air which Bixiou engraved in his memory for one of those celebrated caricatures in which he contested the supremacy with Gavarni.

Léon went to speak with one of the doorkeepers who came and went constantly from this hall into

that of the sittings, with which it communicated by
the corridor in which were stationed the stenogra-
pher of the *Moniteur* and some persons attached to
the Chamber.

"As to the minister," replied the doorkeeper to
Léon at the moment when Gazonal approached them,
"he is there; but I do not know if Monsieur Giraud
is still there; I will go and see—"

When the doorkeeper opened one of the wings
of the swing door by which entered only the
deputies, the ministers or the commissioners from
the king, Gazonal saw come out a man who
appeared to him still young, although he was forty-
eight years of age, and to whom the doorkeeper
pointed out Léon de Lora.

"Ah, you are here!" said he, giving a grasp of the
hand to Léon and to Bixiou. "Ah! you rogues!
what are you doing here in the sanctuary of Law?"

"*Parbleu!* we come here to learn to talk nonsense," said Bixiou; "without that, one would get
rusty."

"Let us then go into the garden," replied the
young man, not thinking that the Southerner was of
the company.

On seeing this unknown well dressed, all in black,
and without any decoration, Gazonal did not know
in what political category to classify him, but he
followed him into the garden adjoining the hall and
which extends along the quay formerly called Quai
Napoléon. Once in the garden, the ci-devant young
man gave utterance to a laugh which he had been

suppressing since his entrance into the *Salle des Pas Perdus.*

"What is it that amuses you?—" said Léon de Lora to him.

"My dear friend, in order to be able to establish the sincerity of the constitutional government, we are compelled to utter frightful falsehoods with an incredible assurance. But, for myself, I work by the day. If there are days in which I lie like a programme, there are others in which I cannot be serious. This is my day of hilarity. Now, at this moment, the head of the cabinet, summoned by the opposition to reveal diplomatic secrets which it would refuse to reveal if it itself were the ministry, is in the act of going through his exercises in the tribune; and, as he is an honest man, as he does not lie on his own account, he whispered to me before mounting to the assault: 'I do not know what to retail to them!—' When I saw him there, I had a wild desire to laugh, and I came out, for you cannot laugh on the bench of the ministers, where my youthfulness sometimes returns to me tempestuously."

"At last!" cried Gazonal, "I find an honest man in Paris! You must be a very superior man!" said he, looking at the unknown.

"Ah, now! who is monsieur?" said the ci-devant young man, examining Gazonal.

"My cousin," replied Léon, quickly. "I answer for his silence and for his honesty as for my own. It is he who brings us here, for he has an administrative process which depends upon your minister; his prefect wishes quite simply to ruin him, and we have come to see you to hinder the Council of State from consummating an injustice—"

"Who is the *Rapporteur?*—"

"Massol."

"Good!"

"And our friend Giraud and Claude Vignon are in the section," said Bixiou.

"Say a word to them, and they will come this evening to Carabine's, where Du Tillet is giving a fête under pretext of the railways, for they are robbing more than ever now on the roads," added Léon.

"Ah, there! but this is in the Pyrenees?—" asked the young man, suddenly become serious.

"Yes," said Gazonal.

"And you did not vote for us in the elections?—" said the statesman, looking at Gazonal.

"No; but, after what you have just said before me, you have corrupted me: on the word of a commandant in the National Guard, I will cause your candidate to be nominated—"

"Well, will you still guarantee your cousin?—" asked the young man of Léon.

"We will form him,—" said Bixiou, in a profoundly funny tone.

"Well, I will see—," said this personage, leaving his friends and returning hastily into the Chamber.

"Well, now, who is that?" asked Gazonal.

"Well, the Comte de Rastignac, the minister of the department in which is your case—"

"A minister!—it is no more than that?—."

"But he is an old friend of ours. He has three hundred thousand livres income; he is peer of France, the king has made him count; he is the son-in-law of Nucingen, and he is one of the two or three statesmen to whom the Revolution of July gave birth; but power wearies him sometimes and he comes to laugh with us—"

"Ah, there! you did not tell us that you were in the opposition down there?—" said Léon, taking Gazonal by the arm. "Are you stupid? Whether there is a deputy the more or the less in the Left or in the Right, will that furnish you with better cloths?"

"We are for others—"

"Let them alone," said Bixiou, quite as comically as Monrose would have said it; "they have Providence on their side; he will bring them out all right without you and despite themselves—. A manufacturer should be a fatalist."

"Good! there is Maxime with Canalis and Giraud!" cried Léon.

"Come, friend Gazonal, the promised actors arrive on the stage," said Bixiou to him.

And all three of them moved toward the persons indicated, who seemed to be sufficiently disengaged.

"Have they sent you out to take a walk, that you go about like that?" said Bixiou to Giraud.

"No: while they are voting on the secret ballot," replied Giraud, "we came out to take the air—"

"And how did the chief of the Cabinet acquit himself?"—

"He was magnificent!" said Canalis.

"Magnificent!" repeated Giraud.

"Magnificent!" said Maxime.

"Well, now! the Left, the Right, the Centre, are unanimous?"

"We have each of us a different idea," observed Maxime de Trailles.

Maxime was a ministerial deputy.

"Yes," replied Canalis, laughing.

Although Canalis had already been a minister, he was sitting at this period in the neighborhood of the Right.

"Ah! you have just had a fine triumph!" said Maxime to Canalis, "for it is you who forced the minister to mount the tribune."

"And to lie like a charlatan," replied Canalis.

"A fine victory!" said the honest Giraud. "In his place, what would you have done?"

"I would have lied."

"That is not called lying," said Maxime de Trailles, "that is called covering the crown."

And he led Canalis some paces away.

"He is a really fine orator!" said Léon to Giraud, indicating Canalis.

"Yes and no," replied the Councillor of State; "he is hollow, he is sonorous; it is rather an artist in words than an orator. In fact, it is a fine instrument, but it is not music; thus he has not and never will have *the ear of the Chamber.* He believes himself necessary to France; but in no case can he ever be *the man of the situation.*"

Canalis and Maxime returned to the group at the moment when Giraud, deputy of the Left Centre, had pronounced this verdict. Maxime took Giraud by the arm and led him away from the others to make to him, perhaps, the same confidences that he had just done to Canalis.

"What an honest and worthy fellow!" said Léon, indicating Giraud to Canalis.

"It is those honesties which kill governments," replied Canalis.

"In your opinion, is he a good orator?—"

"Yes and no," replied Canalis; "he is verbose, he is fine-drawn.   He is a workman in reasoning, he is a good logician; but he does not comprehend the great logic, that of events and of affairs: thus he has not and he never will have *the ear of the Chamber—*"

At the moment in which Canalis issued this verdict on Giraud, the latter returned with Maxime to the group; and, forgetting the presence of a stranger whose discretion was not known to them as was that of Léon and of Bixiou, he took the hand of Canalis in a significant fashion.

"Well," said he, "I consent to the proposition of Monsieur le Comte de Trailles, I will make the interpellation to you, but with a great severity."

"We will then have the Chamber with us in this question; for a man of your capacity and of your eloquence *has always the ear of the Chamber,*" replied Canalis. "I will reply,—but promptly, to crush you."

"You may be able to bring about a change in the Cabinet, for you can bring about on such a ground whatever you wish of the Chamber, *and you will become the man of the situation—*"

"Maxime has hoodwinked both of them," said Léon to his cousin. "That rascal there finds himself in the intrigues of the Chamber like a fish in the water."

"Who is it?" asked Gazonal.

"An ex-rogue on the way to become an ambassador," replied Bixiou.

"Giraud!" said Léon to the Councillor of State, "do not go away without having asked of Rastignac that which he promised me to say to you in relation to a case which you will judge the day after to-morrow and which relates to my cousin here; I will come to see you to-morrow on this subject, in the morning."

And the three friends followed the three men of politics at a distance, directing their steps toward the *Salle des Pas Perdus.*

"Look, cousin, see those two men," said Léon to Gazonal, showing to him a former minister, very celebrated, and the chief of the Left Centre, "there are two orators who have the ear of the Chamber and who have been facetiously surnamed the ministers of the departments of the Oppositions; they have so well the ear of the Chamber, that they pull it very often."

"It is four o'clock, let us return to the Rue de Berlin," said Bixiou.

"Yes, you have just seen the heart of the govern-ment; it is necessary to show you the helminths, the ascarides, the tœnia, the Republican, since it is necessary to call it by its name," said Léon to his cousin.

When the three friends were installed in their fiacre, Gazonal looked mischievously at his cousin and at Bixiou, like a man who is about to launch a flood of oratorical and Meridional bile.

"I was strongly suspicious of this great drab of a city, but since this morning, I despise it! The poor province, so shabby, is an honest girl; but Paris, it is a prostitute, greedy, lying, an actress, and I am very well content not to have left any more of my skin here—"

"The day is not ended," said Bixiou, senten-tiously, winking at Léon.

"And why do you complain stupidly," said Léon, "of a pretended prostitution to which you are going to owe the winning of your suit?—Do you believe yourself more virtuous than we are and less of a comedian, less grasping, less prompt to descend any path whatever, less vain than all those with whom we have played as with jumping-jacks?"

"Suppose you try me—"

"Poor fellow!" said Léon, shrugging his shoul-ders, "have you not already promised your electoral influence to Rastignac?—"

26

"Yes, because he is the only one who has laughed at himself."

"Poor fellow!" repeated Bixiou, "you suspect me, I who have done nothing but laugh!—You are like a little cur wearying a tiger.—Ah! if you had seen us ridiculing anyone!— Do you know that we can drive out of his wits a man of perfectly sound judgment?—"

This conversation conducted Gazonal to the house of his cousin, where the sight of the rich furnishings cut short his speech and put an end to this debate. The Southerner perceived, but later, that Bixiou had already made him *pose.*

At half-past five, at the moment when Léon de Lora finished his toilet for the evening, to the stupefaction of Gazonal, who enumerated the thousand and one superfluities of his cousin and who admired the serious air of the valet de chambre in full function, the *pedicure of Monsieur* was announced.

Publicola Masson, a little man, fifty years old, whose face recalled that of Marat, entered, depositing a little box of instruments and placing himself on a low chair in front of Léon, after having saluted Gazonal and Bixiou.

"How are affairs?" asked Léon of him, abandoning to him one of his feet already preparatively washed by the valet de chambre.

"Oh! I have been obliged to take two pupils, two young persons who, despairing of making their fortune, have abandoned chirurgery for the *corporistique;* they were dying of hunger, and yet they have talent—"

"Oh! I was not speaking to you of pedestrian affairs, I am asking you where you are in your political affairs—"

Masson threw at Gazonal a look more eloquent than any species of interrogation.

"Oh! speak, he is my cousin, and he is almost one of yours; he thinks himself Legitimist."

"Well, we are getting on! we are marching! In five years from now, Europe will be all ours!—Switzerland and Italy have been zealously worked, and, when the occasion arrives, we are ready.   Here, we have fifty thousand men armed, without counting the two hundred thousand citizens who are penniless—!"

"Bah!" said Léon, "and the fortifications?"

"Pie crusts, which will be swallowed," replied Masson.   "In the first place, we will not allow the cannon to be brought; and then we have a little machine more powerful than all the forts in the world, a machine invented by a doctor who has cured more people than the doctors have killed during the whole period in which they have been operating."

"How you go on!—" said Gazonal, who shuddered at the sight of Publicola.

"Ah! it is necessary! we come after Robespierre and Saint-Just; it is to do better; they were timid, for you see what has happened to us,—an emperor, the elder branch and the younger branch!   The Montagnards did not sufficiently prune the social tree."

"Ah, there! you who are going to be, as it is said, Consul or something like Tribune, do not forget," said Bixiou, "that I have been demanding your protection for the last twelve years."

"Nothing will happen to you, for we shall want loustics,* and you can take Barère's trade," replied the pedicure.

"And I?" said Léon.

"Ah! you, you are my client; it is that which will save you; for genius is an odious privilege to which too much has been granted in France, and we shall be obliged to demolish some of our great men in order to teach the others to learn to be simple citizens—"

The pedicure spoke with an air half-serious, half-waggish, which made Gazonal shiver.

"So," said the Southerner, "there will be no more religion?"

"No more religion *of the State*," replied the operator, emphasizing the last three words, "each one will have his own.   It is very fortunate that at this moment they are protecting the convents; it is there that we are preparing the capital of our government. Everything is conspiring for us.   Thus, all those who pity the people, who *bawl* on the question of proletariats and of wages, who work against the Jesuits, who occupy themselves with the amelioration of, no matter what,—the communist, the humanitarian, the philanthropist, you understand, all those people are our advance-guard.   While we are

---

* Loustics—buffoons in the Swiss regiments formerly in the service of France; professional jesters

gathering the powder, they are weaving the fuse to which the spark of a circumstance will set fire."

"Ah, so! what is it you wish then for the happiness of France?" asked Gazonal.

"Equality for the citizens, the cheapness of all commodities—we wish that there shall no longer be those who are in want of everything and millionaires, blood-suckers and victims!"

"That is it! the *maximum* and the *minimum?*" said Gazonal.

"You have said it," replied the pedicure, decisively.

"No more manufacturers?"—asked Gazonal.

"There will be manufactories for the benefit of the State, we shall all be usufructuaries of France—. Each one will have his ration as on a vessel, and everyone will work then according to his capacity."

"Good!" said Gazonal, "and, while waiting till you can cut off the heads of the aristocrats—"

"I pare their nails," said the radical Republican, who put away his tools and who finished the jest himself.

He bowed very politely and went out.

"Is it possible? in 1845—" cried Gazonal.

"If we had the time, we would show you," replied the landscape-painter, "all the personages of 1793; you could talk with them all. You have just seen Marat; well, we know also Fouquier-Tinville, Collot-d'Herbois, Robespierre, Chabot, Fouché, Barras, and there is even a magnificent Madame Roland."

"Come, in this theatrical representation, the tragedy has not been missing," said the Southerner.

"It is six o'clock: before we take you to see *Les Saltimbanques*, which Odry plays this evening," said Léon to his cousin, "it is necessary to go and pay a visit to Madame Cadine, an actress who cultivates a good deal your *Rapporteur* Massol, and to whom you will have this evening to pay assiduous court."

"As it is necessary for you to conciliate this power, I am going to give you some instructions," added Bixiou. "Do you employ workwomen in your manufactory?"

"Certainly," replied Gazonal.

"That is all I wish to know," said Bixiou; "you are not married, you are a great—"

"Yes!" cried Gazonal, "you have guessed my strong point, I love women—"

"Well, if you will execute the little manœuvre which I am going to prescribe to you, you will know, without expending a liard, the charms which one tastes in the intimacy of an actress."

When they arrived in the Rue de la Victoire, in which the celebrated actress lived, Bixiou, who was meditating a trick upon the suspicious Gazonal, had barely finished indicating his rôle to him; but the Southerner had, as will be seen, comprehended it at the first word.

The three friends mounted to the second story of a handsome enough house, and found Jennie Cadine finishing her dinner, for she was playing in the second piece on the boards of the Gymnase. After the presentation of Gazonal to this fair puissance, Léon and Bixiou, in order to leave him alone with her, invented a pretence of going to see a new piece of furniture; but, before leaving the actress, Bixiou said to her, aside:

"It is Léon's cousin, a manufacturer worth millions, and who, to gain his suit before the Council of State against the prefect, thinks it worth while to seduce you, in order to have Massol on his side."

All Paris knows the beauty of this young première; the stupefaction of the Southerner on seeing her may then be readily understood. Received almost coldly at first, he soon became the object of the good graces of Jennie Cadine during the few minutes that they remained alone.

"How," said Gazonal, looking with disdain at the furniture of the salon through the door which his confederates had left partially open, and in computing that it was about equal to that of the dining-room, "how is it that a woman like you is left in such a dog-kennel?"

"Ah! see!—what would you have! Massol is not rich, I am waiting till he becomes a minister—"

"What a lucky man!" cried Gazonal, giving vent to the sigh of a provincial.

"Good!" said the actress to herself, "my furniture will be renewed—I can then rival Carabine!"

"Well," said Léon, re-entering, "my dear child, you are coming to Carabine's this evening, are you

not?   One will sup there, one will play lansquenet."

"Will Monsieur be there?" said Jennie, gracefully
and ingenuously.

"Yes, Madame," said Gazonal, dazzled with this
rapid success.

"But Massol will be there," rejoined Bixiou.

"Well, what does that matter?" retorted Jennie.
"But let us go, my jewels, I must be off to my theatre."

Gazonal gave his hand to the actress down to the
closed carriage which was waiting for her, and he
pressed it so tenderly that Jennie Cadine replied,
shaking her fingers:

"Eh, I have no spare ones!"

When they were in the carriage, Gazonal undertook to take Bixiou by the waist, exclaiming:

"She has bitten!—. You are a fine scoundrel—"

"So the women say—" replied Bixiou.

At half-past eleven, after the theatre, a carriage
conveyed the three friends to the house of Mademoiselle Séraphine Sinet, better known under the
name of Carabine, one of those *noms de guerre*
which the illustrious lorettes take or which is given
to them, and which was derived perhaps from the
fact that she has always killed her pigeon.

Carabine, who had become almost a necessity for
the famous banker Du Tillet, deputy of the Left
Centre, was living at this time in a charming house
in the Rue Saint-Georges.   There are in Paris
houses the destinies of which does not vary, and

this one had already seen seven occupations by
courtesans.   A stock-broker had lodged there, about
1827, Suzanne du Val-Noble, since become Madame
Gaillard.   The famous Esther there caused the Baron
de Nucingen to commit the only follies of which he
had been guilty.   Florine, and she who was facetiously named *the late Madame* Schontz, had alternately shone there.   Wearied of his wife, Du Tillet
had acquired this little modern house and had installed in it the illustrious Carabine, whose lively
wit, whose cavalier manners, whose brilliant disso-
luteness, formed a counter-weight to the works of his
domestic, political and financial life.   Whether Du
Tillet and Carabine were or were not at home, the
table was served, and splendidly, for ten plates
every day.   The artists, the literary people, the
journalists, habitués of the house, dined there.   In
the evening there was play.   More than one member of each of the Chambers came to seek there
that which is bought in Paris at its weight in
gold, pleasure.   The eccentric women, those meteors
of the Parisian firmament which are classified with
such difficulty, brought there the richness of their
toilets.   One could there be very witty, for everything could be said there, and everything was said
there.   Carabine, rival of the not less celebrated
Malaga, had thus come to inherit the salon of Florine, become Madame Nathan; of that of Tullia, become Madame du Bruel; of that of Madame Schontz,
become Madame la Présidente du Ronceret.   On
entering, Gazonal only said one word, but it was at

once legitimate and Legitimist: "It is finer than
at the Tuileries—" The satin, the velvet, the bro-
cades, the gold, the objects of art which abounded
there so occupied the eyes of the provincial that he
did not at first perceive Jennie Cadine in a toilet to
inspire respect and who, hidden behind Carabine,
watched the entrance of the pleader while conversing with her friend.

"My dear child," said Léon to Carabine, "this is
my cousin, a manufacturer who fell on me from the
Pyrenees this morning; he knows nothing yet of
Paris, he has need of Massol for an action before
the Council of State; we have then taken the liberty of bringing to you Monsieur Gazonal for
supper, recommending to you to leave him all his
reason—"

"As Monsieur pleases; wine is dear," said Carabine, who surveyed Gazonal and saw nothing remarkable in him.

Gazonal, dazed by the toilets, the lights, the gold
and the chatter of the various groups who, he
thought, were occupied with him, could only stam-
mer these words:

"Madame—, Madame—is—very good."

"What do you manufacture?—" asked the mistress of the household, smiling.

"Laces! And offer guipure laces to her!—" whispered Bixiou in Gazonal's ear.

"Des—dent—, des—"

"You are a dentist!—Say, Cadine? a dentist! you
are *plundered*, my little one."

"*Des dentelles,—*" returned Gazonal, comprehending that it would be necessary for him to pay
for his supper. "I will do myself the greatest
pleasure in offering you a dress,—a scarf,—a mantilla of my manufacturing."

"Ah, three things? Well, you are nicer than
you appear," replied Carabine.

"Paris has pinched me!" said Gazonal to himself, perceiving Jennie Cadine and going to speak
to her.

"And I, what shall I have?—" asked the actress
of him.

"Why—my whole fortune," replied Gazonal,
who reflected that to offer everything was to give
nothing.

Massol, Claude Vignon, Du Tillet, Maxime de
Trailles, Nucingen, Du Bruel, Malaga, Monsieur and
Madame Gaillard, Bauvinet, a crowd of persons,
entered.

After a conversation apart with the manufacturer
concerning his case, Massol, without promising anything, said to him that the report was yet to be
made, and that the citizens could confide in the intelligence and in the independence of the Council of
State. At this cold and dignified answer, Gazonal,
despairing, believed it necessary to seduce the
charming Jennie Cadine, with whom he was desperately in love. Léon de Lora and Bixiou left their
victim in the hands of the most roguish of the
women of this bizarre society, for Jennie Cadine is
the only rival of the famous Déjazet. At the table,

where Gazonal was fascinated by the silverware of
that modern Benvenuto Cellini, Froment-Meurice,
and of which the contents were worthy of the interest of that which contained them, the two jokers
were careful to place themselves at some distance
from him; but they followed with a sly eye the
progress of the witty actress, who, instigated by
the insiduous promise of the renewal of her furniture, gave herself for a theme the winning over of
Gazonal.   And, never did a lamb of the Corpus-
Christi allow itself to be conducted with more complacency by its St. John the Baptist than did
Gazonal in obeying this siren.

Three days later, Léon and Bixiou, who had not
seen Gazonal again, came to seek him at his hôtel
about two o'clock in the afternoon.

"Well, cousin, a decree of the Council gives you
your case—"

"Alas! it is useless, cousin," said Gazonal, lifting
to the two friends a melancholy eye, "I have become
Republican—"

"What is that?" said Léon.

"I have no longer anything, not even to pay my
lawyer," replied Gazonal.   "Madame Jennie Cadine
has notes of mine for more money than I have
goods—"

"The fact is that Cadine is a little dear, but—"

"Oh! I have had it for my money," replied Gazonal.   "Ah! what a woman!—Well, the province
cannot contend with Paris; I am going to retire to
the Trappist Monastery."

"Good!" said Bixiou; "you are reasonable. Now, then, recognize the majesty of the Capital—"

"And of capital!" exclaimed Léon, offering to Gazonal his notes. Gazonal looked at these papers with a stupid air.

"You will not say that we do not understand hospitality: we have instructed you and saved you from poverty, regaled, and—amused," said Bixiou.

"And *gratis!*" added Léon, making the gesture of the street gamins when they wish to express the action of *pilfering*.

Paris, November, 1845.

LIST OF ETCHINGS

VOLUME IX

.

www.ingramcontent.com/pod-product-compliance
Lightning Source LLC
Chambersburg PA
CBHW030945110726
47900CB00004B/1139